"Joe, we had good reason for what we did."

Allison could hear the pleading note in her voice. "Surely after all this time you can accept that."

"I'm not having this conversation, Allison. I don't want to talk about the agency, or Tackett, or any lame offer he sent you to make. Unless you want to pick up a paintbrush and dig in, you need to leave."

"Just...give me a chance to change your mind."

"And how do you plan on doing that, Allison? Wait. Let me guess." Joe set the water bottle on the ladder and with one swift motion pulled his shirt over his head. "You and me, Slick. Right here, right now. Remind me how convincing you can be."

Heat slapped at her cheeks. Her knees felt loose. He was unbelievable. *She* was unbelievable. While part of her loathed his over-the-top he-man tactics, another part couldn't help admiring the hard, sculpted plane of his bare chest.

Shame sidled in, jacking her chin high. "That wasn't what I had in mind, Joe."

Dear Reader,

Welcome back! I've missed you! I'm so very excited to be able to take you on another journey to Castle Creek. After Harlequin Superromance released *The Other Soldier* last summer (July 2012), I received a number of emails expressing hope that I'd give Joe Gallahan his own book, since readers were curious to know the motel owner's story. I have to admit I was curious about him myself. :-)

Forgiveness plays a pivotal role in *Staying at Joe's*. As the book opens Allison and Joe are both harboring grudges, along with a double dose of heartache. It takes a lot of soul-searching—and sly encouragement from certain matchmaking elders—for the two to realize the life decisions they made were based on bad assumptions. Now not only do they need to forgive each other, they need to forgive themselves. (I just hope that Joe forgives *me* for everything I put him through!)

By the way, in the latter part of the story Allison samples a rather unusual cake. Occasionally my mother finds all kinds of glee in baking this cake, challenging the unwary to name the two secret ingredients—which no one has ever been able to do! Then, giggling maniacally, she reveals the mystery and the partakers refuse to believe that they ate—nay, *relished*—such a peculiar blend. If you'd care to have a copy of this recipe (which really is quite delicious!) please send me an email at kathy@kathyaltman.com and I'll fix you right up. Or send me an email even if you *wouldn't* care for the recipe—I'd adore hearing from you!

Thank you again for coming back to Castle Creek!

All my best,

Kathy Altman

Staying at Joe's

Is this book good?

Kathy Altman

It is getting
interesting after 50 pages!
read on. Sue loves Joe.

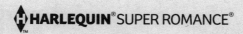
HARLEQUIN® SUPER ROMANCE®

Recycling programs
for this product may
not exist in your area.

ISBN-13: 978-0-373-60792-1

STAYING AT JOE'S

Copyright © 2013 by Kathy Altman

Printed in U.S.A.

ABOUT THE AUTHOR

Kathy Altman writes contemporary romance, romantic sus-
pense and the occasional ode to chocolate. When she's
not plotting romance novels or writing reviews for *USA
TODAY's Happy Ever After* blog, she's probably putting in
her forty hours a week as a computer programmer for the
air force, watching the Ciarán Hinds version of *Persuasion*
or making other people feel superior by letting them win
at Scrabble. Find Kathy online at www.kathyaltman.com, or
email her at kathy@kathyaltman.com—she'd adore hearing
from you!

Books by Kathy Altman

HARLEQUIN SUPERROMANCE

1790—THE OTHER SOLDIER

Other titles by this author available in ebook format.

To my own personal PR crew—Mom, Mary, Jerry, Bill and Stephen—you all keep me going and I love you more than ham.

To Toni Anderson—I couldn't have done justice to Joe without you.

To Kathy Jones—how lucky am I, to be your friend?

And to the sweetest, most thoughtful romance fans ever—Barb Kopsic, Carol Shaffer, Rhonda Sipe, Carol Opalinski, Mary Kennedy, Julia Broadbooks, Louise Hackworth, Edie Faile, Yvonne Cruz, Judy Kuhns, Marlee Soulard, Dolores Finley and especially Linda Esau.

You all are the best and I couldn't appreciate you more!

ACKNOWLEDGMENTS

For a newly published author, writing that sophomore book (the second published book) is notoriously stressful. Actually it's downright agonizing. If your first book was well received, you can't help but fret that readers will find the second a complete and utter letdown. If that first book tanked, you'll spend every waking moment worrying that the second will disgrace your name beyond all hope of redemption and obliterate any chance of a writing career while everyone reading your words is rummaging for antacid or scrambling for a paper shredder as black rain erupts from the skies and cats begin to bark and small children everywhere demand brussels sprouts for breakfast—

Ahem. Let me pull myself back from the brink and thank the amazing people who made this return to Castle Creek possible. My most heartfelt gratitude goes to:

My ever-patient sweetie, Dan, for his expertise on building renovations;

Harlequin Superromance editor Karen Reid, for a rockin' set of revisions;

Robin Covington, Entangled author extraordinaire, whose blog introduced me to Matt Nathanson and helped build my soundtrack;

and the brave, insightful and kindhearted Toni Anderson, Robin Allen and Debby Collier, for cheerfully reading early drafts of Joe's story and generously helping me brainstorm.

Big squeezy hugs to you all.

CHAPTER ONE

THINK OF IT as just another pitch. One more client to woo. Schmooze and booze. Deal and seal. *Nothing new here, Allie.*

Except they weren't in a high-end restaurant. He wasn't a client. She wasn't sipping wine. And she'd never been so bone-deep desperate.

Nor so ready to rely on bondage and torture, should the whole schmooze-and-booze thing end in an epic fail.

Though the thought of duct taping Joe Gallahan did cheer her immensely. She rolled her shoulders up and back, wiped her palms on her linen pants and stepped into the open doorway of the motel room. And blinked.

She'd never seen him in jeans. Two years of working together and three months of dating and she'd never seen him in anything with the slightest resemblance to denim. He'd never been the casual type. Not when it came to clothes, anyway. Then again, it had been nearly a year since he'd left—of course he'd changed. She had, too. Just...not as noticeably.

He stood with his back to her, in a sweat-stained T-shirt and faded, paint-spattered jeans. A pair of scuffed boots added to the construction worker look she was having a hard time wrapping her brain around. And his hair—once kept regularly trimmed—had now grown so long that the shaggy ends flirted with his shoulders.

She inhaled deeply and the thick, sharp smell of paint made her wish she hadn't. She fought the urge to cough. A cough would give her away. A cough would mean she couldn't change her mind.

As if she even had that option. Her pulse kicked up and her fingertips tingled. *Easy, Allie.* Too much at stake to chicken out now.

At least he seemed sober.

She straightened her spine and moved into the room, watching as Joe pushed the roller up and down the wall in the classic W pattern. The muscles of his back and arms alternately bunched and relaxed. Allie dragged her gaze away from his body, annoyed by flashes of erotic memories.

More than his appearance had changed. It seemed that he'd learned a little DIY somewhere along the way. Or had he always known how to do this home repair stuff? It wouldn't be the first time he'd surprised her.

A hot flush of resentment bubbled up and prickled across her skin. If it weren't for Joe Gallahan she'd be back in urban Virginia, less than six miles from the nation's capital, sitting behind a gold-etched nameplate advertising her hard-earned position of

"Account Executive." And collecting the paychecks to prove it.

Instead she was still a PR rep, stuck with this ridiculous assignment in oh so cozy Castle Creek, Pennsylvania, hoping she wouldn't get paint on a blouse she couldn't afford to replace and preparing to plead with a man she'd just as soon tie up, slather with honey and roll onto a colony of fire ants.

Then again, she was lucky she still had a job. Though sending her off to meet with her ex-lover put her boss next in line for the whole fire ant thing.

Stroke by stroke, a thick coat of pale blue covered a hideous shade of green. Allison's stomach lifted then dropped, like a roller coaster cresting that first big hill. He wouldn't be happy to see her—which at least put them on equal ground.

"Hello, Joe," she said.

He went still. The paint roller remained suspended in the air, the muscles of his forearms suddenly pronounced. He turned, slowly, his expression as inviting as his ramshackle, middle-of-nowhere motel. He stared at her and she stared back, fighting the urge to grab handfuls of his shirt and shake the stuffing out of him while screaming, *Why?*

He moved before she did, thank God, bending down and balancing the roller across the paint tray. When he straightened, his hands went to his hips in a familiar "I'm waiting to be impressed" pose.

"Allison Kincaid," he said.

Silence, except for the low-pitched hum of the fan

blowing the fumes toward the open window. Her gaze roved his face. The start of a beard darkened his jaw—yet another difference between this version of Joe and the clean-shaven, designer-suited marketing shark she'd known a year ago. Her throat closed again. If she was having a hard time reconciling the two, Tackett would, too.

Which promised a whole new set of complications. *Damn it.* Her neck muscles went tight. No matter their history, she had a job to do. A job to *keep*.

He cocked an eyebrow. "Want to tell me why you're here?"

Forget "woo the client." What she really wanted to do was kick his arrogant ass all the way back to Virginia. She risked another inhale, and willed her voice to remain steady.

"Tackett sent me," she said.

His laugh was immediate and harsh. "The answer is no." He pulled a tool from his back pocket, squatted and pried open a can of paint.

She didn't blame him for saying no. She didn't want him to say yes. But she had her orders.

She ventured farther into the room, heels clunking across water-stained plywood. "You don't know the details."

"I don't need to."

"You should hear this."

"You should leave."

"It's not that simple."

"Sure, it is." He finished pouring paint into the tray

and with his fist thumped the lid back onto the can. "Turn around. Walk out the door. Get in your car. Drive away." He stood, his gaze narrowed. "Don't come back."

"Joe." She passed her keys from one hand to the other, the jingle a taunting echo in the near-empty room. "I wouldn't be here if my job didn't depend on it."

"Then maybe you need another job." He snatched up a bottle of water, gave the cap a vicious twist. "How long did it take you to drive up here? Five hours? Six? To ask a favor of me? On behalf of *Tackett?* You're out of your mind."

"You're not the only one here with a grievance."

"You have a grievance? Do what I did. Quit your job. End of grievance."

"Can we at least talk about Tackett's offer?"

"Not interested. Go home."

"Won't you at least—"

"Go. Home." He took a swig of water, the plastic crackling in his grip. She glared at him, half hoping he'd choke. She hadn't expected this to be easy, but she'd figured after all this time he'd feel *some* remorse for what he'd done to her. Instead he was still fixated on what had happened his last few weeks at the agency.

Tackett had told her to apologize. Fat chance.

"Tackett and I had good reason for what we did," she said. "Surely after all this time you can accept that."

"I'm not having this conversation. I don't want to talk about the agency or Tackett or any lame-ass offer he sent you to make. Unless you want to pick up a paintbrush and dig in, you need to leave."

"Just give me a chance to change your mind."

"And how do you plan to do that? Wait. Let me guess." He set the water bottle on the ladder and with one swift motion pulled his shirt over his head. "You and me, slick. Right here, right now. Remind me how convincing you can be."

Heat slapped at her cheeks. Her knees felt loose. He was unbelievable. *She* was unbelievable. While part of her loathed his over-the-top he-man tactics, another part couldn't help admiring the hard, sculpted plane of his bare chest.

Shame sidled in, jacking her chin high. "That wasn't what I had in mind."

"Once upon a time it was all you had in mind." He balled up his shirt and tossed it aside. "Let me guess why you're here. One of my former accounts is launching a campaign and he's asked for me as lead. Tackett smelled big money and picked you to play fetch, said if you didn't bring me back to Alexandria you could kiss your Christmas bonus goodbye. Am I right?"

"This isn't about a bonus," she said carefully. His scorn made it easy to keep her gaze from straying south of his. "This is about my job."

He shot her a look that was pure disdain. "When Tackett decided to filch my biggest clients, you backed him instead of me. At a time when work was all I had left. And you expect me to hook up with the agency again? Screw that."

Hook up. Screw. She'd smirk, if only her lips would cooperate. "You know darned well we were trying to—"

"Give it up, slick."

"At least now I know for sure why you did it."

"Did what?"

"Are you kidding me?" Her keys gave a furious rattle as she clasped her hands behind her back to keep from yanking at her own hair. "You're actually going to pretend you don't know?"

"Know *what,* exactly?"

"What you *did.*"

"Why don't you remind me?" He crossed his arms over his bare chest. Another time, another place, and she'd have started to drool.

"You cost me my promotion," she said, letting the resentment ring loud in her voice. "And you almost got me fired."

JOE SCOWLED. What the hell was she talking about? "Want to run that by me again?"

"Tackett found out about you and me. Want to know how?"

Judas Priest. Joe exhaled. He already knew how.

"Danielle Franks told him," she said, her tone not quite casual enough to hide the bitterness. "And you know how he feels about fraternization. So Danielle got the promotion he'd promised me."

"And you're here because you think I told Danielle."

"I'm here because Tackett sent me to bring you back to handle a client who won't work with anyone but you. The company needs you for two months, tops. The fact that *you* lost me my promotion is the reason I offered to scrub every toilet in the building in exchange for Tackett picking someone else to 'play fetch.' Obviously he didn't accept my offer."

Okay, that hurt. Which pissed him off even more. That son of a bitch Tackett was too damned clever for his own good. No doubt the old man figured Joe would jump at the chance to "reacquaint" himself with Allison Kincaid. Instead he wished she'd kept her pretty little materialistic ass back in the city.

"I'm sorry for what happened," he ground out. "But not sorry enough to go back."

"What a surprise. Some things never change, do they?" She shook her head, eyes dark with disgust. "No one mattered but you. *Your* clients, *your* projects, *your* schedule. Everything else came in second. Then something doesn't go your way and bam! You're gone, and the rest of us are left scrambling to meet your commitments."

"Didn't go my way? My brother *died*."

"And that's why you're hiding out in this hellhole? Because you're feeling sorry for yourself?"

Joe set his jaw. Was it wrong to be so damned

angry he wanted to put a fist through a wall—preferably one he hadn't already painted—and at the same time be so incredibly turned on by the hints of nipple he could see through her blouse? He stomped over to where he'd lobbed his shirt, snatched it up and stomped back.

"If you think I told anyone about us, you don't know me."

"Exactly the point I tried to make a year ago."

Another direct hit. She'd learned a lot from her boss. Still, she had it right. He owed her. *Hell.*

"Fine. I'll give Tackett a call."

"And tell him what? That I can handle the client myself? You think I didn't try that? Mahoney made it clear. He doesn't get you, he gets another agency."

Mahoney, huh? Joe grunted. He knew as well as she did that client should be hers.

"Maybe it's a sign," he said. "That it's time for you to move on."

"It's a *sign* that it's time for you to step up and fix the mess you made. Mr. *DIY.*"

"You always did put T&P first."

"They never let me down."

"Until Tackett decided to make an example out of you."

"I repeat. *They* never let me down."

"You really want to start comparing scars?" he asked softly.

She clenched her teeth. "I want to keep my job."

"The agency means that much to you."

"The paycheck means that much to me."

"So it's the money." He should have known. "What, is the gold plating wearing off your toothbrush?"

"You self-centered, egotistical son of a—"

"Children, children, please." They swung toward the door. Longtime Castle Creek resident Audrey Tweedy marched toward them, clapping her hands as if urging a classroom of first-graders to settle down after recess. The seventy-something woman had a voice like a pixie and a body like a lumberjack, and Joe couldn't remember ever seeing her without that purple barrette holding her gray hair out of her face.

For one wild, despairing moment, he considered making his escape through the window. But he'd just replaced the screen. And Audrey was faster than she looked.

She wagged a thick finger. "I could hear you kids all the way out in the parking lot. That's not good for business, Joseph Gallahan."

"I'm not open for business."

"That's not the point." She gave him a disapproving look—he was getting a lot of those lately—then leaned toward Allison, her expression complicit. "I could tell the trouble right off. You two are having a meat crisis."

Allison went still. "A *what?*"

Joe ran a hand over his face as Audrey rummaged through a bright green purse—the one with the over-size "P" on the side. She pulled out a can of Vienna sausages. "You're grumpy. That's what happens when you don't get enough protein. Have a weenie."

Joe held up his hands, palms out. "I'll pass." His gaze cut to Allison, who was staring at the old woman in fascinated dismay.

Audrey gave him a tsk-tsk and shrugged. She jammed the can back into her purse and turned to Allison, thrust out a hand. "I'm Audrey Tweedy, dear. Welcome to Castle Creek. Care for a weenie? No?" She patted her monster of a purse. "I could fit a whole ham in here if I wanted to. I could show you where I got it, if you'd like. The purse, not the ham. 'Course, the initial on the side costs extra."

"What does the 'P' stand for?"

Audrey shot Joe a "where'd you find this one?" look. "Protein." She turned back to Joe. "Which you, Mr. Vegetarian, obviously don't get enough of."

"I had scrambled eggs for breakfast. With cheese. And, Aud? I'm a little busy right now."

She sniffed. "The way you eat, Joseph, you'd think you didn't have any teeth. You need something that'll work that jaw—something besides insulting your visitors. And you're not getting rid of me that easily. Have some jerky."

He stared down at the bright yellow stick of processed who-the-hell-knew-what. "You never give up."

She turned to Allison. "You eat meat, don't you, dear?" Joe tried not to choke while Allison managed a nod. With a smile worthy of a denture commercial, Audrey swung back to face him. "Sounds like you two have some problems to work out. Why don't you invite your friend here to stay awhile?"

Oh, hell, no.

Joe gave her his best "mess with me and I'll break out my pneumatic drill" look. Audrey countered with her "humor me or I'll hide a dead perch in your pickup" glare.

"Sounds like Allison doesn't have much of a job to go back to," Audrey continued smugly. "And, Joseph, you and I both know you could use a hand around here. She has two."

Allison thrust out her hands, fingers spread. "Uh, and they both just had a manicure."

"Go ahead, Joseph. Invite her to stay."

He heard Audrey's words but they didn't register. He'd finally given in to the urge to look at Allison, really look at her, for the first time in a year. She watched him back, head tipped to the side, hazel eyes narrowed, chin indignant. She'd changed her hair. Instead of the short, sleek, behind-the-ears style he remembered, she'd let it grow so a smooth, butter-colored curtain skimmed her shoulders. Not as smooth as when she'd first walked in, though. One side looked kind of poufy, as if someone had given her a noogie.

Or she'd just rolled out of bed.

He drew in a breath and focused on Audrey, who looked mighty pleased with herself as she stood there in her pink pants, spotless white trainers and olive drab Go Army T-shirt. A gift from his buddy Reid Macfarland, no doubt. Joe sighed.

"Don't you have anything better to do, Aud?"

"Better than helping two conflicted souls find grace and understanding? Really, Joseph, how self-centered do you think I am?"

He wasn't touching *that* with a ten-foot salami. Meanwhile, Allison was looking a little wild-eyed.

Audrey gave her a sympathetic smile. "Does it bother you, dear? That he's one of those pesky vegetarians?"

"Pes*co*," Joe growled. "I'm a pes*co*-vegetarian."

"You did call this place a 'hellhole,'" Audrey continued, her voice suddenly all schoolmarm. "If you stayed you could help change that."

Allison shook the noogie right out of her hair. "That's not an option."

Joe watched her back away toward the door. He should be feeling smug. Why wasn't he feeling smug?

"Surely, dear, you could spare a few days to help out an old friend—"

"Audrey Tweedy, you're supposed to be holding a table for us at the diner. If we don't head over there now, we won't get any chocolate mousse." Hazel Catlett appeared next to Allison, tapping her watch. Her gaze slid to Joe's naked chest and her eyes sparked as bright as the neon-orange color on her lips.

"Goodness gracious me. I see what held you up."

Hell. The Castle Creek paparazza had arrived. Joe

shook out his shirt and scrambled to find an opening. Hazel, meanwhile, was brandishing her cell phone.

"Why didn't you text me?" she fussed at Audrey. The moment before Joe shoved an arm inside his T-shirt he heard a chiming sound, and Hazel shot him a wicked wink. "You've been holding out on us, Joe Gallahan." Squinting at her phone's display, she hummed her approval at the photo she'd just snapped. "We've got that fund-raiser for the citizens' center coming up. What do you say we have a wet T-shirt contest? You know, the man-chest kind? Honey, who are you?" Another chime as she snapped a pic of Allison.

"She's a friend of Joe's, visiting from Virginia. Allison Kincaid, meet Hazel Catlett. She and her sister, June, have the most adorable salt-and-pepper schnauzer named Baby Blue."

Allison blinked. Joe did his best to turn a laugh into a cough and Audrey thumped him on the back. With her purse.

Ouch.

Hazel glanced from Joe to Allison and back again. "You really *have* been holding out on us." She sidled closer to Allison, keeping her gaze on Joe. "Tell me the truth, hon. Does the bottom half look as good as the top?"

"Let's go get that mousse," Audrey said, and tugged on her friend's arm.

"I'm coming, I'm coming." Hazel flapped a hand

at Joe then elbowed Allison. "Ironic, isn't it? A piece of beefcake like that, being a vegetarian?"

"I'm standing right here," he said.

"And God bless you for it," Hazel beamed.

Audrey led Hazel out the door while Hazel played with her cell phone, no doubt sending copies of that damned photo to the entire population of Castle Creek. As soon as they cleared the door, Allison rounded on him.

"I'm not staying."

"And I'm not going back. Glad we understand each other. Goodbye."

She let loose a strangled sound of exasperation and stalked over to the window. The fan-borne breeze huffed through her hair and his traitorous fingers itched to follow. His gaze skimmed downward. *Damn.* He shoved his hands in his pockets and forced himself to look away from the luscious lines of her ass. Tried to focus on the probability that the pants hugging that class-A ass had cost more than what he'd shelled out to tile ten bathrooms.

Then again, hadn't he spent thousands on suits during his stint at T&P?

He scowled. If he'd lost her that promotion, then he damned well owed her. He hadn't said a word to Danielle. But she'd been hovering over him as he cleaned out his desk and the instant she spotted the photo of Allison she'd figured it out. And apparently had gone running straight to Tackett.

And Allison thought he'd turned tattletale. Because

she'd rejected him. Because the company had stripped him of his clients. Not a bad way to get revenge, if he'd been that kind of man.

But things had changed since then. *He'd* changed. And right now revenge was sounding pretty damned good.

"I'm serious." She turned from the window, her arms wrapped around her waist so tight it was a wonder she could breathe. "I have to get back. And you have to come with me."

Obviously, she wanted to be here as much as he wanted to be back in the nation's capital. Maybe Audrey's idea wasn't such a ball-buster, after all. Keeping Allison around for a while would be hell, yeah, but he could string that old bastard Tackett along and at the same time score some free menial labor. He pictured Allison trying to handle a roller while fighting to protect her manicure and smiled inwardly. At the very least, he'd get some comic relief.

And maybe, just maybe, she'd see that life in the country—life with *him*—wouldn't have been so bad after all.

Scratch that. He'd keep her here because she could help, nothing more. Though he wouldn't mind getting her naked.

His brain stuttered on the word "naked."

"Are you even listening to me?"

The buzzing in his ears climbed an octave. As his gaze focused on Allison, he took in her furious pink face and it was all he could do to keep from grinning.

"Two weeks," he said, then paused. Had he said that out loud? He gave a mental shrug. "You give me two weeks and I'll give the agency four."

He expected her to go ballistic—looked forward to it, in fact—but she didn't give him the satisfaction.

"It's been a year," she said calmly. "Can you really still be holding a grudge?"

"There's a saying. Something about a pot, a kettle and the color black?"

Her arms dropped away from her waist and she clenched her fists. "We hadn't even been dating for three months when you suddenly asked me to dump everything and follow you up here. Expected me to walk away from my job, my apartment, my life in the city, everything I worked so hard to achieve. And for what? Cracked sidewalks and moldy floorboards? This was your dream, Joe. Not mine." She relaxed her hands and wiggled her fingers. "But that's in the past. In the here and now, I'm about to lose my job and you can prevent it. So will you?"

He ran his hands down the front of his T-shirt, smoothing out the wrinkles, pretending to consider. *In the past, like hell.*

"Two weeks," he repeated. He pictured her trading in her designer duds for a pair of his old coveralls and this time freed the smile. She snapped her spine straight.

"I'm glad you find this amusing." She marched to the doorway. "And I'm glad you can afford to… to humor your inner Bob the Builder fantasies up here in Mayberry-by-the-lake." She swiveled back to face him, as graceful as a model at the end of a runway. "By the way, T&P authorized me to offer you a bonus. Ten thousand dollars. Considering you've already been here a year and the sidewalk has more cracks than the San Andreas Fault, I'm thinking you could use the money."

That did it. Fury kicked at his temples and he tried for a calming inhale, but the air had turned dense. Disappointment, he realized. His throat was thick with it.

It always came down to money.

"Tackett would be proud of you, Kincaid."

"How about you, Gallahan? Anyone proud of you?"

It hadn't taken her long to zero in on that soft spot. In another life he would have admired her. Praised her. Pointed her out as an example to new-hires. Now he pitied her. Almost as much as he wanted to find out if she still tasted the same.

She must have seen something in his face she didn't like because her chin went back up in the air. "So you won't consider coming back."

"The moment you consider picking up a drywall taping knife."

She stared at him for a couple of beats. "Afraid you lost your edge? That you can't do the job?"

He grunted. "Your job security depends on two weeks of kissing up to the guy who screwed you out of a promotion. Literally. Maybe you'd better stick to worrying about yourself."

"I had to try." She hesitated. The already rigid line of her shoulders tensed. "You're looking good, Joe," she said quietly. Her gaze locked on to his. "I'm glad." She turned and walked out, her posture suddenly soft.

He reclaimed the paint roller, dipped it and faced the wall. Struggled to find the strength to raise his arms.

She still talked a good fight, but sometime during the past year her confidence level had taken a massive hit. How much of that was his fault? He looked over his shoulder, at the empty doorway.

He needed a whiskey.

Make that a double.

ALLISON SEETHED AS she guided her Camry around the pits in the motel parking lot, then slowed for a pair of squirrels that tumbled across the pavement toward a scraggly pine.

Damn Joe Gallahan and his miserable excuse for a motel, anyway. *She* was the injured party here. *She* was the one with the grievance. Yet there *he* had stood, acting all smug and superior, like the advertising hotshot he used to be. Though to be fair, despite the unruly, sun-streaked hair and construction worker getup, the hot part still applied. Or maybe it applied *because* of those things.

Good grief. Could she *be* any more pathetic?

She pulled out onto the highway, shaking her head over Hazel Catlett swooning over Joe's bare chest and Audrey Tweedy knitting her brow over his protein consumption.

Joe Gallahan, still a sensation with the ladies. Her giggle turned into a groan and her fingers clamped tighter around the steering wheel. Sudden tears blurred her vision and she blinked, panic overtaking frustration. Time to pull over before she wrecked her car. Or worse.

Two minutes after passing a sign indicating a picnic area ahead, she parked in a small gravel lot and made her way along a path that led through a grove of shaggy pine trees down to the lake. Arms wrapped around her waist, shoulders hunched, she lingered above the beach, squinting across the choppy, platinum waters toward Canada.

He knew what he'd done. That confused look on his face? Had to be an act. He knew.

Mist-laden air swirled around her, flashing rainbows whenever the spray caught the waning sun. She dragged in a deep breath, smelled fresh water, decaying fish and seaweed. Over the hissing rush of the surf she heard a series of echoing thuds—oars, maybe, banging against the rim of a rowboat? Another breath, and gradually her panic began to recede. Despite the occasional drone of a car traveling the road behind her, she felt more alone than she had in a very long while.

Which was ridiculous. She was on edge only because she was used to having half a dozen people demanding half a dozen things from her, all at the same time—usually during her lunch hour. This "being alone" thing...she never did handle that well. She needed to get back to work. Back to her old self.

Though if she went back without Joe her old self would be out pounding the pavement, looking for a job in a bleak economy. Her stomach gave an unpleasant wriggle.

Maybe that's why seeing Joe upset her so much. At Tackett & Pike, she was doing what she wanted to do. What she'd struggled to learn the skills to do. She reached out to the nearest tree and snagged a pinch of pine needles. Rolled them idly between her thumb and forefinger, releasing a sharp, sweet scent. Yeah, *that* was why she'd dreaded this visit.

She steered her mind away from Joe Gallahan, sprinkled the needles into the wind and stepped out of her pumps. Cautiously, she ventured out onto the beach, the sun-warmed stones grinding and clattering beneath her. A glint of green caught her eye and she bent over to get a closer look. Her cell rang, and a glance at the incoming number roused a sigh from the deepest, darkest pit of her belly.

She thought of the produce stand she'd passed on her way into town, pictured the heaping quarts of strawberries lined up for sale. She pasted a bottle of rum, a tray of ice and a blender into the picture, bit back a whimper and answered her phone.

"Mr. Tackett."

He grunted. "See, the way you just said my name right there, that tells me you don't have good news.

And I need good news, Kincaid. The *company* needs good news."

The man was doomed to disappointment. Unfortunately, so was she.

"He's not interested, Mr. Tackett."

"*Make* him interested."

She'd get right on that. As soon as she solved the energy crisis and invented a toilet seat that put itself down.

"Why don't you arrange for the client to contact Joe directly?" She bent over, left palm braced on her knee, and scoured the beach for another glimpse of that green. "Mr. Mahoney would have more success talking him around, seeing that Joe's—" *a chauvinist pig* "—more likely to respond to a man."

Tackett's laugh was sly. "You and I know better."

Her eyes fluttered shut and her chin sank to her chest. What had she been thinking, all those months ago? She'd compromised her professional image by getting involved with a coworker. A coworker with a reputation for being a player.

Tackett's disapproving hum dragged her back to the here and now. "Did you offer him the bonus?"

"It made things worse."

"Because you didn't do it right."

She held the phone away from her ear and hefted it in her hand. She looked at the lake, and back at her phone. If she threw it just right she could probably get four, maybe five good skips out of it. But it wasn't worth losing her job over. Losing the promotion sucked enough.

"Mr. Tackett, I know how to negotiate a deal. The thing is, both parties need to be interested."

"Well, what did he *say?*"

"That he wouldn't consider it."

"Bastard's holding out for more money."

She had no trouble recalling Joe's contempt at the mention of a bonus. "I don't think so."

"Then what? The cliché about everyone having a price is only a cliché because it's true. So figure out Gallahan's price."

Trouble was, she already knew it. And she had no choice but to pass that information on to Tackett. Because if he found out about Joe's proposal before Allison told him about it, it wouldn't matter if Joe came back to T&P and brought a dozen big-name clients along with him. She'd still be out of a job.

So, while crossing her fingers and envisioning a giant neon sign endlessly flashing the word NO, she told Tackett about Joe's proposal. He interrupted before she had a chance to tell him she'd rather spend a winter in Greenland.

"There's a multimillion-dollar account at stake, here. Mahoney refuses to work with anyone else so I don't care how you do it. Hammer a nail, bake a cake, perform the dance of the seven veils. Just get Joe back here. Take the two weeks. Stick to him like syrup on a pancake. And, Kincaid? Don't come back without him. Do what it takes, you hear? You show up two weeks from Monday without Joe Gallahan, you'll be clearing out your desk."

Her stomach dropped to her knees and her neon sign went from flashing NO to BETTER LUCK NEXT TIME, SUCKER.

She rolled her lips inward and disconnected the call. She had to go back. She had to *cave*. To *him*. Her head drooped and her spine sagged. How did she get herself into these messes? After several moments of pointless self-pity she found herself scanning the rocks at her feet.

Before she did anything else, she'd find the source of that glint of green. Maybe she'd snag herself a good-luck charm—she needed all the help she could get. She hitched up her pants and dropped into a crouch, blinking against an annoying eyeball burn.

There. With a quiet squeak of glee she scooped up the square of tumbled glass. The stone felt sleek and cool against her skin. She stroked her thumb across the surface worn smooth by the water.

Her phone rang again. She glanced at the caller ID, lost her balance and almost fell on her ass. Forget the strawberries. Straight rum would do just fine.

The strident sound continued. She rose out of her crouch, her thumb hovering over the connect button. But only for a millisecond.

No way she could handle this. Not now.

Seconds later a much-too-cheerful chime signaled the caller had left a voice mail. Nerves prickled in her chest as she pocketed the piece of polished glass, entered her password and held the phone to her ear.

"Where's my money, bitch?"

CHAPTER TWO

OH, NO. OH, no, no, no, no, *no.* Staring blindly down the rocky expanse of beach, Allison listened to the remainder of the message. Her mother had hit Sammy up for another two thousand. He'd staked her, even though he'd promised to cut her off. And she'd lost it all playing blackjack.

Allison swallowed against the bitter panic rising in her throat. Sammy wanted his money, and he wanted it now. All of it.

I'm talking lump sum, bitch. No more of this payment shit.

She didn't have it. Her mother knew it. Sammy knew it. Which was why he'd previously offered to take payment in trade.

The bastard.

In his dreams.

God, what a nightmare.

Her fingers started to ache. She relaxed her grip on the phone, felt suddenly graceless as rocks shifted and rattled beneath her feet.

She'd call Sammy back. Try to negotiate more time.

She stumbled forward, almost stepped on a half-decayed fish. Her throat tightened. The bottom line was, she would have to deal with Joe. Assuming he hadn't changed his mind. Though why would he? Having someone he considered a traitor at his beck and call for the next two weeks? Considering how he felt about Tackett and his methods—and her, by association—no way he'd make it easy on her.

But she could handle it. For a guaranteed paycheck at the end of every two weeks she could handle anything. She *had* to.

Sammy was the most merciless—hence the most successful—moneylender in the Washington metropolitan area. But if she could convince him that padding loans was bad for business, maybe he'd cut her a break.

She shoved her feet back into her pumps. She'd downsized her apartment, her car, her wardrobe. In view of the debts her mother had racked up—not to mention the money she'd siphoned out of Allison's bank account—a PR rep's salary didn't stretch anywhere near far enough. Allison had looked for other jobs, with no luck. Not a shocker, given the state of the economy.

She *had* to keep her job. Yes, her mother had messed up. Big time. But no matter what she'd done, there was no way Allison would let her own mother spend her days fretting that one of the people in line with her at the supermarket might just be someone sent by Sammy to deliver a "friendly reminder."

She marched back to her car. She'd return to Castle

Creek first thing in the morning because she'd had more than enough of Joe Gallahan for one day, thank you very much. And since T&P was paying her expenses, she'd snag a room at the Hampton Inn the next town over, call room service and order up a strawberry daiquiri.

Or two.

Then she thought of Joe as he'd been a year ago and winced.

Club soda would have to do.

THE FAMILIAR RUMBLE of a truck outside the room provided just the excuse Joe needed to set aside his trowel. He winced as metal clanged on ceramic. No, the relentless throbbing in his *head* was just the excuse he'd needed. Or it should have been. But instead of pausing and taking something to ease the pain he'd decided to punish himself. Not for drinking—hell, he'd have to punish himself every damned day for that. No, his crime was in wishing, even for a moment, that Allison Kincaid had come to see him simply because she'd wanted to.

Not because she'd had to.

He pushed up onto his knees and went still, the sudden greasy churn in his gut making him grateful he was inches away from a toilet. *Hell.* He breathed in deeply, slowly. The nausea passed.

With a grunt he pushed to his feet, grimacing at the stiffness in his legs, the ache behind his eyes. He brushed the grit from his palms and studied the floor.

Once he got it grouted and scrubbed and got the walls repainted, he could cross another unit off his list.

Three down, six to go. He had ten rooms altogether, but the one at the far end was currently his personal gym, and no way was he giving that up. No matter what Allison had implied the day before, he *was* making progress. He already had a good head start on this room and, hell, he and a crew had spent an entire month replacing the roof—

He blew out a frustrated breath. Why did it have to come back to her? Why should he care what she thought? This was why he'd moved four hundred miles north. To get away from the expectations and the guilt. The responsibility. And the woman who'd cared about her job more than she'd cared about him.

He lifted his hands over his head and leaned left, then right, in a careful stretch. Here in Castle Creek he had no one depending on him but himself. And whenever he let himself down, he invited himself for a drink at Snoozy's and got over it. Life was good.

He was well rid of her.

So why did he suddenly feel so damned restless?

Two truck doors slammed. Parker had brought Nat with her, a realization which both cheered and saddened him. If the kid kept seeing him like this, it wouldn't take long for her to decide he was more zero than hero. He sucked in another deep breath, swiped the hem of his T-shirt over his face and headed out to the parking lot.

Parker Macfarland, a tall, pretty redhead with an

unfortunate love of baggy overalls, held up a hanging basket dripping with purple and red blooms. "A little something to cheer up your lobby, since you insisted on painting it brown."

"Not brown. Buff."

She rolled her eyes. "It's still brown."

He took the basket and kissed her on the cheek. "Thank you, my sweet." He managed a grin, pleased by the gift, and by the conspicuous absence of a certain nine-year-old. He made a show of sniffing the flowers.

"Funny thing," he said. "These smell like fresh-baked muffins."

Parker's carbon-copy daughter popped out from behind the pickup, a foil-covered plate in her hands. "Surprise," she shouted.

Joe staggered backward, hand to his heart. Giggling, Nat offered him the plate.

"Tell you what, sport. Can you hold on to that for me? I need to wash my hands." He led them through the lobby and headed for his apartment while Parker found a place to hang the basket of flowers and Nat helped herself to a glass of milk. Joe closed himself inside his tiny bathroom and took a swig of Pepto, praying Nat wouldn't push a muffin on him. He purposely avoided looking in the mirror.

When he returned to the lobby, Parker was trying to explain why it wasn't the best idea for Nat to share her milk with the geraniums. She turned to Joe and made a "what will she think of next?" face.

"I hope you don't mind us dropping by so early. I drew up some plans for your landscaping and I was hoping you'd look them over, let me know what works for you and what doesn't."

Joe frowned. "That's great, but...you sure you have time? With Reid overseas, I figured you'd be struggling just to keep the greenhouses going."

"With Reid overseas, I'll take all the work I can get. Helps keep my mind off...you know."

He did know. Parker's first husband—Nat's father—had been in the Army, like Reid. Only he hadn't survived his tour in Afghanistan, a tragedy that Parker's new husband, Reid, had been responsible for. Several months ago, Reid had shown up on Parker's doorstep, determined to make amends for the friendly-fire disaster. They'd ended up falling in love. Just two months ago, and only two weeks into his marriage, Reid had been deployed for the third and final time and Parker was terrified that something would happen to him, as well.

"Anyway." She smiled brightly. "Don't forget Nat's out of school for the summer, if you need extra help. She and Harris have already picked up where Reid left off, clearing junk from the outbuildings."

"How's the old man feeling?" Had to be tough for someone as active as Harris, a former Marine, finding out he had a heart condition.

"Ornery, since we're all making sure he takes it easy."

"We play poker during our breaks." Nat swiped

the back of her hand across her mouth and flashed a smile. "Harris owes me fourteen ice cream cones."

"Yeah? I like ice cream. Maybe you guys could deal me in sometime."

The smile turned sly. "I found something yesterday. I brought it for you."

"Another surprise? You'll spoil me, kid. Well, first, I have a surprise for you. Bring your milk. I want to show you something out back."

Parker's eyes went wide. "Oh, no. We're not going back there. That grass has to be three feet tall. You won't catch me wading through that sea of ticks."

"Gross." Nat gave an exaggerated shudder.

"Just follow me."

Despite the threat of ticks, Nat jogged ahead of them and disappeared around the front left corner of the building. When Joe and Parker rounded the same corner, Nat was already standing at the rear edge of the motel. She glanced back, looking nervous.

"I saw something."

Joe moved in front of her and scanned the trees. "Like what?"

"I don't know. It was at the edge of the woods."

"An animal? A person?"

"I think it was a person, but I—I'm not sure."

Parker palmed her daughter's shoulder. "Could it have been a deer?"

"Maybe. I only saw it for a second."

"I'll check it out." Joe tugged once on Nat's ponytail. "Be right back."

He crossed the field, his boots making scuffing sounds as he waded through the layer of freshly cut grass. The sharp, sweet scent of the leavings reminded him of his brother. Braden had reveled in the smells of a lakeside summer. Joe's stride faltered and his chest went suddenly hollow.

"See anything?" yelled Nat.

Shake it off, man.

He held up a hand to buy himself time, and finally registered a trail through the dew-damp grass, parallel to the one he'd just made. Kids, cutting through the woods on their way to the lake? Wouldn't be the first time. As long as they didn't start lighting matches he had no problem with it.

He paused at the edge of the field, peering into the shadowed depths. Watching. Listening. The occasional dart of a squirrel, the stirring sound when a gust of air pushed through the leaves. With a series of loud nasal screeches, a blue jay warned him to mind his own business.

Good advice. *Excellent* advice. He strode back across the field, doing his damnedest to pull away from the thoughts of his brother and the plans they'd made. When he reached Nat and Parker he stopped, and shaded his eyes with the flat of his hand.

"You must have scared off whatever it was." Nat peered around him, ponytail dangling. "You okay?" She nodded.

"Thanks for checking." Parker wandered a few feet into the newly shorn field. "When did you do this?"

"Couple days ago." He raised his eyebrows at Nat. "What do you think?"

"Of the grass?"

He reached behind the square wooden structure that stood outside his back door—if he didn't have something sturdy protecting his garbage cans, the raccoons would scatter trash all the way to the lake—and retrieved a battered pair of wooden sticks. Each stick had a slight hook at the bottom.

"Of our hockey field," he said.

"Cool!" Green eyes sparked.

Parker shot him a look drenched with gratitude. He winked and offered one of the sticks to Nat, who was bouncing up and down. "I'll rake up the cuttings and rig a couple of goals. I figured with softball over, you might be ready to try something new, Nat."

The girl took the stick and proceeded to whack at a nearby dandelion. The bright yellow head popped off and sailed across the field and Nat giggled.

"When can we start?"

"No way you're bringing that home with you," Parker said quickly. "I can see it now—petals all over the greenhouse floor. Please give that back to Joe. He'll let you know when the field is ready." When Nat protested, Parker gave her an arch look. "Aren't you forgetting something? In the truck?"

Nat shoved the stick at Joe and ran off. "Take your time," Parker hollered after her. Thumbs tucked in the straps of her overalls, she turned back to Joe.

"You're not looking so hot."

"Reid would be relieved to hear you say that."

"I'm serious."

He shrugged. "Didn't get a lot of sleep last night."

"Because of Allison?" He reared back and she chuckled. "Hazel was here. You know what that means. All of Castle Creek is clued in by now."

So much for privacy. Yet another reason to be pissed at yesterday's visitor.

"You two were coworkers?"

He took his time putting the hockey sticks away. "She's a PR rep for an advertising firm near D.C. I worked there as an account exec before moving here."

"And you quit because your brother died?"

Parker wasn't the pushy type. She'd back off if he asked her to. But she'd brought muffins. And he still owed her for patching him up after that brouhaha at Snoozy's bar.

"That was one of the reasons. I had a hard time handling it. Afterward I was ready for a change."

"So with Allison here, you're reliving some tough times."

He hesitated. She showed him any more compassion and he'd be draped all over her, weeping like a grand showcase winner on *The Price Is Right*.

Apparently she sensed that, too, because she changed the subject. "Thanks for taking such good care of Nat. It makes it easier for Reid, knowing you're looking out for her. You should have heard the two of them on the phone when she told him you'd taught her to rappel—she was so excited and he was so jealous." She put a hand on his arm. "I don't know if you realize how much she depends on you. We both do. We *all* do."

He managed a nod. As nice as it was to hear, he could feel the familiar heaviness pressing against his rib cage, coiling like a cobra around his windpipe. He breathed in deep, filling his lungs. An open field at his back and still that closed-in feeling.

Parker gave him a sympathetic smile edged with concern. "Too much touchy-feely? You're looking a little green. Even more than before, I mean."

Nat came back around the corner, a cardboard box cradled in her hands. Joe's throat went tight again. The way the kid was beaming—he had a bad feeling about this.

When she reached him she gently pressed the box into his stomach. He looked down, and stifled a groan.

Nat clapped her hands. "Isn't she cute? And she's just what you need, 'cause you're always complaining about mice. What're you going to name her?"

"I...don't know."

"I could name her for you, if you want."

He looked up, away from the kitten's anxious amber gaze. His arms quivered as he toyed with the idea of pushing the box right back at Nat. But the cat chose that moment to let loose an entreating mewl.

Oh, man.

"We found three," Nat said. "Harris and I each got

a black-and-white one. I brought you the orange one 'cause she's special."

A muffled sound, coming from his right. Was that...was Parker *laughing* at him? He threw her an ominous look.

The kitten meowed again and Joe's hands tightened on the box. "Uh...what did Harris say when you gave him his?"

Nat watched him, her face expectant. "He said 'thank you.'"

Another muffled laugh before Parker finally came to his rescue. She scooped the kitten out of the box and cradled it to her chest. "Maybe Joe needs to think about it," she told her daughter gently. "A pet is a big responsibility. He might need to work his way up to it."

Too bad he couldn't enjoy his sense of relief, since it came along with a hefty dose of guilt. Then he saw the hurt in Nat's gaze and the relief evaporated altogether. He dropped the box, reached out and carefully freed the cat from Parker's arms. He held the kitten aloft and turned it this way and that, wincing as the needle-sharp claws dug into his skin.

"Looks like a mouser to me." He held the kitten against his shoulder and regarded Nat solemnly. "Thank you, sport. I'll take good care of her."

"I knew you'd love her!"

"I don't have any—"

"We brought supplies." Parker gave Nat's arm a light shake. "C'mon, kiddo. Let's get Joe set up and

then be on our way. He has things to do and so do
we." While Nat skipped ahead, Parker made a face,
reached over and stroked the kitten's downy head.
"You don't have to keep her. I tried to convince Nat
she should ask you first, but she just couldn't resist
bringing her along."

"Smart kid."

"We'll take her back if it doesn't work out." He
must have looked grateful at that offer because Parker
looked disappointed. Still, she knew how hard he
worked to keep his life simple. For some reason she—
and most of the women he knew—considered that a
challenge. And no one could complicate a situation
like a woman.

They walked in silence. She stopped him before
they reached her truck. "I am sorry, Joe. About your
brother. I didn't even know you had one, until Hazel
mentioned him."

"It's not something I talk about. But thanks." He
sucked in a breath as the kitten tried to climb his
neck. "For everything."

Ten minutes later, Joe had yet to figure out where
to put the damned litter box. The bathroom was too
small, the kitchen didn't bear thinking about and the
bedroom was off-limits—the last thing he wanted to
hear in the middle of the night was the scrape of claws
on plastic. He finally slid the tray under the reception
counter, out of sight of the guests but close enough
so he'd know right off when it needed cleaning. In

went the cat. She immediately started digging, flinging sprays of clay onto the floor.

He had a name for the creature, all right. But he doubted Nat—or her mother—would appreciate it.

The kitten made him think of Allison. He remembered hearing her once say she wanted a cat but spent too much time at the office to make it practical. He'd mocked her at the time. He looked down at Nat's gift, currently chewing on an electrical cord. With a sigh he snatched her up.

How about you, Gallahan? Anyone proud of you?

His neck muscles went tight. Damn her for bringing the memories back. For reminding him of the life he'd left behind. Of the person he'd been and never wanted to be again. Of disillusionment and betrayal. Of what he wanted and could never have.

He was tired of money and he was tired of manipulation, in all its forms. Still, he'd already accepted one responsibility today. What was one more?

With that thought, he set the kitten down, snatched up his phone and followed the orange ball of fluff into the kitchen. It bothered the hell out of him that he still knew the number by heart.

"Tackett here."

"Vince. It's Joe."

A pause. Tackett was trying to decide how to play it. Joe wasn't in the mood for games.

"Let Allison handle the client. She's more than capable."

"Mahoney wants you."

"Unless he's passing through northeast Pennsylvania and needs a room for the night, I can't help him." Joe squatted and scratched at the leg of his jeans. The kitten tensed then pounced, and Joe couldn't help but smile. "Give her the promotion. She's earned it."

"So did Danielle Franks."

"Got a feeling they earned it in very different ways."

"You get back here and give Mahoney what he wants and I'll make sure Allison gets what she wants."

Fine. A bluff it would be. Slowly, Joe straightened. "You're not hearing me. I'm not coming back."

Another pause, this one measured by a series of heavy breaths. But when Vince spoke again his voice carried a casual shrug. "Then Allison's done at Tackett & Pike."

Son of a bitch. "You're willing to sacrifice one of your best employees for Mahoney's account?"

"I'll sacrifice every schmuck in the whole damned company for Mahoney's account."

Joe swung around and glowered through the window over the sink. He frowned at the tree line, wondering what exactly Nat had seen earlier.

No. What he was doing was trying to ignore the guilt that had been squirming in his gut ever since Allison had laid into him. The very last thing he wanted to do was return to the rat race—hell, T&P had more rodents than Joe had ever had to chase out of his motel. And he knew damned well that as soon as he stepped foot in Alexandria, Vince would start his campaign to keep him there on a permanent basis.

Allison's elegant face flashed through his thoughts and he scrubbed his fingers through his hair, as if he could scour the image away. He didn't have a choice. But before he could voice his surrender, Tackett barked into the phone.

"Put her on."

"She's not here. She came by yesterday, delivered her pitch, I said 'hell, no' and she left."

"Only you didn't, did you? I talked to her afterward. She told me about your offer and I gave her the two weeks you asked for. Guess she decided to wait until today to seal the deal. So when she gets there, why don't you set her up with some hard labor? None of that sissy stuff. She's a cocky little thing— it'll serve her right. And make sure she knows she's staying with you. I'm not paying for a hotel when you can put her up at your place."

With his free hand, Joe gripped the edge of the sink and watched his knuckles turn white. "Don't play me, Tackett. I come back with her and she keeps her job. And you give her that promotion. And I want that in writing. Understood?"

"Let's wait and see what you can do for Mahoney."

"That wasn't the deal, Tackett. You screw her on this and so help me God I'll convince Mahoney to take his business elsewhere. Then I'll convince him to take your staff along with him. And if that doesn't put you out of business, I'll open my own agency and do it myself."

"That's not ethical," Tackett blustered.

"You wouldn't know ethical if it grabbed you by the balls."

Joe let go of the sink and shook the ache from his fingers. While Tackett lectured him about proprietary information agreements, Joe heard a noise, like something ripping. He tracked the kitten to the bathroom, where she was attacking the cover of a paperback he'd tossed in the corner. He nudged her out with his boot and shut the door. Non-disclosure agreements aside, the threat he'd made was an empty one. He'd start his own agency the day Tackett aced sensitivity training.

He pressed the End button, cutting off Tackett's monologue, and scowled down at his phone. How the hell did she tolerate that asshole? And more importantly, *why?* But of course he knew. The money. Apparently whatever she was spending her salary on was worth putting up with Tackett and his crap.

As much as he wanted to despise her for it, he'd once felt the same.

HE LIFTED HIS head and peered through the trees at the motel across the field. The field that didn't provide the cover it once had, thanks to the meathead owner and his lawnmower. The dude had no idea he was wasting his time sprucing up this dump.

His breath knifed in and out of his lungs and sweat

slicked his skin. Despite his jeans and sweatshirt and the seventy-degree weather, he felt cold as shit.

He huffed out a quiet snort. Make that cold as *frozen* shit.

No one came back around the corner. The coast was clear. The girl had seen him, but he'd bet that the adults had rolled their eyes and patted her head and discussed in hushed, condescending tones how she must have made it all up. All part of the parental conspiracy to eff up the kiddies.

A hot, sharp anger set his hands to shaking. He gripped his thighs and held his breath, started the usual silent count, felt the fury fade. No sense in unleashing it until he needed it. Slowly he rose out of his squat and leaned against the nearest tree, pine needles rustling under his feet. The uneven bark bit into his shoulder.

He should have backtracked as soon as he'd heard the truck. But he'd almost been inside. Almost had what he needed. And he'd almost been caught. He couldn't blow this. *Wouldn't* blow this. Next time, he'd know.

He turned his back to the motel, and made his way deeper into the sun-dappled woods.

Joe wasn't in #4, where she'd left him the afternoon before. Allison carefully made her way back up the sidewalk toward the office, stepping over and around the cracks that rendered the concrete path less than

high-heel friendly. If she'd known what she was getting into, she'd have brought her cross trainers.

Maybe even a Taser.

Then again, what if she *did* fall and break her
neck? She wouldn't have to humble herself by accepting Joe Gallahan's deal. And she wouldn't have to
learn how to use that drywall thingy he'd mentioned.

But she wouldn't have the satisfaction of paying
off Sammy, either.

She yanked open the office door and heard a faint
buzzing sound as the door closed behind her. Tugging
off her sunglasses, she stalked toward the counter.
Behind it, a set of pocket doors stood closed. She assumed Joe's office was in the back. Possibly his living quarters, too.

She eyed the bell, tempted to slap it a few times.
But of course the buzzer had already alerted Joe he
had a visitor. Antagonize him before she had a chance
to announce she'd changed her mind? Kick things off
by giving him a reason to change his? Not a good
idea.

"Be right out," he hollered from behind the doors.

She jumped, and dropped her keys. After scooping them up off a pretty hardwood floor, she took
a closer look at the space around her. Brightly col-
ored prints and a hanging basket loaded with purple and red blooms accented clean, neutral walls.
A wooden bench under the front window, a floor
lamp with a patterned shade and a brown-and-scarlet-

striped runner in front of the counter added welcoming touches to an otherwise Spartan room.

Given the state of the motel's exterior, she could only imagine the kind of work Joe had done to make the lobby look this good. Had he done it all himself? And when had he learned to do this stuff, anyway? He'd bought his D.C. condo furnished and his only contribution to the décor had been a few photos of him and his brother.

Regret pinched at her heart. She reached out to touch a flower.

Behind the pocket doors came a thump, then a curse, then a series of rattling thuds that shook the walls. By the time Joe groaned, Allison had already shoved open the doors.

He was stretched out on the floor, facedown, hands under his shoulders as he prepared to push himself up. She rushed forward and squatted next to him.

"You all right?" she asked, even as a familiar bitterness climbed her throat.

"Yeah." He pushed himself onto his knees and lifted his head, his face inches from hers. She stared into his red-rimmed but clear, blue gaze—clear being the operative word. Her surprise must have shown in her eyes because his narrowed. "Not alcohol related," he said flatly. He sat, his back against the wall, and slowly exhaled as he stretched his legs out in front of him.

She dragged her gaze away from a body that in the past year she could see had scored some heavy-duty muscles. She blinked a few times, and concentrated on the floor around them. She saw nothing nearby that could have tripped him up.

"What happened?"

He ran a hand through his hair and pointed. "That."

He was indicating the room at the end of the short hall—she could see shelving and one end of a couch, so she assumed it was his living room. She shook her head, on the verge of asking him what he was talking about, when a tiny orange tabby hopped around the corner and bounced toward them.

Joe scooped up the kitten and tucked it into his shoulder. The tabby proceeded to chew on his hair.

"You have a cat," Allison said stupidly.

"One determined to break my neck, it seems."

She stood, and backed away. That Joe had fallen for a kitten—in more ways than one—disturbed her to no end. Joe wasn't a kitten kind of guy. Dead plants were more his speed. She thought of the geraniums thriving out in the lobby and bit her lip.

"Mind holding her? So I can get up without busting my ass?" The cat dangled from his large hand.

The little tabby was adorable. Still Allison had no intention of letting those claws anywhere near her silk blouse or linen pants. She took the cat gingerly in both hands and held it out in front of her, as if she'd accepted a ticking bomb.

Joe sent her a mocking glance. Once he was on his feet he relieved her of his pet and nodded toward the lobby.

"Let me remind her where the litter box is. Then we can talk."

Allison trailed behind him, assuring herself she was checking out his backside only to make certain he wasn't limping. "What's her name?"

"I haven't decided yet. Not on anything G-rated, anyway."

He plopped her into the tray under the counter and straightened. Allison didn't miss his wince but chose to ignore it. The last thing she needed was for him to think she actually cared.

Grow up, Allie. "Sure you're okay?"

He nodded, one eyebrow raised. Damn him. "Something to drink?"

"No. Thanks." She crossed her arms, watching as he sauntered into the kitchen and opened the fridge. "You're not surprised to see me."

"I talked to Tackett."

"Of course you did. You are so not my favorite person right now."

"Feeling manipulated, are you?"

"Touché." She tapped her fingers against her upper arm. "So. We're stuck with each other."

"Looks that way." He watched her. Waiting for her to beg him to reconsider, no doubt. He'd be waiting a good long time.

"I didn't come prepared to stay, let alone work," she said.

"I can see that." He looked askance at her outfit. "You ever handle a hammer?" She opened her mouth and he added, "Successfully?" She closed her mouth. He grunted and paused before speaking again. "Ever think about working somewhere besides the agency?"

"You mean because Tackett's a sexist ass?" She shook her head. "I've invested a lot of years at T&P. It's time I started seeing some dividends. And by the way, I can learn to use a hammer." She hesitated. "Are you going to make me use a hammer?"

He took another swallow of water and set the bottle on the counter. "Be right back." When he reappeared he held up a pair of white coveralls that looked roomy enough to hold them both. Allison's thoughts fled from that unwelcome but cozy image when he tossed the coveralls in her direction. "For you."

"Are you kidding me?"

"You'll need work boots, too. I suggest you make a run to the hardware store."

"Boots. From the hardware store."

"You'd be surprised. Get something sturdy. No hot pink rubber raingear." He pulled a piece of paper from his pocket. "Pick this stuff up for me, too, would you? Put it on my tab. When you get back I'll give you a tour. And for the record, from now on we start at seven."

"I'm assuming you have a separate room for me. One with clean sheets and a working toilet."

"And if I don't?"

"Then you get to bunk with the cat."

"The cat sleeps with me."

"Huh. Now if I were the type to make tasteless jokes—"

He held up a hand. "You'll get your own room." In four steps he was across the lobby and at the door. He pushed it open. "Hardware store's on State Street. You can't miss it."

When she made to walk past him he stopped her with a hand on her arm. His nearness, his scent, the warmth of his fingers and their movement over the silk of her blouse made her shiver. *Damn it*. She pushed fear into her eyes but the awareness in his told her he wasn't buying it.

Don't look at his mouth, don't look at his mouth, don't look—

Her gaze lowered. His lips formed a smug curve, and for one desperate, self-hating moment she considered running. But she'd be running from the only solution to her problems.

"If I'm going to delay renovations for a month," he said, "just to hold the hand of a man convinced there's a market for PowerBars for pets, then I get two full weeks of labor from you. No complaints, no backtracking, no games. Agreed?"

She shrugged free of his touch. "It's cleaning products that Mahoney's into this time. And you and I both know it's all one big game to you. Always has been. But don't worry, I'll do my part. Your part is to keep your hands to yourself."

"You might change your mind about that. You might discover power tools turn you on."

Oh, for God's sake. "You start putting your hands where they don't belong and I'll start swinging my hammer. And my aim—" her gaze dropped suggestively "—might leave a lot to be desired."

"There's nothing wrong with your aim, slick. The problem has always been your choice of target."

ALLISON ZIPPED UP the front of her "uniform" and let loose a laugh that came out sounding disturbingly frantic. What in God's name had she gotten herself into? The only paint she'd ever applied had been to her fingernails. And any experience with hand tools had almost always ended in bloodshed and bandages.

She grimaced at her pale-faced image in the mirror and thought back to Joe's earlier comment. By describing himself as a target he'd made it sound like she'd plotted against him a year ago. He didn't understand she'd been trying to save the company's reputation. And Joe's along with it.

You always did put T&P first.

No. She'd done what she had to do. He didn't remember it right. How could he, considering he'd been in a constant state of drunk at the time?

She bit her lip, turned her back on her reflection and regarded the piles of clothes on the bed. At least she'd found an honest-to-goodness mall, instead of having to do her shopping at a hardware store. When she'd arrived in Castle Creek the day before she'd planned on staying no more than an hour or two. Thank God for company credit cards.

Someone pounded on her door and she jumped.

"Move it, Kincaid. We have work to do."

This could *not* be the same guy who'd cuddled a kitten two minutes after the thing had nearly made him break his neck. She'd picked up and already delivered his stupid PVC piping. What more could he want?

But of course, she knew. He wanted to teach her a lesson. She'd invaded his territory. Tried to make him feel guilty. The last place an ad-man wanted to be was on the receiving end of a sales pitch.

She closed her eyes and pulled in a slow breath. Pictured herself sitting behind that Account Executive nameplate, handing a bewildered and infuriated Sammy a stack of cash, wandering around an elegant apartment double the size of the place she lived in now.

Walking her mother into rehab. Again.

More pounding. She squeezed her eyes tighter and pictured a line of fire ants marching toward a trussed up Joe.

"Don't make me come in there."

She stalked to the door and yanked it open, bracing herself for a litany of smart-ass comments. Joe looked down at her clunky, sand-colored boots, and with the toe of his own boot nudged the nearest one.

"Show me."

She hiked her pants leg and he nodded.

"This way."

She followed him down the sidewalk, admiring the snug fit of his jeans despite herself. He stopped three doors down, in front of #5, and she raised her gaze just in time. Or maybe not, because he shot her an amused look as he searched his pockets for the keycard.

"How's your room?" he asked idly.

"Fine." Allison adjusted the clip in her hair and thought back to the soft lemon walls, the cozy tiled bathroom and the down comforter on the bed. She lowered her arms and sighed. "That's not true, actually."

She almost missed it—the subtle tightening of his fingers on the card.

"Problem?"

Huh. What she said mattered to him. Or rather, what she said about the *motel* mattered. Her chest cramped. He'd been a natural at advertising. Reveled in the challenge, expertly wooed his clients, basked in his many successes. But how much had he really cared? How much *could* he have cared, if he'd been able to walk away from it all?

Well, then. She'd have to *make* him care.

"Kincaid?" One eyebrow went up. "Problem with your room?"

"No. No problem. Just the opposite. The room is lovely."

That one eyebrow remained suspended while wariness leaked in to replace the mockery. The fact that he didn't believe her ticked her off, but she wasn't going to beg the man to take a compliment. Besides. She'd cured herself of begging him a year ago.

He pushed open the door and stood back to let her in. She stopped on the threshold and stared.

"You have *got* to be kidding me."

He'd traded an elegant capital-city condo with a killer location and a doorman for *this?* For God's sake. One glimpse and *she* needed a drink.

The paneling on the walls bore so many scrapes and gashes, there wasn't a lot of brown left to see. The ceiling sagged. The carpet was stained beyond color recognition—except for the duct tape holding it together. And even with the window wide open, the room smelled like well-used gym shoes.

She could only imagine the condition of the bathroom.

"You turned *this*—" she tipped her head in the direction of her own room "—into *that?*"

"First step is pulling up the carpet. I'll let you handle that while I fix the sink next door. After that we'll be yanking out paneling."

"Wouldn't it have been easier to burn the place down and start over?"

"Maybe in the beginning. Yell if you need anything."

She backed out the doorway. "No way I'm working in there. Not without a tetanus shot and a hazmat suit."

"What's the matter? Afraid you'll break a nail?"

Yes, as a matter of fact. "More like step on one."

"That's what boots are for." He motioned at the room with his chin. "You don't go in there, deal's off."

"You'd like that, wouldn't you?"

"Yeah. I would."

Tackett wouldn't, though. The unspoken words danced like dust motes in the air between them.

"Fine," she grumbled at last, rolling her eyes and drawing out the word so it came out *fiiii-nuh.*

With the faintest trace of a smirk, Joe pointed to a five-gallon bucket just inside the door. A mask and a pair of leather gloves lay on the carpet beside it, and from the bucket's rim hung a well-used hammer.

"Use the claw side to pry the carpeting free of the tack strips along the walls. Then start rolling."

He made it sound so easy. But she'd *almost* rather accept Sammy's sickening proposition than crawl around in the filth at her feet. She shuddered. She'd have to go out and buy herself a loofah. Or twenty.

Joe swept out an arm, as if offering paradise. "I'll leave you to it."

"Thank you so much." Her hands tangled as she stared at the ruined carpet. "What if there's something under there?"

"There is. It's called a floor."

An hour later, Allison had called Joe Gallahan every dirty name she could think of. She'd hoped to have the entire carpet up before he came back, just to show she could, but pulling the thing up had proved to be a lot harder than she'd imagined. It was heavy and thick with dirt, and kept sticking to the floor. Finally she'd resolved herself to cutting it free, inch by disgusting inch.

A mixture of sweat and dust coated her face and the back of her neck. It trickled down her spine and soaked into the waistband of her panties. Her skin crawled and she wondered if Joe had another pair of coveralls because she couldn't help fantasizing about burning the pair she was wearing. Hell, she might as well burn her entire outfit.

How did he do this all day? Her knees and lower back were killing her.

With a groan she sat back on her heels and surveyed the section of floor she'd uncovered. She'd never thought of herself as a complainer. But here, in a run-down motel, amidst cigarette butts and mouse droppings, she wanted nothing more than to indulge in a good cry. When her throat thickened in automatic response she pushed her mask up off her face and grabbed her water bottle. A few deep swigs and the tightness eased.

A mouse scurried across the floor, inches from her knees. Allison shrieked and jolted to her feet. The water bottle went flying and slammed against the wall with a sloshing thud. She was almost at the door when Joe appeared, a wrench in his hand and concern on his face. Sweat formed a dark V on the front of his T-shirt and slicked his muscled arms. All that moisture her body had been producing nonstop over the past hour? Apparently she'd used it all up, because her throat chose that particular moment to go bottom-of-the-well dry.

CHAPTER THREE

JOE'S GAZE WHISKED over her, as if checking for
blood, then scanned the room. "What happened?"

"I um, saw a, um…mouse."

His shoulders relaxed and he leaned against the
doorjamb. She could see he was trying not to smile.

"It's not funny. They're…unhygienic."

"Is that even a word?" She glared and he shrugged.
"I've had an exterminator out here but the suckers
are persistent." He released the smile. "My guess is
they're all female."

That smile took indecent liberties with her insides.
When his mouth took on that playful curve, it reminded her of less-hostile times. Of blissful, sultry,
between-the-sheets times.

Easy, Allie.

Her cell rang and she tugged off her gloves. Got
a good look at what was left of her manicure and bit
back a whimper. She plucked her phone from her
pocket and peered at the incoming number.

"I should take this."

Something flickered across his face and he jerked
a nod. "I have to go, anyway. A friend of mine needs
help. Why don't you knock off for the day? Try the

diner in town if you're hungry, and I guess I'll see you in the morning." He glanced at the lopsided roll of carpet on the floor behind her, then at the phone in her hand. "Good job, Kincaid."

She continued to stare at the doorway long after he'd left. He was as distant as he could be. Calling her by her last name, keeping himself busy with other projects so they wouldn't have to work together. Exactly what she needed him to do, if they were going to make it through the next few weeks without any messy conversations, let alone power tool mishaps.

So why did she feel slighted?

It was almost as if the effort involved in yanking carpet and refitting pipes had chipped away at the bitterness they shared. Well, it had to stop. She needed her bitterness. She and her bitterness were BFFs.

When her cell started a second series of rings she closed her eyes and pressed the phone to her ear. "Hi, Mom."

"You talked to Sammy."

Fine, Mom, thanks. And how are you?

Allison exhaled. "You and I agreed you wouldn't see him, and he and I agreed he wouldn't loan you more money. But you did, and he did, and I got a threatening phone call. I had to do something."

"He cut me off." As usual, Beryl Kincaid's words were muffled—she did most of her talking around a mouthful of butterscotch candies.

"Mom. We've been over this. What happens if you can't pay your rent and Carlotta kicks you out?"

The moment she asked the question she'd have given anything to take it back. She'd already had to make it clear—more than once—that she wouldn't sacrifice her privacy. Not on top of everything else.

"I'm working on that," her mother said, and Allison sagged against the nearest wall. "I wouldn't mind a roommate who's a little more appreciative. I made the cleverest centerpiece for the dining room table and you know what Carlotta said? She said it was tacky.'"

A crinkling sound. Her mother had popped another candy into her mouth.

"*Tacky.* Can you imagine? I spent hours on that piece. I put a little stuffed bear in a doll's chair with a curved back—you know, kind of like a throne?— gave him a jar and a honey dipper and drizzled wood glue all over him. I wish you could have seen him, he looked so adorably messy. Oh, and I glued a bee to his nose and put a tiara on his head." She paused, and sucked on her candy. "Maybe I should say *her* head. Anyway, I think the tiara glows in the dark."

"That sounds…creative." Poor Carlotta.

Her mother gasped. "Next time I'll paint hearts on the jar and I'll have the perfect Valentine's Day gift. I could make a fortune, don't you think? And ruffles. I should add ruffles." Allison could hear her mom scribbling on a piece of paper. "Anyway, after all the time I put into the centerpiece, Carlotta didn't want it. So I gave it to Sammy. *He* was thrilled. Well, not at first, but when I told him to give it to his girlfriend he perked right up."

Allison turned and rapped her forehead against the wall. "You need to stay away from Sammy. He's not your friend, Mom."

"He's a better friend than Carlotta."

Allison sighed. "Aren't your craft projects and your job at the mall enough to keep you away from the tables?"

"I get bored easily. You know I do. And when money's at stake, hours go by like seconds."

"Money has been at stake for as long as I can remember. The tables are killing you, Mom. They're killing me. I can't stand by while you dig yourself in deeper and deeper with that creep. One way or another, you're going to end up in the hospital."

"Now you're being ridiculous. Sammy would never hurt me."

"We stop paying and that's exactly what he'll do." She pushed away from the wall and surveyed the room. As messy as it was, it couldn't compare to the wreckage that was her life. But she was a daughter, with a mother who'd once risked everything to protect her.

She had to ask. "You making your meetings okay?"

"Of course I am," her mother snapped. "And I wish you wouldn't feel the need to ask every time we talk."

"I care about you. I want you to get better."

"You mean you want me to stop being a burden."

"Mom—"

"But I think I've found a way to fix that."

Oh, God. Oh, no. "What do you mean?"

"You'll find out. How long will you be away?"

"Two weeks." Because Joe Gallahan was determined to be an ass. "Mom. No more gambling. Promise me."

"It's not a gamble when it's a sure bet."

"Mom?"

"Trust me, Allie girl."

"Mom."

She'd disconnected.

Allison gritted her teeth and glared down at the phone. She really should have chucked the damn thing into the lake.

AN HOUR LATER she was combing her damp hair and trying to convince her empty stomach it could survive until morning when she remembered the packet of M&M's she'd stashed in the glove compartment. She might be too tired and achy to check out the diner Joe had mentioned, but she could certainly limp as far as her car. When there was chocolate at stake, she'd *crawl* if she had to.

She shimmied into a pair of jeans and a black, short-sleeved shirt, wishing she'd had the chance to wash her new clothes. But at least she didn't have to climb back into those grime-encrusted coveralls. Not yet, anyway.

After scooping up her keys she walked barefoot to her car. A sleepy gray haze had crept into the summer evening, heralding dusk. Cool air, crisp as a Granny Smith apple, had her thinking of porch swings, oversize sweatshirts and glasses of red wine. On second thought, scratch the wine.

She forced her mind away from the thought of alcohol and what it could do to a person—to a *couple*—and looked around. Crumbling asphalt, exterior walls that looked like someone had painted them with mashed-up peas, flowerbeds sporting more weeds than blooms, a construction Dumpster that was no doubt as practical as it was unsightly. But there was also a brand-new professional sign towering over her car, a gracious lobby and…her room. A room that had been more than renovated—it had been lovingly decorated.

By a woman? She hadn't considered that before. That Joe might be involved. But why should she consider it? And why should she care?

She glanced again at the sign. Sleep at Joe's. Clever. And something that two days ago she was certain she'd never do again.

The ball of her foot landed on a sharp-edged rock. She hissed in a breath, her limp more pronounced as she approached her car. Suddenly she caught a whiff of something fruity and her stomach perked up. She and Joe hadn't talked about meals—they hadn't really talked logistics at all. His earlier recommendation of the diner probably meant she was on her own, food-wise.

Though judging by today, she might be on her own. *Period.*

Supposedly Joe was looking for payback, but he

hadn't seemed to get much of a kick out of Allison on her hands and knees in filth. And she'd thought for sure he'd enjoy mocking her reaction to the mouse. Instead he'd taken it in stride. Well, mostly.

With a frown, she rummaged through the glove compartment. Nothing edible. She sighed. Next on the agenda? Find a supermarket. And put M&M's at the top of her list. She needed all the help she could get dealing with not only Tackett and Joe, but her mother's pleas for money.

And the next time Beryl Kincaid called, Allison would let voice mail do its thing. She might get more sleep that way. Because she knew that if her mother had her way, they'd both be living out of Allison's car.

She shut the car door just as a dusty blue over-size pickup pulled into the lot and parked beside her. Joe. Allison curled her toes into the pavement, feeling suddenly naked. He rounded the hood of his truck, a mouthwatering package of muscle, denim and shadowed jaw. Considering he had eyes only for her Toyota, she obviously didn't have the same pulse-pounding effect on him.

Which was good. Great, in fact. Things were complicated enough.

Still, it smarted.

"I meant to ask." Joe hitched a thumb at her car. "What happened to the Beemer?"

She shoved her fingers into her back pockets. She didn't want to lie. But she didn't want to tell the truth, either. "Got something against Camrys?"

He looked as if he wanted to say more, then shrugged. "Didn't see you at the diner."

"It's been a while since I last pulled up fifty-year-old carpet. I had a hard enough time getting in and out of the shower."

Instantly she regretted her provocative words, but Joe didn't take the unintentional bait. Though why should he? Their bantering days were long gone. He merely nodded, then turned back to his truck. Moments later he held up a crisp white bag.

"I brought you a sandwich."

"Ham?"

"Extra pickles."

Her mouth watered. She squinted. "In exchange for…"

"An answer. To one question."

"Do I get to ask one, too?"

"Did you bring me dinner?"

They stared at each other over the roof of her car. In his eyes she could see that bitterness she'd been wondering about. She sighed.

"Let me guess. You want to know if it bothers me. That Tackett's basically holding my future for ransom. Am I right?" An incline of his head signaled that she'd guessed correctly. Her gaze dropped to the bag in his hand. "You realize you're doing the exact same thing."

"There's a difference between two weeks and an entire career. And unlike Tackett, I honor my word. After I've served my four weeks he'll ask for more.

He'll offer a bonus if I stay, forget to pay me if I don't. I won't be staying. You shouldn't, either."

"So now you're looking out for me. How very—" *Wait a minute.* She pushed away from the car, a blush of fury scorching her from head to toe. "You *want* me to quit. To get back at the old man. Or are you hoping you won't have me to deal with once you're there?" When he didn't answer she swallowed against a pang of…something…and glowered. "You don't like that question? Fine. Here's another one."

A muscle car drove past the motel, engine growling, radio blaring an energetic song. Allison blinked back inexplicable tears.

"Were you and Danielle lovers?" she asked.

Joe took his time positioning the bag on the hood of her car. When he looked back up his face had lost all expression. "We were barely friends."

"That's not what I asked."

"No. We were never lovers. I had you. I didn't need anyone else."

She released the breath she'd been holding, but the pressure in her chest didn't ease. She turned away. "Good night, Joe."

"You forgot your sandwich, Allison."

It would be churlish to refuse, though her appetite had vanished. At least he'd stopped calling her by her last name. When he did that he sounded like Tackett.

She reached for the bag. So did he. He didn't let go. Instead he held out his free hand. "Truce?"

"So this is a bribe."

"More like a peace offering." When she hesitated he wiggled his fingers. "Come on. I'm not asking to be friends. You don't want to be here and I don't want to go back. But we're stuck with each other. And two weeks is a long time to trade dirty looks. So what do you say? Truce?"

"Well." It was easier just to give in. She put her hand in his. "You did say extra pickles."

"JOE?" NO ANSWER. Another rap of her knuckles on the glass, but the lobby remained dark. Damn. She had no way of knowing whether he'd already gone to bed or just couldn't hear her knock. And she'd never thought to ask for his cell number.

She shivered in the cool night air and glanced around. At each end of the motel lurked a tall, skinny pole, the beams from the lights at the top casting broad puddles of pale yellow onto the broken pavement. The light glinted off the windshield of Joe's truck. He was definitely here.

She drew in a resolute breath and marched around the side of the building. The sooner they got this settled, the better.

The dew-damp grass slicked her toes, making her feet slide in her flip-flops, every step a rubbery squeak. She hesitated at the corner—no lights back here but for the dim bulb over the door. A pair of moths flirted with the scrawny light, making tiny little pings whenever they connected with the glass.

She yanked at the hem of her top, skirted the

wooden box that protected his garbage cans and stepped onto the slab of cement that served as a porch.

Nothing but darkness on the other side of the square window in the door. For God's sake, it was only ten o'clock. He'd always been a night owl— surely he couldn't have changed that much?

Then again, there didn't seem to be a lot to do in Castle Creek. Especially after dark. Except maybe— Allison's breathing hitched and a prickling heat swept across her skin. An image of what Joe could very well be doing in the dark had her snatching her hand away from the door and stumbling back a step.

After her encounter with the mouse, Joe had said he had to go help a friend. Maybe that friend was female? And maybe she was in his apartment at this very moment, in his *bed,* and they were shaking their heads at the idiot outside who couldn't take a hint?

Embarrassment shoved her back another step and she started to turn away. Then suddenly he was there, looming on the other side of the windowpane. *Not* naked. Not from the waist up, anyway. The door swung inward.

"Come in before the moths do," he said.

She hesitated. Something in his voice… His hair was rumpled, his feet bare and he wore sweatpants and a T-shirt—clothes that could be pulled on in a matter of seconds.

Or off.

She blinked away an unwanted memory. "I don't want to interrupt…anything. You alone?"

"Mostly."

She started to ask what that was supposed to mean when she heard the kitten, meowing softly in the background. *Funny guy.* She gave a half shrug and sidled past, holding her breath so she wouldn't breathe in the scent of bed-warmed male.

He shut the door behind her and turned, hand still on the knob. "There a problem?"

"Could you turn off the light?"

"Come again?"

It took real effort to keep her mind from going in an X-rated direction. *For God's sake, Allie, grow up.* "The outdoor light. Those poor moths."

He stretched a hand to the wall. The room went black. Allison blinked and thrust out her hands, feeling suddenly off-kilter.

Asking him to turn off the light might have been a mistake. Still, she couldn't get that pinging noise out of her head.

"Anything else I can do for you?"

Damn that "throw me to the floor" voice of his. "I know it's late, but I hoped we could talk."

"No."

She frowned in the abrupt silence. Then the refrigerator gurgled and she found her voice. "It won't take long."

"Not gonna happen."

Huh. So maybe "mostly" alone didn't involve the kitten, after all. Maybe "mostly" meant his date was asleep. Or maybe Allison needed to remember that just because they'd declared a truce, it didn't mean he was happy she was here in Castle Creek.

She clamped her teeth together. "Fine. We'll talk in the morning. Sorry I bothered you."

"My answer will be the same when the sun comes up." A whisper of fabric—she imagined him folding his arms across his chest. "I mean, I'm assuming you're here to wriggle out of our deal, right?"

"I didn't come to wriggle out of anything. I came to have a rational conversation. But obviously this isn't a good time." She took a step toward the door. He didn't move. She blew out an impatient breath. "If you don't get out of my way I can't get out of your hair."

"I can offer more than conversation."

A mingling of anger and longing sapped the strength from her knees. Had she considered him funny at one time? Try hateful. She sneaked a step to the left and sagged against the counter. Not one of her better ideas, coming here at this hour. Though she wouldn't admit to it now, she actually had hoped to talk Joe into letting her leave. Now all she wanted to do was scuttle back to her room and lock herself in.

"If you mean coffee," she managed, "I'm in. Anything else and you're out of your mind." *Like me.*

He grunted, but that was all the reaction she got. His breathing remained steady—unlike hers. She let her hands slap back against her sides.

"Are we really going to just stand here in the dark?"

"I like the dark. It hides a multitude of sins." When

she didn't—couldn't—respond, he laughed softly. "Follow me."

He paused beside her, and ran his fingers down her arm to her wrist, the heat of his touch suggesting an erotic promise she almost wished he could keep. He tugged lightly. She let him lead her out of the kitchen and down the hallway, past a tiny bathroom to the seating area she'd caught a glimpse of before. He let go of her wrist and pressed a palm to her back, encouraging her to cross the threshold.

A rickety-looking card table sat in front of a pair of windows overlooking the field behind the motel. On top of the table sat a bronzed, bottom-heavy lamp, which shed its light on a thick book of crosswords, a mason jar full of pencils, a clear glass tumbler and a half-empty bottle of whiskey. A cold, crawling bleakness filled her belly. She wandered into the center of the room then slowly turned. He watched her, his mouth forming an arrogant slant, his navy eyes glazed with a falseness she'd learned to despise a year ago.

"You've been drinking." Inwardly she winced at the accusation in her voice. *None of your business.* Not anymore. Still, she couldn't help mourning the day-old hope that just that moment unwound itself from around her heart and slunk away. She took a breath and added quietly, "I thought you'd given it up."

"I gave up getting drunk. Drinking? Not so much."

She jerked her chin at the bottle of Glenlivet. "This is what you meant when you said you weren't alone."

He shrugged. "I'm guessing I don't need to hunt up a second glass."

A mewling sound. They both looked down in time to see the kitten launch herself at Joe's leg. He bent and plucked her free of his sweatpants, cradled her in his arms and scratched her belly. A soft, satisfied rumbling filled the room.

Allison swallowed, but the ache in her throat refused to recede. An overwhelming sadness crowded her chest, pressing painfully against her heart, and she shook her head.

"I can't do this again. I *won't* do this again."

"If you're talking about renovating it's obvious you've never done it before."

"You know exactly what I'm talking about." She strode back to the doorway but Joe stayed put. Why hadn't she realized the moment he'd opened the door? The moment he'd spoken? She could have left then, instead of finding herself in the position of having to bluff her way past him.

"Excuse me," she said briskly. "I have to pack."

"You leave, I stay."

Damn him. "You gave your word."

"So did you."

"When I thought you were sober."

"Does it matter? We made no stipulations."

"We did, actually. Something about keeping your hands to yourself?"

He took his time looking her over, from her flip-flops to her brand-new jeans to the baby doll pajama top she hadn't bothered exchanging for a shirt. His gaze seemed to settle on her shoulders, and she found herself wishing stupidly that she'd taken the time to brush her hair. She was worse than pathetic.

"Just so we're clear," he drawled, "the same doesn't apply to you."

Despite herself, despite…everything…a heated thrill of remembered pleasure zinged straight from her heart to her belly. *Stop that.* She struggled to focus on all the long-ago nights she'd been desperate to touch him, to lose herself in his caresses, but instead had lain frozen and aching on her side of the bed. Why? Because he'd been too drunk to realize she was there, let alone to make love to her.

Did he really think it would be that easy? Did he think it was even an *option?*

You've thought about it, too. She had. Of course she had. At one time they'd been good together. Very good. And as different as he'd seemed to be…

Now she knew that only his appearance had changed. And that he'd found a new hobby. Everything else that counted had stayed the same.

"Is this part of the plan? Seduce the woman who plotted against you? Make her fall for you all over again so she'll beg you to let her stay? Then of course you'll respond with, 'Sorry, my sweet. Offer expired. Let me get the door.'" She tipped her head. "I can see the poetic justice."

"Nice touch, that thing with the door." He leaned over and released the cat onto the sofa. When he straightened, brushing the orange hairs from his T-shirt, his expression had loosened. "No plan. Just fond memories. I miss the look of stunned bliss on your face when you come."

She sucked in a breath. "Damn you and damn that bottle, Joe Gallahan. What you miss is your old life. You're just too proud to admit it."

"I am *not* drunk. I've been drinking, yeah, but it takes more than a few swallows of hooch to knock me on my ass. And you're wrong, slick. I sure as hell don't miss my old life. Right now? I'm missing my beauty sleep. So unless you want to join me…"

"Haven't we punished each other enough?"

"Hardly." He yawned, then scrubbed a hand over his hair and headed toward his bedroom. "Lock the door behind you. Don't forget we start at seven tomorrow."

"This is ridiculous," she said to his back. "There's no reasoning with you."

"Yet you persist."

Because that's what idiots do. She sighed. "Why is it so important for me to stay?"

At the door to his bedroom he turned. "Because I can make you. I may not wear a suit anymore, but I still like to call the shots." He bared his teeth. "Almost as much as I like to drink 'em."

JOE LAY ON his back, one hand cupped around the kitten sprawled on his chest, the other pressed to his head. The cat was snoring, every fur-coated rumble like a buzz saw ripping through Joe's brain. How the hell could something so small create such a massive sound? And why hadn't that handful of pills kicked in yet?

Gingerly he raised his head high enough to aim a one-eyed squint at the clock. Almost time to roll. Yee-haw. He lowered his head again, and groaned when it connected with his hard-ass pillow. If he weren't expecting Allison he'd stay in bed, at least until he could blink without sending pain shooting through his skull.

Then again, if he weren't expecting Allison he wouldn't have polished off that bottle of whiskey last night.

Two weeks. Damn. He'd better stock up.

He closed his eyes, pictured her in her borrowed getup and shifted on the bed. Who knew a determined woman sweating through an oversize pair of coveralls could be such a turn-on? Too bad she'd never let him anywhere near that zipper. He let loose an aching moan.

And then, of course, there was the outfit she'd showed up in last night. Tight jeans and some silky, floaty, barely there top with short sleeves. Pale pink, like the polish on her naked toes. When they'd stood in the cool darkness of the kitchen, where he could hear the excited hitch in her breathing, and smell the familiar spicy peach scent she'd stroked across her skin, all he'd wanted to do was strip her, push her against the wall and lick every inch.

But he hadn't wanted her to smell the booze on him. Because he'd known she'd react...well, exactly how she had reacted. Which was why he'd led her to the living room after all. Where she could see for herself what he'd been up to.

As often as he'd fantasized about taking a horizontal trip or two down memory lane the last couple of days, he knew it would never happen. Allison Kincaid had never been the type for casual encounters. And shame on him, anyway, for lusting after a woman he didn't trust any more than he trusted Vince Tackett.

What he should have done was get up early this morning and hit the treadmill. An hour-long run would have helped take the starch out of his libido.

Who you kidding, asshole? He'd had to practically crawl to the bathroom to get the ibuprofen.

He exhaled, deposited the kitten on the bed beside him and pushed himself up. The pounding in his head didn't get any kinder, but at least he no longer felt the need to hurl.

I don't want to be here. Haven't we punished each other enough?

So much for a truce. Not that either of them had really wanted it in the first place. Damn it, why'd she have to go all judgmental on him? It was no surprise she hadn't appreciated his comment about calling the shots. But he deserved some payback of his own and he was going to get it.

He sure as hell wasn't going to get anything else.

He stroked a palm down the length of his hard-on, his groin somehow managing to out-throb his head. He imagined Allison sinking to her knees in front of him, licking her lips and humming deep in her throat....

He called himself one of the names he'd considered for the cat, peeled off his boxers and staggered to the shower, desperate for the temporary relief of a hot water massage and a personal hand job.

He was showered and dressed and considering a little hair of the dog when the buzzer sounded. Allison called out then appeared in the doorway wearing jeans and a bright green top, the grimy coveralls over one arm, her pale blond hair neatly gathered in a plastic clip. Her eyes were heavy-lidded, her ivory cheeks still flushed with sleep, and it was all he could do not to flash back to the rare mornings they'd awakened in the same bed, him reaching out, her instantly arching, pressing close and hot against him—

Judas Priest. How the hell could he still want her, after everything she'd done and who she'd become? He angled away from her. Busied himself pulling mugs out of a cupboard.

"You stayed," he said curtly.

"You didn't give me a choice." She looked around, probably for the kitten, and draped the coveralls over the back of the nearest chair. "Are you feeling as miserable as you look?"

"Just about."

"Good."

He banged the mugs down onto the countertop, then flinched.

"I've been thinking," she said, with just the tiniest trace of smugness. "I know there are...things we don't like about each other. Things we both did that we're finding hard to get past. Simply put, if we have any hope of getting this job done, we have to overlook these things—all of them. For now."

"You mean, so Tackett can have his way."

"So we can *all* move on."

"To D.C. Where I get to be Tackett's lackey. Got any pointers for me, Kincaid?"

Her lips went tight and she shook her head. "Got any coffee for me, Gallahan?"

It was like they were playing Go Fish. He set his jaw and slid a mug across the counter, hiding a wince at the loud scraping sound. "Help yourself." He watched her, wondered what she'd do if he offered her a little Irish to go with her brew. As she hefted the pot, her gaze veered to his yolk-smeared plate in the sink and he closed his throat against an instinctive invite. She already had him by the short hairs. Damned if he'd offer up his balls, too.

And anyway, he didn't have any eggs left, though where the hell they went, he had no idea. The loaf of bread seemed shorter, too. He hadn't had *that* much to drink. Maybe he'd started sleep-eating? Wouldn't be much of a stretch, considering what he'd dealt with over the past few days.

"Thanks for the coffee," she murmured.

"Bring it with you." He grabbed his own mug and headed for the door. But she didn't move, didn't even seem to hear him, her attention focused on the microwave he kept on top of the chest-high refrigerator. The kitten bounced into the room and was headed for the food dish when Allison suddenly reached out and stabbed a button on the appliance. The high-pitched *ping* startled the cat. Tiny claws scratched feverishly over the linoleum as the kitten scurried out of the room.

All Allison had done was zero out the remaining seconds on the display, but she was smiling as if she'd set the thing to detonate the next time he used it.

An hour later they had the carpet in #5 rolled up to within four feet of the far wall. They knelt in opposite corners, each working a hammer into the space between the carpet and the tack strip. As awkwardly as Allison handled her tools, she worked faster than he did. It was the damned hangover.

And his tendency to stop every minute or so and look over at her.

She'd shocked the hell out of him when he'd ordered her to wrestle a carpet lined with decades of grime and she hadn't told him to go screw himself— because she sure had every reason to. She was used to wining and dining clients in high-end restaurants, facilitating million-dollar contracts and shopping for PR party duds at cutesy designer boutiques in Old Town. Yet here she was, wearing ill-fitting, stain-

resistant cotton and big-ass boots, helping him renovate a country motel without giving him anywhere
near the grief he deserved.

Which would be more impressive if it weren't so
obvious that the job—the *money*—meant everything
to her. And he was dying to know why. What was
the something she needed so desperately? Or was it
a some*one*?

He shifted, relieving the pressure on his knees.
How many times did he have to tell himself—?

Suddenly a wolf spider with a body the size of a
goddamned golf ball popped out from under the carpet. Joe yelled and fell back on his ass. He stared at
the spider as it scuttled toward the door, then over at
Allison, whose eyes were rounder than the fried eggs
he'd forced himself to eat for breakfast.

He started to laugh, and she started to laugh, and
at the sight of her dirt-smudged face lit with unre-
strained humor, the late morning sun gilding her hair
and gleaming on her pale skin, he realized that he
had screwed himself. Big time.

Because at that precise moment, what he wanted
most in the world was the freedom to pull her into
his arms, kiss her breathless, inhale her sweetness
and absorb her heat. And that freedom was the last
thing she'd ever grant him.

He jerked to his feet. "I have paperwork. We can
finish this later." He motioned with his chin at the
nearest wall. "Next step is tearing down the paneling. Feel up to tackling that yourself?"

She rose more slowly, her face adopting the polite and professional mask she'd always worn for T&P clients. She nodded. "My trusty hammer and I won't let you down."

"Don't forget your goggles," he said, and got the hell out of there.

He HOVERED AT the edge of the tree line, his gaze sharp on the open window. Surprisingly the meathead who'd convinced himself he could run a motel had had the sense to ventilate the room while painting it. Kind of a shame, really. 'Cause with all those fumes trapped in that tiny space, one flicker of flame was all it would take to burn the whole place down.

Whoosh. And a hellish history would be...history.

He shivered, glad that despite the bright morning sun he was wearing his hoodie. Not that he had much choice. If he had to make a run for it he'd just as soon nobody got a good look at him. An inhale rewarded him with a whiff of the lake—seaweed roasting on summer rocks. An answering ache in his stomach. He distracted himself by concentrating on the task at hand.

Pay attention.

Meathead must have finished painting because he'd moved on to the next room—and he had a partner now. Pulling up carpet—how much help could that skinny blonde be? Didn't matter. What did matter was that his chances of being caught had just doubled. Uneasiness sparked at the base of his spine. He worked up a mouthful of saliva and spit.

He'd come too far, waited too long to back out now.

Keeping his eyes on that fifth window, he loped toward the only door on the back side of the building. Locked, of course. Meathead was smarter than he looked. But not smart enough to install a keycard lock, like the ones on the guest room doors. With the help of a torque wrench and a paperclip, he was in.

He carefully closed the door behind him, shoved back the hood of his sweatshirt and looked around. Three times, now, he'd broken into this dump. Still, he took a moment to bask in his accomplishment, to enjoy his triumph over the new owner and his cheap-ass locks.

At least, that's what he let himself believe. The real reason for his hesitation was too complicated—too painful—to think about.

At the end of a long, narrow counter was a once-white stove, now yellowed with age, pushed into the corner. On the other side of a faded strip of linoleum crouched an undersize refrigerator. Beside it stood a small sink and a square of countertop big enough to support all four feet of a stainless steel toaster, the gleaming mass of which mocked the rest of the kitchen.

He squeezed his eyes shut, and curled his fingers into his palms, fighting the desperate need to bash, to bellow, to burn the whole godforsaken pile down to the goddamned ground. One shaking hand went to the pouch at his belly, pressed against the slim bulk of the lighter he kept there.

Not yet. He didn't understand why, but he just knew he had to wait.

He opened his eyes, inhaled, yanked open the refrigerator door. Milk, cheese, apples, salad stuff. And the ever-present beer. He rubbed at the sudden tightness in the center of his chest.

The dude needed to shop. And he'd eaten the rest of the eggs, damn him. But he still had potatoes. And ketchup.

His belly let loose a pleading gurgle as he contemplated hash browns and toast. But he couldn't risk taking the time to cook again, let alone wash up. With a grunt he grabbed an apple and hit the cabinets next. Not much he could take that wouldn't be missed. Finally he eyed the loaf of whole wheat bread on the counter and sighed. Peanut butter and jelly it would have to be. Again.

He was drying the knife he'd used when the buzzer in the hallway sounded. *Shit.* Luckily the pocket doors were closed, but he should have thought to check them before.

Someone mumbling. It was Meathead. And he sounded pissed.

Soundlessly he set the knife on the counter, wrapped a paper towel around his sandwich and backed quietly down the hall and into the bathroom. He wedged himself into the narrow space behind the door, the backs of his legs mashed up against the toilet. Meathead would definitely see him if he poked his head in—or if he had to use the john.

Shit. Shit, shit, *shit.*

A muted rumble as the pocket doors slid along the track. Footsteps pounded on the linoleum. A frustrated sigh, the slam of a cabinet door, the soft rush of water as Meathead held a glass under the faucet.

The thick smell of peanut butter rose up around him, and his belly begged loudly for a bite. He held his breath. A *clack* as the water glass was put on the counter, more muttering, then footsteps coming closer, and closer.

Even as he fought to hold his breath, to keep quiet, the memories crowded in. Ugly, aching, relentless snatches of the past. Sweat dribbled from his scalp and into his ear. A rushing sound, punctuated by the echoing thud of his heart. He pressed his left fist to his mouth while the fingers of his right hand curled into the sandwich. If Meathead found him, he wouldn't get another chance. He'd have to run, lay low and wait a hell of a long while before coming back.

A soft sound, near the floor. His stomach went into free fall. He looked down and saw a little orange tabby looking back up at him and almost pissed himself as his muscles loosened. The dude had a *cat?* Since when?

The thing meowed, like it thought it might like a bite of his sandwich. He swallowed a groan. With his left foot he nudged it back toward the door. It meowed again, and launched an attack on his boot.

"I hear you, girl. Where are you?"

Give me an effin' break.

He shook the cat free of his boot and pushed it into a slide. The cat scooted on its ass out into the hallway and hit the opposite wall with a tiny thump.

"There you are. Ouch, damn, you really need to stop climbing my leg. Tell you what, let's get some fresh air. You can drool at the birds while I kick my own ass for thinking I could get one over on a woman."

Meathead continued talking nonsense to the cat as he headed back up the hallway. *Front door, front door, front door.* If he saw the back door was unlocked, he might get suspicious.

The buzzer sounded. He emptied his lungs. Silence settled over the little apartment.

So the dude's new helper had him by the balls. If that was all Meathead had to worry about, he should count himself lucky.

He relaxed his hands and rested his forehead against the wall's cool, cracked plaster. Gradually his heartbeat slowed. He sidled free of the toilet, opened his hand and scowled down at the remains of his sandwich. The sooner he did what he came to do, the sooner he could move on. Find someplace soft to sleep. Something decent to eat.

And, shit. Maybe he'd even get himself a cat.

ALLISON WANDERED INTO the center of the room, boots thumping across the subfloor. *What just happened?* One second they're laughing, and the next…

She shook her head, tamping down the hurt that she knew was ridiculous to feel. What was she thinking, anyway? This was *business.* Nothing more, nothing less. Wondering whether she and Joe could be anything but bitter ex-lovers would win her nothing but aggravation. She'd do well to follow his example and keep her distance.

Especially since he was still drinking. Did she really want to get sucked into that alcohol-infused chaos again? She already had one addict in her life.

Just as well she was in the mood to do some damage. Maybe if she exhausted herself she'd manage to get some sleep tonight. Troubles with Joe aside, this…village he lived in was too damned quiet. And dark. And Stepford-like.

Hammer in hand, mask and goggles in place and teeth in a determined clench, she approached the nearest panel. After wedging the claw in between the seams, she levered the hammer to the side. The paneling gave way a lot easier than she expected and she stumbled forward and smacked her forehead against the wall. *Good going, Allie.* She backed up, rubbing the heel of her hand over what promised to be one heck of a bruise. And all for nothing, because instead of freeing the edge of the paneling she'd actually splintered it.

She tried again, a little lower this time, and managed to create a gap between two sections. She dropped the hammer on the floor, tucked her gloved fingers around the panel's edge and pulled. Harder, and harder still. The thin board finally broke free and she staggered backward.

By the time she'd leaned the grime-covered panel against an adjoining wall, her arms felt heavy and she was breathing as if she'd just run laps around the motel.

She dusted off her palms and smirked at the space she'd opened up. Thick motes of dust floated and bobbed in front of her. Skinny strips of insulation and thick electrical wires dangled between the studs. It looked like an especially fat coil of cable was wedged between…

Hold on. *What the—?* She tugged off her goggles. Craning her neck, standing on tiptoe, she took a closer look.

And let loose the mother of all screams.

CHAPTER FOUR

THIS TIME SHE was halfway up the sidewalk before Joe appeared. She collapsed against the stucco siding and struggled to catch her breath while he came to a stop in front of her, hands on hips, chest rising and falling in sync with hers.

"You scared the hell out of me," he said. "Please tell me it was just another mouse."

She grabbed his arm, her hand shaking so hard his muscles vibrated. "There's a s-snake. In the wall."

He pulled away and looked her up and down. "Did it bite you?"

"N-no."

"Was it poisonous?"

"I didn't think to ask."

"Where did it go?"

"It didn't go anywhere. It didn't move."

"Judas Priest." He rammed a hand through his hair. "Okay. So you saw a dead snake. You wait here. I'll get a broom and a dustpan."

She laughed, a little wildly. "Forget the broom. Got a wheelbarrow?"

"How big is it exactly?"

"You're the one with the tape measure. You figure it out."

"Tell you what." His drawl sounded more condescending than patient, damn him. "You show me where it is, and I'll take it from there."

"No way I'm going back in there. You shouldn't, either. We need to call someone."

"Like who, the local snake patrol? You wait here. I'll check it out."

"But—"

"Be right back." He jogged down the sidewalk and disappeared into the room. Five seconds later she heard "Son of a *bitch.*" Slowly he backed out onto the sidewalk, then lunged forward and pulled the door shut. When he turned to look at her, his face was almost as gray as his T-shirt. "You could have warned me."

"I tried to." The fact that *he* was nervous doubled her freak-out factor. She wrapped her arms around herself and backed toward the office.

"That's a *python,*" Joe said, pointing at the closed door. "How the hell did a *python* end up in my motel? If that thing had got hold of either one of us, we wouldn't have had a chance."

Exactly what she needed to hear. She slumped against the building, unable to stop shaking. The thought of that thing slithering toward her, coiling around her...

"Aw, hell." Suddenly Joe stood in front of her. He

reached out, hesitated, dropped his hands to his sides. "I didn't mean to scare you."

"I'm thinking we can blame that on the snake," she muttered. Though the fact that he'd been about to pull her into his arms was nearly as frightening. How bizarre would that be, to have Joe Gallahan as her personal protector? Joe, who had the power to take away her only source of security?

Her gaze avoided his. "Do you think it's dead?"

"No."

"Should we call Animal Control?"

"Doesn't exist in Castle Creek. Even if it did, I doubt they'd handle something like this."

"So what do we do?"

"We get someone here who can help." He watched her a moment longer, then freed his cell from the holster on his belt. She distracted herself from visions of slow suffocation by guessing who he was calling.

"Police?" she asked. "Fire department?"

He shook his head and held the phone to his ear. "Librarian."

TWENTY MINUTES LATER, Noble Johnson arrived, followed by two members of Castle Creek's Volunteer Fire Department. Noble stepped out of his pickup wearing steel-toed boots and motorcycle leathers, carrying a hard hat in one hand and a hockey mask in the other. Joe didn't know whether to mock him or high-five his good sense. Though none of that gear would matter if the snake decided to play Ring Around the Rosie.

After the introductions were made—Allison did an admirable job hiding her shock at the librarian's mammoth proportions—Noble and the two firefighters checked out #5. Joe had no idea if the snake had stayed put and he'd had no desire to find out. When the three men emerged from the unit, they were shaking their heads and bumping knuckles.

"That's a first for us," the dark-haired volunteer—Burke—said. "We've trapped and released possums, 'coons, skunks and the occasional fox. But we've never seen anything like this."

Joe looked at Noble. "It is a python, right?"

Noble removed his hard hat and passed a hand over his bristly white-blond hair. "Burmese," he said, his expression avid. "You can tell by the color—brown with gold markings. Unless it's a caramel. Either way it can grow to more than twenty feet, weigh a couple hundred pounds."

Joe heard a feminine gasp behind him. Before he could react Burke moved to Allison's side and murmured in low, soothing tones. Joe glared, then realized if he had to be pissed at someone, it should be himself. Why couldn't he stifle the urge to look out for her? She sure as hell had never looked out for *him*.

When he realized how pathetic that sounded, he scrubbed a hand over his mouth and wondered how many beers he had left in the fridge.

"I've read about cases like this." The second firefighter, a thin man with thick auburn hair, cracked his knuckles. "Happens all the time. Idiots think it's cool to own a snake until they realize it eats like a lion and shi—er, craps like a horse. So they release it into the woods, figuring it can take care of itself." He shook his head in disgust. "It doesn't even occur to them that pythons aren't native to Pennsylvania."

Noble scratched his head. "That snake's been having a field day, chowing down on all them mice you got in there."

"So how come I still have mice?"

"Just think how many you'd have if he weren't hanging around."

"Good point. All right. No matter how it got in there I have to get it out. Call me crazy, but I have a feeling it wouldn't be good for business. So what do you suggest?"

Noble looked at the firefighters and they looked back at him. Noble nodded. "I'll get my .45."

"No!" When everyone turned to stare, Allison flushed and hiked her chin. "It's not the snake's fault his owner didn't want him anymore." She gazed at Joe, hazel eyes entreating. "Please don't let them kill it."

He tried not to resent the compassion she was showing for a damned snake. "Correct me if I'm wrong, but weren't you the one screaming loud enough to rattle the windows?"

Her expression changed, and carried a clear message. *Want me to announce how a spider had you squealing like a little girl?*

He winced. "You're not saying I should keep the thing."

"Of course not. But he doesn't deserve to die."

"Neither do we." This time everyone looked at Noble. The big man's cheeks turned as red as the geraniums hanging in the motel lobby. "I mean, c'mon. That thing is frickin' *huge*."

Allison shoved her hands in the pockets of her coveralls. "What about the zoo?"

A faded red Jeep careened into the parking lot. A few seconds later, Snoozy, the usually slow-moving bar owner, hurried around the hood toward them. Joe raised a hand in greeting. "Wonder what he's doing here."

"Probably heard it on the scanner. Looking for something to do, since the bar don't open for a couple hours." Noble turned back to Allison. "Zoo's not a bad idea. But most of 'em have all the reptiles they can handle *because* of situations like this. I'd say call in a trapper but I doubt we could find one specializing in Asian pythons."

Burke frowned. "Meanwhile, the thing could make a break for it and start killing pets. Or worse."

Oh, hell, no. "I won't be responsible for that. Let's call the vet." Joe reached out and squeezed Allison's arm. "The kindest thing would be to have him euthanized."

"Don't you dare." Snoozy charged into the middle of the group. "Where is she?"

"She who?" Joe exchanged a look with Noble. He hadn't seen Snoozy so worked up since the big bar fight. "You mean the snake?"

Snoozy nodded eagerly, his eyes more red-rimmed than ever. "Show me."

"You sure? Could be dangerous."

But Burke had already pointed to #5 and Snoozy, his droopy moustache quivering, tugged Joe toward the room. At least they had two firefighters and an ass-kicking giant nearby, in case anything went wrong.

They stepped through the doorway and Joe opened his mouth to warn the other man to keep his distance but Snoozy scurried right up to the open wall, hands clasped at his chest. "Mitzi," he cried. "Oh, Mitzi, it really is you."

Noble crowded in beside Joe. *Mitzi?* he mouthed. Joe moved forward, gaze locked on the python. He— *she,* apparently—had moved since he'd seen her last. She was still coiled in between two studs, but not as tightly—her tail hung nearly to the floor. And he could see her head now, about the length of his hand and half as wide. She didn't seem aggressive, but what the hell did he know?

And Snoozy, standing too damned close to the thing, continued to croon, his voice quivering with emotion.

"Snoozy, man." Joe hoped like hell that thing had already eaten breakfast. "Is that your snake?"

The bar owner turned and nodded, eyes wet. "My

ex-wife ran away with the bastard who delivered our upright freezer. But before she left, she turned Mitzi loose."

Ouch. "How can you be sure it's Mitzi?"

Snoozy glowered at him. "You'd know, if you had children."

Noble scratched his belly. "So what do you want us to do, Snooze?"

Snoozy turned back to his snake. "I want you to help me find a big box. And then I want you to help me put her in it."

Joe exhaled. Somehow he'd known that was coming. "I'll see what I can do," he said, and squeezed past Noble and the firefighters. Allison waited farther up the sidewalk, eyes as liquid as Snoozy's. Joe felt something shift in his chest as he walked toward her.

"How long ago did his wife leave him?"

"Six, seven years."

"And the snake's been here all that time," she said, mostly to herself. "Are you going to help him...you know...contain her?"

"Long as I get to handle the end that doesn't bite."

She managed a smile then looked away, toward the string of pine trees that separated his property from the vineyard next door. "It's really something," she said. "The way the people in this community look out for each other." She peered back at him. "You fit in here."

He could see it in her green-flecked eyes. She knew that once he went back to Virginia, it wouldn't be for good. Wise girl.

A pine-scented breeze danced past, and she brushed silky hair out of her eyes. "Want me to help you find a box?"

He gave his head a quick shake, like a boxer who'd failed to dodge a mean left hook. "There's no telling when that snake last had a meal." He forced a grin. "What I'd really like you to do is keep an eye on my cat."

"YOU DO REALIZE I'm never going back there." Allison's hands were fisted in her lap, her shoulder blades pressing into the back of the booth as she willed herself to stop shaking. But her muscles didn't pay any more attention than Joe did.

"I'll have the vegetable soup and a grilled cheese," he was saying, to a stick-thin girl in an oversize black polo shirt.

Allison ground her teeth together. How could he eat at a time like this?

"How can you eat at a time like this?" she demanded.

"I'm hungry. And in Cal's Diner, if you don't eat, you better be ready to explain why." He surrendered his menu to the waitress. "Any cinnamon rolls back there?" She gave him a reverent nod and tucked the menu under her arm. Joe rubbed his palms together and leaned back. "We'll take two, please. Thanks, Rachel."

She tore her gaze away long enough to dart a wary glance at Allison. "The regular kind?"

"The regular kind," he agreed. Instantly Rachel's shoulders relaxed and she let loose a giggle. The teen had one hand splayed over a jutted hip while the other toyed with the tail of a neat French braid. Adoring brown eyes clung to Joe's face, tighter than a gob of gum clinging to the bottom of a shoe.

Somehow Allison resisted the urge to drop her face into her hands. Had she ever tittered at Joe like that?

Probably.

Definitely.

Dear God in heaven.

"Hey, Gallahan." An older man sitting at the lunch counter swiveled his stool around and faced their booth. A sly smile creased his sun-reddened face. "Got a good one for ya. Why'd the two pythons get hitched?"

Joe grinned as Allison shuddered. She pressed her palms to the seat on either side of her thighs and let her fingers take up a steady drumming.

"I don't know, Harris," Joe said. "Why did they?"

The old man slapped his knee. "'Cause they had a crush on each other!"

The entire diner exploded in laughter. And that's when Allison realized the curious glances they'd been collecting weren't so much because she was a stranger, but because of how they'd spent their morning.

"This is big doin's in our town," Joe drawled, leaning across the table so she could hear him over the uproar. "Next year this time they'll probably be holding a festival in Mitzi's honor."

"I bet I can top that!" A teenage boy in a bright orange shirt and board shorts shouted from across the diner. "What do you do if you find a snake in your toilet?"

A few *ewws* and muffled squeals, then the diner quieted, taking on an expectant air.

"What *do* you do?" someone prompted.

"You wait till he's finished!"

A second eruption of laughter. The kid sat down amidst a flurry of back slaps and wet, rattling thwacks as plastic tumblers full of chipped ice collided in celebratory toasts.

"All these people know each other?"

The level of noise meant Joe hadn't heard Allison's question. He slanted forward and turned his head. She leaned in and repeated herself, then lost track of her words as her gaze roved his tanned, unshaven cheek, the tips of sun-kissed hair curling around his ear, the determined push of his chin.

Easy, Allie. For God's sake, she shouldn't have to constantly remind herself to back off the guy. Was she so hard up she'd consider putting the moves on the man who had single-handedly derailed her career?

She had to be careful. With all that she had going on with her mother, her job and now Joe, she was feeling…unsettled. Something Joe wouldn't hesitate to take advantage of. He'd proven that the night before.

With a soundless groan, she collapsed against the

back of her seat. Here she was, already preparing to blame Joe for any hanky-panky that might happen between them—in essence giving herself carte blanche for a hookup. Could she be any more shameless? Or mercenary?

Or *desperate?*

That particular hookup would never—*could* never—happen.

Joe's mouth formed a sardonic curve. "It's a small town. You live here and sooner or later you'll meet everyone in it."

Oh. Right. She'd asked a question. Luckily he didn't seem to notice her distraction.

"You think this is crazy, you should have seen the place after that cow Priscilla Mae won the crown in the Miss Lilac competition."

Allison stared. He didn't…did he…? He just called some poor girl a *cow.* She shot upright and filled her lungs with outraged air, but then he laughed.

"Priscilla Mae, dairy cow. Pride of the county. Must have netted a dozen blue ribbons at the state fair."

"She has beautiful eyelashes." Rachel was back. Empty-handed. And judging by the annoyed look she tossed to her left, Allison wouldn't be getting her coffee anytime soon. Damn it, she *needed* that coffee.

"That was awfully brave of you, helping to pull Mitzi out of the wall and everything." Rachel blushed as she stared down at Joe. "They say snakes aren't slimy like they look. What'd her skin feel like?"

Joe looked over at Allison and she went still. She knew that expression. She exhaled, welcoming the resentment that sparked to life inside her chest.

If only she could decide who deserved her bitterness more. Herself, for feeling the least bit gratified by his "you doing okay?" face? Or Joe, for thinking her so fragile she couldn't handle a little verbal rehash of their adventure?

Then his frowning gaze dropped to the edge of the table—her side of the table—and she realized *why* he was concerned. Oh. Huh. Who knew fingers tapping on vinyl could make so much noise?

She wedged her hands beneath her thighs.

A waitress a few years older than Rachel, with flawless skin as dark as her coworker's was pale, paused at the teen's elbow. "I hate to interrupt, but you've got orders up. And you need to refill your drinks." The woman hurried away while Rachel rolled her eyes.

"Duty calls," she said to Joe. "Maybe you could tell me about Mitzi later." She angled away from Allison and lowered her voice. "My shift ends at nine."

Allison hid a cringe, her own embarrassment forgotten as she agonized for the smitten teen. Being in love was hard enough. Being in love as a teenager? Brutal.

Joe's skin had browned over the past year, but there wasn't enough tan in the world to hide the flush creeping up his throat. "I don't think that's a good idea. We wouldn't want anyone to get the wrong impression. Listen, why don't you ask your parents to take you by the bar one day before it opens for business? I'm sure Snoozy would love the chance to show Mitzi off." He smiled carefully. "Oh, and do you think we could get our coffee now, Rachel?"

Reluctantly she backed away. "I'll bring it as soon as it's ready. You like it young, right?" She stumbled to a stop, mouth gaping open, cheeks flushed fire-engine-red. "I mean, *fresh*. You like it *fresh*. Coffee drinkers don't like to drink—" she swallowed a squeak "—stale coffee." She clutched the menu to her chest. "Do they?"

"You're absolutely right. They do not. Make that decaffeinated, okay?" When she left he looked at Allison. "You're jumpy enough."

She couldn't help it. She rubbed her palms up and down her arms—she'd shucked the coveralls but hadn't been brave enough to return to her room to shower, let alone change her clothes—and forced her mind away from the image of a V-shaped head and the blank-eyed grip of sharp teeth.

She snatched up the ceramic box jammed with packets of sweetener, dumped the contents onto the table and started organizing. "I'm not going back."

"I heard you, slick." His gaze fell to her hands. "How about we talk after we eat?"

Her fingers slowed then went back to arranging. It may have been a year since she'd last spent any time with Joe but she knew that tone. Business would *not* be discussed until he was good and ready. Fine. But the moment they were alone she'd tell him exactly what he could do with the nickname "slick."

There. All done. She patted the neat row of packets and pushed the sweetener away, averted her gaze from the question in Joe's eyes and studied the diner's counter, currently swollen with customers. The L-shaped structure was fronted by a row of stools upholstered in alternating mustard-and ketchup-colored vinyl—a bright contrast to the black-and-white floor. On the Formica countertop, newspapers, coffee cups, elbows and polished-steel napkin holders jockeyed for space. A pair of black-lacquered wrought iron stands bookended the longer stretch of counter, offering an array of pies and—Allison craned her neck. Were those brownies?

Then she spotted Rachel and her tidy French braid. The teen was bent at the waist, facing away from the booth, her head lowered into what looked like a chest freezer. The other waitress hurried over, said something and Rachel thrust a brightly wrapped ice cream sandwich up behind her back without lifting her head.

Allison linked her arms and leaned forward, elbows on the table, teeth scraping across one corner of her bottom lip. She couldn't help feeling bad for Rachel—was there anything worse than humiliating yourself in front of a hot guy?

She turned back to Joe and caught him staring. The intensity in his eyes made her thighs go tight, her stomach shimmy. She dropped her gaze to his chest, couldn't help but notice his loose-fitting T-shirt did nothing to hide his intriguing new muscles. *Stop that.*

"I thought getting away from the motel might help you relax," he said slowly. She glanced up, saw him looking at her hands and realized she'd reclaimed the sugar container. She pushed it away.

"The price you pay for a vivid imagination." She jabbed her chin in Rachel's direction. "You handled that well, by the way."

His mouth quirked, but at least he didn't call her on her clumsy attempt to change the subject. "She's a sweet kid," he said. "We got along great until her boyfriend dumped her and she decided to try for someone older. What can I say, she has excellent taste. She's just ahead of her time."

She hated herself even as she asked the question. "Anyone special in the here and now?"

He lost the grin. "Not since you."

NOT SINCE YOU.

He hadn't meant to say it like that. Like he had regrets.

Those were beside the point.

Allison's cheeks were the same pink as the packets she'd reorganized, what, seventeen times? But her gaze remained steady on his.

"Do you ever regret it? Your decision to move here?"

Maybe not so beside the point.

Rachel chose that moment to arrive with Joe's soup

and sandwich and two cups of coffee. Wordlessly she emptied the tray. When he murmured his thanks she dropped into a small curtsy, froze, gave a small whimper and fled.

Poor kid.

He picked up his spoon. "I have regrets. Moving here isn't one of them."

Greedily Allison wrapped both hands around her mug and Joe frowned. He'd assumed her trembling was a delayed reaction to finding herself nose-to-nose with a ten-foot-long reptile. Maybe there was something more to it….

"I have a jacket out in the truck. Want it?"

"Careful. Someone might think you actually care."

O-kay. He picked up a sandwich half. "And you? Any regrets?"

"About staying in Virginia? No. This place has its attractions, but it's not my idea of a good time."

"There's more to it than indentured servitude and lame-ass jokes, you know."

"Uh-huh. Like the fresh country air and the—" she toasted him with her mug "—'young' coffee."

He glared, but she only laughed. "What are they?" he asked, his voice too gruff for his liking. "The attractions you mentioned."

She set her mug back down on the table, hesitated long enough that he started on his lukewarm soup. After a while she looked up, her expression wary.

"We both know I made the right decision."

He waited.

"I thought about it a lot, you know, and I realized something. You *wanted* me to turn you down."

He rested his spoon against the side of the bowl. "Is that so?"

"It's the only reason you asked. You knew I'd say no. Counted on it. You wanted to punish yourself. And moving here was part of the penance. Moving here on your own? Icing on the atonement cake."

He settled back against the booth's cracked vinyl padding. So now she thought she could read minds. He let the anger surge.

Slowly, deliberately, he leaned forward again. When she pulled away he gave serious thought to stopping her, to holding her in place with a hand on hers, to closing the rest of the distance between them. To showing her just how much her know-it-all attitude pissed him off.

And turned him on.

Instead he let his gaze wander over her smooth, pale face, down past her don't-mess-with-me chin and slender throat, to uneasy shoulders and a just-the-right-size pair of breasts he damned well should have worshipped more. The denim at his crotch stretched tight and he shifted. Two seconds ago he'd been angry. Hell if he could remember why.

"Maybe once you're done punishing yourself you'll find your way back to Alexandria," she said.

Ah, *that* was why.

"For you? Or for Tackett & Pike?"

She pulled her coffee closer. "For T&P, of course."

Of course. "Just so we're straight, I asked you to move here because I wanted you with me."

"What you wanted was for me to beg you to stay. We both know you didn't want to leave that life behind."

"You keep saying that. 'We both know.' Who's *we?* Got a python in your pocket?" He shoved aside his half-empty dishes. "You realize anything else about me over the past year?"

"Nothing I can say in public."

"Because I'll blush? Or because you think I want to hide I had a drinking problem?"

A breathless quiet settled over the diner. Allison stared across the table. A chorus of speculation surrounded them before the usual din settled in again. The hiss of fat on a hot griddle, the clack of plates meeting Formica, the high-pitched *ping, ping, ping* of the cash register. Rachel sidled over from the next table, her gaze rapt. She hefted the remains of his grilled cheese. "Want me to wrap this up? You could come by and finish it later."

You had to give the kid credit for trying. "I'll take it to go," he said firmly. Her smile drooped and with a flick of her braid, she swung away.

The other waitress—Olivia, he thought her name was—swooped in, deposited their cinnamon rolls, flashed a smile and scurried back to the kitchen. Allison didn't look at him as she picked up her fork.

"So what makes a cinnamon roll *ir*regular?"

Nice job with the subject change, slick. "Sometimes Cal shapes them into hearts."

"Oh." She glanced over at Rachel then said it again, stretching the single syllable into a ten-second monologue.

"Remember Noble Johnson?"

"The librarian in leather."

"Right. He kicked up a fuss about the hearts and threatened to start buying his breakfast at the Dinky Mart. Since Noble orders two rib eye specials every morning, Cal had a change of heart. So to speak."

Allison chuckled as she settled her elbow on the table and rested her chin in her hand, and Joe felt an odd swell of pride. She still knew how to shake off a sulk. He'd forgotten how stimulating it had been, switching from bantering to bickering in the blink of an eye, but always, *always* with an underlying affection.

Until.

"Poor Noble. Got his heart broken, did he?"

"No. He's saving himself. Won't eat a heart-shaped anything until he has someone to share it with."

"That's...sweet." She drummed her fingers against her cheek. "You haven't asked if I'm seeing anyone."

He stabbed his fork into his cinnamon roll. "I don't have to."

"What does that mean?"

"You never had time for anything but the job."

"That's true," she mused, surprising him again.

He'd expected her to go all defensive on him. Still, it rankled that she sounded more proud than wistful.

She watched him while he ate, her gaze tracking every bite. Damned if she didn't remind him of Chance, Nat's black Lab, forever lurking at the table's edge, trembling in anticipation for the moment the bearer of the fork dropped something tasty.

He coughed into his fist. Probably best not to mention he was mentally comparing her to a dog. Then again, outrage had always looked good on her.

Desire looked even better. Hot, pulsing, throw-me-down-*now* desire—

He set down his fork and swallowed hard. Her fingers stopped mid-drum.

"Can we talk now?" she asked.

He had something much more…gratifying in mind. But that's where his fantasy would have to stay. In his mind.

He nodded toward the untouched plate at her elbow. "Not interested?" Luckily she didn't seem to notice the strain in his voice.

"No. It looks delicious, but—" she gave him a once-over so hurried he almost missed it "—I'd regret it later."

He could read between the lines. He'd just been pumped up and shot down in a matter of seconds. He nudged his plate aside. "Life is too short to cut yourself off. Relax. Indulge. Enjoy."

Judas Priest, he sounded like an ad for flavored coffee creamer.

"Back to the subject at hand," she said firmly. "Our arrangement did *not* include hundred-pound Burmese pythons."

"It didn't include loaning out my favorite pair of coveralls, either, but look at me, I've adapted."

"You can't hold me to the deal."

"The deal stands."

"Ever heard of extenuating circumstances? And by the way, those circumstances could have strangled us in our sleep, thank you very much."

"Strangled *you* in your sleep. My bed's all the way at the other end of the motel. Anyway, the snake's gone." She opened her mouth but he didn't give her a chance to speak. "You agreed to stay at the motel a full two weeks. 'No complaints, no backtracking, no games.' That was the deal. *If* you recall."

"I've been looking for you." A cheerful, twenty-something blonde with long, curly hair appeared beside the booth. She aimed a curious glance at Allison. "Both of you."

Joe shifted to make room. "Got time to sit?"

"Not really. After I do some stuff for Snoozy I have to get right back to the bar."

"Stay for just a minute. I'll introduce you." She crowded in beside him. "Allison, meet Liz Early. Snoozy thinks she works for him but we all know who's really in charge. Liz, this is Allison Kincaid, a former coworker from Virginia."

"And snake savior, according to my boss. Snoozy's

half in love already." Liz thrust her hand across the table. "Nice to meet you, Allison."

Allison smiled. "It's nice to meet you, too. I'm happy your boss has his pet back, but I have to say I wish someone else had found her."

Liz shuddered. "Totally. I made him promise to give me a decent raise if she ever gets loose. At least now I know he'll do everything he can to make sure she stays put."

Joe grinned at Allison. "Told you she was the brains of the outfit."

"Anyway, the reason I'm here—" Her gaze snagged on Allison's untouched cinnamon roll. She froze, and her eyes went wide. "Look at that," she said, her voice hushed.

Joe winked at Allison. "I don't think loud noises will scare it away."

"Shh." Liz shoved a palm in his face, her gaze never wavering from the plate. "Give me a moment to revel in its glory." After a few seconds she licked her lips and looked over at Allison. "I planned to score one of these while I was here, but Cal said he was out. Is that…I don't suppose…"

"Help yourself." After a token protest, Liz accepted a fork. She ate quickly, and when she'd swallowed the last bite she leaned back in smiling bliss. Joe gave her a few seconds then tugged lightly on her hair.

"You were about to tell us the reason you're here."

"Hmm? Oh!" She snapped upright. "Jeez, I have to get back to work. But first I need to invite you to the bar tonight. Snoozy's throwing a welcome home party for Mitzi and he'd like you both to be there." She licked the back of the fork, slid out of the booth and beamed down at Allison. "Especially you."

"Instead of celebrating that snake he should be eating it."

Joe winced. Even if he didn't recognize the girl-ish pitch, the comment alone was enough to give her away. He twisted in his seat and nodded a greeting, grateful that Liz was in his way, preventing him from standing. Because if he moved any closer he'd be well within striking distance, and he was in no mood for another Attack of the Giant Purse.

"How you doing, Aud?"

But Liz didn't give Audrey a chance to answer him. "Audrey Tweedy, that's a horrible thing to say! How would you feel if someone suggested Hazel and June barbecue Baby Blue?"

"Now, dear, that's a very different thing. Even for a schnauzer, Baby Blue is scrawny. He'd barely qualify as an appetizer for a family of four. But that python? She could feed all of Castle Creek."

"You know as well as I do that Snoozy would never let that happen."

"Let me know if he changes his mind. You'd be surprised how delicious snake can be. I have a fab-ulous recipe for a soy sauce marinade with ginger and honey. Oh, and I imagine I'm invited to the party, dear?"

Liz hesitated then exhaled. "Only if you promise to remember Mitzi's a pet, not a food source."

"Of course. You can trust me, dear." She adjusted her neon green purse—the one big enough to transport not only Joe's circular saw but his nail gun, as well—and nodded sagely. "I can be very discreet."

"Yes. Well. I have to go. Snoozy will be wondering where I am. See you all tonight. Oh, and since you two are the guests of honor, Snoozy said not to bring anything. Nice to meet you, Allison." With a friendly wave and a final warning glance at Audrey, Liz scurried toward the door.

The old woman rounded on Joe. "Now, Joseph, please tell me you're not going to make your friend here go back to that…that jungle of yours. What'll you find next, a water buffalo?" She snorted, then immediately became earnest. "Although, buffalo is the perfect red meat. It's high in protein and low in fat. I should talk to Cal about putting it on the menu. Which reminds me. It's past my lunchtime and I'm craving a burger." Her eyes glinted as she looked down at Joe. "In fact I think I'll make it a double. With extra bacon."

"Chicken tenders on the side?" Joe suggested wryly.

"Maybe even a lamb chop. Extra rare."

"And a turkey leg, just to round things out?"

"With mincemeat pie for dessert," she finished triumphantly. A handful of diners around them laughed while Audrey dug in her purse. Joe craned his neck.

What would she pull out this time, a can of SPAM? She surprised him by pulling out what looked like a business card, which she handed to Allison.

"Here's my address, dear. You're welcome to stay with me until this snake business is all settled."

Oh, hell, no. "It *is* settled. The snake is gone."

"I hear Snoozy doesn't have a proper pen for the thing. What if it gets loose again? Where do you think it'll go? The same place it's been for the past umpty-ump years, that's where."

Allison was steadily tapping the edge of Audrey's card on the table. Next she'd be emptying the salt shaker on the table and counting crystals.

Joe shook his head. "Mitzi's not going to get loose. After all that time he spent grieving for her, there's no way Snoozy will risk losing her again." He glanced at Allison, but his words hadn't had the desired effect. Her jaw remained rigid, her gaze fixated on the door. *Damn it, Aud.*

His favorite busybody gave an encore snort and headed for the counter. Joe paid the bill and ushered Allison outside. The sky was a faint, splotchy gray, the air thick with the smell of hurriedly trimmed lawns and the promise of rain.

"Oh, my God," muttered Allison, over and over as he guided her toward his truck. Beneath his palm the small of her back vibrated with tension. He shut the passenger door behind her, rounded the hood and climbed into the driver's seat, turned and braced himself for a blast of fury.

But when she swung around to face him, he saw that she was laughing.

JOE SCOWLED. "You want to tell me what's going on?"

"I'm sorry," she gasped. "I-it was just all suddenly too much. The snake jokes and Rachel's head in the freezer and barbecuing pets and—" a fresh bout of laughter seized her and she bent at the waist, chin to her knees, panting for air. "And here I f-figured life in the country would be boring."

"Glad you find us entertaining."

That sobered her. "I didn't mean it that way. Seriously, you didn't find any of that funny?"

"So all that talk about Mitzi wasn't making you nervous?" He sounded angry. She sat up, concentrated on breathing and swiped at her face.

"The thought of Mitzi finding her way back to the motel definitely gives me the heebie-jeebies. But like you said, Snoozy wouldn't let her get away again."

"Great. Terrific. I'm glad that's settled. But when I asked what was going on, I meant with the tapping. And the counting and the organizing and that thing this morning, when you couldn't relax until you'd cleared the leftover seconds from the microwave. Want to tell me what that's all about?"

She swallowed, and stared straight ahead. Had she really thought he wouldn't notice?

"Um," she managed. "That would be a 'no.' And by the way, thanks a lot for thinking I was making fun of your friends."

"Nice try. But I still want an answer." He scooted closer and reached for her, and an unwelcome tingling started, deep in the pit of her belly. Damn it, how could she both detest him and lust after him at the same time? But all he did was push the hair out of her face. "You have a bruise."

"You should see the dent I left in the paneling."

His frown deepened. "Allison, tell me what's going on with you. Please."

CHAPTER FIVE

ALLISON TURNED HER head away, out of reach of his touch. God help her, she was starting to like this country version of Joe way too much. Where had all this compassion been a year ago?

And just how much did you show him?

She rested her elbow on the door frame and tucked her hair behind her ear. "There isn't much to tell," she said. "Whenever I get overly anxious, I...also get a little compulsive. I can usually head it off by finding a distraction. But when I'm in a controlled environment, like in a car or a meeting or—"

"Or a diner."

"Right." She turned her head, found his mouth inches from hers and for a split second lost track of her thoughts. A faint rumble of thunder rolled across the sky and a memory of a rainstorm, of a parked car and slow, drugging kisses behind steam-veiled windows flashed through her brain. She struggled to inhale, and it was like trying to breathe through a wet towel.

"That's when things can get a little dicey," she murmured, her eyes riveted on his mouth. "Whenever I'm feeling trapped."

Thunk, thunk, thunk, thunk. They both jumped. Allison jerked her head toward the side window and spotted Audrey outside, holding aloft a takeout bag.

"Extra bacon *and* pepperoni," she said loudly through the window, and winked. "See you kids at Snoozy's." She turned and made her way toward a beat-up, cranberry-colored Lincoln, her purse banging against her ample hip.

Allison put a hand to her chest. "I think I just got heartburn."

"When did it start?"

"The moment she mentioned pepperoni."

"I meant the OCD."

"Oh." He shifted away and she breathed a little easier. "I've been dealing with this most of my adult life." No need to tell him the past year had been the worst by far. There wasn't a person on the planet who didn't have to deal with some sort of stress. "And by the way, I have compulsions, not full-fledged OCD. Most people misuse the term. True OCD is debilitating because you spend every minute of every day fighting a specific fear. There's no vacation from it, no cure. My urges are nothing in comparison."

He studied her, his mouth grim. "So you were dealing with this while we were together. How did I not notice?"

Wasn't it obvious? Considering the number of hours they'd dedicated to the job, he'd had as much time for her as she'd had for him. But he didn't seem to expect an answer.

He turned in his seat and started the truck. "How about once we get back to the motel you pack up your stuff. Get that room at the Hampton Inn. You'll be more comfortable there."

"You know I can't do that. Tackett will freak if he thinks I'm jeopardizing our deal...or wasting T&P's money." And she needed Tackett's approval before she could use the company credit card, anyway. Snake infestation aside, she already had a place to stay. These days, every dollar counted.

"That's it, isn't it? That's why the compulsions. You're in a situation you can't control. Tackett's calling the shots."

"He's my boss. He usually does."

"How often does he banish you from civilization for two weeks so you can entice an ex-boyfriend back to the firm?"

No response. They pulled out of the lot behind Audrey, and Joe gestured at the Lincoln. "How about Audrey's place, then? I know she's peculiar but her heart's as big as that aircraft carrier she's driving."

"She'd probably make me eat scrapple."

"And pickled pigs' feet." When Allison groaned, Joe didn't take time to gloat. He was too busy trying to avoid rear-ending Audrey, whose foot spent more time on the brake than the accelerator as she waved at pedestrians—tourists and residents alike—and offered a ride to anyone carrying a shopping bag.

Allison took the opportunity to study the scenery she'd been too wired to notice before. If she'd decided the previous night to venture out on her own to find the diner, she wouldn't have had any trouble. Downtown Castle Creek consisted of three parallel, tree-shaded streets lined with shops, businesses and wrought iron benches—the perfect venue for a weekend stroll. The WWII-era storefronts were shabby but cheerful, made distinctive by brightly striped awnings that stretched along the street like a parade of half parasols. The sidewalks were uneven brick, the streetlights old and ornate. And each bench was bookended by what looked like fountains of pansy blooms.

Allison wanted to ask Joe to stop and let her out so she could walk the streets herself. Get lost in a world without debts and deadlines, if only for a little while. But her discovery of Mitzi had already cost them most of the day—and she had a bargain to keep.

Funny how a little coffee and camaraderie—not to mention making an ass of herself—could weaken her resolve to pack up and go home.

It looked like someone finally took Audrey up on her offer of a ride and she steered the monster Lincoln into a parking space. Joe sighed his apparent relief and glanced over at Allison—he watched her watching the town.

"What do you think?"

"It's charming. Eclectic. Quiet. Very quiet. I'm guessing this place doesn't see a lot of action after ten."

"You'd be surprised. More than once we've had livestock wandering down State Street after hours.

Trust me, cleaning up after that is an all-night effort. Most of the town pitches in, though."

They drove past Cooper's on the right and Allison chuckled. "Which explains the huge selection of rubber boots for sale at the hardware store."

"Gil Cooper is a practical man."

Silence again. The mood in the cab shifted. A sidelong glance showed Joe scowling through the windshield as the shops gave way to houses that looked more Victorian than twentieth century. He angled his head left and then right, stretching his neck.

"I'm sure Tackett warned you to keep close to me," he said abruptly. "How close?"

"Closer than syrup on a pancake." She thought she'd done a decent job mimicking Tackett's exaggerated Southern accent, but Joe wasn't smiling. She sighed. "Don't start that again. He didn't tell me to sleep with you." Not outright, anyway. "Just because I love my job doesn't mean I'm willing to sell myself."

"He know that?"

Heat crept into her face and her fingers tingled with the urge to slug him. She lowered the window, welcoming the fresh, metallic tang of impending rain. "Seems I've been worrying for nothing, Joe. You'll fit right back in at T&P. Tackett and Mahoney will worship you. I'd forgotten how much of a jerk you can be."

"I'd forgotten how self-righteous you can be."

She bounced in her seat, maneuvering around to face him. "I take it back. I didn't forget you're a jerk because you've been one ever since I arrived. But you've now officially outjerked yourself."

He smirked. "You do realize what that sounds like?"

Oh, for God's sake. "Don't even try." But despite her annoyance the image crashed into her consciousness. Joe, naked, head flung back and teeth bared, muscles bunching as he worked a straining erection.

Her lungs went flat. She scrambled to recover the anger she had every right to feel.

The truck slowed as Joe braked for a red light. "Do you really?"

"Really, what?"

"Love your job."

She answered without thinking. "I used to."

"What changed?"

"The light," she said, and pointed. "It's green."

Her cell rang and she recognized the ringtone. Tackett. No way she wanted to talk business. Not with Joe right there. She plucked her phone out of her purse and pressed Ignore. She felt Joe look over at her, but she didn't offer an explanation.

After several long moments, he broke the silence. "I've been trying to figure it out. You've never been the greedy type. Nice clothes, nice car, nice apartment, yeah, but for you it was more about image." He glanced at her decidedly non-designer jeans. "Hell, you're more careful with Tackett's money than he is. So what gives? Why so desperate for that promotion?"

"Not desperate. Deserving."

"Okay, both. So what's the deal? Someone else need the money? Your mom. Has she been sick?" He jerked his head toward her. "Are *you* sick?"

She made a deep-throated sound of impatience, but at the same time couldn't help feeling warmed by his concern. "No one is sick," she said. "You just need to butt out."

A muscle worked in his jaw. "Speaking of butts, it's time we get ours back to work."

"If that means what I think it means you can forget it. I gave in on the rest of it. But there's no way I'm tearing down any more paneling."

"Forget the paneling. I have something more cerebral in mind."

"That sounds like code for paperwork."

"You're in the mood to count. Let's go with that."

"Way to use my weakness against me."

He shot her a look. What, now she wasn't allowed to sound bitter? "A friend of mine drew up some landscaping proposals," he said evenly. "I want to take some measurements and lay out some beds, see how much digging we'll be doing."

"Who's *we?* Got a python in your pocket?"

He quirked an eyebrow. "Touchy."

"Don't you mean touché?"

"I mean touchy. You always were sensitive." His voice went gruff as he tossed her a scorching glance. "Unbelievably sensitive."

Except for one tight little ripple of need she couldn't suppress, she was proud of herself for not reacting to his words. "Maybe you should keep your eyes on the road," she said.

"View's not as good."

"So suffer." Time for a subject change. "This friend of yours. She help you with the decorating, too?"

"Parker? God, no. She cares about interior design even less than I care about the spittlebug."

"The spittlebug."

"Ever see a little mound of foam on a leaf? That's a bug, camouflaging itself with its own spittle. Apparently it weakens strawberry plants."

"Uh-huh." She poked her tongue against her cheek. "Sounds to me like you do care."

"Only as a friend. Besides. She's married."

"No, I meant—" Allison wrinkled her nose. "Never mind."

"I know exactly what you meant. You forget, I know *you*."

She pulled a few breeze-blown wisps of hair out of her eyes and smoothed them behind her ear. "You used to."

Silence, except for the air rushing in through the half-open window.

Joe scratched his chin. "About those measurements."

"You do realize it's going to rain."

"A little wet never hurt anyone."

And just like that, he had her back to picturing him naked.

IT NEVER DID RAIN. The skies had cleared, leaving Joe and Allison the afternoon to measure distances, pound wooden pegs into the ground and string plastic ribbon. It was a lengthy process. Joe might have been the carpenter, but it was Allison who insisted on measuring everything twice. If not for the satisfaction on her face every time they achieved a perfectly straight line, he'd have thought she was deliberately trying his patience.

What he'd accused her of earlier… Well, maybe he had been a little out of line. But she sure as hell didn't have the market cornered on resentment—though she was better at hiding it.

"See this stake, Joe?" She called to him from twenty feet away, where she hovered over a corner peg. "It's your head." She went at it with a hammer like she was saving Castle Creek from Dracula himself.

Ouch. Seemed her resentment had come out of hiding.

He fumbled the spool of ribbon he'd been rewinding and eyed the pulverized peg. "Where the hell did that come from?"

She swiped a wrist across her forehead and tossed him a feral smile. "I've been pounding Tackett into the ground all afternoon. I've moved on to you, now."

He set his jaw and sauntered closer, enjoying the trace of alarm pulling her eyes wide. "So. You want to compare scars after all."

"I want you to stop making asinine accusations. If you think I'm capable of prostituting myself for T&P, then you never really knew me at all."

"I thought I did. Until I got some nasty surprises."

She dropped the hammer and lifted her chin. "You mean, like having your ex-boyfriend rat you out when you didn't do anything other than try to save his reputation?"

"*Save* my reputation? You and Tackett reassigned every damned client I ever had. You ruined my reputation." No denying his drinking had been a factor. But she graciously refrained from stating the obvious.

"It can't be ruined if Mahoney still wants you. And speaking of ruined reputations, I have you and Danielle to thank for mine."

So they were back to that. "Neither one of us made you sleep with me." Her eyes went wide and she swelled up like a black cat on Halloween. Next she'd start spitting. "Fine," Joe growled. "I'll tell you what happened."

"Don't bother."

"That's great. That's terrific. You know what you need to do? You need to stop pretending what you did was for my own good. With you, it's always been about the agency. Took me a while, but I finally figured out I'd always come in second."

"You think I don't know how that feels?" She marched away and scooped up the stakes they hadn't used and marched back. "You said your job was all you had left after your brother died. Well, guess what? The Joe I knew died right along with his brother. My job was all *I* had left and you nearly took it from me, out of spite. Which means I have just as much reason to resent you as you have to resent me."

"No, slick, you don't. You left me high and dry."

"You're the one who moved away. And at the time you may have been high, but you certainly weren't dry."

Joe was only surprised that it had taken her so long to bring it up. "You're a real ball-buster, aren't you?" he said softly. Damn, she was cold. His gaze fell to the stakes she cradled in her arms like a child. He looked away.

He didn't know what the hell he'd expected her to say. He wasn't sure there was anything she could say to fix things. Then again, there was nothing left *to* fix, was there?

"This is getting us nowhere. How about we call another cease-fire?" He squatted, and stuffed the spools of ribbon into his workbag. Shifted around so she couldn't see his hands were shaking. "I need to get cleaned up and get over to Snoozy's."

"Me, too."

Oh, hell, no. "Just because you were invited doesn't mean you have to go."

"We're the guests of honor. It would be rude not to."

He straightened, and dusted off his palms. "Let me put it another way. I don't want you there."

"Guess I'm lucky you're not in charge of the guest list."

"It'll be chaotic," he warned. "Like today at the diner."

"Afraid I'll end up counting ice cubes, or sorting people by the color shirt they're wearing? Or maybe you're afraid everyone will think we're an item?"

"They already do."

"So why don't you want me to go?" A gust of wind pressed her shirt to her breasts, and stirred the tendrils of damp hair clinging to her cheeks. He had a sudden urge to push her down among the dandelions and kiss her until desire replaced the gleam of challenge in her eyes.

Damn, he needed a drink.

"Be honest," he said. "Hanging out with the locals, eating cheese and crackers and faking an interest in lake fishing? That's not your idea of a good time."

"You want me to be honest? Like you were honest at the diner when you talked about your drinking problem and used the past tense?"

"Fine. I don't want you there because I won't be able to relax with you glaring at me every damn time I take a sip of beer, and on top of that, having to pretend we're friends. As far as drinking goes, I don't have a problem. I control it when I need to, let go when I want to. So you can stop with the lectures. And do *not* come to the party just because you think I'll need a designated driver."

The sudden mist in her eyes told him he'd hurt her.

He should probably feel worse about it, but damn it, he didn't want to remember how it used to be between them. Before *and* after those months when whiskey had become his world.

"You don't have to pretend anything," she said tightly. "And I'm coming to the party because it's the right thing to do."

"And you always do the right thing." She frowned and he fisted both hands around the stiff leather of his tool belt. "So why weren't you there?"

The moment he asked the question, he could have kicked his own ass. Already he could feel grief putting a chokehold on his voice. But it was too late to take it back.

"What do you mean? Why wasn't I where?"

He swallowed. "My brother's funeral. Why didn't you come?"

Judas Priest, he couldn't believe he was putting himself through this. He already knew she simply hadn't cared enough to come. Did he really need to hear her say it?

She stared at him, a dawning horror pushing the color from her face. "But...you told me not to."

"I *what*?"

"I had every intention of going. In fact, I planned to drive you. But you called and said—" She swallowed, and looked away.

"What did I say?"

She crouched, and dropped the stakes into a pile next to the canvas bag. Slowly she straightened, and slid her hands into her front pockets. "You told me there was no sense in both of us missing work that day. That since I'd never met your brother I shouldn't bother...pretending to mourn."

Son of a bitch. "I said that? I don't remember."

"There was a lot you weren't remembering, then. That's why we reassigned your clients."

"All this time, I thought..." He bent again over the bag, took his time rearranging the contents. When he stood upright again, Allison's eyes were brimming with the remorse he'd once hoped to see—and now knew he didn't deserve.

She pulled her hands free, reached out to him but didn't make contact. "It's just as much my fault. I should have gone, anyway. I knew you didn't mean it. Knew it was just the whiskey talking. But I thought it'd be easier on both of us if I stayed away."

"I'm sorry," he gritted. He didn't know what else to say. Didn't know what to think.

Had to get the hell away from her.

He hefted his tools and turned toward the lobby. Spotted two boys, maybe fifteen or sixteen, headed into the woods behind the motel. One of them was drinking out of a plastic sports bottle. The other was smoking.

"Hey!" he yelled at them, and felt Allison jump beside him. "Careful with that cigarette!" The boy with the water bottle lifted it toward Joe in acknowledgment. The other boy gave him the finger.

Joe grunted, and watched them disappear into the

trees. "One of these days those woods are gonna go up in smoke." He turned back to Allison, gave her a stiff nod. "You're right about the party. It'll mean a lot to Snoozy, having you there."

"Joe." She laid a hand on his arm. "Tell me what happened with your brother."

He pulled away. "Meet me out front at seven."

SHE'D LET HIM DOWN.

Allison pressed a hand to her chest and rubbed at the stinging tangle of regret. A year ago, she'd been so caught up in her own hurt and resentment that she hadn't seen how much Joe had needed her. How alone he must have felt. How lost.

No wonder he was bitter.

She shut the door of her room and slapped at the safety bar, then remembered Mitzi and flipped it open again in case she needed to make a speedy escape.

Escape. God, how she wanted to go home. She missed her desk, her color-coordinated file system and the calculator her mother had given her as a college graduation gift. She'd had it engraved—*You can count on me.*

Allison steered her mind away from the irony of *that* thought, snagged a fresh pair of underwear from the dresser and headed for the shower.

The spray of warm water pummeled her face, her throat, her breasts. Her arm muscles shrieked as she lifted her hands to wash her hair but she didn't flinch, more concerned about what was going on in other parts of her body.

Like a hot, throbbing emptiness…

Damn Joe Gallahan and his tool belt. She wished with all her heart he hadn't put the wretched thing on. The combination of work boots, faded denim, male sweat and rigid tools sliding in and out of worn leather had made it tough to remember why she was so mad at him.

Hazel Catlett was right. Joe would rock a wet T-shirt contest. And she hated him for it. Hated herself even more for the buzz of excitement that thrummed in her veins at the thought of going out with him tonight—of standing next to him in a crowd, of feeling his heat and breathing his scent while the beat of loud music pulsated behind her breastbone.

While need pulsated in every last corner of her body.

She shifted the water to cold and squealed. The high-pitched sound bounced around in the confines of the shower, mocking her.

Joe had apologized for believing she'd intentionally let him down, but it didn't excuse his crack about what she was willing to do for Tackett. And he was still bitter about losing his clients.

Which was all just as well. It would only make it easier for her brain to call the shots, and not her body.

Once out of the shower she dressed quickly, not anxious to spend a lot of time alone in her room—in case she really *wasn't* alone. Silly, but she couldn't shake the feeling she was being watched. Even out-side, when she'd followed Joe around the perimeter of the motel as he explained Parker Macfarland's am-bitious plans for sprucing up the grounds, she'd had the feeling they weren't alone.

God only knew what other kinds of creatures lurked behind the motel's walls. Or maybe those teen-age boys had been watching from the trees?

She shivered, and snatched up her purse and key-card.

She forced her thoughts to something more pro-ductive—like her plans for future success.

Luckily she'd brought her electronic notebook along with her, but she could always use a supply of the old-fashioned kind. Maybe she could pick up a few notepads at the dollar store she noticed in town. After all, she did her best thinking with a cup of cof-fee, a pencil and a fat pad of lined paper.

And she had some serious thinking to do.

First she'd double her efforts with her prospects list and make plans for some hard-core recruiting. She needed to brainstorm ways to lure clients away from the agency's competitors. She could make cold calls and squeeze every last penny out of her expense ac-count taking potentials to breakfast, lunch and din-ner if she had to.

The more work she shouldered when she got back to T&P, the less time she'd have on her hands to brood about Joe. How he didn't trust her enough to tell her about his brother. How his genuine remorse made her wish things had turned out differently.

And why, even after he believed she'd turned her back on him when he'd needed her most, he had still asked her to move away with him to Castle Creek.

HE WOULDN'T HAVE cut himself shaving if he hadn't been in such a hurry. And he wouldn't have been in such a hurry if he hadn't spent the better part of an hour alternately staring out the kitchen window and eyeing the bottle of whiskey on the counter. In the end he'd had fifteen minutes to shower and shave, once he'd managed to turn his back on the Glenlivet.

He'd allowed himself just a single glass of the good stuff, to take the edge off the shock Allison had given him. But as soon as they got to Snoozy's, he had every intention of cutting loose, even if it did mean handing over his truck keys.

He'd spent a year resenting Allison for something she'd never done. And when the truth had come out, *she'd* apologized to *him*. If that didn't call for one hellacious hangover, he didn't know what did.

With one minute to spare, he smoothed his palms down the front of his navy pullover—anything more than jeans would stand out at Snoozy's, but he'd dressed up his usual T-shirt by covering it with a V-neck sweater—and patted the cat settling herself at the foot of his bed.

"Don't wait up."

Once he'd locked up he saw Allison standing

beside his truck. Like him she wore jeans, but she'd dressed hers up with high heels and that slinky-looking blouse she'd had on the first day she appeared at the motel. Which pretty much guaranteed he'd be on nipple watch all damned night.

He stifled a groan and forced his gaze upward. She'd curled her hair, so that it fell to her shoulders in mild waves. As he watched, she leaned over to brush at her knee. Her hair swung forward, and he had a sudden vision of her making that very same move—while straddling his naked body.

Damn it to hell. He should have worn a looser-fitting pair of jeans.

CHAPTER SIX

NEITHER OF THEM said much during the fifteen-minute drive to the bar. Joe pulled into the parking lot, which bore a marked resemblance to his own—he and Snoozy were both in desperate need of a visit from a paving company. But that was one of the last items on his list, and it probably hadn't even made Snoozy's. His customers didn't come for the pristine parking lot. They came for the brew and the crew.

He switched off the engine. Allison leaned forward, her gaze roving over the bar's shabby exterior, every gouge, crack and water stain visible in the lingering daylight. Yeah, it would have looked better in the dark. But like he'd told his buddy Reid, the beer was cold, the cheese plate was free and the pool table was mostly level.

From inside the bar came the faint, catchy sounds of a Shania Twain song. Already Allison's shoulders had picked up the rhythm. Joe watched her graceful motions, his pulse picking up its own rhythm. *Chill, Gallahan.* No way was he going to compound his mistakes by putting the moves on her. Besides, he had a feeling that right about now she'd welcome a pass from him about as much as she'd welcome a hug from Mitzi.

Two soccer-mom types came out of the bar, laughing loudly, releasing a blast of music and energetic conversation behind them. They continued to giggle as they stepped to the side and passed a pack of cigarettes back and forth. The smell of secondhand smoke and overcooked popcorn sidled into the truck's cab.

"We should get in there." Allison grabbed her phone and tucked her purse under the seat, hesitated and turned to face him. "Look. I know you don't want me here. Not at the party, not in Castle Creek. I get it. And you get why I can't wait to be back in D.C. But we made a deal, and…why don't we just make the best of it? Like you said before—a cease-fire, right?"

Ouch. She couldn't have made it clearer she wanted the hell away from him. But if he had his way, making *the best of it* would involve the two of them getting naked.

She started to cough, and sounded like she was strangling on her purse strap, and that's when he realized he'd spoken the thought out loud.

He blamed it on the nipples.

Thunk, thunk, thunk, thunk. Audrey at the window again.

"Let's go 'make the best of it,'" he said, and hopped out of the truck.

"Come on, children, the party is starting without us." Audrey stopped Joe with a hand on his arm.

"There's a tray on my front seat. Grab it for me, would you, please?"

"Let me guess. Sausage balls."

"Bran muffins and fruit. Someone had to bring the fiber. Cheese is like meat, you know. Too much and it'll clog your plumbing." Her glance traveled from Joe to Allison and back again. "And if you ask me, you've been looking a little plugged up lately."

Joe felt heat climb his cheeks as he made a break for the Lincoln. After retrieving Audrey's tray he followed the women inside, noting Allison was careful not to catch his eye.

Plugged up.

Was it that obvious?

The regulars had managed to claim their usual spots at the bar, but if one of them got up to use the can, they might as well just hang out in the bathroom—the toilets could very well be the only seats left in the house. Someone shouted Joe's name and he looked to the right, toward the pool table, saw Noble and his two firefighter buddies surrounded by half a dozen women. Telling tall tales about snake wrestling, no doubt. Joe produced a grin, and gave Noble a thumbs-up.

When he turned back he spotted the Welcome Home, Mitzi banner. It was draped across the mirror behind the bar, and decorated with fluorescent yellow happy faces. Normally something like that would have looked as out of place as a flower arrangement in a man cave, but Snoozy's was famous for something much more bizarre.

And at that moment, Allison spotted it. Snoozy's pride and joy—or what used to be his pride and joy, until Mitzi had come back into his life. In the left front corner of the room, a hot pink salon chair faced an ornate-framed mirror tall enough to tower over Noble Johnson. The mirror, sporting a leopard-print-scarf-looking thing, sparkled from a recent cleaning.

Allison gaped. "What is that?"

"Something his ex-wife left behind."

"But...I thought he was happy she left."

Snoozy appeared in front of them, taking an unprecedented break from morose. His moustache practically quivered with glee. "Glad my guests of honor could make it. Wouldn't have a reason to celebrate without you. Good to see you, too, Audrey. Liz was telling me you were 'specially concerned about Mitzi. No need to worry. The vet gave her a clean bill of health. Said she'd live a good long time."

Audrey took the tray from Joe and shoved it at Snoozy. "How much does she weigh?"

Oh, man. Joe rolled his shoulders back and bounced on the balls of his feet, ready to run interference.

"Hundred and ten pounds, four ounces." Snoozy winked. "But that was before lunch."

Audrey harrumphed and walked away, lips moving as she calculated serving size.

Snoozy scratched his head and watched her go, then set the tray aside. He led Joe and Allison over to the pink chair and gave it a slap. "You're probably wondering about this here chair, Allison. Well, you see, I kept this as a reminder. In case I ever thought about getting married again. It nearly took every-thing out of me. You know, like Samson, after Deli-lah cut his hair. Nope, never thought I'd want to take another risk like that...." He offered Allison a shy smile. "Though lately I've been thinking differently."

Joe blinked. He had to give ol' Snooze credit. The man had taste.

The bar owner was gesturing at the antishrine he'd created. "But the time has come to get rid of all this. I'm raffling it off tonight, as a matter of fact. This'll be Mitzi's spot. That way she'll never be lonely." He gave Joe the elbow. "If you're interested in the raffle, be prepared to lay down some serious cash. Noble musta bought a hundred tickets already."

"Noble?" As soon as he spoke, the big man himself loomed behind Snoozy. He and Joe bumped knuck-les—they'd come a long way from pounding each other into Snoozy's beer-soaked floor. "What do you want with this thing, man?"

"It's for the library. Thought the kids might get a kick out of it."

"It looks like a throne," Allison said. "Who wouldn't want to read a book curled up in a chair this cool? What a wonderful idea."

Noble got an aw-shucks expression on his face and moved a step closer to Allison. Snoozy frowned, and crowded in from the other side. Allison's eyes went wide. Joe smirked, and turned his attention to the chair's pristine, flamingo-pink vinyl.

"I don't know, man. You better hide the scissors."

"How're you planning to get it over there? Gonna borrow yourself another minivan?" Snoozy asked.

Noble gave the bar owner a red-faced scowl. "Nothing wrong with a minivan. I'm a big man. I need lots of room. Besides, it's perfect for hauling books around."

"If that helps you sleep at night."

"Right, Snooze, and I guess you think chicks dig that death trap you drive?"

"So, um, how's Mitzi doing?" Allison asked loudly.

The moment she spoke, Snoozy stopped glowering at Noble and stood a little taller. Noble rolled his eyes and headed back to the pool table, muttering about head room and safety features.

"She's settling in nicely," Snoozy said. "She'll be more comfortable in a bigger space, but she does seem happy to be home."

"You don't think she's lonely?"

"Not anymore, thanks to you."

"She doesn't seem…fretful?"

Snoozy looked puzzled. Joe kept his own expression carefully blank.

"She's thinking Mitzi might have left behind a bunch of babies."

Snoozy's face lit up like one of the bar's neon signs. "Wouldn't that be something?" He sighed, and aimed a light kick at the base of the pink chair. "You know,

Mitzi hissed at this here thing when I brought her in. All these years and she remembered who it once belonged to. Now, that's loyalty for you." His Adam's apple bounced and he turned an accusing glare on Joe. "And you wanted to shoot her."

"If we'd known she was yours, Snooze, we'd have called you first thing."

"Well. You might not want to get too close for a while. Give her a chance to forgive you."

"You told her?"

"I thought she had a right to know."

Allison gave a choking cough, and immediately Snoozy's expression turned contrite. "What can I get you to drink?" he asked. "Anything you like. On the house."

"Club soda with lime?" Her eyes had started to water. This time Joe recognized the signs of a laugh fighting to get out. He tried to look appropriately concerned, even patted her back.

Snoozy pointed a finger at him. "And a draft for you. Coming right up."

THE INVOLUNTARY LAUGH bubbling up inside her petered out as Joe guided her toward the food tables pushed against the back wall. What kind of shape would he be in by the end of the evening if Snoozy kept offering him beer? Anxiety gnawed. The smell of overripe popcorn edged her stomach closer and closer to nausea.

He made the necessary introductions as they

threaded their way through small clusters of guests, but between the noise and the number of names tossed in her direction, she had little hope of remembering much. She did recognize Liz Early behind the bar, so she gave her a wave. Liz beamed, and responded with a furious flapping of her own hand.

"You've made a friend for life," Joe murmured, and the low timbre of his voice made her shudder. *Stop that.* "It's not everyone who would sacrifice one of Cal's cinnamon rolls for a stranger. She's handling the music tonight, so let her know if you have any special requests. She'd probably play the song five times in a row for you. Ten, if you ask real nice."

A tall, graying man wearing black pants and a black polo shirt strolled up and gave Joe a light slap on the back. Allison recognized him from the diner— she'd seen him in the kitchen.

"Cal, man, we were just talking about you." After Joe introduced him to Allison, Cal promised he'd "take care of her" next time she came into the diner. Then some of the cheer seeped from his face.

"I sure am glad you're breathing life back into that old motel. Not only will you fancy up that stretch of road, you'll bring more business into town. Of course I won't mind that one bit. Anyway, it's about time some good came out of that place."

Joe nodded grimly. "I got bits and pieces of the story when I was at the courthouse arranging for permits. What I heard was pretty bad. What's it been, about ten, twelve years now?"

"Something like that."

Allison looked from one man to the other. "What happened?"

Cal exhaled. "Child abuse. The worst kind. I never did hear what happened to the kid involved." He looked down at the floor and rubbed the back of his neck, then squinted up at Joe. "I need to get back to the diner, but I do have a question before I go. You, uh, planning on painting the outside of that motel?"

"Got something against green?"

"I like my peas on a plate. Not on the side of a building."

"I'll take that into consideration," Joe said solemnly. Cal walked away and Joe nudged her toward the tables. "You have to be hungry. If you ate anything at all today, I bet it was peanut M&M's. I'll fix you a plate."

He had to stop doing that—proving he paid way more attention than she'd ever given him credit for.

He selected two paper plates and waved them over the jumble of platters and plastic containers spread across two folding tables. "What sounds good to you? Pasta salad? Chicken parmesan? The ubiquitous deviled egg?" He turned, took one look at her face, dropped the plates and hustled her into the nearest corner, where someone had stashed an oversized trashcan. "You look like you're about to throw up everything you didn't eat today."

"I'll be all right. I think it's the smell of the popcorn." She pulled in a deep breath and managed a wry smile. "Plus, that forgetting-to-eat thing probably isn't helping."

"I should have made sure you ate breakfast." Some emotion she didn't recognize flashed in and out of his gaze. He backed away. "Let me grab you that club soda."

He was back almost immediately with their drinks. "Snoozy sends his earnest apologies. Audrey managed to corner him. I got out of there before I found myself tapped as referee. Work on this and I'll be back with some food. Don't worry, I'll go with bland."

He was gone before she could stop him—food was the last thing she wanted. A drift of blessed fresh air swept across her skin and she peered through the crowd toward the front of the bar, where Snoozy was propping open the door. An uneasy wistfulness welled up inside her.

She sipped her drink and stared at the bottle of beer Joe had placed on the corner shelf beside her. A plate appeared in front of her and she jumped.

"You okay?"

"I was thinking about that poor little girl."

"Little girl?"

"The one Cal talked about. From the motel."

"It was a boy." They exchanged somber looks then Joe nodded at her stomach. "Feeling better?"

"I am. Thanks for looking out for me."

He started to say something then shrugged. "The better you feel—"

"The harder I work. So you've said."

"About that." He drank a mouthful of beer, took his time setting the bottle back on the shelf...took even more time positioning it so the label faced out. And at last he met her gaze.

"Are you...could you possibly be..."

"Hey, handsome." A tall, slender woman with a mass of long, white-blond hair sauntered over. She had a small digital camera in one hand and a plastic cup of lime-green punch in the other. "Why are you two hiding out over here? If you're looking for privacy you should have stayed back at the motel."

Joe smiled, and held his plate out of the way as he gave the woman a hug. "Allison and I used to work together." To Allison he said, "Ivy Millbrook runs the local dairy farm."

"Nice to meet you, Allison. I've heard a lot about you. Of course, I've heard more about poor Mitzi."

Joe retrieved his beer. "If you're calling her 'poor Mitzi' that means you've been talking to Snoozy. Have you seen her yet? Trust me, that snake had it made."

Ivy waggled the camera. "Ah, yes, the proud father's making introductions. I've never seen him so animated. I bet you two were just as animated when you found her." She laughed, then for Allison's benefit pulled a sympathetic face. "I heard about all the joking at the diner. That place is like one big kitchen party. Living in D.C., you're probably used to more anonymity."

"It was a little overwhelming at first." Allison didn't dare look at Joe. "But everyone is so friendly."

"Don't tell me—I can read between the lines. Rachel waited on you, didn't she? Bless her heart—she's been in love with Joe since day one. She can be a little cross, but that's only because Priscilla Mae beat her out for Lilac Queen. Did you at least try one of Cal's cinnamon rolls?"

Joe shook his head. "Liz charmed it out of her."

"Shame on you." Ivy punched him lightly on the biceps. "You need to take better care of your guests. You know how Cal likes to show off for visitors. Hey, why don't you bring Allison out to the farm? I can give her a tour, and then show *you* where I'd like those bookshelves."

"Oh, no, you don't. I told you the moment you brought them up I don't have—"

"Time. I remember." She rolled her eyes at Allison. "What are we going to do with this guy? So allergic to commitment he won't even take on a little DIY project."

"Because I'm busy with my own *little* DIY project. And I think you're missing the irony of calling it DIY. Anyway, didn't Seth offer to do it for you?"

"There are many things I'd love Seth to do for me. But the bookshelves aren't going in my bedroom."

Silence. Ivy winked at Allison but looked all innocence for Joe. "TMI?"

"Instead of filling Allison in on your love life, why don't you tell her about Priscilla Mae?"

"She was one of yours?"

"She still is." Ivy's smile was affectionate. "She's too old to provide milk but not too old to be the farm's main attraction. Kids love having their picture taken with her. You should come see for yourself. Breathe some fresh air, learn about dairy farming, maybe even milk a cow or two."

Joe grunted. "You have more than a hundred animals out there, including horses and chickens. I don't think what she'll be breathing is fresh air."

Ivy ignored him. "So what do you say?" When Allison didn't answer right away, Ivy laughed. "It's not as bad as it sounds. Besides, one slice of my cheesecake will more than make up for the muck you get on your boots. Even if you can't make it by the farm, don't you dare leave Castle Creek without trying one of Cal's cinnamon rolls. In fact, I'd love to meet you for coffee before you go. That is, if Mr. Fixit here ever lets you take a break. Not counting tonight, I mean."

Allison promised to give her a call and Ivy headed in the direction of the punch bowl. Joe nodded at Allison's plate.

"You need to eat," he said, gently but firmly.

She stabbed her fork into a fat strawberry as a roar of approval went up around the pool table. "What's got everyone so excited over there?"

"Bet it's Burke. That guy can clear a table faster than…well, faster than Mitzi can clear a motel room."

"Very funny." She speared a blueberry this time,

and motioned with her chin toward the crowd. "Do you play?"

He stared at her fruit salad. "How about we trade questions again? I'll answer yours first."

"O-kay." And here she'd just gotten rid of her nausea. She put down her fork and reached for her drink.

"I've been known to play pool," he said. "But I'm better at poker. My turn to ask a question. Are you pregnant?"

She choked. Wait, *what?* Club soda sloshed. Joe rescued her cup as she stared down at the puddle on her plate, struggling to decide if she'd heard him right. When she didn't say anything, Joe set his jaw.

"You should have told me first thing. I'd never have—" He looked around, rubbed his fingers over his chin and lowered his voice. "You're working too hard. And even though you're wearing a mask, breathing in all that dust can't be good for the baby. You need to go back to D.C., stick close to your doctor."

Yep. She'd heard right. He thought she was pregnant.

Allison stared, vocal cords rigid as she wavered between anger and astonishment. And an overpowering desire to fall down laughing. Not that she was an expert on babies, but didn't making one usually involve sex?

Which meant motherhood was completely out of her current realm of possibility.

She finally managed to recover her voice. "Are

you kidding me with this? What on earth makes you think I'm having a baby?"

"You're not?"

"No."

"Good. That's good." He picked up his beer, drained it and nodded at her glass. "Ready for another?"

She ignored a trickle of uneasiness. If he drank too much, she'd simply confiscate his keys. She'd done it before, she could do it again.

Difference was, this would be the last time.

"Why is that good?"

He made a gesture with the empty bottle, as if searching for the words. Then his expression turned grim and his arm dropped to his side. "What if something happened while you were here? Something… irrevocable? It would be my—wait." Regret flickered across his gaze. "Unless you're *trying* to start a family."

"No." God, no. Maybe someday, but— "Why did you think I might be pregnant?"

"You asked for club soda instead of wine, a whiff of popcorn made you sick and…well, raising a kid can't be cheap. It would explain why you need money."

So would a mother with a gambling addiction.

"But I should have known better," he said.

"What do you mean by that?"

"You don't like to get involved in something unless you know the outcome. Which is why you didn't want to go back to the motel today. Not so much because of the snake, but because you don't like surprises."

She blinked. He'd all but accused her of being predictable—might as well just call her dull. "Would *anyone* like that kind of surprise?" she murmured.

"Are you talking about discovering Mitzi?" An elegant, fifty-something woman with short blond hair eased closer. Allison swallowed an envious moan. The woman's Misook pantsuit was spectacular—and made Allison mourn anew the loss of her designer wardrobe.

"Eugenia." Joe helped himself to another hug. Huh. She'd never known him to be a hugger. "Allison, this is Eugenia Blue, owner of the finest dress shop in town."

The woman laughed and held out a slim hand. "I own the *only* dress shop in town."

"If your store is anything like your outfit, it has to be a hit."

"Why, thank you. With this economy, it's *taken* a hit, but I'm hanging in. You should come by. We could dip over to the diner for coffee." She put a manicured hand on Allison's arm and leaned in. "Have you heard about Cal's cinnamon rolls?"

Allison laughed. Did everyone in this town have a sweet tooth? "As a matter of fact, I have. Trying one is at the top of my 'do before you leave town' list."

Right under "Joe."

Her own thought shocked her. She didn't mean it. Of course she didn't mean it. Still, her face grew warm.... At least she hadn't said the words out loud.

Eugenia must have sensed something because she

cut her eyes at Joe. "Who knows? Maybe you'll decide you like Castle Creek too much to leave."

Joe didn't give her a chance to respond. "Where's Harris tonight?"

"At home with Natalie. Parker and I decided to enjoy a girls' night out, so we volunteered Harris for an evening of Barbie dolls and Ellery Queen."

"The show from the seventies?"

"Reid turned her on to it."

"That's quite a combination." Turning to Allison, Joe said, "Harris was at the diner when we were there earlier. He's the one who told the joke about the pythons getting hitched."

The knee-slapper. "So Harris is your husband?"

Eugenia hesitated, and licked her lips. Joe frowned over at the older woman, looking like he wanted to comfort her. Meanwhile Allison could have kicked herself—she'd obviously said the wrong thing. She scrambled for something else to say, something innocuous to break the tension.

Saved by the bell, so to speak, her cell rang and it was all she could do not to slump to the floor in relief. She plucked her phone from her pocket, eyed the screen and offered Eugenia an apologetic smile. "I should take this." Of course, even if it was Sammy on the other end of the call she'd have taken it. No sense in standing there gawking while Eugenia Blue struggled to find a suitable answer to Allison's artless question.

She excused herself, and headed for the parking lot.

"Maggie, how are you?" She hadn't talked to her former college roommate in months. Yet another testament to Allison's preoccupation with her job. "Is everything okay?" She held her breath. Considering how out of touch they'd become, she had a feeling her friend was calling with bad news.

"That's what I wanted to ask *you*. You could have called me yourself, Allie. You don't have to be embarrassed. Things like this happen."

Allison frowned as she leaned against the bumper of Joe's truck. "What are you talking about?"

"You know. The loan."

Dear God in heaven. Allison's nausea came back full force. She bent forward at the waist and gulped in air. "Please tell me my mother didn't call you and ask for money."

"But…she did. She said you'd made some bad investments and if you didn't make a payment in the next few days, you'd lose your condo. I promised to put a check in the mail tomorrow."

Oh, no. Oh, God. Mortified heat flashed through Allison, making her dizzy. The lengths her mother was willing to go to get back to the blackjack table… She swallowed, and pressed her hand to her forehead. "Please do not do that, Maggie. The money isn't for me. It's for my mother. She has a gambling problem."

"Oh. Oh, Allison, I'm so sorry."

"So am I." The door to the bar opened, releasing strains of Jim Stafford's "Spiders and Snakes." Allison's lips twisted—she'd bet her last handful of M&M's that Snoozy was at that very moment hunched over Liz's laptop, desperate to fast-forward to another song. Along with the music drifting through the open doorway came the sound of friendly laughter, the muted thwack of pool ball hitting pool ball, and a man and a woman with their arms wrapped so tightly around each other they looked like they'd been caught naked in a blizzard. As they walked past, the man dropped his hand from the woman's shoulder and squeezed her butt. Allison looked away and the woman giggled before they disappeared behind an SUV.

Allison should have known her mother wouldn't give in so easily.

"Thank you for being so willing to help me, Maggie," she murmured into the phone. "I can't apologize enough for what my mother tried to do."

"It's not your fault, Allison. But you should know that she asked for Dee's number."

Allison tipped her head back and opened her mouth wide in a silent scream. It hadn't occurred to her that she'd need to warn her friends about her mother. As soon as she got back to her room, she'd send an email to everyone on her contacts list. But first—

Two seconds later she had her mother on the phone.

"You told me you had a sure bet. By any chance would it have something to do with extorting money from my friends?"

"Borrowing. I'm *borrowing* money from your friends. And you should be flattered. They're anxious to help. And why not let them, if it makes them happy? People need to feel needed."

"So you're saying you're doing them a favor."

"Exactly."

She could picture her mother beaming. Her fingers tightened around the phone. "Who else besides Maggie have you called?"

"I don't think that's any of your business, Allie girl, and I don't—"

"*Who else?*"

Her mother sniffled. "Dee. And I don't see why I can't accept the money. She has plenty to spare. She must, since she promised to send—"

"I don't want to know. I'm calling her right now and telling her not to write that check. And I'm warning all my other friends about you. This is unbelievable, Mom. I never thought you'd exploit me like this. Get help. And get it from someone else. I'm all tapped out."

In more ways than one.

She disconnected the call and concentrated on breathing. On dislodging the searing weight that pressed against her chest. Between the work schedule that left her little time for socializing and her mother's greed, Allison would be lucky to have any friends left.

Her cell rang again. Tackett this time.

When it rains, it pours.

But she couldn't ignore him forever.

Minutes later she ended yet another call feeling

drained. *Give me good news, Kincaid.* Was Gallahan still on for D.C.? Was she making herself indispensable? Did she think he would consider coming back on a permanent basis?

Yes. Hardly. For Joe's sake she hoped the hell not.

Of course, out loud, she answered yes to every question. At the same time she wondered when exactly she'd accepted that Joe didn't belong in D.C. He belonged here. *She* was the one who belonged in D.C. And the thought wasn't as comforting as it used to be.

Her own mother. *God.*

"You all right, dear?" Allison hadn't even heard Audrey come outside. The older woman stood on the pavement in front of her, legs spread and arms akimbo. She'd dressed for the party by exchanging her pink pants for a pair of baggy jeans. And over top of her Go Army T-shirt she wore some sort of faux leather jacket. In the dim light it was hard to tell but... Allison looked closer and winced. Yep. Snakeskin.

"Shall I fetch Joseph for you?"

Blinking furiously, Allison pushed upright. As much as she wanted to crawl under the covers and hide—her own covers, in her own bed, in her own apartment—she could wallow in self-pity later. Probably in the shower, where everyone in the movies pretended no one could hear them cry.

"No, thank you." She cleared the thickness from her throat. "I came out to take a call and got distracted by the stars. Amazing how many you can see when there aren't any city lights to turn night into day."

"Such a poetic prevarication. I'll say good-night, then. Don't forget to eat some fruit."

With a wave Audrey headed for her Lincoln. Allison swiped at her cheeks and watched her go. She breathed in, caught the scent of engine exhaust laced with something blooming—gardenia?—and went back inside.

Joe looked pensive as he stood with the crowd surrounding the pool table, where Noble played with a bearded man wearing navy coveralls. When Joe spotted Allison he waved her over, and bent down so she could hear him.

"Everything okay?"

She wasn't even going there. "Yep. What about you? You're looking solemn."

He raised his beer. "Not for long. Hey, Snoozy's looking for you. He wants to take us upstairs to see Mitzi." She jumped when he suddenly shouted along with the crowd and pumped his fist in the air. Someone must have made a tough shot. She couldn't have seen it if she'd wanted to—the guy in front of her was almost as big as Noble.

"Oh, and that's Pete Lowry," Joe said, bending again. He gestured at Noble's opponent. "He owns the local service station. Said you should give him a call if you ever have trouble with your Camry."

"How…nice." And that was her undoing. Here a perfect stranger had offered to look out for her, while her own mother didn't think twice about taking advantage. Tears scalded the backs of her eyes and she whirled toward the bathroom. Joe said something, asked some question. "Restroom," she managed, and hurried to the rear of the bar before she fell to the floor in a howling mess.

The restrooms were at the end of a short hallway. She tried the door marked Ladies and found it locked. *Please hurry.* She folded her arms and slumped against the wall to wait.

Beneath the too-strong, citrusy scent of air freshener lingered the sour smell of cigarette smoke. The linoleum was faded and curled up at the edges, the dark paneled walls—what was it with this town and paneling?—covered with dusty plaques of pithy sayings. I Only Drink to Make You More Interesting. Don't Cry Over Spilled Milk—It Could Have Been Beer. If You're Drinking to Forget, Please Pay in Advance.

She was desperately trying to follow the Don't Cry advice when Joe suddenly appeared in front of her. He took one look at her face, grabbed her hand and tugged her through an unmarked door.

CHAPTER SEVEN

SHE HEARD JOE swipe his hand along the wall before light flooded the storeroom. Allison angled her body away, desperate to hide her distress. Joe closed the door and came up behind her, his concern as tangible as the heat of his body.

"What happened?"

She shook her head and prayed he would drop it. But she knew better. Knew she'd feel better, too, if only she could tell him. But, of course, she couldn't.

"Bad news?" he asked, in that deep, troubled voice, and suddenly she didn't care about the conflict between them—she needed to feel all that solid, country-Joe concern wrapped around her. She turned, and pressed into him, buried her nose in the side of his neck. Wrapped her arms around his waist. Enjoyed the soft feel of his sweater so much that she squeezed him.

A little too hard, apparently, because he grunted. Then his arms came around her and he squeezed back.

Warm. Firm. Strong.

And so very tempting.

"Want to talk about it?" he murmured.

No. She didn't. What she did want, with every aroused ounce of her femininity, was to taste him. Had his flavor changed? Would her tongue still tingle when it made contact with his skin? She had to find out.

Yes, she was desperate for a distraction and Joe provided a handy one. Would it be wise to kiss him? No. Spontaneous? Definitely. He'd implied she couldn't be impulsive. Cared too much about being in control, he'd said. Well, who could blame her?

Everyone in her life *except* her had control. Her mother ruled her finances. Tackett called the shots at the office. And Joe...Joe had the upper hand, here. In more ways than one.

So maybe it was time for a little spontaneity.

She lifted her head and pushed Joe back against the door. He gave a half-grunt, half-groan when she body slammed him, trapping him from knee to chest. Then she curled her fingers into his sweater, stood on the tips of her toes and sank her teeth into his chin.

He sucked in a breath and reared away. The back of his head thumped against the door and for a long, wordless moment he stared down at her. When she followed up her bite with a lick his expression morphed from shock to desire, his eyes narrowing with sexy intent. She knew that look. It had always made her vibrate, as if someone had flicked a switch, sending a relentless electrical current through her body.

And apparently someone was still manning that switch because she was pulsing like a Cuisinart.

Though so much about Joe had changed, his effect on her body remained the same. Which would probably turn out to be a very bad thing, but at the moment, she couldn't bring herself to be anything but grateful.

She could see the moisture from her mouth on his chin, the smudges of red where her teeth had scraped him, and she shuddered with the need to bite him again. Hard. Heat pulsated from her thighs to her hands.

Do you know what you're doing?

But she'd stopped thinking the moment her body had touched his. Her nails dug into his chest and she wriggled against him, his muscular length both fresh and familiar at the same time.

His chest rose and fell rapidly against hers while his fingers tightened on her hips. From the back of his throat came a deep, primal noise of appreciation. His arms slid up and around her. He lowered his head, skimmed his mouth along the side of her neck and up behind her ear. The warmth of his breath on her skin had her craving a much more intimate, rhythmic heat.

The thought of opening herself up to Joe again like that—literally and figuratively—sent nerves sparkling through her chest, and her lungs felt suddenly too small. She turned her head and touched her tongue to the stubble along his jaw, inhaled and caught a hint of sandalwood. Realized she wasn't the only one shaking.

She moved her hands to his ribs and around to his back, pressing even closer, wondering how she'd managed to go for so long without touching him.

He shifted his hold, stroking his hands up under her hair and cradling her head. She licked her lips and felt him jerk. Felt something else, too, high and hard against her stomach. Her core went molten. His breathing intensified.

Then he pushed her away.

EVEN AS HE slid out from between Allison and the storeroom door, Joe was calling himself all kinds of foul names. But, damn it, he'd only meant to console her. She'd looked so…unhappy. So fragile.

He touched his fingers to his chin. Yeah. Fragile like a tigress in heat.

His erection sat up even straighter, like a student determined to be teacher's pet, and Joe set his jaw. If he didn't stop thinking about her mouth, he'd have to hide out in the storeroom all night.

The small space echoed with uneven breathing, and the scrape of his boots on cement as he turned to face her. She stood with her arms crossed, skin flushed and ice edging into her eyes. But the hurt lingered.

He hadn't meant to make her feel rejected. But he didn't want to lose himself in the moment, either. He might accidentally tell her how much he'd missed her.

How watching her charm Liz and indulge Snoozy, how seeing the regret she felt for upsetting Eugenia and the gratitude she felt toward Pete, had all made Joe realize she wasn't the materialistic snob he'd accused her of becoming. The person he'd needed to believe she'd become.

She lifted her chin. "Why did you push me away?"

And she was a hell of a lot more forthright than he remembered.

"It's not what you want," he gritted. "*I'm* not what you want. You're not thinking clearly."

"You're the one who's been drinking."

Not anymore. Not tonight. He'd keep his distance from the bar—and from her—even if it killed him.

Muffled sounds of cheering and laughter reached them. Someone must have finally won at the pool table. When he didn't speak, Allison swung away, rubbing at her arms and studying the contents of the storeroom.

Lopsided stacks of cardboard boxes bearing liquor logos lined two walls. A floor-to-ceiling wine rack, the bottles intermingled with packs of paper towels and spools of toilet paper and towers of cardboard coasters occupied the third. Most of the remaining space in the room was taken up by a haphazard stack of broken chairs, a plastic bin overflowing with dirty aprons and towels, and a battered stepladder. The place reeked of stale beer and mildew.

"You're not going to forgive me, are you?" she asked.

He yanked his gaze away from the Shelves of Blessed Oblivion and took a moment to consider.

Best thing he could do for either of them was remain silent. Let her believe the answer was "no."

Gradually her chin lowered, and her expression emptied. "I'm ready to leave whenever you are."

He knew damned well she didn't mean the party, or even the bar. But, damn it, they were sticking to the deal. He'd negotiated two weeks, and they were only two days in.

She'd see the before and after—for one room, anyway. As long as the electrician and the building inspector could fit him in, and if he and Allison got a move on, they just might be able to get the drywall up and painted, the bathroom tiled, and the new carpeting in before they left for Virginia. Then maybe she'd understand, if only partially, why working for T&P couldn't compare.

He opened the door. "Let's go find Snoozy so he can show us how happy Mitzi is to be back home. After that we'll head back to the motel. It's been a long day."

"It certainly has." She marched past him, head up, shoulders back, and he felt again that tingling of pride he had no right feeling. He had to keep his distance, or risk letting her down again.

His gaze dropped to her ass as he followed her out to the bar. Judas Priest, it was going to be a long two weeks.

TWO HOURS AFTER arriving back at the motel, Allison sat in the center of her bed, knees to her chest, eyes alert, ears strained for unusual sounds. Like slithering. Or hissing.

Or fang sharpening.

So much for believing Mitzi couldn't escape. But the daylight made it easy to believe that ghosts and goblins and vampires weren't real. And that pythons wouldn't be lonely for the only home they'd known for half a dozen years.

Damn that Joe Gallahan. She never should have let him talk her into saying goodbye to Mitzi. But Snoozy had been so eager to show them her new temporary digs—the bathroom in his loft upstairs. Mitzi liked to soak in the tub, he told them. The entire time Snoozy talked, the python watched them from where she was curled up, around the base of the toilet.

Allison counted to ten, pulled in a breath, counted to ten again. Eyed the phone on the nightstand. Imagined herself dialing the motel office, waking Joe, asking if she could spend the night on his couch. He'd laugh so loud he'd drown out the sound of a python winding its way across her bed—

She shuddered and leaped to her feet, and bounced in a circle as she scanned the mattress.

A desperate glance at the clock revealed it was nearly one in the morning and her gaze landed again on the phone. She rolled her lips inward and bit down hard. There was nothing for it.

She'd have to sleep in her car.

She half-bounced, half-walked to the edge of the bed and jumped, then gathered up a pillow, a blanket, her purse and her car keys and hurried to the door. At least she wouldn't have to bother Joe for a flashlight—the security lights were plenty bright.

She unlocked the car, made a nest in the backseat, climbed in and hit the locks again. Then she settled on her side and prepared to get some much-needed sleep.

Her eyes shot right back open. Was he kidding with these lights? She pulled the blanket over her head and squeezed her eyes shut. Shifted to her left side. Her back. Her right side. Considered reclining in the front passenger seat but was too tired to climb over the console. And too lazy to get out of the car just to get back in again.

She jammed the pillow over her head and started counting backward from one hundred: *100, 99, 98…* she remembered the shock on Joe's face when she'd shoved him against the storeroom door, and how his mouth lowered toward hers…*97, 96, 95…*Joe, concern on his face as he handed her a plate of food. Anger in his eyes as she accused him of petty revenge. Laughter smoothing the tension from his jaw after a harmless spider knocked him on his ass. She gave a sleepy giggle and yawned, snuggling deeper under the blanket…*94…93…92…*Joe cheering on his friend at the pool table—

Bam, bam, bam, bam, bam. Allison gasped and shot upright, heart thrashing against her ribs. She blinked frantically—why was it so dark?—then batted the blanket away from her face. Someone was at the window. She shrank back, pressing into the corner, then recognized Joe. He peered through the glass, his expression as black as...well, as black as the parking lot would be if it weren't for all these asinine streetlights.

"What the hell do you think you're doing?"

"Trying to sleep." She scooted back down and covered her head. "So go away and leave me to it."

"You can't stay out here. It's not safe."

She flung herself upright again and scowled at him through the glass. "Oh, but it's perfectly fine to shut me up in a room infested with cold-blooded, man-eating, squeeze-the-life-out-of-you predators."

"One predator. And we removed her."

"What if she had a boyfriend?"

"I thought we settled this."

"In a room full of people. In the middle of the day."

He straightened. She heard him sigh. He bent down again. "Come inside. Stay with me. You'll be safe."

"I may not be a zoologist but I do know that not all predators are cold-blooded."

He growled, and for some reason the sound turned her on. Good grief. After all they'd been through tonight. She flopped back down and closed her eyes.

"You can have the bed," he said through the window. "I'll take the sofa. We'll figure something out tomorrow. Just come inside. Please."

"I'm fine where I am."

"Don't be—"

She kicked at the door. "Go. Away."

Another growl, then silence. She waited. More silence. She opened one eye and tipped up on her elbow, just in time to see Joe disappear through the office door.

He'd keep her safe, he said. He had to be kidding. She hadn't felt safe with him since the first morning he'd arrived at T&P toting a hangover. The black moods, the excuses, the stumbling into her apartment when she'd felt obligated to open the door because otherwise he'd end up passed out in the hallway—

Rap, rap, rap.

She shrieked then bolted upright for the umpteenth time. What *now?* Joe stood outside the car, a pillow under his arm. Oh, *hell,* no.

"Go away," she yelled.

"Open the door, slick."

She threw the blanket over her head and lay back down.

"Either you sleep in the motel or I sleep out here with you. Which will it be?"

"I don't need you to babysit me. I'm fine."

"Who says I'm doing this for you? Some psycho killer comes along and slits your throat and my dreams of running a motel empire die right along with you. Can you live with that?"

Oh, for God's sake. With a frustrated growl, she rummaged for her keys and pressed the button to unlock the doors. Joe climbed into the front passenger seat and proceeded to spend the next several minutes playing with the seat adjust buttons until she threatened to turn the radio on and tune into an '80s-only station. When he finally settled down he'd reclined so far back that she didn't even have to straighten out her arm to touch his hair.

"What about your cat? Aren't you worried one of Mitzi's offspring will turn her into a midnight snack?"

"I'm counting on the Garp effect."

"The what?"

"*Garp*. You know, the movie. Based on the John Irving novel? Garp and his wife are standing in front of a house they're considering buying when an airplane comes crashing down and takes out the entire second floor. And Garp decides *this* is the house he wants to live in."

"Because…he's looking for a fixer-upper?" She really should have changed position, so her feet instead of her head were behind Joe. That way, if the recline button he'd worn out suddenly failed and he came crashing down on her, he wouldn't end up flattening her skull.

Plus it was more intimate this way, with their heads so close they could almost whisper—as if they were lying next to each other in bed. She squeezed her eyes shut, disturbed by a surge of yearning.

They'd been so unhappy with each other at the end, and obviously still had so much bitterness between them. Their lives were too different to even entertain the idea that they could have a functioning, healthy relationship.

So *why* was she wishing for a second chance?

Guilt? Loneliness? Whatever it was, it was more than physical need. And it was damned inconvenient.

"Because," Joe said, "the odds that another aircraft will ever crash into that house again are astronomical." He yawned. "The house had been plane-proofed, right before their very eyes."

"So you're saying odds are there will never be another snake taking up residence in the walls of your motel." When he hummed in agreement she punched at the back of his seat. "Are you kidding me with this? How do you know that at this very moment, there aren't a gazillion mini Mitzis slithering among the rafters, on the hunt for someone to squeeze?"

"First of all, they're not rafters, they're studs. Second of all, if Mitzi had a boyfriend, I think we'd have spotted him by now. And if Mitzi had had a gazillion babies, don't you think we'd have glimpsed at least one? Trust me. Nothing's going to get into the rooms I've renovated. They're sealed up tight. Between the drywall joint tape, the paint and the caulking, no creepy crawlies will be invading your space."

"I don't care. I'm not going back in there."

He heaved an exaggerated sigh. "How about if I get someone from Pests R Us to come by tomorrow and take a look? Will that make you happy?"

"Depends on what they say."

"If they say there are no snakes in the motel, can we sleep in our beds tomorrow?"

"Yes."

"Good." He shifted impatiently. "Because I won't be getting any sleep out here, I can tell you that."

"Is the seat that uncomfortable?"

"It's those damned streetlights."

She couldn't help it. She laughed. "Good night, Joe."

"Maybe for you."

Allison smiled into her pillow, lulled into relaxation by Joe's even breathing and the squeaking, rhythmic chorus of the crickets outside. Then something squawked, and made a chittering sound. She held her breath.

"Joe. Hear that?"

"Yeah." He sighed the word. "It's a raccoon. He won't bother us. Go to sleep."

"Okay." She tried. She really did. But she was suddenly too wired to sleep. "Joe?"

It took him a few seconds to answer. "Yeah?"

"How about Pumpkin?"

"Suddenly you're hungry?"

"I mean, as a name for your kitten."

"No. Go to sleep."

"Why not?"

"I am not going to yell out 'Pumpkin' every time I need my cat to come running."

"Fine." She readjusted her pillow and tried to relax. Not happening. Her eyes popped open. "Joe."

"Yeah?" he drawled.

"I'm sorry I said the wrong thing. To Eugenia."

"No way you could have known. She proposed and

Harris turned her down. They're together, they're just not married."

She winced. "I also want to apologize for what happened in the storeroom. You wanted to comfort me and I tried to turn it into more. Can we go back to the hands-off policy?"

"I don't know. Can we?"

She didn't know what to say to that, so she didn't say anything. For a while.

"Joe?"

"That's my name."

"Are they really called Pests R Us?"

"What's the matter? Sorry the name's already taken?"

"Bite me."

He chuckled and rolled onto his left side and spoke into the space between the seats. "Whatever happened to that idea, by the way? Of starting your own firm?"

Her fingers curled into the blanket. "The timing. It wasn't right." She held her breath, hoping he wouldn't pursue the topic. He didn't. Instead he grunted, and faced forward again.

Long moments passed before Allison realized she may never get a better chance to ask something personal. Not that Joe would necessarily agree to answer. But it was worth a try.

"Joe?"

"Still here." He mumbled something else along

the lines of "unfortunately," but Allison refused to take the hint.

"What was your brother like?"

O-KAY. HE HADN'T SEEN that one coming. Joe stared at the inspection sticker at the base of the windshield—was she aware it expired this month?—and rubbed at his chest. A strong breeze nudged at the car, and tumbled a gray-looking azalea bloom along the sidewalk.

"Why?" Joe winced when the word came out sounding gritty.

"I just… You never talked about him."

He heard what she didn't say. *I'd like to know what you're not forgiving me for.*

"Braden pretended to be tough," he finally said, and cleared his throat. "Wore muscle shirts, had a habit of scraping his knuckles across the bricks of our front steps so it'd look like he'd been fighting. Even got a tattoo when he was thirteen. Kept the bullies away."

"From him or from you?"

His silence was answer enough.

"It sounds like you two were close." The blanket rustled as she changed position. He pictured the fabric gliding across her skin, slipping to reveal a bare leg or hip or belly, and his body tightened. Couldn't ask for a better distraction from—

"What did he do for a living?"

Damn it. He pulled his thoughts out of the backseat. "He was a mechanic. And a cabinetmaker."

"So you both inherited the carpentry gene. From your father?"

No way in hell was he going there. "My turn. How much trouble are you in?"

"Excuse me?"

"You're so determined to get me back to Alexandria that you'll pass up a king-size bed in a comfortable hotel just to avoid breaking our deal. You're sleeping in your *car*. That doesn't seem desperate to you?"

"I already admitted I was desperate."

"So why not tell me the rest of it? Starting with why you were so upset at the bar tonight?"

"That's private."

"Like memories of my brother are private?"

"Is that why you shared them? To guilt me into answering your questions?"

He sighed. "Not everyone is out to exploit you, slick. We meant something to each other, once upon a time."

"This isn't a fairy tale."

"Tell me about it." He reached for the rearview mirror, made a show of adjusting it so he could get a good look at her. "Sleeping Beauty, you're not."

"Bite me twice."

"If you insist." He pushed up and around and started to climb into the backseat. Allison shrieked, and hit him with her pillow.

"Kidding! I was kidding!"

He brushed the hair out of his eyes and gave her his fiercest scowl. "So you'll go to sleep?"

"Yes."

"No more questions?"

"I promise."

He grunted, and lay back down. Yawned, and realized he missed his cat. Which he would *not* be naming—

"A motion detector. You could put one in every room and that way—"

"Don't make me come back there."

"That wasn't even a ques—"

He whipped around again. Allison shut her mouth, flung herself onto her left side and started to snore. Joe stretched out again and folded his arms across his chest. A long while later he realized he was still grinning.

A DEEP, DROWSY growl coaxed Allison toward consciousness. The sound tumbled gently through her, leaving a delicious heat in its wake, and she responded with a low-pitched, approving hum before rolling toward the other side of the bed. But instead of warm masculine skin, she got a face full of carpet. *What the—?*

Above her head, someone swore.

She blinked awake, registered birds singing in the distance, the scent of cinnamon-laced air freshener, a rustling sound nearby. Joe. Her Camry. The motel parking lot. And oh, dear God, muscles as cramped as…well, as the backseat of a compact car.

She opened her eyes wider. The gray morning light revealed a single candy-coated, chocolate-covered peanut inches from her nose. Brown? No, red. Good to know she wouldn't starve to death if she ever got stranded in her car during a blizzard.

She pushed herself off the floor and rolled back onto the seat, threw an arm over her head and smacked her knuckles against the window. *Damn* it.

"Good morning," she mumbled.

Joe struggled into a sitting position and scrubbed his hands over his face. "Please tell me we're not doing this again tonight."

"Depends." She yawned, pressed her feet against the window and pushed into a stretch. "Does our deal still stand?"

A few beats of silence, then he grunted. "Deal's on. But you need to go home."

"What?" She jolted upright. "Wait." But he was already out of the car. She scooted over to the door, fumbled for the handle and scrambled out onto the pavement. The blanket twisted around her legs. *For God's sake.* She struggled to kick herself free as she hurried after him, feeling like a crippled penguin when she couldn't manage more than an awkward, flapping string of half steps.

"Wait." She muttered a breathless litany of curses

as she stumbled over the loose gravel scattered across the lot. "What do you mean, I need to go home? Joe? Joe! If I show up without you I'll lose my job."

CHAPTER EIGHT

JOE GRUNTED, AND yanked open the office door. When she followed him inside he rounded on her. "I need a shower. And coffee. Then we'll talk."

"Wait. Just...wait a minute." She finally managed to shimmy free of the blanket. She gave it an irritated flap, draped it around her shoulders and glared. "When Tackett called last night I promised you were committed to coming back. He insisted I stay the entire two weeks. So you can't send me home. Not yet."

"'Course he wants you here. He wants us to be lovers again. That way T&P gets a two-for-one deal."

The way he said it, so matter-of-factly, nipped at her ego. That he was right made her feel guilty, as if she were in on the scheme. And maybe on some level she was. She'd never approved of her boss's tactics, yet she had no intention of walking out on their deal.

"Is that why you pushed me away last night?" she asked. "So Tackett wouldn't get his way?"

"I pushed you away because you deserve better than a handful of hookups for—how did you put it?— 'old times' sake.'"

"Thanks. I think."

"Plus, I didn't want to have to wonder whether it was you or Tackett screwing me."

Shock sucked the air right out of her chest. "You really are a son of a bitch, aren't you?" she whispered. She swung away, heaved against the door and somehow found herself out on the sidewalk. Keycard. She needed her keycard.

"Allison, wait." Joe moved in front of her and gripped her shoulders. She kicked out blindly, but only managed to get herself tangled up in the blanket again. *Damn* it. Good thing he didn't laugh, because once she got herself free...

He pulled her toward him slowly, carefully, and held her close, palms pressed to her back.

"I ought to knee you," she muttered into his shoulder.

"You should. I'll remind you later. Right now I need to tell you I'm sorry. I am a son of a bitch. I'm worse than a son of a bitch." He leaned away, raised his hands to smooth her hair. "I'm grumpy as hell because I haven't had my coffee yet and I spent the night cooped up with you less than two feet away smelling good enough to eat and I couldn't touch you. Well, I could have, if I'd climbed into the backseat, but you know what I mean."

He looked at his hands and lifted them away, backed up a step. "Can we start the morning over?"

She glanced at him sharply, but his face didn't indicate anything other than a desire to shake off a bad mood. She forced herself to stop imagining what might have happened if he *had* climbed into the backseat. "Fine." He raised an expectant eyebrow and she rolled her eyes. "Good morning."

"Good morning to you, too. How about some coffee?"

"I'd love some."

"Follow me."

While Joe fussed with the coffeepot, Allison excused herself to use the bathroom but was cut off by the kitten who bounded down the hallway, making a beeline for the kitchen. Joe yelped as she climbed his sweatpants, and Allison couldn't help but laugh.

"She missed you."

"She missed breakfast." Carefully he worked her paws free, tucked her in the crook of his arm and set about filling her food dish. A rush of affection caught Allison by surprise, and she ducked into the bathroom. When she came back out, Joe offered her a slice of apple.

"How about I take you over to Ivy's after breakfast? I'll get the pest people over here today. If they give us the green light we can start work again tomorrow."

"What if they can't come today?"

"I'll make it worth their while."

She blinked. That wouldn't be cheap. "You'd do that for me?"

He busied himself gathering mugs and pouring coffee. "It's a sound business decision. If you're ner-

vous about being here, others will be, too. How do
you feel about French toast?"

She stared at him, at his sleep-tousled hair and
warm blue gaze. He wore sweatpants snagged by the
claws of a marmalade kitten and looked exhausted
after keeping Allison company all night. Dear God
in heaven, she was in trouble. Big, fat, hairy trouble.

"You know what," she started, and nearly cringed
at the quiver in her voice. "I'm not all that hungry
and...the sooner we can get back to work, the better. Would you mind if I headed over to Ivy's now?"

"Now?" Joe frowned. "Because I was an ass?"

She managed a smile. "Because it'll be easier if
I just get out of your way and let you do your thing.
Trust me—I'd have no trouble calling you an ass if
you earned it."

"True enough." He watched her a moment more,
then shrugged. "I'll give her a call."

As Joe drove away from Ivy's after promising to return for a late lunch, the dairy farmer who looked
anything but, even in jeans and rubber boots that
reached up to her knees, stared at her guest in fascinated disbelief.

"Did you really spend the night in your car?" When
Allison nodded Ivy gave her an admiring once-over.
"You're tougher than you look. Good for you for not
letting that snake run you out of Castle Creek."

"I didn't have an option. It's...complicated."

"No kidding." She gestured Allison to follow her

to the house, which wasn't at all what Allison had expected. Instead of a weathered farmhouse with a wraparound porch, Ivy lived in a cozy brick A-frame with a glassed-in sunroom slanting off the left side.

"Joe seems grumpy. I'm guessing he didn't get any action in that car of yours last night?"

Allison sputtered a laugh and followed Ivy up the front steps. "That was never the plan. We're not... We're just friends. I think I ticked him off by turning down his French toast this morning."

"I never heard it called that before. Ever tried it with syrup?"

Allison gurgled a response and Ivy grinned. "Don't mind me. I'm in a bit of a dry spell and the only action I get these days is the vicarious kind." She led the way into a sunny kitchen with pale green walls and a dark polished floor. "Since you didn't get any—and by 'any,' I mean breakfast—let's see what I can do."

"Please don't go to any trouble," Allison managed, even as she wondered if Joe kept syrup in his cupboard. "Coffee and fruit will be fine. You must be crazy busy, running an operation like this on your own."

"I have an amazing manager who is no doubt ecstatic to have the place to himself for once. And it's a nice treat, having the morning off."

Allison smiled her gratitude and gazed around the room, at the baskets mounded with produce, the lush hanging plants and the bright red and yellow pottery on display. "What a gorgeous space." Huh. "You helped Joe decorate?"

"I gave him a few suggestions. When he wouldn't take those I offered him design advice instead."

Allison gasped out a surprised laugh.

Ivy handed her a cup of coffee. It came with a wink. "Okay, I'll behave. Let me hull some strawberries and put some muffins on a plate and we can have our breakfast in the sunroom. I'll tell you all there is to know about running a dairy farm."

WHEN JOE GOT back to the motel after dropping off Allison, the Catlett sisters' baby blue Buick—the car they'd named their schnauzer after—was parked in the lot. Joe sagged against his seat. The trio of old ladies meant well, but they could stretch a man's patience further than old man Katz could stretch a nap.

Joe pulled up beside the car and recognized June behind the wheel. It looked like she'd come alone. Aw, hell. Apparently it was time for another heart-to-heart and he'd bet his brand-new 8-amp rotary hammer that the subject of this particular chat would be Allison Kincaid.

With a heavy exhale he got out of the truck. June stayed put. He knew what she expected—the Buick acted as her confessional. He opened the passenger door, slid inside and did his best to look penitent.

"June."

"Joseph." She beamed over at him and he couldn't help but smile in return. Like her sister, she preferred her hair short and her makeup bright. Today she'd painted on some kind of metallic green color, all the way from her eyelids to her eyebrows. Together with her navy pantsuit, goldfish earrings and shell necklace, she looked…seaworthy.

"So what's up?"

Her smile turned mysterious and she faced forward again, tapped her fingers on the steering wheel. It wasn't often June was at a loss for words. Which meant this wouldn't be the usual 'we need to find you a nice girl' conversation.

Or would it?

Had Audrey shared her concerns about his being "plugged up"?

Judas Priest, just shoot me now.

To distract himself he studied the car's interior. He spotted an open box of cough drops—likely the source of the too-sweet cherry odor. A travel mug adorned with a purple lip imprint was jammed into the console. The inside of June's seat was marred by a tiny rip, probably made by one of Baby Blue's toenails. The door to the glove compartment sat slightly askew—

"Was there a point to this visit?" he asked.

June shot him a look, reached over to the floor beside his leg and yanked up her purse. Something inside made a clinking sound. No jerky then, thank God.

She settled the bag on her lap and gave the side pocket a pat. "Know what I have in here?"

"Salt and pepper shakers from the diner?"

Another glower. "Of course not."

"Nail polish? Baby food? Sperm samples?"

She slapped his knee. "Enough with the sass."

"Why don't you show me what you have, then tell me why it is you think I need to see it?"

Her expression turned speculative as she considered his words and Joe felt a flush sidle into his cheeks. June chuckled, pulled two items from her purse and propped them on the dash between them. Joe's cheeks went from hot to cold in an instant.

Son of a bitch.

He slumped back against his seat and stared. June reached out a reverent finger and touched the faded labels barely clinging to a pair of mini liquor bottles. *Empty* mini liquor bottles.

"Do you know why I carry these around with me?"

He swallowed. "In case you can't find a bathroom?"

Another slap on the knee. "Don't be rude. And before you start asking, no one said anything to anyone. No one had to. We live in a small town, Joseph. Besides—" she knotted her hands in her lap "—it doesn't take much for one alcoholic to recognize another."

"You think I'm an alcoholic."

"Don't you?"

He shifted in his seat, and fought a hot rush of anger. Struggled to find the respect her admission deserved. He came up empty. Like June's little trophies.

God save him from interfering old ladies.

She watched him, an expectant gleam in her eyes. He sighed. What would it hurt to play along? The sooner she said her piece, the sooner he would *have* peace.

"Why *do* you carry those bottles around with you? To remind you of what you can't have?"

"And to remind me of how empty my life will be if I start drinking again."

He rubbed his palms back and forth over his thighs. "Why bring this up now?"

"Audrey expressed some concerns after the party last night."

"Wait, she followed me around? She *spied* on me?"

"We prefer to call it an 'affectionate hover.' We all care about you, Joe. We've been concerned for a while, now."

He grunted. "Okay, so what did your *spy* tell you?"

"That you started drinking heavily about a year ago when you thought Allison didn't care. And now you're drinking heavily because she *does*. Kind of a losing proposition, don't you think?"

She didn't really want to know what he thought, but he was going to tell her anyway.

"What I think is that this is none of your business, June, and you should have better things to do with your time. I know I do. Just because I like to drink doesn't mean I'm an alcoholic." He opened his door.

She rummaged in her purse again, pulled out a brochure and held it out. "Humor an old lady."

She really was chapping his balls. He grabbed the brochure and slapped it against his palm. "Is there some kind of covenant against drinking? Some Castle Creek bylaw I'm breaking? I don't drink and drive, I don't have a wife to beat in a drunken rage—who exactly am I hurting?"

She smiled softly, leaned over and patted his cheek. "The most important person in the world, Joseph. Yourself."

WITHIN HALF AN HOUR Allison had learned the number of breeds of dairy cattle there were (six), how many gallons of milk the average cow produced per day (six to seven), and how to put cow manure to good use. Not only did Ivy sell it as compost to Joe's friend Parker who owned a greenhouse business, but she also let the manure dry so it could be used as a bedding similar to sawdust. To top it all off, Allison had also heard *way* too much about artificial insemination. So when her hostess took pity on her and suggested a walk, Allison practically leaped out of her chair.

The sun was bright but friendly, the air fragrant with moist earth and pollen-laden flowers as they tramped across the fields that were as green as sliced kiwi. Ivy introduced Allison to a countless number of horses, goats and chickens, then led her to a special paddock so she could meet the celebrity Holstein herself—Priscilla Mae.

"She does have beautiful eyelashes." Allison leaned

over the fence and patted the cow's glossy black-and-white hide as the Holstein munched on a pile of hay. The former Lilac Queen didn't seem so impressed with Allison.

"Ready to tour the barn?"

"You're going to make me milk a cow, aren't you?"

"I'd never hear the end of it from Joe if I didn't."

Allison lifted her shoulders up and back and drummed her fingers against her thigh as she followed Ivy toward the barn, a structure that looked like it could easily fit Joe's entire motel inside it. The closer they got, the more the smell of grass and flowers gave way to dung, and the more Allison had to wonder—would it be worse to be hugged by a python, or kicked in the head by a Holstein?

A rhythmic beeping sound put that thought on hold. Ivy stopped, and held up a hand to shield her eyes.

"He's early."

Allison squinted across the field and spotted a large panel truck backing slowly toward the barn. When the truck stopped and the driver jumped out, Ivy's breathing developed a little stutter. The brown-haired man strode to the back of the vehicle, said something to someone in the barn and tugged on the truck's rear door to slide it up and out of the way.

Allison understood the stark appreciation on Ivy's face. The man had all kinds of muscle, and moved with a lazy, mesmerizing grace.

"Who's that?"

"Seth Walker. He owns the feed store."

"*He's* the one who offered to build your bookshelves?"

"Gorgeous, isn't he? He's also kind and genuine and the hardest working man I know."

"But?" It was obvious there was one.

"But he's looking for something long-term."

"The bastard."

Ivy's laugh sounded forced. "He has kids." She saw the question in Allison's eyes and shrugged. "I don't do kids. Not ones I can't give back to their parents, anyway. I don't do long-term, either. So I get to look and not touch, twice a week, every week. Which means I'm more frustrated than a purse snatcher in a men's locker room."

Allison knew the feeling. "Should we go help him?"

"I'd rather help myself." She sent Allison a belated wink. "Let's go inside. It's safer in the house."

They spent the next twenty minutes debating the merits of boxers versus briefs while making sandwiches—chicken salad for them and smoked salmon for Joe—and cutting up fruit for lunch. When someone knocked at the front door they looked at each other. Ivy set down her knife.

"Yours or mine?"

"It's too early for Joe. And he's not 'mine' anyway."

Ivy gave her a "yeah, right" look as she wrapped up a sandwich. "Come on. I'll introduce you."

The brown-haired man stood on Ivy's porch, a ball

cap in one hand, a clipboard in the other. Bits of straw clung to his shirt, and his face and arms glistened with sweat. He smiled in Allison's direction, but his eyes were locked on Ivy.

"Seth." Ivy accepted the clipboard, scrawled on it and handed it back.

"Ivy." He tucked the clipboard under his arm and nodded at Allison. "You must be Joe's friend."

"Allison Kincaid. It's nice to meet you."

Ivy tossed her braid over her shoulder. "She's hanging out with me until the pest control people finish with the motel."

"Lucky Allison." A lopsided smile revealed a dimple. "Somehow I need to find the time to stop by Joe's. See how the reno's coming along."

"You'd have plenty of time if you didn't spend so much of it here," Ivy teased.

"You'd miss the view." He slapped his hat against his thigh and backed toward the steps. "Gotta go. Supposed to meet Gil Cooper for a trail ride and I have a bike tire that needs pumping first." He ambled down the steps, turned and walked backward to his truck.

"Pleasure to meet you, Allison. Hope you decide to stick around. Castle Creek might be small, but it's got a big heart. Great place to raise a family."

"Wait." Ivy jogged down the stairs, handed him the sandwich she'd wrapped in foil and put a hand on her hip. "You know you can call on me if you're ever looking for something to ride besides that bike."

"And you can call on me, when you realize you deserve to be treated better than a piece of exercise equipment."

Allison winced as Seth stalked to his truck, slammed his door and drove away without looking back. Slowly Ivy climbed the porch steps.

"Sorry about that. It's what we do."

"If you don't mind my asking, how long have you been doing it?"

"Too long. I don't know, over a year now? Ever since he took over the feed store. I guess part of me keeps expecting him to give up, stop coming by."

"And the other part?"

"He's right. I really would miss the view." She sighed, and sank down onto the top step. "Now you know all about me and my dysfunctional love life. Tell me about you and Joe."

Allison sat beside her, and busied herself brushing at the dried mud on her jeans. "There is no me and Joe. Like I said, we're just friends. I came to recruit him for a temporary job back at the agency. He agreed to take the job if I agreed to help him with the motel for two weeks."

"But why? You have experience with renovations?"

"Hardly. It's…complicated."

"Where have I heard that before? And by the way, it usually is." She stared out at the driveway for several seconds, then huffed out a laugh. "Did he tell you about the bonfire?"

"Bonfire?"

"Right after he moved here. Someone spotted smoke behind the motel and called the fire department. Turned out Joe was burning his suits." She nodded at Allison's shock. "I know, right? Anyway, he held one back, for weddings and funerals, but the rest? Gone."

Allison couldn't believe it. All that Armani, up in smoke.

Obviously he'd been determined to eliminate reminders of his old life. And here she was, part of a conspiracy to drag him back into it.

"After that day it was as if he'd lived in Castle Creek all his life. Everyone wanted to be his friend." She nudged Allison with her shoulder. "That crack I made, about Joe being allergic to commitment? He likes to think it's true but everyone in town knows differently. Not only is he committed to reopening the motel, which means more visitors and more money for the town, but he always steps up to help out. He just doesn't want to admit it. Like a few months ago, when Parker's truck broke down and she couldn't make a delivery, he came to her rescue without even being asked. But you'll never hear from him that he helped save her business that day."

Ivy stood, and tucked her fingers in her back pockets. "You're wondering why I'm telling you all this. Well, it's just…Joe's been here a year and as far as I know he's never been on a date." She hesitated. "Do you know why he moved to Castle Creek?"

"His brother died, and Joe was looking for a fresh start."

"Do you know how Braden died?"

"A car accident." Something about Ivy's expression... "Wasn't it?"

"If you don't know, then maybe there really isn't anything between you two."

For some idiotic reason, that hurt. "You're saying there's more to it."

"A lot more." Ivy sat down again. "Last month I crashed a poker game. Had this crazy idea of seducing Seth into taking me home with him. That didn't work out, so I decided to stay and hang out with Joe after everyone else left. I could tell he was down and I figured it was because his buddy Reid had deployed."

"Iraq?"

"Afghanistan. Anyway, it turned out it was the anniversary of his brother's death."

Allison propped her elbows on her knees and dropped her face into her hands. "Oh, my God." She should have realized. Could Tackett's timing with this assignment have been any worse?

"So he broke out the Glenlivet and we had ourselves a couple of toasts. The story he told... I'm not surprised he fell apart like he said he did. What does surprise me is how quickly he pulled himself together again. On his own, too."

There was no missing the edge of disapproval in Ivy's tone. Allison leaned back on her hands and stared out at the road. "You think I should have been there for him."

"Someone should have been." Abruptly, Ivy rose and paced the porch. "I…and every other single woman in town…have been coming up with some pretty creative scenarios to explain why he's not interested in dating. For example, he fell in love with a woman married to a mob boss, the mob put out a hit on him and his lover made him promise to leave town and never come back. Or maybe Joe's wife fell in love with their neighbor, who convinced her to murder *his* wife so they could be together, but Joe figured it out and turned her in, and to this day he still visits her in jail. My personal favorite? Joe fell madly in love with an ex-CIA agent who retired to run a motel, and as the agent lay dying she vowed to be reincarnated. Now he's waiting for the re-embodiment of her soul to grow up and find him so they can be together again."

Good grief. At least with that last scenario, Joe actually had a reason for saddling himself with that money-pit motel. "That's…wow."

"I know, right? We're talking about collaborating on a book. Point is, now we know the identity of the woman who broke Joe's heart."

"Ivy. I didn't break his heart. He decided to move here, I decided to stay in D.C., end of story. If he was grieving, it wasn't because of me, it was because of his brother."

"I'm sure that was part of it. But when he first

came to Castle Creek he mentioned someone. A former lover. He never said a name, and now he doesn't have to. I saw you two at the party last night. So what happened? It was the drinking that broke you up, wasn't it?" She bit her lip. "Was he violent?"

Allison shot upright. "Never. And our history is not something I'm prepared to talk about, Ivy."

Ivy leaned over and patted her shoulder. "Good for you. I knew there was a reason I liked you right off. I hope you two can work things out, Allison. But I'll shut up now, because here comes our tragic hero."

JOE KEPT HIS wary gaze on the two blondes flanking the front door. Ivy was tall and slender, eyes mischievous, smile leaning toward haughty. Allison was shorter, curvier, her smile more secretive than confident, and her eyes...

Complicated, vulnerable, "don't you dare" eyes.

He climbed the porch steps, and somehow resisted the urge to lay claim to Allison with a lip lock.

"Ladies," he drawled.

Ivy stepped forward and shocked the hell out of him by brushing at his pecs. "You look like you've been crawling through cobwebs."

"Maybe because I have." He replaced Ivy's hands with his own and shifted away. He caught her wink then from the corner of his eye spotted Allison's stern posture. He hid a grin as he wiped his boots on the mat.

Allison crossed her arms. "So what's the verdict?"

Ivy ushered them inside. "Why don't we talk in the kitchen? We can put lunch on the table while Joe fills us in."

He washed up at the sink and Ivy offered drinks. Allison accepted a glass of iced tea while Joe opened a pair of pale ales. He found it interesting that Allison couldn't seem to meet his gaze. Because he'd accepted a beer? Somehow he resisted the urge to chug the thing.

"What did Pests R Us have to say?" she asked.

"'Sleep at Joe's' is officially snake-free. Mice are another matter." He grinned. "They also said to tell you their name isn't copyrighted."

Funny guy. "What about big scary spiders?"

"Hey." Joe pointed a menacing finger.

Ivy leaned against the sink. "Snoozy will be disappointed Mitzi doesn't have any grandchildren after all. So what'd the guy do, use one of those peekaboo cable thingies like the military types use on TV when they want to see into a room?"

"You got it. He drilled holes in the paneling and fed it through. Only he called it a 'fiber-optic scope.'"

"I like peekaboo thingie better."

"You would."

A burst of salsa music. Ivy stretched across the island, scooped up her phone and headed for the doorway. "Sorry, guys. Be right back."

Joe waited until she turned the corner. "What's up with you?" He raised the bottle. "Ticked I accepted a beer?"

"You know what, Joe, it's none of my business whether you drink or not."

She was right. Still, it stung.

She turned her attention to a dish towel on the counter, one with fringe along the bottom. With slow, deliberate movements, she began to comb the tangles out of the fringe. Yet another compulsion. He'd consider it cute if it didn't signal she was stressed.

"Ivy's very protective of you," she said. "She scolded me for not being more supportive after your brother died. I have a feeling she's not the only one who feels that way. I'm guessing Castle Creek will be happy to see the last of me."

He'd have to make sure Ivy knew the fault was his. "But you're looking forward to that, too, aren't you?"

"Do you really have to ask?"

"Yeah. And you really have to answer." When she bristled, he had his reply. "Humph. You like it here."

She opened her mouth and he braced himself for a denial. But she hesitated, and her shoulders sagged. "So what? You're as confused as I am," she said softly. "You order me around and call me Kincaid and make fun of my high heels and tell people to put me to work shoveling manure—which Ivy didn't, by the way—yet you also spend the night with me in my car so I'll feel safe, and take care of me like…"

Like he never had before. Ouch.

She pushed the towel away. "You're trying to get rid of me, and at the same time you're trying to show me just how sweet a deal I passed up."

His blood began to thrum. "Maybe we should concentrate on that sweet deal thing." Except that was the last thing they should be doing. The last thing *he* should be doing. Maybe June was right. Maybe *Allison* was right. His fingers tightened around the bottle in his hand.

She'd been here three days and he'd greeted two of those days with a hangover. Would have had one this morning, too, if he hadn't worried the alcohol would do more talking for him.

And it wasn't because Allison was here. It was because *that's* what he did. Had been doing, for more than a year now. He drank too much.

He had a drinking problem.

He went still, and waited for the jolt in his chest. For some kind of inner thunderclap. For *something* to acknowledge the realization he'd been fighting for far too long. Nothing happened.

Because he'd already known. And it didn't change a thing. Why should it, when he had no chance with Allison, anyway? Yeah, he had a problem. *His* problem, not hers. Bad enough he had to deal with it. He couldn't drag her down with him again.

Still. She was so damned adorable. And he'd missed her so damned much.

He kicked his conscience out of his head, set his beer on the counter and moved around the island. Allison backed away and ended up trapped in the corner between the sink and the refrigerator. He stopped. He needed her to listen and the closer he got, the more she'd panic and the less she'd hear.

"I miss you," he said. *Good going, asshole.*

"You miss the life you used to have."

"Would you stop putting words in my mouth?"

She looked away. When she looked back her eyes were sad. "Nothing has changed."

"I've changed." He had. A little.

Her gaze dropped to the remains of his beer. "Not enough," she said, and she sounded so damned prissy she set off a throbbing in his groin. Something clued her in and she flushed bright red. "This is business," she said, a little desperately. "Nothing more."

"Even though we both feel more."

She shrugged. "Leftovers."

Okay, that pissed him off. He backed away, out of reaching distance. Otherwise he just might drag her down to the floor and show her what his taste buds were really craving for lunch. And it had nothing to do with leftovers.

Then again…

He'd achieved what she'd accused him of planning that very first day—making her want him. Trouble was, she wasn't following the next step in the plan. She wasn't begging to stay.

So maybe he'd settle for just plain begging.

Before she could blink he took the three steps needed to bring him up close and personal. He rested his palms on either side of her and leaned in. She stared up at him, eyes wide…breath trembling past oh so soft lips.

"I have one question," he murmured, his gaze hot on her mouth. "When did I ever make fun of your high heels?"

"I am so sorry you two—" Ivy rushed back into the room and stopped short. "Make that really, *really* sorry. But I have to go. My manager's wife was in an accident. She's at the hospital and I need to be there."

Joe exhaled, and pushed away from Allison. "You okay to drive?"

"Thanks, I'll be fine. But here—" she opened the refrigerator, removed a tray of sandwiches and shoved it at him "—take this with you." She pulled out a bowl of fruit, then half a cheesecake. "These, too."

Allison rushed forward to take the sandwiches before they ended up on the floor. "Is there anything we can do before we go?"

"Just lock up." She pointed at Allison as she snatched up her purse. "And I really do want to go for that coffee. Call me." She hurried out of the kitchen. Seconds later the front door opened and closed.

Quiet descended. Outside, one of Ivy's horses gave a shrill neigh, and a chorus of moos sounded in response. Joe stared at Allison, who couldn't seem to look him in the eye.

"I'm guessing you're glad my hands are full," he said dryly.

She lifted her head and glared. "Last night in the

car we agreed we'd reinstate our hands-off policy. If there was one thing I thought I could count on, it was you keeping your word."

"Point taken." He set the fruit and the cheesecake on the counter, picked up his beer and walked to the sink. Hesitated. He wanted to pour it out. Meant to pour it out. But why let her think he wanted to change for her? Why let himself think he had a chance?

He'd already proved he couldn't keep his distance. Fine. He'd make sure she kept hers.

Abruptly he lifted the bottle to his lips and drained it, forced a satisfied sigh and set the empty in the sink. "Let's head back to the motel. We'll do some damage to these sandwiches, then pick up where we left off on #5."

The drive back was...subdued. Allison helped Joe carry the food into the kitchen, politely declined a sandwich, gave the cat a quick cuddle and left to change into her coveralls.

He'd wanted distance—and he got it.

He picked up a sandwich, put it back down, picked it up again, tore half of it off and dumped the filling in the cat's dish. An orange blur launched itself at the salmon.

Restlessness wriggled under his skin, poked and prodded at his muscles, had him pacing the length of the tiny kitchen. He couldn't wait to get back to work. And after that he'd punish himself on the treadmill.

He swore. Yeah. Like he could outrun his problems. On a treadmill.

Maybe what he needed was to focus on someone else's problems. Someone like Allison, who, come to think of it, never did reveal why she'd been so upset at the party. Whatever had made her fall apart, he was certain it involved more than him or Mitzi or the job she was so determined to cling to.

Maybe he could help. He damned well owed it to her to try. He could talk and still keep his distance, couldn't he?

The back of his neck prickled with sweat as he washed his hands and headed for the bedroom and a clean shirt. Two minutes later he was striding down the sidewalk, the unsteady punch of his heart taking him back in time, reminding him how edgy he'd been during his first date with Allison. She'd been curious, asking all kinds of questions, determined to see the man beneath the slick veneer. Meanwhile he'd been determined to see the body beneath the sexy dress. But they hadn't even made it through their salads before he began to wonder why the hell it had taken him so long to ask her out. But that was then....

He was halfway to her room when he heard her talking—and it wasn't in her happy voice. Which meant she was probably on a call with Tackett. It also meant she'd left her door open—she must have been on her way out when her cell rang.

He turned back toward the office. She deserved her privacy. Then he heard a male voice, one he didn't recognize, and he froze. Whoever the man was, he was angry.

And he was in Allison's room.

Joe broke into a run.

CHAPTER NINE

ALLISON'S HEART KEPT up its frantic bounce as she glared across the room at the scruffy lowlife poised in front of the open window. The intruder glared back, his lean body stone-still, his left foot barely touching the floor. His mouth was tight with pain—he must have twisted his ankle while scrambling to escape. If it weren't for the threat in his eyes, *and the whole hired thug thing,* she might have actually felt sorry for him. He looked young—like barely-out-of-his-teens young.

Didn't mean he wouldn't hurt her.

"I already talked to Sammy," she said, and resented the desperation in her voice. "So why'd he send you?"

This was bad. This was very, very bad. She'd brought a loan shark's hired muscle straight to Joe's motel. The good people of Castle Creek would have her tarred and feathered within the hour.

Footsteps pounded down the sidewalk. Allison looked over her shoulder and Joe exploded through the doorway. He scanned the room and went rigid, thrust her behind him and locked gazes with the intruder.

"Did he hurt you?"

She shook her head, lips pressed tight so they wouldn't wobble. "You still think no creepy crawlies can get in?"

"Tell me what happened, Allison." Joe put out a hand toward the stranger in the universal "don't shoot us, stab us or maim us in any way" gesture. That's when Allison started to shake. Could this guy be *armed?*

The young man did look unstable, with his angry eyes, every-which-way hair and grubby clothes. Yet he remained still, except for the ragged breathing he struggled to bring under control.

"I—I opened the door and startled him," she said. "He dropped something and made a break for the window."

Slowly Joe backed up, nudging Allison toward the door. "Okay, you son of a bitch. We're going to the office to call 9-1-1. You'll have maybe ten minutes before the sheriff arrives, so if you don't want to end up in cuffs you'd better get the hell out of here."

Allison stopped moving. Her nose ended up between Joe's shoulder blades. "We can't do that."

"Can't do what, let him go? Screw that. He's hurt. He won't get far."

"I mean, we can't call 9-1-1."

Joe shot her an incredulous glance, and over his shoulder she saw the same astonished look on the stranger's face. "Why the hell not?"

She bit her lip. "It'll complicate things."

"It'll—" Joe looked from her to the intruder and back again. "Judas Priest, do you *know* this guy?"

"Not personally. But I know why he's here."

Eyes ablaze, Joe grabbed her by the arm. "What the hell are you mixed up in?"

"Let her go." Joe and Allison both jumped at the rusty sound of the intruder's voice. Allison stared. He was *defending* her?

Joe jerked his chin at him. "You." Another jerk, at the small bench under the window. "Sit." The young man ignored him, and for the moment Joe returned the favor. He aimed his narrowed gaze at Allison instead. "And you. Out with it."

"He wants money."

"Most burglars do."

"I'm not a burglar," their visitor said hotly.

Joe grunted. "Well, you're sure as hell not here to take a meter reading."

"You can't keep me here." His voice was sounding strained. He took a few limping steps toward the door. "Get out of my way."

"Not until I know why you're here."

"I got lost. And I wouldn't be here if you'd get the eff out of my way."

Joe dropped his arms, stood tall and jabbed a finger at the bench. "Sit down and shut up. Or I call the cops. Now." The intruder hesitated, then hobbled backward and sat, expression mutinous. Jaw equally rigid, Joe turned back to Allison. "Who. Is. He."

Her stomach churned and she wanted nothing more

than to collapse down onto the bed. But then Joe would be looming over her, and she was already feeling intimidated enough, thank you very much. Plus, she needed to be able to scramble out of the way should Sammy's minion make a run for it.

She settled for leaning against the nearest wall. Damn it, she hadn't wanted this to come out. She sighed. "He works for a loan shark."

The young man shot to his feet. "I do not." His face went pale and he sank back down onto the bench, holding his left leg.

Joe rounded on Allison. "You took money from a *loan shark?*"

"Not took. Borrowed." She turned from Joe and frowned at their visitor. "You don't work for Sammy?"

He shook his head.

Joe scrubbed a hand over his face. "There's no car out front. How did you get here?"

No response.

"If you didn't come for money, what did you come for?" As Joe spoke he moved to shield Allison—making it clear to everyone in the room what he'd thought the young man had been after. Allison couldn't help but shudder, though she hadn't gotten that vibe from him. When she'd first spotted the intruder, he'd seemed as shocked and scared to see her as she'd been to see him.

"I would never do anything…like that." He pushed to his feet, revulsion twisting his features.

The tension in Joe's back eased slightly. "Then why are you in this room?"

His gaze darted toward the floor on Joe's left. The something he'd dropped. Joe bent and scooped it up. Red tinged the other man's unshaven cheeks.

"A paperback?" Joe stared down at the murder mystery Allison hadn't had time to crack open. She moved closer, and watched as comprehension mingled with the fury on Joe's face. "Have you been *living* here?"

Their intruder recoiled, gave his head a quick, negative jerk.

With deliberate motions Joe set the book on the dresser and rested his hands on his hips. "Out back, then. In the woods."

Silence.

"You scared the hell out of a little girl. And you've been stealing food. Time for you to move on. Leave now and I won't call the police."

"He's hurt." Allison gestured at his ankle. "How do you expect him to leave?"

"Through the door." Joe nudged Allison out of the way and stepped aside, waved a hand toward the parking lot. "Let's go."

The young man pushed away from the wall and started for the door. Step, hop. Step, hop. Even from across the room Allison could hear the grind of his teeth.

"For God's sake, Joe, he can hardly walk. We need to get him to a hospital."

"No. I won't let you take me there." He spit out the words and kept moving.

Allison put a hand on Joe's arm. "He has no place to stay and he's obviously not getting enough to eat. We have to do something."

"You make an idiotic decision like doing business with a loan shark and expect me to take your advice?" He passed a hand over his eyes. "Don't you know dealing with a loan shark is illegal?"

It was Allison's turn to grind her teeth together. "So making him suffer is supposed to punish me?"

"Hell." Joe pushed his fingers through his hair. "You're right." He stepped in front of the young man. "Just tell me you're not one of those asshole vandals back to finish the job."

He froze, and Allison frowned. "What vandals?" she asked.

"Couple months ago I'm running errands in the city when I get a call from the sheriff's department. Someone reported a break-in here at the motel. Deputies got here in time to put out a fire. The call came from—" he stopped, and peered at the young man "—inside the motel."

He faced Joe squarely. "I didn't start the fire. But I did make the call."

"Then I owe you one." Joe offered his hand. The young man hesitated for the longest while then finally accepted the gesture. Joe motioned toward the parking lot. "Let me pull the truck up. I'll take you to the hospital so you can get that ankle checked out."

"No."

"No hospital. Okay. How about the clinic?"

He shook his head. "No doctors."

Allison stepped forward. "Will you let Joe take a look? He used to play rugby. He knows all about sprains."

A couple of beats, then the young man nodded. Joe exhaled. "Good. Stay put. We'll be right back."

Panic slid across his face. Joe quickly held up a palm. "No tricks. I said I owe you one. But if you try to take advantage of this—"

"I won't."

"Then wait for us." Joe took Allison's hand and led her outside. He swore under his breath all the way to the office. Once inside she followed him into the kitchen, where he retrieved a first aid kit from the cabinet above the refrigerator.

"When were you going to tell me about this Sammy?"

"I wasn't. It's none of your business."

He grabbed a bottle of water from the fridge and slammed the door shut. The whole thing shook. "You thought a loan shark had sent someone after you. Sent someone here, to my motel. Yet it's none of my business?"

"Exactly."

His eyes went dark and narrow. He wheeled around and strode from the kitchen and back outside. Reluctantly she followed. The last thing she wanted was for him to discover the truth.

Because he'll realize you're an idiot?
No one asked you.

Awesome. Now she was talking to herself *and* answering back.

Joe was pacing the sidewalk. "Whatever kind of trouble you're in, you obviously believe it could have followed you here. Therefore, I have a right to know."

"Fine. *Fine.* I owe some money." He waited. "I thought he was here to collect." More waiting. Finally he gave a baffled shrug.

"You make a good living and you have excellent credit. Why not go to a bank? And don't you dare tell me it's none of my business. Not now." His expression turned suddenly ferocious. "Tackett. If he's dragged you into something dirty, so help me God—"

"No," she cried. If Joe thought her boss had anything to do with this he'd never return to D.C. "He's not involved."

"Convince me. I deserve to know what we're dealing with, here."

He was right. She ignored the crumbling sensation in her chest and licked her lips. "It's my mother, okay? She gambles."

He swung away, stepped off the sidewalk onto the parking lot and stared out at the road. Turned back and spread his arms. She concentrated on the water bottle and the first aid kit he held, rather than meeting the contemptuous disbelief in his eyes.

"You write me off for drinking, yet you're working your ass off to cover the debts of a chronic gambler?"

"She's my mother." Allison hadn't talked to Beryl Kincaid since that hideous conversation outside the bar, but she knew she inevitably would. Of course she would. She was her *mother*.

"They're her debts. You're enabling her."

"I don't need you to judge me."

"No. What you need is for me to knock some sense into you."

"Don't you touch her!"

They turned to see their intruder standing outside Allison's door, one hand braced against the stucco, the other curled into a fist.

Joe let his arms fall back to his sides. "Take it easy, man. It was a figure of speech. I would never hurt her. I would never hurt any woman." When the young man didn't move a muscle, Joe gestured with the kit. "You'll just have to take my word for it. Now let's take a look at that ankle." He hesitated then started to lower himself to the curb. Joe shook his head. "Inside." He didn't bother looking at Allison as he followed her would-be protector back to her room.

Seemed Joe was finally getting the message. There were just too many reasons they would never be a good fit. She pulled her lips in and trailed after them.

"Feels better already." The young man demonstrated by putting weight on his foot as he headed for the bed.

"I'd still like to take a look." Five minutes later Joe pronounced a mild sprain and handed over the water bottle and two ibuprofen.

Allison pointed to an ACE bandage. "Shouldn't you wrap it?"

Joe busied himself repacking the kit. "A doctor once told me that actually prolongs inflammation. Said the best remedy is to elevate the ankle, then alternate hot and cold baths." He stood, and massaged the back of his neck. Allison knew what he was thinking. *What were they going to do with this guy?*

"What's your name?" Joe asked.

No answer, except for the crackle of plastic as he took a deliberate swig of water.

"Do you have any family? Anyone we can call for you?"

Still no answer, except for the curl of his lip.

"How long since you've had a hot meal, man? Not counting eggs, I mean."

The lip curl took on a hint of humor. "Week or so."

"Then I'll take you to get something to eat. We can talk about what to do next."

"Don't bother."

"I'm not asking. Let's go."

The panic was back in the young man's eyes. "I don't do people."

"We'll go to Snoozy's, then. More private than the diner." Joe pulled Allison aside. "You'll be all right here on your own?" His voice was clipped and impatient, his gaze remote. Which she should have been celebrating, not mourning.

"I can't go?" she asked

"He might not be as forthright with you there." His eyebrows scrunched. "You and I need to talk later."

Oh, for God's sake. He wasn't going to let this thing go. Which was exactly why she hadn't wanted to tell him in the first place. "I don't think so," she said.

"Think again." Then his face changed. "Hell, I can't leave you here alone. What if this Sammy character really does send someone after you?"

"He won't. He knows I'm coming back to D.C. When I saw someone in my room I made an assumption."

"I hope you're not as cavalier about this as you sound. Those kinds of people mean business."

"I have it under control."

Sure you do.

Joe started to say something then shook his head. "Lock up after us."

The young man limped past her and she gave a little wave. "I'm sorry I called you a creepy crawly."

With a disinterested grunt he followed Joe out of the room. Allison flipped the bolt into place.

She really did have a way with men.

MARCUS HESITATED INSIDE the door to Snoozy's, and blinked in the dim light. The place didn't smell like he'd expected, not like smoke or sweat or booze. It smelled like French fries. And old leather. He jammed his hands into the pockets of his jeans and watched Meathead settle at a table in the corner.

A flat-screen TV was tuned to a news channel, the no-nonsense voices of the newscasters masking the frenzied rhythm of his heart. What the hell was he doing here? In a *bar*? With a dude he knew very little about, other than he liked to lift weights, read old-fashioned spy novels and drink whiskey?

Sweat sprouted on the back of his neck and his hands started to shake. So what if he'd been swallowing drool ever since they left the motel. He hadn't had a decent meal in weeks, but he knew damned well—lunch would come with a price. At the very least, Meathead would expect him to talk.

And the more he talked, the more he risked giving himself away.

And he was never giving anything away again. Never.

Meathead waved him over. Screw that. So the dude had figured out he'd been living in the woods. Whatever. He'd find somewhere else to hang until he'd done what he came to do. He was outta here. As he turned to leave, a hot blonde carrying a tray of dirty dishes and a damp rag paused beside him.

"Can I help you?"

He told himself not to stare but he did, anyway. She had wide blue eyes and lots of crinkly hair, and she smiled like she meant it.

"You look hungry. Lucky for you, we just pulled a chicken pot pie out of the oven. But our wings are popular, too, and people drive in from all over for one of Snoozy's hamburgers. From Erie, even." She leaned in. "But whatever you do, don't order the chili. My name's Liz. Go ahead and take a seat. I'll bring you a menu."

She walked away, and his stomach growled a threat he figured it was better not to ignore. He reluctantly made his way to the table in the corner and took the seat across from Meathead. Liz was right behind him. She greeted Meathead with a smile he totally didn't deserve, shot Marcus a curious glance and took their drink orders.

Meathead ordered a beer. If Marcus weren't so hungry, he'd have left right then.

"Problem?"

Marcus shook his head. He'd wait until *after* he'd eaten before pissing off the guy buying him lunch.

"Tell me something." Meathead sat back in his chair. "If Allison and I hadn't cornered you, what would you be eating tonight?"

"An apple. And a muffin. Pumpkin, I think."

"I knew I hadn't eaten the last one."

"Figured we were even 'cause I—"

"Yeah, I know. You saved my motel from burning to the ground." He must have seen something in Marcus's face because his suddenly went wary. "What?"

Marcus shook his head and picked up the menu. If he was so determined to give himself away, he might as well do it on a full stomach.

"You just passing through?"

"Something like that."

"On your way to where?" Marcus scowled and lowered the menu and Meathead held up his hands. "Hey, man, I'm not asking for an address. Just curious."

"South, maybe. Winter sucks here."

"Unless you happen to *like* snow. Which I totally do." Liz stood by their table, pad in hand. "You boys ready to order?"

Marcus reached for his iced tea. His throat had gone dry. She smelled like peanuts and flowers, and he had a sudden urge to touch her hair.

For the twenty minutes it took them to finish their meals, Meathead grilled him, but he didn't learn much more than what he had already discovered when they'd placed their orders—Marcus liked his cheeseburgers with ketchup and mayonnaise.

With a bemused shake of his head, Meathead pulled out his wallet. "How's the ankle?"

"Good." Good enough to run, if he had to.

"Tell you what. I could use some help with the motel. You want to hang around, I'll put you to work. Give you room and board in return. What do you say?"

He'd say it was too damned good to be true. "What kind of work?"

"Demolition, sheetrock, painting, cleanup—maybe even some landscaping. Whatever needs doing."

The demolition part sounded good. But at the moment, the room and board sounded better. He hesitated, finally pushed the question past a throat gone inexplicably tight. "Why?"

"I owe you one. But there is a condition."

Marcus jerked to his feet. "I don't do conditions."

"Now, don't get your dress over your head."

"Do what?"

"Sorry. Favorite expression of a friend of mine. The condition is, you have to give me a first name. Doesn't have to be real. But I have to call you something."

Marcus shifted his weight, and clenched his teeth against the pain that clawed at his ankle. His first name. What would it matter? Let the dude feel like he'd scored a point. He'd be long gone before anyone figured out why he'd really come to town.

"Marcus," he muttered. As soon as he said it, a gray-haired man emerged from the hallway at the back of the bar, a large box in his arms. He was looking over his shoulder, laughing with someone behind him. When he faced forward Marcus stopped breathing. Blindly he reached for the back of his chair, and gripped it so hard his fingers went numb.

"You all right, man?" Frowning, Meathead tossed a couple of bills on the table and moved closer, blocking Marcus from the gray-haired man's view. "Let's get you back to the motel so you can put that foot up." Meathead held out an arm, as if expecting him to lean on it.

"I'm hurt, not helpless."

Slowly Meathead lowered his arm. "I understand."

"And I'm not an idiot. I know patronizing."

"That wasn't patronizing. You got defensive. I got careful." He dug his keys out of his pocket, never breaking eye contact. "Just so you know, I'm not looking for anything more than a solid day's work. You get your own room. No one can get in. Long as you lock the window," he added dryly.

Marcus tensed. What exactly did this guy know? And how the hell did he know it?

His gaze traveled from the empty beer glass on the table to the man standing beside him. Meathead lifted an eyebrow.

"Something on your mind?"

"I've had some trouble with drunks in the past," he said, and braced himself.

Meathead grimaced, and let a few seconds of silence go by. "It's no secret I like to drink. And yeah, sometimes I drink too much. But I would never—" He frowned. "You're safe from me," he said finally.

He headed for the door and Marcus followed slowly. Safe? Maybe. Time would tell. Least the gray-haired man had already left. Marcus annoyed himself by scanning the room for a final glimpse of the blonde. She'd disappeared, too. Just as well. Meathead held the door open for him, gave him a nod as he limped by.

"Marcus, huh? That's a good name."

Marcus pressed his lips together. If that was true, then it was the only good thing about him.

ALL THE WAY back to the motel, Joe battled his conscience. He wanted to help Marcus—whether the kid knew it or not, he was desperate for guidance—but wasn't it time Joe put Allison first? He'd made a snap decision she could end up paying the price for. And damn it, she deserved better.

Keep saying it. Eventually you'll mean it.

He'd started to tell Marcus he would never hurt anyone. Considering what he'd done to Allison—not to mention his brother—that was a lie.

He tightened his grip on the steering wheel, watched idly as tiny drops of water speckled the windshield. Maybe they'd finally get that rain they were promised the day before. He cast a sidelong glance at his grim-faced passenger. What did Marcus do when it rained? Huddle under a tree and wait it out?

He flicked on his windshield wipers, considered the comfortable interior of a high-dollar vehicle he took for granted. Thought about the shock on Marcus's face when he'd offered him a job. He didn't think the kid was dangerous, just angry and resentful. Stubborn, too.

Still, he had no way of knowing for sure. Allison was sleeping in his motel. She was his responsibility. Already he'd let her down by allowing a stranger to find his way into her room. Judas Priest, what if the intruder *hadn't* been an angry kid, but someone bent on violence?

He gave his hair an impatient scrub and turned into the motel parking lot. "Look, man. I have to be honest with you."

Marcus already had a grip on the door handle. "I get it. No sweat. I'll be on my way."

"I'm not asking you to leave. But I should have checked with Allison before asking you to stay."

"You and she…?"

"No, no. In fact, she'll only be here another week. And then I'm following her back to Virginia for a month. But she was here first." He shifted toward his passenger, careful not to move closer. Marcus was as twitchy as a kid sitting in a classroom five minutes before the last bell rang—on the last day of school. "So, do you mind waiting in the truck while I talk to her?"

Marcus stared through the windshield, now streaked with narrow ribbons of rain. He shrugged, but Joe knew what he was thinking. That Allison would tell Joe to send him away. He didn't know her like Joe did.

Ironic as hell, wasn't it? She'd agree with Joe that Marcus deserved a second chance. But she'd never agree to give Joe one. And as tempting as it may be to use that argument to win his own do-over, it was time he accepted it wasn't going to happen. Shouldn't happen. He let people down. That's what he did. She'd already experienced his particular brand of betrayal and he wouldn't put her through that again. She had enough to deal with.

He slammed out of the truck, welcomed the warm, wet shock of summer rain. Butt-kicked his mind from imagining Allison out there with him, the soft, slick skin of her face in his hands, her mouth moving under his. He pulled in a long, deep breath, and knocked on her door.

Thirty seconds later he was using a borrowed towel to wipe the damp from his face while Allison stood at the round table by the window, where she'd been working on her computer. She looked apprehensive, and no wonder. He had plenty to say to her, but first things first.

"Here's the deal. Marcus is outside in the truck."

"Marcus?"

"He finally came through with a name. Whether or not it's real..." Joe shrugged. "I'd like to put him up for a while, give him a chance to get back on his feet. He's agreed to help out with the renovations. But I won't let him stay if it'll make you uncomfortable."

"Where would he go if I said no?"

"I'll drive him over to the next town. Get him a room there. Assuming he'll want to stay in the area till I get back from D.C."

"It's nice of you to help him out. And I appreciate that you're asking me how I feel about the whole situation. But as long as he doesn't have any plans to slither through the wall and suffocate me in my sleep, I'm good."

Joe nodded his thanks. "The moment you feel the slightest bit uneasy having him around, you let me know."

"I will. It's only for a week, anyway."

"Twelve days."

"But who's counting?"

They both were. For very different reasons. He tossed the towel on the bed. Opened his mouth. She rushed into speech.

"I talked to Ivy. She said her manager's wife has a broken collarbone and a few cuts, but she'll be okay."

"Glad to hear it. Nice of you to call her. But once I let Marcus know he has a place to stay, you and I need to talk."

"No, we don't."

"The *hell* we don't. You could be in danger. And I'm supposed to stand by and do nothing? Screw that. You need my help and I'm giving it to you."

"I'm not your project. You coming back to Alexandria to handle Mahoney is all I need. And I'm not in danger. My payments are up to date." She gestured with her chin at the door. "You need to go. Marcus is waiting."

"*Your* payments? Damn it, we need to talk about this. About what you're letting your mother do to you."

"I'm doing what I have to do."

"No. You're doing what *she* has to do. Jesus, Al. Why would you take that on? Why would you sacrifice everything to pay her debts? She can't know what you're doing. There's no way she'd allow you to waste your money—your *life*—supporting her vices."

"None of that is your business. And how many times do I have to tell you? My name is Allison."

Had he...? He had. Hell, he hadn't called her "Al"

since before his brother died. He rubbed at his forehead. "My motel. My business." He dropped his hand and snagged her gaze. "My friend."

The hostility in her expression faded, giving way first to confusion, then sadness and finally resignation. "My mom kept me safe. From a father who couldn't keep his fists to himself. She took beatings meant for me. I *do* owe her. I owe her everything."

A furious burn started in Joe's chest, and spread until his entire torso smoldered with a bitter energy. She'd never told him. Never even hinted. No wonder she had compulsions. He'd have them, too. Had one right now, as a matter of fact.

To kick someone's abusive ass.

"Where's your father now?"

Her glance was cautious, as if she sensed the aggression behind his words. "I don't know. I haven't seen him since I was ten. He was in prison for a while—maybe he's still there."

Good place for him. Joe moved closer. "If your father was beating your mother it wasn't your fault. You don't have to spend the rest of your life paying for something you had no control over."

That's when it clicked for him. She'd had no control over her father's temper, her mother's addiction, Joe's drinking, Tackett's unreasonable demands. It all made sense, now. Allison was tired of being at the mercy of others. She needed to feel in charge, for once. Not because she was manipulative, but because she was hurting.

A long overdue megawatt lightbulb went off in his head. He'd been feeling all of that, too, and he'd let the booze have control over him because it was just easier not to fight.

But Allison was fighting. She was fighting hard. Didn't he owe it to himself to do the same? Hangovers, tremors, forgetfulness—they'd all become his new normal. And despite all the lame-ass things he'd done in his life, he deserved to be free of the hold alcohol had on him. Didn't he?

His muscles suddenly felt loose, and his stomach churned. Could he give it up? The one thing that got him through each and every day? And damn, if he tried and didn't make it he didn't know what the hell he'd do—

"You need to go," Allison choked. She plucked his damp towel off the bed and backed toward the bathroom. "Marcus is waiting."

He had a lot to think about. He went.

ALLISON LINGERED IN her room for half an hour after Joe left, giving him time to get Marcus settled, and herself time to come to terms with the fact that she'd actually told someone about her father. It wasn't something she discussed. Ever. But if it meant avoiding another misguided lecture from Joe, she was glad she'd blurted it out.

She pulled on her coveralls and headed for the office, and shivered in the gray curtain of rain that bordered the sidewalk. At least the weather wouldn't prevent them from working. Thanks to the discovery of Mitzi, and Allison's wild imagination, they'd lost more than a day on renovations. No doubt Joe realized by now that he'd made one lousy bargain.

At the reception desk she tapped twice on the bell. Her hands quivered just the tiniest bit but she was determined—though the first mention of the situation with her mother and she was shutting him down.

She heard him walking down the hallway, and braced herself.

He came around the corner, a pen and a pad of paper in his hands and...reading glasses on his nose? She blinked, could actually feel her antagonism leaking out of her as she leaned on the counter and propped her chin in her hand.

"You look rather scholarly."

His cheeks grew ruddy and he tossed the pad onto the counter. "Don't you mean old?"

Actually she'd meant sexy, but no way she'd admit that.

She pushed upright. "I'm reporting for duty. Put me in, coach. Unless it involves paneling—then I think I'll develop a torn ligament, or jock itch or whatever it takes to get me benched."

Joe peered at her over the top of his glasses, but what he had no doubt meant to be a disapproving expression looked more like a come-on. She entertained a sudden, brief fantasy—Joe, bare-chested and intent, leaning over her in bed, his eyes locked on hers as he slowly removed his glasses and set them on the bedside table, then turned back to her, the scorching purpose in his gaze promising his undivided attention, and so much more—

"What we need to do is get some groceries."

The mundane words chased away her fantasy. Too bad it couldn't do anything about the damp state of her underwear. She drove her teeth into the inside of her lower lip and forced herself to pay attention.

"I put Marcus in #1, told him to take it easy today and we'd hit it hard tomorrow. In the meantime we have some meal planning to do. What do you say— up for a trip to the supermarket?"

"As long as we're coming back with M&M's."

"That's understood." Then he did take his glasses off, and her belly did a little shimmy. "Let's go see what our patient might need."

While Joe knocked at Marcus's door, Allison continued on to her room to grab her purse and lose the coveralls. Then she made her way back to Marcus's room and peeked in to find Joe scribbling on his pad and Marcus hovering awkwardly by the bed. The television was off—somehow she'd had a feeling he wouldn't have any patience with afternoon programming.

She set the book she carried on the table under the window. "You have to promise not to tell me who did it."

He gave her a wary nod, his gaze lingering on the paperback. Joe read from his list. "Orange juice.

Potatoes. You like ketchup on your eggs? Probably should get another—"

"In the cupboard. Behind the peanut butter."

"Scratch the ketchup." Joe never looked up to see Marcus flush. "I suppose you two will want bacon as well."

Fifteen minutes later, Joe and Allison were in the refrigerated aisle of the supermarket, arguing about orange juice while a sale on animal crackers was announced over the PA system.

"The pulp is good for you," Joe insisted.

"I don't like to chew my juice."

"Just get one of each," spoke a little voice behind them.

They turned. A young girl with freckles and shoulder-length russet hair stood watching them, a gallon of milk cradled in her arms. Joe pulled her into a one-armed hug.

"Hey, sport. You're exactly right. We'll get one of each." He put the juice into the cart while the girl tipped her head at Allison.

"You're the lady who found the snake. I'm Nat."

"I'm Allison and, unfortunately, yes, I did find the snake. I think they heard me screaming in Canada."

Nat giggled and Joe tugged gently at her hair. "Nat brought me the kitten."

The girl's face brightened at Joe. "What'd you name her?"

"Nothing, yet. I'm still thinking."

"She doesn't have a name?"

"She'll have one soon. I promise."

"But it's been days," she said plaintively, drawing out the last word.

"You don't want me to saddle her with a name that doesn't suit her, do you?"

"I just want you to care enough to give her one." Nat raised her chin and hefted the gallon of milk. "Excuse me. I have to go find my mother."

They watched her walk stiffly away, a study of huffiness in pink. Allison's amusement evaporated when she noticed the stark regret on Joe's face.

"I did it again," he said.

"Did what?"

The grocery list crumpled in his hand. "Let someone down."

"Joe, it's an easy enough fix. You just have to come up with a name."

He was shaking his head as he turned up the nearest aisle, scouting out the next item on the list. "It's never an easy fix."

Allison let it go.

She waited until they'd loaded the groceries and were on their way back to the motel before asking the question she had no right to ask. "Was it your brother you let down?"

The truck slowed and his jaw flexed. "Among others. Speaking of which…" He checked the rearview mirror and sped up again. "I want to help you. I want to pay off that loan."

She stared at him, sputtered, stared some more.

"Don't be ridiculous." She should have known he wouldn't leave it alone.

"I have investments. I can afford it." He shot her a dark look. "I understand your need to get free of the grip of something that's slowly strangling you."

"You don't understand anything. If you did you wouldn't even consider making such an offer."

"I made the offer because I care about you."

"I don't need you to care about me. I need you to respect me."

For a long while there was silence in the cab. Then Joe exhaled. "Fair enough," he said.

A handful of beats later, Allison huffed out a humorless laugh. "That almost worked."

"What do you mean?"

"I ask about your brother, you distract me. Big time."

His body stilled. Then he flipped on his turn signal and pulled off into the nearest parking lot, which happened to belong to the produce stand Allison had spotted on her way into Castle Creek. Due to the unfriendly weather, the lot was nearly empty. With an impatient flick of his wrist Joe turned off the truck and they sat in silence, cocooned in the dry warmth of the cab while rain drummed a steady rhythm on the roof. Outside, hopeful workers in bright yellow plastic ponchos arranged quarts of strawberries on rough wooden display stands.

Joe shifted to face her. She barely resisted folding her arms over her chest, which would only have made her look childish and defensive.

Though that was pretty much how she felt.

"Why the sudden interest?" His voice was bleak, and he had a damned good point. But the answer was clear.

"I know you better now. Over the past few days I've learned more about you than I learned in the three months we were dating."

"For example?" His tone was skeptical, but there was no mistaking the curiosity in his eyes.

"You have an affinity for unconventional old ladies. You know construction phrases like 'grade beam' and 'barge rafter.' You cook a mean fried egg. You have a big protective streak. And you're a sucker for the underdog." She turned to face him as well, her knee sliding up onto the seat. "Last year we were so caught up in the sneaking around and the...the physical stuff...that we never took the time to talk. Really talk."

"'The physical stuff'?"

Of everything she'd said, *that* was what he'd zeroed in on? "If I said 'screwing,' would that make you feel better?"

He shifted again, banged his wrist on the steering wheel and swore. "I don't see the point of this."

"You said we were friends."

"And friends force deep dark secrets out of each other?"

"You forced one out of me."

"So now we're playing *show me yours and I'll show you mine?* I thought that particular game was off the table."

Table, bed, kitchen floor…she'd play it wherever he wanted to. *Easy, Allie.* She fiddled with a loose thread on the hem of her jeans.

"We trade questions. That's what we do. Besides, Ivy knows. She said that you two talked about it on the anniversary of Braden's death."

"Now you're jealous of Ivy?"

"Yes, I am. I'm not sure why, since you and I aren't—" She shrugged. "I guess, after all we've been through, it makes me sad that she knows and I don't."

Joe turned and opened his door, letting in a chilly swirl of rain-speckled air. Allison put out a hand.

"Wait. Where are you going?"

"This is exactly the kind of thing whiskey was invented for. But since we don't have any, coffee will have to do." He got out of the truck and jogged toward the green-and-white striped canopy. That's when she saw the sign under the giant strawberry. Hot and Cold Beverages for Sale.

Her palms went slick. He really had no desire to tell her. Suddenly she wondered if she really wanted to know.

When he came back she leaned across the seat to take both cups of coffee from him while he got in the truck. Drops of rain silvered his windbreaker and glistened in his hair. She looked away.

"Thank you," she said.

She took a sip—strong, but not stale—and realized he'd taken time to add cream and sugar. "It's good."

"It's warm."

For a short while the only sounds in the truck were the creak of thin plastic lids and the huff of careful breaths. Then Joe stopped pretending to be fascinated by the design on his cup.

"My mother was an addict, too. Prescription drugs were her thing. My brother and I were only kids—we didn't know what was going on. But we knew something was wrong. It didn't occur to my father to put her into rehab, or maybe he just figured she wasn't worth the money. Anyway, he kicked her out."

Allison caught her breath. "Did you ever see her again?" The jerk of Joe's chin roused an ache behind her breastbone. "I'm sorry," she whispered.

"So were we. My brother and I. My dad, not so much. But he hadn't counted on how hard it would be to raise two young boys. And the guilt... He couldn't take it. He shut down. Braden and I, we took care of each other. Grew up, got decent jobs, made plans together. Too bad I never took the time to realize he hadn't forgiven my mother for leaving. Or my father for not giving her a choice. Eventually he followed her example. Turned to drugs."

"Oh, God."

"I was working too hard to notice. When his car ran off the road—" With extra care he placed his cup into the holder between them then fisted his hands in his lap. "It wasn't an accident. And he wasn't alone."

"You mean...he tried to—"

"—kill himself. And my father, too."

Oh, God, oh, God, oh, God. Allison needed to walk, to scream, to *move*. She reached out but Joe thrust up a hand.

"Maybe now you understand why I don't talk about it."

"Your dad. Is he..."

"He survived. But he refuses to see me."

Allison stared out the window into the gloom brought on by the rain, his truths, her failures.

"No wonder," she murmured, her throat thick with anguish. "No wonder you had to escape."

"I'm not proud of that. That I made the same mistake as Mom and Braden. I've always been a drinker, struggled with it especially in college, but I had a handle on it. Or thought I did. Anyway, maybe if I'd turned to you instead of booze...who knows where we'd be today."

And if she'd put him first, ahead of T&P... Allison felt his gaze, his need for her to face him. But there was no sense in rehashing the past. His drinking had only hurried the inevitable. If his move to the country hadn't ended them, her mother's problems would have.

After what seemed like an eternity, he switched on the engine. "I guess where we should be is back at the motel, putting these groceries away."

She gave a silent exhale of gratitude and gulped

at her lukewarm coffee. "And checking on Marcus." The underdog.

"I can't help feeling I made a mistake, asking him to stay."

"I thought maybe he…reminded you of your brother." When Joe sucked in a breath she rushed to add, "Anyway, don't worry about me. I'll lock my door. And stick close to you."

Silence. To fill it she blurted the first thought that entered her head. "What was it about Castle Creek that drew you here?"

He shook his head as he turned back onto the highway. "You don't give up, do you?"

She waited. Nothing. "Um, that was a rhetorical question, right?"

"That was our plan. Braden's and mine. To buy a run-down motel in the country and renovate it. I kept telling him to wait. That we needed more capital. Now I have plenty of capital and no brother." He cleared his throat. "Sometimes waiting is the wrong thing to do."

AFTER PUTTING AWAY the groceries, Allison and Joe checked on Marcus. He'd been sleeping, but it didn't take him long to get to the door—staying off his ankle seemed to have helped. At some point he'd apparently started the book Allison had given him— it lay on the bedside table beside a glass of water, a folded-up piece of paper neatly marking his place. After Joe offered up any of his books to Marcus that he might be interested in, he asked him what he wanted to do for dinner. Allison suggested she bring him a plate of Ivy's sandwiches and Marcus accepted before she'd even finished the sentence. And since she had work waiting on her laptop, Allison told Joe she'd eat in her room, as well.

Joe didn't argue. Of course, she hadn't expected him to. No doubt he looked forward to locking himself up in the motel office so he could stick pins into a voodoo doll that had butter-blond hair and snappy fashion sense.

The rain had a way of making Allison sleepy, but of course as soon as she was ready to go to bed, it stopped and she was wide-awake. Since she'd already answered emails and finished a few outstanding reports, she downloaded a book and settled into bed, her laptop on her knees, but the story failed to keep her interest. She thought with longing of the gym in #10—an hour on the treadmill would certainly wear her out—but she'd forgotten to get a key from Joe, and bothering him at this hour was not an option.

She turned out the light and lay down, started imagining what Marcus's story might be, like Ivy and her friends had done for Joe. The sole heir to a fortune controlled by a ruthless and demanding father, Marcus had recently discovered he was adopted and was searching for his natural parents. She yawned. Too far-fetched. Maybe he was a college student who'd been backpacking across the country, when he got conked on the head during a mugging in

Erie and he's been wandering ever since. Wait. What if he was actually the *mugger*...?

An insistent banging dragged her out of a hard-won sleep. *What the—?* With a long, drawn-out hum of frustration, Allison shifted onto her back and blinked up at the ceiling. No way could it be morning. Which meant the light seeping in through the gap in the curtains was the artificial kind. Which also meant it was nowhere near time to get out of bed.

More knocking. For God's sake, enough with the banging already. Didn't she hear enough of it during the day? She yawned, then finally realized that if someone was knocking at her door at—she lifted her head and squinted over at the table by the bed—1:00 a.m., there had to be a reason. And it probably wasn't a pleasant one.

She shoved at the covers, sat up and had just scrambled to her feet when the door swung open.

CHAPTER TEN

JOE STOOD IN the doorway, keycard in hand. The scream withered in Allison's throat. When he spotted her, his entire body sagged and she frowned. He had on sweatpants but no shirt, and his feet were bare, as if he'd just rolled out of bed. But the intensity in his face had little to do with desire. Panic slithered down her spine, like a fat drop of ice water.

"What is it? What's happened?"

"You didn't throw the bolt," he growled softy. He strode forward and grabbed her hand, pulled her out into the night and shut the door behind them.

"What's going on?"

Instead of answering, he tugged her along the sidewalk, the naked soles of her feet slapping against the damp concrete.

"Joe." She stopped, and struggled to reclaim her hand. "You're scaring me."

He put a finger to his lips and glanced at the door to Marcus's room. He'd put him beside her in #1. She'd wondered from the beginning if Joe had given her #2 to remind her of the two weeks she'd promised—of course, it had only ended up reminding her of the two grand her mother had frittered away.

The glow from the nearest streetlight angled across his face, revealing the disquiet in his eyes. And a lack of focus that told her he'd been drinking. He wasn't drunk, but he wasn't all Joe, either. She wanted to cry.

His grip tightened. "I had a nightmare. I needed to know you were safe."

The hot knot of disappointment blocking her throat shrank a little. He motioned with his head toward the office and started pulling again. Silently he led her through the lobby, down the hall and across the living room to his bed. He held the covers and she slipped underneath, shivering at the feel of his left-over warmth, the masculine smell that lingered on the sheets. She gazed up through the dimness as he leaned over her and snagged the extra pillow. He hesitated, staring down at her, then straightened and turned away. The couch squeaked. A muffled flap as he shook the afghan free of its fold.

He'd worried about her. And then he'd come for her. He could have just slid into bed beside her, but instead he'd brought her back here, where she could sleep alone, but not be lonely. He'd wanted her to feel safe.

He'd wanted to make sure she was safe.

She rolled over, buried her face in his pillow and drifted back to sleep.

JOE SAT UP, kicked his feet free of the blanket and scrubbed a hand over his face. Did he smell...was that...*bacon?* He finally registered the couch beneath him, and the details of his late-night errand arrived in a flash. *Allison.*

He pushed to his feet and looked around for his pants. That's when he realized Allison couldn't be in his kitchen making breakfast because she was still in his bed.

She lay with her back to him, both arms hugging his pillow, her legs under the covers a long, tempting line. He hadn't paid much attention to what she'd been wearing when he'd brought her in here last night—he'd been too intent on getting her where he could keep an eye on her. But he did recall a lot of naked leg.

He forced his gaze upward.

The dim light stole the luster from her hair but his memory supplied the color. He smiled, remembering how he'd pursued her once he'd finally gotten his head out of his ass and noticed her. He'd teased Allison that her hair was the same color as the butter that wouldn't melt in her mouth until she finally agreed to go out with him. She'd probably said yes to the date just to shut him up.

He took a step closer, his fingers itching with the need to touch her. Last night he'd breached the hands-off policy, but he'd had to do it, for his own peace of mind. He couldn't do it again, though, not if he had any intention of hanging on to that peace.

Besides, he had breakfast to supervise. He grabbed a shirt and headed for the kitchen.

Marcus hovered at the stove, spatula in hand, dark

hair standing on end. He wore a different shirt, so he must have retrieved his things from wherever he'd been hiding out in the woods. First order of business after breakfast? Acquaint Marcus with the washing machine.

"Morning."

The kid's entire body jerked. He fumbled the spatula and it landed on the floor with a loud slap. His cheekbones darkened as he scooped it up, making an awkward little motion toward the stove.

"Thought I'd cook. Didn't mean to wake you. Sorry."

So that was how you got the kid to say more than one word at a time. Scare the hell out of him.

With a heavy-duty yawn, Joe took the spatula and set it in the sink. "No problem. But we do need to keep it down. Allison's still asleep." Marcus gave him a look and Joe bristled. "It's not what you're thinking."

"I'm thinking you wanted her safe." His voice cracked, and he practically buried his nose in the skillet.

Joe stood there feeling like a first class ass, and tried to ignore the shredding in his chest. He yanked out a drawer and found a clean spatula, handing it to Marcus like an apology.

"No offense, man."

"This can wait if you want to—" Marcus motioned with his head at the doorway.

Joe cast a longing glance in the direction of his

bedroom and shrugged. "No, I'm good. Not like I was gonna get any, anyway." He froze. "Sleep, I mean." He launched himself at the cupboard, grabbed a glass and poured himself some juice. "By the way, at the risk of being uninvited to this incredible feast, I have to say I distinctly remember locking the—"

"Won't happen again."

Joe held Marcus's gaze and nodded, took a swig of OJ and set the glass aside. "What can I do to help?"

A buzzer sounded. "Take out the biscuits."

"You made biscuits?" Joe grabbed a pot holder and Marcus shifted to the right so he could pull the baking sheet from the oven. A dozen fluffy, perfectly browned biscuits crowded the tray. Joe's mouth watered as he gazed around at Marcus's handiwork— cheese and mushroom omelets, home fries with fresh parsley, sliced strawberries and homemade biscuits. And of course, bacon.

"Damn." Joe looked around for a place to set the tray. "And here I was hoping to impress Allison with a batch of French toast. Where'd you learn to cook like this?"

Marcus hesitated. He bent his knees and adjusted the flame under the potatoes, then turned. Judging by the "well, it was good while it lasted" look on his face, Joe wasn't going to like whatever the kid had to say.

"Jail."

Joe scratched his jaw. "Didn't see that one coming." He retrieved the spatula and loosened the biscuits, one by one. "Why'd you tell me?"

"You asked."

So the kid was either a smart-ass, or just plain honest. Or maybe both.

"What got you locked up?"

"Assault."

"The other guy deserve it?"

"Worse."

"Which means you have a temper."

"I got counseling. But I get it. I'll head out now." Marcus offered his hand. "Thanks—"

"Go if you want, man. But I'm not asking you to."

Marcus frowned. "You were scared for her."

"I had a bad dream. I needed her near me. None of that's your business, if you decide to stay. Anything else you need to tell me?"

"I made a pledge. I won't do it again. Hit someone, I mean. Just so you know I'm not that guy anymore." He turned back to the stove.

Joe rubbed his neck. *I made a pledge.* Was that all it took? After his revelation about Allison, about what she deserved and what he deserved and how his life revolved around the next drink, he'd decided to give quitting a try.

He'd managed two hours.

"Good morning."

They both looked over to see Allison standing just inside the kitchen, the afghan around her shoulders covering a roomy nightgown that stretched to her knees. In her arms she cradled Joe's kitten.

"Something smells good."

"Thanks to Marcus. Sit down. I'll get you some coffee."

She set the kitten down and washed her hands at the sink—not an easy maneuver considering she was trying to keep a grip on the afghan at the same time. Joe settled her at the table with a cup of coffee, then set three places. All the while trying not to think about how having her here in his kitchen seemed natural.

It seemed the kitten had taken an interest in Marcus. Or maybe it was the bacon he was carrying. Either way she scampered up his pants leg and clung to his hip as he moved to the table. Before he sat he gently disengaged her.

"What's her name?"

Joe winced. "She doesn't have one yet."

"Harsh."

Allison gestured at Marcus with her coffee cup. "He's right. It is harsh. You have to give her a name. How about Ginger?"

"Right. Because that's so much better than Pumpkin. I might as well name her Fluffy."

"Tigerlily." Marcus helped himself to a biscuit.

Joe looked at Allison, Allison looked at Joe, Marcus looked for the butter dish and the cat looked disapprovingly at her empty food bowl.

"You can preserve your machismo by yelling

'Tiger' when you need her, and call her by her full name when she's naughty." Allison beamed across the table. "Marcus, it's perfect."

Joe tossed the kitten a pinch of bacon. "Tigerlily it is." He nodded his thanks at Marcus, whose cheeks were as red as the strawberry jam he was spreading on his biscuit. "Can we eat now?"

After breakfast Joe and Marcus did the dishes. Allison offered, but Joe sent her to her room to get dressed—they had paneling to yank. As he dried a platter he thanked Marcus again for breakfast.

"You interested in taking care of meals while you're here? Breakfast and dinner? Throw in some help with the reno and I'll put you on the payroll."

"Aren't you leaving?"

"In a little over a week. Let's see how it goes. If you're still here, maybe we can talk about you playing caretaker while I'm gone." When Marcus didn't say anything, Joe shrugged. "Just an idea. No pressure if you're not up for it."

"Payroll sounds good," said Marcus, but instead of looking at Joe, he stared at the cat.

"Good." Joe hesitated then draped the dish towel over the back of a chair. "Now let's go do some damage."

MARCUS WAS STANDING in front of the roadside vegetable stand when it hit him. Just how much Meathead had entrusted him with. His meals, his power tools, his money, his truck—how could the guy know

Marcus wouldn't take off with his ride? Or shit, even murder him in his sleep? One call to 9-1-1 about a little fire and suddenly Marcus had the run of the place. Made no sense, especially since the only reason he'd made that call was to save the motel for himself. No one but him had the right to burn that place down.

Didn't matter what Meathead or his lady did for him. Ten years ago he'd made himself a promise. And he was finally about to keep it. He couldn't let any misguided do-gooder make him forget what he'd come back for.

But until the time was right, he might as well enjoy having the chance to cook. He'd always found it soothing, even in prison. The bonus was, he seemed to have a knack for it. And the praise felt good.

He gazed down at the plastic bag in his hand and the lone tomato it contained. *Don't be an asshole.* He shook his head and scanned the bin for another. He was thinking maple-glazed salmon and salad for dinner—

"Hello, again."

He stiffened. If he hadn't recognized her cheerful voice he'd have known her by her sweet summer scent. The realization both saddened and annoyed him. He couldn't afford to "know" anybody. Hadn't she figured out he wasn't the friendly type?

Liz Early shook out her own plastic bag and crowded in beside him under the faded canopy. But instead of studying the produce, she was peering up at him.

"You're cute. Quiet, but cute."

He moved away from the tomatoes, started toward the cantaloupes, pictured Liz's curves and went hot. No way he could act disinterested while checking melons for ripeness. He cast a desperate glance around and zeroed in on the broccoli—the least erotic vegetable on the farm. Well, not counting cabbage.

She followed him, watching closely as he pinched and poked and considered. What the hell was her deal? He wanted to tell her to get the eff away but was afraid his voice would fail him. After a while she turned and leaned back against the rickety table, head tilted, fingers shoved into the front pockets of her jeans.

"You look like you know what you're doing." He didn't glance at her, didn't answer, didn't betray he'd even heard her. She leaned closer, her shoulders hunching, her shirt gaping to reveal a lacy, emerald-colored bra.

Okay, so maybe he looked. Who would blame him?

"Do you?" she asked, with a suggestive smile. "Know what you're doing?"

He scowled. "Do you?"

"Depends on what we're talking about—vegetables or sex?" When he didn't respond she gave a good-natured shrug. "I'm only teasing. So, how long are you here for?"

"As long as it takes," he snapped, and cursed himself as wariness chased the mischief from Liz's eyes. But that was exactly what he wanted to do. Chase her away. So he let the apology dissolve on his tongue. Grabbed his wallet and headed for the cashier.

Little Miss Perky was right behind him. "How long have you known Joe?"

"Not long." He paid for his items and swung toward the pickup. He was starting to feel like Peter Pan must have felt when Tinker Bell was bouncing around him all the time. What he needed was a flyswatter.

"Why don't you come back by the bar sometime? You might not be old enough to drink but I'm guessing you're close. Got anything against older women?"

"Not interested," he growled, and dug the keys out of his pocket.

"How about the diner, then? You can buy me a cinnamon roll."

The diner that Calvin Ames owned? Marcus's fingers fisted around the keys. "Not gonna happen."

She moved in, real close. "That's too bad," she murmured. "Because you seem lonely."

"Yeah?" He yanked open the door. "You seem desperate."

That did it. She fell back a step. "Well. I guess we're not both consenting adults after all." Her tone made it clear it wasn't the "consenting" part he no longer qualified for. She spun around and marched back over to the tomatoes.

Despite himself Marcus watched her go, all the while feeling the pull of something unexpected. Something visceral. Something he'd have to work even harder to ignore than Liz Early herself.

ALLISON WAS BACK on her hands and knees, slicing at decades-old carpet, while Joe had returned his attention to removing the paneling next door, in the room they'd found Mitzi. Marcus had gone out to run some errands. In addition to ripping up carpet, Allison was also trying desperately not to dwell on the comment Joe had made after confiding the heartbreaking story of his brother's death.

Sometimes waiting is the wrong thing to do.

She knew that sleeping with Joe would only complicate an already difficult situation. But even more than the physical craving that Allison was finding harder and harder to ignore, the truths they'd shared, the hurts they'd confessed—she felt a connection with Joe she'd never imagined she could, even in their early days. And despite his mocking threats upon her arrival in town, he'd taken care of her like no one else ever had.

So what was she waiting for? They had only a few short weeks together. Once he handled Mahoney's account in D.C. he'd return to Castle Creek and she'd have lost her chance to fall asleep and wake up in Joe's arms.

To let a strong, sexy, caring man make her come.

She shuddered, and sat back on her boot heels. Thing was, as long as Joe continued to drink, she couldn't start down that path with him again.

"You look like you're praying over it."

She sucked in a breath and looked over her shoulder. He stood behind her, dangling a water bottle straight from the fridge. She peeled off her gloves, accepted the bottle gratefully and pressed it to her throat.

"My prayers were answered if you're here to take over for me."

He moved into her line of vision and leaned against the wall, took a swig from his own bottle. "You'd rather tackle paneling?"

"Never mind." She sat back on her butt and stretched out her legs, sighed with pleasure. "Find anything interesting in the walls?"

"Nothing moving, if that's what you mean."

"Glad to hear it."

"So." Abruptly he dropped into a crouch in front of her, between her outspread feet. "I talked to Mahoney."

"About the campaign?"

"About you."

She frowned. "What about me?"

"Mahoney does want me on the campaign. Even after ditching me a year ago." He locked gazes with Allison, his thumb scraping at the label on his bottle. "Did I really pitch power bars for pets to a roomful of women looking to promote weight loss supplements?"

"Yep. And you even hired someone in a dog suit to hand out candy."

"Damn. Mahoney mentioned a few other…incidents I don't remember—or at least I don't remember them the way he does. I'm surprised Tackett didn't fire me before I had a chance to quit."

"I think he wanted to keep his options open."

"Now we know why." Joe paused, as if choosing his words carefully. "I'm sorry I accused you of being in league with the bastard. I am sorry for everything I put you through."

"We both jumped to conclusions. And I wasn't as supportive as I should have been after your brother died." It felt good to say it. She hadn't realized how much she'd needed to. "I'm sorry for that."

He rose slowly out of his crouch. Allison pulled her knees to her chest and wrapped her arms around her legs. Joe motioned with his water bottle.

"And you should know. Mahoney never said he wouldn't work with you. He's apparently heard good things."

"What does that mean?"

"That you have choices." His gaze dropped to her fingers, which were drumming a silent, frantic rhythm on her shins. "You can choose to let me pay off your mother's debt, or not. You can choose to work with me on Mahoney's account and take it over when I'm gone, or stick with your prior accounts. And by the way, Mahoney paid a signing bonus—you work with me and we'll split it. Or you can choose not to do any of that, and quit T&P. Start fresh at another firm. Or if you do a good enough job with Mahoney, I bet he'll hire you freelance. Point is, you have options."

"I…that's…thank you. For talking to Mahoney."

"You'll let me know, then. If you pick any *options* that involve me?"

"I'll let you know," she agreed solemnly. And realized why the freedom to choose didn't thrill her like it should have. He hadn't made it personal—there was no option to stay in Castle Creek with him. And why should there be? She'd made it more than clear she'd never consider such a thing. He had no reason to put himself out there again like that.

And she shouldn't want him to.

She got to her feet and brushed at her butt. "Better get back to work before my boss—*ouch.*"

She jerked her left hand forward and cradled it in her right, peered down at the splinter lodged in her palm. Damn it. If only she hadn't taken off her gloves.

"Let me see." Joe took her hand and gently rubbed a thumb over the palm. His nearness, the smell of wood shavings and sweat and the deliberate stroke of skin on skin kindled a fervent need, deep down in her belly. It took every last bit of bravado she possessed to resist yanking her hand away. "We'll need tweezers," he said. "Come on up to the kitchen, where there's more light."

He kept her wrist in his grip as he led her to the office, much like he'd led her to his bed in the middle of the night. Where he'd lifted the covers for her, leaned over her, wanted her. Then turned away because of that ridiculous hands-off policy.

Hands-on, she wanted to shout. *Please* put your hands on me. Around me, over me, in me.

But Marcus could be back at any moment. And did she really want to seduce Joe when she was wet with sweat and smelled like carpet crud?

Tonight, her body whispered....

Cold shower, her brain cried.

Joe fetched the first aid kit, joined Allison at the sink and rinsed the tweezers in hot water. When he bent over her hand a small hank of dark blond hair fell forward, and dangled over his eyebrow. Allison grimaced. As antsy as she was, she had no patience for temptation. Screw that cliché about fingers aching to brush the stray lock of hair back into place. What she really wanted to do was grab the scissors and snip the damned thing off. It was just too tempting to reach out and touch it.

She looked for somewhere else to focus, *anywhere* else to focus, and noticed the recycle bin in the corner by the back door. It was full of empty liquor bottles.

"That's quite a collection you have there," she said lightly.

Joe looked up at her, then over at the corner. His fingers tightened on her hand. "I'm trying to cut back."

"Cut back?" Her chest went suddenly light and she found it hard to swallow, almost as if her heart had floated up into her throat. Her leg started to bounce, her boot heel tapping on the kitchen floor. "Or quit?"

"Keep still." His brow furrowed and he probed carefully for the tail of the splinter. Seconds passed. "I thought I'd take it one day at a time," he finally said. He lifted his head, and the combination of resolution and panic in his eyes made her hope like she'd never hoped before.

"You can do it, Joe," she breathed.

"I appreciate the vote of confidence." Irony tinged his words. Slowly she pulled her hand free of his.

"I let you down last year."

"I let myself down. You told me I had a problem, I just wasn't ready to hear it. Still not sure I am. Now let's get this over with so we can get back to work."

His sudden brusqueness confused her. But before she could question him on it, Marcus walked into the kitchen. He looked wary, as if he'd sensed the tension the moment he'd entered the lobby. Why hadn't she heard the buzzer? While Marcus unpacked the groceries, Joe wordlessly reclaimed her hand, caught the tail of the splinter and eased it out. A splash of isopropyl alcohol, an adhesive bandage and she was ready to get out of Joe's way.

"Thank you," she murmured. He nodded, and turned away to help Marcus.

FOR THE REST of the day, Allison concentrated on yanking up carpet. Ironic, since two doors down in #4, Joe, Marcus and Noble were laying carpet— a pretty blue-and-gray pattern that blended well with the freshly painted pale blue walls. Noble had beamed when she'd applauded the choice—apparently Ivy hadn't been the only one giving Joe decorating advice. The next opportunity Allison had, she planned on asking Noble if there was anything he couldn't do.

As the afternoon light waned, Allison finished uncovering the subfloor and had the carpet rolled up against the wall, ready for the short trip to the huge garbage bin outside. She'd let the guys handle that task.

After chugging the rest of her water, she grabbed the hammer, muttered a quick prayer and went on to the next job—stripping the paneling.

Not because she wanted to prove she could do it. Screw getting back on the horse and all that. What she really wanted was to wear herself out. Sweat every last ounce of moisture out of her body and make her muscles cry for mercy, so that at the end of the day she'd be too tired and sore to do anything but sleep.

Let alone plan a seduction.

Of course, she'd have more confidence in her plan if her blood weren't fizzing with a hot, urgent need to rediscover Joe Gallahan, inch by tempting inch. Especially after seeing for herself what she hoped was his resolve to quit drinking. Hope was heady stuff.

Shake it off, Allie. She wedged the hammer's claw into place, and pushed.

Half an hour later she'd ripped out two sections without finding anything scarier than a collection of mangled nails and bits of insulation. Then someone called her name, and she turned to see Marcus standing just outside the doorway, trying not to crowd her. She was touched, but also slightly frustrated. She knew evil, and Marcus didn't have it in him.

She tugged off her mask. "I'm not afraid of you," she said gently.

Silence, then, "Because you have a hammer?"

She smiled, leaned over and hooked the hammer on the rim of the bucket. Pulled off her goggles and moved toward the door. "Because you have kind eyes."

His expression blanked and he backed up a step. "You need glasses."

Her stomach growled. "I need food."

"We're cooking with the phone."

"I'm sorry?"

He walked with Allison to #4, letting her have the sidewalk. "Noble doesn't like salmon, so we're getting take-out."

"Damn," she muttered. "I was really looking forward to that maple glaze."

"Tomorrow," he promised. He stuffed his hands in his pockets, and for the first time she noticed the blue and gray fibers clinging to his jeans. "We're ordering subs and salads. Joe's calling it in. I'm picking it up."

The timbre of his voice made it clear that wasn't something he was looking forward to doing.

"I'll go. It'll be good to get out," she said, and when relief practically oozed out of his pores, she knew she'd made the right decision. "Tell Joe I want the usual. I'll just grab a quick shower and be on my way."

When Allison returned with the food, they ate in the motel parking lot in the gathering dusk. Allison and Noble perched themselves on the tailgate of the truck Noble had borrowed to transport the library's newly acquired salon chair, while Marcus and Joe settled on the tailgate of Joe's pickup. As the light faded the crickets started to sing their scratchy song, and the safety lights began to buzz, hum and glow.

While Noble provided Allison with a mini-seminar on Oliver Hazard Perry and the Battle of Lake Erie— apparently one of the biggest naval battles of the War of 1812—Allison found herself distracted by the interactions between Marcus and Joe. Marcus sat as close as he could to the edge of the tailgate without falling off. Joe maintained a relaxed pose, careful not to make any sudden movements, or even physical contact. He knew as well as Allison did that Marcus was skittish. And it wasn't because he was shy.

Somewhere along the way, he'd suffered, and Joe was looking out for him. Like Braden had looked out for Joe.

She blinked back a hot rush of tears, and when Noble frowned in concern she distracted him by offering the uneaten half of her sandwich.

AFTER WORKING HER ass off all day, Allison's body was one big, aching, overworked muscle. Her stomach was full. She'd indulged in a long, hot, relaxing shower. She hadn't had coffee since breakfast.

And she'd even tried to calm her mind with the yoga corpse pose.

Twice.

Still, she couldn't sleep.

She wished she could blame the loudmouthed cricket that had somehow found its way into her room. But the noisy little insect had nothing to do with the memories that played over and over in Allison's head. The ardent strength of Joe's embrace, when he'd held her in the storeroom. The husky ripple of his laugh. The heady man-smell of his sheets.

So many close calls since she'd arrived in Castle Creek, yet they hadn't managed so much as a kiss. And probably wouldn't, unless she made the first move. Because she'd insisted he not touch her.

What an idiot.

With a frustrated grunt she threw back the covers. If she didn't find that cricket and get him out of her room, she really would be up all night.

She fetched a cup from the bathroom and went on the hunt. She finally tracked the little guy to the alcove where she hung her coveralls. It took several tries, but trap him she did, and then hurried him over to the door. She turned off the light—no sense in giving any cars on the road a free peep at her nightwear—opened the door and lobbed the cricket outside. When she started to scuttle back inside, something, a noise maybe, made her hesitate.

She poked her head out and spotted Joe standing halfway down the sidewalk, in front of #5, still dressed in his work clothes. He had his back to her as he coiled up an extension cord. Wait, he was *un*-coiling it. So he could finish with the paneling? She glanced over her shoulder at the clock. At *midnight?*

Maybe he was having trouble sleeping, too.

She eased back into her room and stood in the dark, teeth pinching the inside of her lower lip, breathing suddenly ragged. What was she afraid of? Rejection? Mockery? Nothing could be worse than this desperate restlessness she was feeling.

According to Noble, after vanquishing that British squadron during the Battle of Lake Erie, Oliver Hazard Perry had announced, "We have met the enemy and they are ours."

Allison knew very well who her enemy was. Fear.

And it was time to take that bad boy down.

CHAPTER ELEVEN

ALLISON HIT THE light switch and hurried into the bathroom to brush her teeth. The cool tile beneath her feet finally registered and she looked down.

She couldn't go over there barefoot. With her luck she'd step on a nail—a ring shank, not some piddling two-penny job. And how cool was it, by the way, that she knew the difference? *Concentrate, Allie.* Nothing like a trip to the emergency room to kill the mood. Which meant she needed shoes.

She eyed her flip-flops. Definitely not nail-resistant. High heels? Match those with her pale blue baby doll pajamas and sleep-tousled hair and she'd look like a centerfold from the fifties. Maybe Joe wouldn't mind, but she didn't want to look like she was trying too hard. Just in case.

With a resigned sigh, she slipped her feet into her boots, and decided not to bother lacing them up.

On her way to #5 she thought of Marcus, and stumbled. If he wasn't tucked in bed where he was supposed to be, she was in for one serious dose of humiliation. Triple that if Joe turned her away. And he might, after she'd ticked him off that afternoon.

She clomped down the sidewalk, feeling like a

bumpkin headed for the outhouse, wishing she'd opted for the flip-flops after all. But if she went back to her room she wouldn't come out again until morning. Second thoughts would drive her right back under the covers.

With any luck, it wouldn't be her feet he'd be paying attention to, anyway.

A car whizzed by and Allison barely resisted the urge to drop to the ground. Maybe they hadn't seen her. Maybe it wouldn't be all over Castle Creek by tomorrow afternoon that Joe's guest liked to DIY in her jammies.

Maybe she should stop stalling.

The smell of lake air and pine trees mingled with the scent she'd dabbed behind her ears, in the hollow of her neck and between her breasts. She thought of Joe's mouth connecting the dots and her bones shook. A wet, heavy anticipation settled between her thighs. She ran her palms down the silky front of her pajamas, and her skin tingled.

But the impersonal glare of the streetlights and the brisk chill in the air did their best to make her feel more tragic than tempting. And what could be more tragic than begging for sex? Still, she'd set the rules. It was up to her to break them. And if she didn't break them soon she'd explode.

Light from the window of #5 splashed onto the sidewalk, and she could hear muffled pounding— both the hammer-in-hand kind, and the rock band kind. She peered through the glass, which trembled with every swing of Joe's hammer. He faced away from her. She could return to her room and he'd never know. She glanced at the door. Closed. She probably wouldn't be able to get in, anyway. And who had the strength to knock?

But a gentle push was all the door needed to swing wide. She moved slowly into the room and into the light, everything inside her, everything contained by her skin, vibrating like storm-charged air between rages of thunder.

She had no idea what she was doing. No clue what he'd think of her for doing it. Still, she needed to show him—everything she couldn't say now, everything she wished she'd said then.

And she was desperate to feel him inside her again.

Despite her heavy boots clunking across the floor, he didn't seem to hear her behind him. He was working on the wall opposite the door, ripping a panel free of the studs, the low-pitched screech of uprooted nails competing with an old clock radio blaring Van Halen's "Jump."

A nervous giggle rose in her throat and she pressed both palms to her mouth. How appropriate.

Joe swore, and the crudeness of the word kicked off a raw excitement in her stomach. He swore again—the panel wasn't cooperating. He let go and stood back, swiped a gloved hand across his forehead. Need warred with common sense as Allison eyed the breadth of his shoulders beneath the sweat-dampened T-shirt, imagined the moist heat of the fabric pressed to her skin.

Thus endeth the briefest war on record.

Had it been less than a week since she'd seen him for the first time in over a year? Since she'd quietly watched him work the paint roller while she floundered for the courage to say his name? Now, instead of resenting her yearning for him, she planned to revel in it. Even if only for a short while.

She pushed her shoulders back.

"Joe."

He turned quickly, anxiety stamped on his features. When he saw the way she was dressed, in her baby doll nightie and unlaced work boots, he fell back a step. But the concern on his face sharpened.

"What is it?" he asked, his voice a low rasp. "What's wrong?"

"Nothing. Nothing serious, anyway."

The tension in his neck muscles eased. His gaze dropped to her feet and his lips twitched. So much for thinking he'd be too distracted to notice her footwear.

Disappointment dragged her heart from her throat back down to her chest, where it belonged. He wasn't going to make this easy for her. So be it.

"I couldn't sleep," she said.

"The noise." He grimaced. "Sorry. I'll call it a night."

She tipped her head. Was that a quiver she'd heard in his voice?

He turned his back, leaned down and switched off

the radio, started tugging off his gloves. Streaks of sweat dampened his hair, making it cling to his neck. If she had her way she'd soon be doing a lot of her own clinging. She moved closer.

"I wish you wouldn't. Call it a night, I mean."

He paused, his head bent, the line of his shoulders taut. "You're not saying you want to help. Not dressed like that."

She shook her head then realized he couldn't see. "No," she murmured. "I don't want to help. I want to watch."

He swung back around, eyes narrowed and glittering.

"But first I want you to take off your shirt."

"Al." The pleading growl of his voice sent a thick, buzzing heat tumbling through her veins.

"Please," she whispered.

He hesitated. Then his T-shirt hit the floor with a muffled slap. Hard chest, taut skin, muscled arms— this time she looked her fill. The harsh rasp of uneven breathing crowded the room. She swallowed, finally lifted her gaze to his and shivered at the smoldering purpose that had turned his navy eyes to black.

She gestured jerkily at the wall. "Why don't you finish what you started? I'll wait."

He started to say something, stopped and lifted an eyebrow. Slowly turned and faced the wall again. This time when he pulled, the upper portion of the sheet broke free.

Which was exactly what she was feeling. Free. As

if she'd escaped the doubt and the resentment holding her back from what she really wanted.

Joe.

Relaxed Joe. Attentive Joe. Country Joe.

Sober Joe.

At T&P she'd always admired his drive and dedication, his intelligence and business savvy, and, of course, his polished good looks—*who could resist a handsome man in a tailored suit?* Euphoric wasn't a potent enough word to describe how she'd felt when he'd finally shown an interest in her, and it hadn't taken long for her to start fantasizing about a future together. Then his brother died and everything unraveled. Joe became a man she didn't know, someone she couldn't trust. And though she missed him after he moved away, her grief was more about the loss of possibilities than the loss of Joe.

In love with love, she'd decided, and did her best to forget him.

But this time it had taken her less than a week to fall for him. Despite the initial animosity, the distrust and the still-present drinking problem, he was giving, funny, compassionate and so damned sexy. And she'd fallen hard. Which meant it would be that much more difficult to say goodbye.

The good news? There would be no surprises this time. No hope for a happy-ever-after. Just the here and now.

"Don't move," she whispered, as slow tingles of anticipation traveled up and down her spine. She stepped closer and took her time admiring his back. Sweat streaked an impressive set of muscles that quivered with tension.

She blew on his skin. He froze, his gloved hands clenched around the edge of the panel. Slowly she raised her palms and settled them on his back, let her fingers press and drift, press and drift, over his shoulders, his delts, on either side of his spine. He let go of the panel, braced his palms against the wall and hung his head. His breathing roughened as her hands skated over him.

Then she leaned forward and bit him.

He jerked. "Judas Priest, you're killing me."

She licked the same spot and felt him shudder. "Remember what I said about finishing what you started?"

"Can we forget about the wall?"

"What wall?" Another bite.

Her teeth had barely left his skin before he turned from the waist and whipped out an arm, tucked her in tight between his body and the paneling. His gaze seared into hers as he anchored the fingertips of his left glove in his teeth and yanked his hand free, let the glove drop to the floor and followed suit with the right. With a groan he slid his fingers into her hair. He lifted her face to his, thumbs stroking the edges of her mouth. She reached out, encountered the leather of his tool belt and pulled him in closer. Something long and hard pressed against her belly, and it wasn't his hammer.

"Want to tell me what this means?" he asked hoarsely.

She looked down. "That despite the work boots, you're into me?"

"That goes without saying. I mean *this*. You. Here. With me."

"You're not going to feed me that line again, are you? That I'm too good for a handful of hookups?"

"Is that what you're looking for?"

"I'm looking for whatever will work for us over the next five weeks."

His thumbs stilled against her lips. "Does this have anything to do with the booze I poured down the drain? Because you and I both know my problem won't disappear that easily."

"It has to do with the fact that I can't sleep for wanting you. And what you said yesterday, about waiting, and how it can be the wrong thing to do. We've already wasted a week." Her gaze dropped to his mouth. "Though I admit it's quite the turn-on, knowing you're not under the influence of anything but lust."

He groaned her name and skimmed his hands down the sides of her neck. "I've wondered," he whispered. "Whether you taste the same." When he dipped his head and pressed his mouth to one corner of hers, then nipped at her lower lip, she started to vibrate. He touched his tongue to the same spot and her hands climbed frantically up his naked chest and knotted in his hair. Their mouths collided.

The kiss was desperate and searching, a frenzied reunion. The scrape of stubble, the clash of teeth, the crush of bodies—the joining of their mouths was as much a scolding as a pleasure. *Why* had they waited so long?

She lifted her left leg and wrapped it around his hip, dragging him even closer, indifferent to the tool belt digging at her inner thigh. She was frantic to ease the ache in her core, the ache that cried out for the hot pressure of his erection. Damn it, he was too *tall*. She pushed up on her toes and wriggled, yanked on Joe's hair to signal—

Suddenly with one hand on her ass and an unflattering grunt he hefted her. There. Oh, yes, *there*. The shock of moisture against her center meant her panties were already soaked. She wrapped her other leg around him and thrust forward. Joe broke off the kiss and supported her with his other hand.

"Welcome back," he rasped.

She tipped her head against the wall and laughed, exhilarated by him, her own daring, their mutual need and the pulsing promise of release. He laughed, too, reclaimed her lips and tangled his tongue with hers. When she started to move he sucked the breath right out of her mouth.

She pistoned against him, slowly at first, then faster, and faster still. The pressure built—agonizing, delicious and demanding. She started to pant. Joe buried his face in her neck and muttered bald, bad words against her skin, his hips holding her in place, his hands kneading her ass, until her climax burst upon her. Her body seized, her center throbbing as fiery sparkles of bliss shot outward.

"Joe," she cried.

"Right here, my sweet." He kissed her slowly, deeply. She sagged against him, dropped her head onto his shoulder.

"Dear God in heaven."

"I don't think he had anything to do with it."

She smiled against his skin, felt him shift position. "You're not going to drop me, are you?"

"As much as I hate the thought of putting you down, we're running a risk, here."

Allison lifted her head—no easy task, since her neck felt about as strong as a blade of grass—and followed his gaze toward the window. She stared at Joe's reflection, at his muscled torso and long legs, the forward angle of his hips, and got turned on all over again.

"Oh, my," she whispered.

He huffed a ragged laugh. "Oh, no, you don't. With the lights on, anyone can see in. We need to take this somewhere else." Gently he eased her legs from around his waist and lowered her to the floor. She clung to his biceps.

"Afraid Audrey's out there?"

He made a face. "Any minute now she'll come busting in, shouting about a meat crisis."

She pressed a palm to the rigid thickness behind his zipper. "I think you might be having one."

He moaned, and reached out. She dodged him and clomped over to the light switch, slapped it to the off position and clomped back, the glow from the light posts illuminating her way. "Where were we?"

"Wait." He caught her hand before she could touch him again. "Not here. Not like this. Let's go to my place. I'll hit the shower—"

"Yes, to your room. No, to the shower." She tugged him toward the door. "And bring the tool belt."

"I think I can keep you entertained without it." He pulled to a stop, unbuckled the tool belt and let it drop. She nearly went down right along with it when she saw how low his jeans rode his hips. Her palms twitched as she recalled the warm, coarse feel of that thin smattering of hair that covered his chest and abs and disappeared behind the solid line of his fly....

He bit out a swear word when he saw where her gaze was focused. Snatched up his shirt and propelled her out onto the sidewalk, took a second to shut the door behind them. Snagged her gaze. Pushed her back against the door and took her mouth. She kissed him just as hungrily, intoxicated by the need she'd roused in him. When she started to wrap a leg around him again he choked out a laugh and pulled away.

"We need to go. Now." He grabbed her hand and

led her toward the office. She resisted when they neared the door to her room.

"Here. We can go in here."

"Yeah?" His mouth tilted as he looked her over. "Can't wait to see where you hid the key."

JUST AS HE'D SUSPECTED, Allison had locked herself out of her room. Not that it mattered, since he wanted her in *his* bed.

Though how the hell they made it to his bedroom without one of them tripping over Allison's bootlaces, Joe had no clue. But finally he had her right where he wanted her. Now to be able to see her...

He groped for the bedside lamp and tapped the base once. A dim light spilled across the bed he was damned glad he'd taken time to straighten that morning. Before he could turn around a soft pair of arms snaked around his waist and two hands busied themselves unfastening his fly. He turned in her arms before she could free him, planted a swift kiss on the lower lip she'd stuck out.

"Let me get my boots off." He dropped onto the edge of the bed, then got distracted by the sight of her standing before him, hair tousled, eyes half-lidded, nipples poking through her pajama top. His gaze didn't make it any farther south. He stretched out a hand but she danced out of reach.

"Naked," she demanded. "Now." She kicked out of her boots and reached for the hem of her top— and lifted an eyebrow. He lunged at his laces, fingers fumbling since he couldn't bring himself to look away from her. Somehow he managed it, ripped off his boot and sock and tossed them aside. She pulled off her top and threw it in the same direction.

"Now the other one," she said. But her words barely registered.

Her breasts were just as he remembered. Perfect handfuls. Flushed pink with passion, the nipples puckered, ripe for the flick of his tongue, the nip of his teeth. He half rose from the bed.

"Hello?" She slid her thumbs behind her waistband. "The other boot?"

He growled and fell back, practically shredded the laces to free his foot. The second boot and sock sailed across the room. Then he shot up off the bed and mimicked her pose, thumbs at his waistband, chest heaving…gaze roving every sinful, satin inch of her.

Her gaze was locked. On his groin. He eased the zipper down and she licked her lips. His fingers shook. So did her best sexy voice when she suggested breathlessly, "On the count of three."

He started. "One…"

"Two…"

"Three."

She had her bottoms off before he did, which was just fine with him. God, she was beautiful. She was also laughing her ass off.

Probably because his jeans had caught at his knees.

"Allow me." She kissed him, her mouth opening under his as her fingers worked his boxers free of his erection. She pushed them over his ass and down, squeezing as she went, sinking slowly to her knees. Her chin caught the tip of his dick and he inhaled sharply then stopped breathing altogether when she paused to give that a squeeze, as well. She tugged his clothing free and made a leisurely climb back up his body, her tongue sliding him nearly into oblivion. He yanked her up the rest of the way, held her face before she could go for another lip-lock.

"I've been sweating all day," he reminded her gruffly. "I really need that shower."

"I like you sweaty." She ran her hands over his pecs and down his biceps, wrapped her fingers around his elbows and tugged him closer. They both sucked air at the long-awaited thrill of skin on skin. With a gratified moan she wreathed her arms around his neck while his hands explored her back, her waist, her ass.

"I never had you sweaty." Her grin trembled. "Sweaty from doing me, yes. But never sweaty from doing hard labor."

Even as her words made him stiffer than he'd ever been, his skin feeling two sizes too small and his lungs burning from lack of oxygen, he got it. She wanted this to be new, untouched by their past. He'd do his damnedest to give that to her.

All the things he hadn't done for her, all the time he hadn't taken to learn her body, to appreciate her passion, because he'd had a meeting or a phone call or a hangover. He'd been a selfish bastard. But she was giving him a second chance and he wouldn't waste it.

He'd do it all now. Take the time now. Now, and in an hour, and in an hour after that, and as often as she'd let him over the next five weeks. His pulse rocketed.

"Everything okay?" she asked, her eyes searching his.

"Not okay. Amazing." He fell back onto the bed and took her with him, rolled and levered over her. She hummed when he nuzzled her neck, gasped when he tongued her breasts, giggled when he blew into her navel. When he kissed his way lower she stiffened.

"Condom," she said suddenly, and reared up, as if prepared to lead the search party. He grasped her hips and held her in place.

"You in a rush, city girl?" He scooted a little lower, gently spread her thighs. "Relax. We won't need them for a while."

"We won't?" she squeaked, her muscles rigid beneath his hands. Then in a different tone, one tinged with hope, she ventured, "Them?"

He responded with a leisurely lick, a direct hit. She jumped and made a strangled sound, fought to close her legs, clutched his hair with one hand. Before she could start yanking he treated her to a few flicks and lazy circles of his tongue. She hesitated, her hips quivering, and he knew he had her.

"Lie back," he murmured. "Let me play."

Sixty seconds later her hips had gone from quivering to full-out bucking. She thrashed on the bed, directing her choked screams into the pillow she held to her face—he suspected more to hide her embarrassment than to control her noise level.

One finger and his tongue were all he'd needed to take her to the edge. To push her over, he added his thumb. She flung her hips up and spasmed, pillow forgotten, hands fisted in the bedspread, throat working as she released a shattered cry.

Softly he blew on the apex between her thighs, wanting to soothe, reveling in the sight of her mindless satisfaction. Eyed the hapless pillow. Hopefully by the time he was through with her she'd have lost her self-consciousness about this particular act.

By the time he was through with her. He knew better. That time would never come. The thought of leaving her behind in D.C.—the thought of leaving her at all—made his heart curl into itself.

But he couldn't help feeling smug as he kissed his way back up a body still racked with tremors. She lay spread-eagled and panting, perspiration gleaming on her skin, astonishment widening her eyes.

"You…you never did that for me before."

"I missed out on as much as you did. Trust me. I plan to make up for it."

She flung her arms and legs around him and pulled him in tight, as if his words had triggered some kind of man trap. His erection pressed into the hot cradle of her thighs and they both groaned. She grabbed his face and bit him on the chin.

"I need you inside me."

CHAPTER TWELVE

WITH A HUSKY CHUCKLE of anticipation she helped him roll on a condom. Then she stretched out on her back, arms over her head, body straining toward his. He'd forgotten how insatiable she could be. He braced himself above her and stared down into her glowing face. The reality of having her in his bed, of having all night to touch her and taste her and make her scream, filled him with a gladness, a rightness he hadn't felt since before his brother's death. He lowered his head, slid his mouth along hers for a lingering kiss.

"Just so you know," he said. "You taste even better than I remember."

He positioned himself between her legs, nudged her knees up and eased forward. She was slick, but so tight she didn't want to take him in. He pulled back and tried again, and just as he pushed she hooked her ankles behind his ass and thrust upward. She gasped as he slid home, her inner muscles gripping him snugly.

He paused, gritting his teeth, somehow finding the strength to resist the urge to thrust again. He blew out a breath and rested his chin on her head. His arms shook. "You okay?" he asked, the question not much more than a grunt.

"Not okay," she said, echoing his earlier words. "Amazing. And by the way…" She swept her palms across his cheekbones, pushed his hair out of his face and grinned. "Welcome back to you, too."

His heart unfurled and he returned her grin. But when he began to move, her hands pushed at his shoulders. Had he hurt her? He went still again, biting back a whimper. She really was bent on killing him.

He was about to ask again if she was okay but her brown-and-green-flecked gaze didn't look the least bit troubled. In fact, the way she studied him… Her lips parted and his breath stalled. Was she about to tell him she'd changed her mind? That five weeks wouldn't be enough? That she liked Castle Creek so much she'd—

"You're softer," she mused.

He blinked. "Not something a man wants to hear when he's inside you."

"You know what I mean. Emotionally. You've changed."

Maybe he had changed. But was it enough? Was it too late? A sudden hopeless fury clawed at his insides. He twisted his mouth into something feral, withdrew from her satin heat and thrust again, deep. Allison gasped, and threw back her head. His thrusts graduated to plunges as her moans and whimpers grew rougher and more demanding and she slammed her hips up to meet his, again and again. He felt the pressure cresting, his balls tighten, the sweet, boiling lure of completion. *Damn* it. He wanted to make it last but there was no way, no way in hell he could draw this out.

"It's been too long," he gritted. "I can't—"

"Joe!" She went rigid, then started to shudder. Her body arched and her fingernails dug into his shoulders and the fierce, rolling clamp of her insides launched him into his own climax. He buried his face in the curve of her neck and for long moments they shook together. It had been *way* too long.

When she finally started to relax he moved, preparing to shift away. But she moaned in protest and lifted her hips, seeking his.

He didn't want to break the connection, either. He did, however, want the woman to be able to breathe. He eased his weight onto his right elbow and used his left hand to smooth the damp hair out of Allison's face.

"I've missed you," he said simply.

Her eyes turned to liquid hazel. "I've missed you, too," she whispered. She swiped the moisture from her eyes, raised her arms above her head and stretched, hummed in appreciation when he palmed her breast.

"You said it's been a while." Her mouth took on a mischievous slant. "So you really have been Mr. DIY."

"A man's gotta do what a man's gotta do."

"Me, too. I mean, that was the first orgasm—"

"You had three. But who's counting."

"—in a year that didn't involve silicone toys or fingers. My own fingers, I mean."

He stirred inside her. "No details," he growled. "Not yet." It'd be damned humiliating if they started something he couldn't finish. He bent, and kissed her on the nose. "In fact, let me get rid of this thing." He eased out of her, and rolled off the bed.

When he returned from the bathroom she was under the covers, propped up on one elbow, watching him with a hungry glint in her eye. But when he slid in beside her she merely cuddled up against him, and put her head on his shoulder. He lay back with one hand behind his head, the other holding her close, and wondered how the hell he'd gotten so lucky as to get a second chance. The start of one, anyway.

Providing he could stay sober.

He knew that any shot with Allison depended on that. And he had five weeks to convince her he intended to change. Five weeks to turn this into a full-blown fresh start.

She rubbed her hand lightly over his chest. "Can I ask you something?"

"Ready to go again?"

She rolled on top of him, and drew her knees in to straddle his hips.

"I'm thinking that's a 'yes,'" he said, and his dick responded appropriately.

She sucked air. "That's very nice, what's happening down there. But there's something I'd like to know first. Something you already offered to tell me."

He fumbled the box of condoms and gave her a wary look. "O-kay."

She took the box from him, ripped off a packet and handed it back. Crawled up his chest and hovered over him, her hands on either side of his head, leaving his junk to feel a draft but putting her breasts within easy reach. Before he could take advantage of the situation, she asked her question.

"How did Danielle find out about us?"

He tightened his hands on her hips. "You didn't want to know before."

"I didn't want to hear anything else one of us might have to apologize for."

"You mean *you* didn't want to have to apologize. Again."

She cocked an eyebrow, and lowered herself to her elbows. "Is that truly the position you want to take?" She held the condom packet by the corner and dangled it over his face. "At this particular moment?"

"Touché." He lifted his hands to her hair, smoothed it behind her ears. "Danielle didn't want me to leave T&P." She tensed, and he lifted to give her a quick kiss. "And no, not for that reason. A few months before everything fell apart, Tackett assigned me as her mentor and I took it seriously. I guess she didn't want to lose that advantage. I gave her pointers, let her shadow me and sat in on her meetings with new clients to help her get things started off right. But when it came to handling accounts she was a disaster. Lost paperwork, missed appointments, shoddy pitches—which was why it shocked the hell out of me when I heard Tackett had given her your promotion. I suspect he was the recipient of her one successful pitch, and it likely involved getting naked."

Allison pushed upright, which put the moist heat of her center in direct contact with his groin. Instant hard-on. But he seemed to be the only who noticed. "If that's true then he's guilty of the same thing he punished me for."

"If you're looking for fair, you're looking in the wrong place. If you're looking for action..." He raised his hips.

A smile flirted with her lips and she did a little shimmy that had his fingers digging into her thighs. But she wasn't going to let him use that condom until she heard the rest of the story. He knew that because she said, "I'm not going to let you use this condom until I hear the rest of the story."

He forced his fingers to relax on her hips and hoped like hell it wouldn't take him long to get through this. Every last muscle was crying out for another release—a release that only she could provide.

"When I was packing up my office, Danielle was right there, begging me not to leave." Allison stiffened and Joe knew exactly what she was thinking— Allison herself hadn't begged him to do anything but understand why they were through. "I kept a photo of you in my desk. She knew what it meant, and must have decided that turning into an informant would make it that much easier for Tackett to justify keeping her on."

"I'm sorry I thought you told her." She was trembling, and it wasn't with passion.

"Come here."

She tipped forward again and he took her into his arms, rolled so she lay on her back. He leaned over her. "I'm the one who's sorry. Sorry I was shallow, narrow-minded and critical." He picked up her hand and pressed it to his mouth, kissed it again when he discovered the bandage he'd placed there earlier. "Sorry it took me so long to realize that you're the best thing that ever happened to me."

She squirmed. "Joe…"

"Maybe if I'd paid more attention, you'd have taken me up on my offer a year ago."

She shook her head and repeated his name, but this time it came out silent. He levered himself over top of her.

"I know. Not gonna happen. I just wanted you to know that I get it. That it was my fault."

She touched her fingers to his mouth, and when she spoke her voice was rusty. "I should have—"

He stopped her words with a kiss, forced a smile because he didn't want her to feel anything like the shame that was ripping through him.

Shake it off, man. He had more satisfying things to concentrate on.

"Now," he said, and proceeded to pat her down

as he worked his way toward the foot of the bed, his smile turning genuine when he heard her breathing quicken, watched her thighs fall open in anticipation. "Where did you hide that rubber?"

ALLISON WOKE SLOWLY, reluctant to leave behind a dream that involved chocolate mousse, whipped cream and Joe. She blinked into the dim light, at a wall that should have been a window, and realized she was hugging a pillow that wasn't hers, in a bed that smelled like Joe.

She'd slept at Joe's. She'd slept *with* Joe.

How long had it been since she'd made such a stellar decision?

She smiled, stretched her arms over her head and rolled, seeking the fireside warmth of Joe's naked body. But his side of the mattress lay empty. She hesitated, wondering what that meant. Damn that man, if he'd gone any farther than the bathroom she'd beat him with her unappeased libido.

"Good morning." The sound of his deep, gravelly voice tingled through her, and she responded with a *mmm* as she remembered all the delicious things he'd said using that voice. All the wicked things he'd demanded. But why was he so far away? She sat up in time to watch him zip himself into a faded pair of jeans.

"No," she moaned. Warm, sleepy morning sex was her absolute favorite. Did he really not remember?

She crawled to the foot of the bed and rose to her knees, put her hands on her hips.

"Why aren't you in this bed?"

"Trust me. It's exactly where I want to be." His eyes were hooded, his face still flushed with sleep. He lifted his hands, looked her over and gave his head a shake, as if he didn't know where to touch her first. Then he swooped, slid his fingers into her hair and pressed a hard, swift kiss to her upraised mouth. He smelled like pine trees and peaches. She wrapped her arms around his naked waist and pulled him close, moaned at the solid caress of his chest.

"Then why are you?" she murmured against his lips. "Leaving me?"

"Someone's at the door."

"Ignore them."

"I can't. Not the way they're pounding. There might be something wrong."

She heard it, then, a frantic rapping on the glass. "Marcus?"

"He knows how to get in if he needs to. No, the only guy I know who knocks like that is Snoozy."

She jerked away. "Mitzi's loose. He came to warn us." She saw the grin he wasn't trying very hard to hide, snatched up a pillow and smacked him. "It's not funny."

"It's also not true. The point I was trying to make is that it's a woman at the door."

"How do you know it's not true?" Then his words

registered and she groaned. "I bet it's Audrey. If she brought scrapple, do I have to eat it?"

He dragged a shirt over his head, leaned down and kissed her again. "Don't go anywhere."

As soon as he shut the door behind him she flopped back onto the bed and made a snow angel in the sheets, enjoying the stretch, anticipating the hard, hot length of him pressing down on her again. She wouldn't think about their limited time together. She'd only think about what they could do to take advantage of it.

But several minutes later, when Joe hadn't reappeared, she realized what she needed to be thinking about was getting dressed. He might need her help.

She put on a borrowed pair of boxers and a T-shirt, opened the bedroom door and heard an agitated Hazel Catlett. Had something happened to Hazel's sister? Or to Audrey? Allison rushed into the lobby, found Hazel shaking her finger while a gray schnauzer sniffed at Joe's bare feet.

Allison's gaze jerked from Hazel's suddenly self-satisfied smile to Joe's pained expression. "What's wrong?"

"Hazel's worried about STDs."

"I-I'm sorry?"

"You will be, honey, if you don't use a rubber." From the outer pocket of the battered brown purse tucked against her belly, Hazel pulled a bright blue strip of condoms. "For you."

Good grief. What was it with these women and

their purses? Allison shuddered to think what June might be carrying around in hers.

Hazel rattled the condoms at her. Allison felt her cheeks burn as she accepted the gift with a murmured thanks. The old woman reached into her purse again and Joe held up a hand, palm out.

"Give them all away and you won't have any left for yourself."

Allison glanced sideways at Joe and he countered with a wink.

"Oh, I'm not going for more rubbers, Joseph." Hazel showed off her cell phone then snapped a picture before Allison could scoot behind Joe. "In case no one believes you've gotten back together."

A long pause. The awkward kind. "We're not together," Allison said.

Hazel's arm dropped like her phone had just gained twenty pounds. "You mean you're just...together."

"That's right."

"Well." She recovered her smile. "At least you got over your grudges. Amazing what a little hot sex can do. Anyway, hon, I just came by to make sure you're still planning to come to my card party."

"Card party?"

Joe scratched his jaw. "I, um, forgot to tell you."

"Lucky I came by, then, isn't it? Lunch and canasta, that's the plan. What do you say, hon?"

Allison cast a desperate glance at Joe, who was grinning, damn him. "I really should be helping out around here...."

Hazel waved a dismissive hand. "He can spare you. And don't forget, Joseph, you have a meeting with Snoozy in about fifteen minutes. I saw him at the supermarket and he said he was coming over to talk to you about Mitzi's pen."

Damn it. Allison barely restrained a growl. So much for going back to bed.

Hazel snapped another picture, pointed at the strip of condoms and gave a thumbs-up, then left. But two seconds later she opened the door again and made kissing sounds. Allison gaped. Was she...did she actually think...was she trying to get them in the *mood?* Then the schnauzer hightailed it from behind the counter, a spitting and fluffed-up Tigerlily right on his tail. Oh. She'd forgotten her dog. Joe scooped up his cat, Hazel disappeared with Baby Blue and Allison buried her face in her hands. When Joe started to laugh she rounded on him.

"A card party? Really?"

With an unabashed grin he put down the cat, moved in close and nuzzled at her hair. "Are we okay, you and me?"

"We'd be better if you hadn't offered me up as a sacrifice to the gossip girls. *And* if we'd managed to have wake-up sex. Now we don't have time because Snoozy's on his way."

"And I need a shower." He backed her up against the counter, his hands roaming. "I haven't given you a crash course in plumbing yet. Want to see my fixtures?"

"These...fixtures. I guess you expect me to be properly impressed with them? *Ooh* and *ah* over them? Maybe even...fondle them?"

His breathing quickened. "Even fixtures like to be appreciated."

"Then by all means." She grinned. "Let's go get wet."

MARCUS GRIMACED AT the freshly tiled floor, now freshly spattered with primer. As was the toilet, and the front edge of the sink. Maybe he should have used that drop cloth after all. Who knew he'd suck at painting? Joe—make that *Meathead*—was going to kill him.

Except he wasn't. The dude wouldn't even yell at him. He'd give him that "yeah, you effed up but we can fix it" look, then either help him fix it, or leave him alone to figure it out himself.

He lowered the roller into the paint tray for a re-load. He should be grateful they'd left him alone. That they trusted him to have the place to himself. Allison had gone to some old lady lunch deal and Joe—*Meathead*—had taken Snoozy somewhere to talk someone else into making a pen for that python they'd found. Meathead said he didn't have the time.

He'd made time for Marcus, though.

He raised the roller and paused. Thought about that snake, hiding in the wall all these years. Just trying to survive. Wondering why she'd been abandoned. Why no one came for her. Thought about what it would have suffered if Marcus hadn't put out that fire those kids had started. Thought about the bigger, better, un-effin'-stoppable blaze he planned to set himself.

Thought about what it would mean to Joe.

What it would mean to *him*.

The emotion slammed him in the throat.

He struggled to breathe, and eventually registered that someone was standing behind him. He blinked, and inhaled, dropped the roller back into the tray and hoped that whoever it was had just walked in.

"The door was open," she said.

Shit. It had to be her.

He raised his head but didn't...*couldn't*...turn around. Couldn't even tell her to get the hell out. Not without giving away the fact that he'd been bawling like a baby a few seconds ago.

Except somehow she knew. She squeezed in at his side, slid a warm palm onto his shoulder and spoke in the kind of voice he'd have given anything to hear when he was a boy. But didn't deserve to hear as a man.

A man. Who was he kidding? Even Meathead called him a kid. He was trapped in between. And he longed for someone to pull him out of his purgatory.

"Hey," she said softly. "What's the matter? What can I do to help?"

He balled his empty fist. He wanted nothing more than to turn and curve down into her embrace, to let her hands and her lips and her whispered words stroke away his pain. But then he'd only want more, because she'd make him feel good. Somehow she'd sensed his need from the first time they met and for some godforsaken reason she wanted to answer it.

But he wasn't worthy of feeling good. She'd figure that out and sooner or later she'd want to know *why*. That's when he'd end up scaring the hell out of her.

Might as well do that now and get it over with.

"What *is* it with you?" He swung around to face her, the sudden violence of the motion startling her into backing out of the bathroom. Deliberately he followed, his jaw set and his gaze narrowed as he herded her toward the door, the paint roller clutched in both hands. "I mean, give me a *break*. I don't want to talk, I don't want to be friends and I sure as shit don't want to screw you. So why don't you go pester someone your own age?"

Liz had folded her arms across her chest and her eyes had dampened the moment he'd turned on her. But after that last crack, outrage replaced the hurt in her expression.

"Just how old do you think I am?" she demanded.

For the first time in…Jesus, how long?…he wanted to laugh. But weeks of homelessness had honed his ability to gauge a situation, and the people in it. Which meant he knew damned well that if he so much as smiled she'd kick him in the balls.

"I don't have time for this," he said instead, and stomped back into the bathroom. For a while she stood outside the door—he could hear the harsh rhythm of her breathing. He leaned over and flushed the toilet to drown out the sound. When she spoke again it was from the doorway to the motel room, and he had to strain to hear.

"Friends don't have to talk, or pretend, or even screw. Sometimes they can just *be*."

He knew the moment she'd left, and found himself resenting the smell of paint that overpowered her fresh summer scent, and aching from the longing her words had roused. He pressed too hard on the roller and the piece of shit broke, the handle gouging into the drywall.

"God *damn* it." His own breath came rough and fast, his muscles coiling as he battled the urge to attack the wall until there was nothing left of the handle. But he knew better than anyone—violence ruined lives. He launched into his breathing exercises and set the broken roller carefully aside. Yeah, he'd hoped to finish painting today. He'd wanted to show Joe—*Meathead,* damn it—that he was serious about earning his keep. About pulling a paycheck. About—

He sucked in a breath. What was he thinking? It didn't matter. None of it mattered. He'd gotten so caught up in pretending to care about fitting in that he'd forgotten why he was there in the first place.

He forced out a laugh as he replaced the lid on the can of primer. Funny, how an empty room could make a noise sound so hollow. With a final appraising glance at the hole in the wall, he went to scare up some spackle.

ALLISON SMILED WEAKLY at the plate Hazel set in front of her. "Um. I don't think I can—"

"Of course you can. Just one bite. That's all I ask." Hazel nudged the plate closer, smiling with lips the color of Pepto-Bismol. She turned and poked at her sister, who wore eye shadow in the very same shade—or maybe she'd just coated her eyelids with her sister's lipstick? "What were you thinking, telling her what was in it?"

"She asked, for cripes' sake."

"Oh, and I suppose if she *asked* how many times I did the nasty last week, you'd tell her that, too?"

Allison's fork clattered against her plate and she grabbed for her iced tea. Dear God in heaven.

"Hazel Mae. How could you think I'd do a thing like that?"

"Oh, I know you would, June Evelyn. You and that mouth of yours that's just as big as Pete Lowry's—"

"Trust me, ladies." Allison sang out, a little too loudly. "I wouldn't ask." *Cross my heart and hope to die.* She scanned the table, desperate for a reason to change the subject. Plump breadsticks, oversize dill pickles, cream-stuffed cannoli—the remains of their lunch didn't help a lick.

Oh. God. *No pun intended.*

She dropped her head into her hand.

"Even if you did ask," June sniffed. "I wouldn't tell you. Some things are simply not for public consumption. Right, Hazel?"

"Right." Hazel swung back around, picked up a fork and pushed it into Allison's hand. *Four times,* she mouthed. She waggled four fingers and winked. Over her shoulder June was alternately stabbing a finger at her sister and tracing a big fat zero in the air.

Allison peered down at the fork in her hand and considered stabbing herself in the eye.

"Maybe she's still hungry for real food." Audrey sat at the other end of Hazel's lace-draped dining room table, sorting the decks of cards they'd used in two hours' worth of canasta. Allison had learned how to play Pennies from Heaven and she'd loved every minute of it. Who'd have thought mild-mannered June Catlett had such a competitive streak? "Want some more ham, dear?"

Hazel answered before Allison could. "No, Audrey, she doesn't want ham, she wants to try my cake." She gave Allison an encouraging smile. "Go ahead, hon. Take a bite and tell us what you think."

It looked delicious. It smelled delicious. But instead of taking a bite of the Catlett sisters' most notorious recipe, Allison would almost rather listen—for the third time—to June catalog all of the advantages of living in Castle Creek while Hazel recounted Joe's good qualities—focusing on the physical ones, of course—and Audrey listed all of the reasons Joe needed a dedicated non-vegetarian as a life partner.

But there were times when politeness demanded sacrifice. Even when it meant eating cake made with canned sauerkraut and beer.

Allison drew in a breath, speared a forkful and closed her lips around it. Chewed. Moaned. Swallowed. And paused.

"Scrumptious," she pronounced, not bothering to hide her shock. "This is one of the best chocolate cakes I've ever had. If you hadn't told me what was in it, I'd never have guessed."

Hazel beamed, June clapped and Audrey got up to make herself a ham sandwich. Baby Blue followed, his hind parts wiggling.

"Glad you like it." Hazel patted Allison on the shoulder and refilled her tea. "You'll have to learn to make it for Joe. It's one of his favorites."

"Hazel." Allison set down her fork. "You have to understand that Joe and I aren't—"

"Who is that, hon? Standing next to your car?" Hazel was peering through the lace curtains, the afternoon sun catching the cut-glass pitcher, backlighting the slices of lemon floating in the tea.

Allison's stomach fell into a slow tumble. *Joe.* But of course that didn't make sense—Hazel would recognize Joe. Even in a shirt.

She did her best to ignore a hot blast of longing, pushed back her chair and joined Hazel at the window. A lean, twenty-something guy stood at her front bumper, head bent, thumbs busily tapping at the device cradled in his hands. The combination of crisp white shirt, tie, close-cropped hair and earnest posture made him look like a salesman. Or a church member sent forth to recruit for the congregation.

But Allison knew that clean-cut appearance hid all kinds of corrupt.

Sammy.

CHAPTER THIRTEEN

OH, GOD. How had Sammy tracked her down?

Why had he tracked her down?

The nerves in her stomach morphed from the turned-on kind to the "I'm about to lose my lunch" kind.

June came up behind them. "He looks lost."

Audrey followed, swiping at the mayonnaise on her chin. "He looks underfed."

"Do you know him, hon?" Hazel's gaze was sharp.

Allison nodded. "He's from D.C." She swiped her palms down the front of her pants and attempted an unconcerned smile. "I'll go see what he wants."

She half expected Hazel to demand an introduction. Luckily all three ladies seemed more than willing to wait inside. And watch from the window, no doubt.

"I'll be right back."

She pushed her hands into her pockets and strolled down the driveway, determined not to give the bastard the satisfaction of seeing her fingers shake. In her right pocket she found the good-luck charm she'd forgotten about—the piece of green glass she'd plucked from the beach. Some luck, since the darned thing seemed to have the power of summoning her least favorite person in the world—first over the phone, and now in person.

Next time she was near the lake she'd stop and toss the worthless charm into the water.

When Sammy heard her coming he snapped his phone shut and looked up, the lack of expression on his face more daunting than any sneer. The driver's side door of a black Mercedes parked across the street opened. A short, powerfully built man stepped out and assumed the bodyguard stance—face impassive, legs spread, hands folded at his belt.

Allison's body shook for one brief, spine-rattling moment. She knew Sammy never traveled anywhere without Mr. Muscle, but the deliberate show of force unnerved her. Especially since rumor had it that Sammy was more than capable of delivering his own "messages." And enjoyed doing so.

Inside her pockets her hands grew slick. Then she thought of her mother at the mercy of these bullies and anger surged. The moment Mr. Muscle stepped away from that Mercedes, she'd start screaming. The image of three old ladies flogging him with frying pans cheered her no end.

Sammy took off his sunglasses and ran his free hand slowly down his tie, his gaze locked deliberately on Allison's chest. "Aren't you going to ask how I found you?"

"I don't care how you found me." That Sammy had approached her at Hazel's house made Allison so angry she wanted to lock him in the bathroom with Mitzi. A week should do it. "And no, I don't know why you're here. The next payment's not due for another two weeks. I'll be back in D.C. by then. I told you that."

"The next payment's due now."

His words punched the air from her lungs. She fell back a step, yanking her hands from her pockets and curling her fingers into fists. His driver watched, irritatingly serene.

"But…we had an agreement."

Sammy shrugged and turned his attention back to his BlackBerry. Allison blinked in the afternoon sun, feeling suddenly trapped and despairing, resenting the muted shrieks and laughter of children splashing in a nearby pool, the distant drone of a plane passing slowly overhead.

"You can't renege on our agreement. How are you going to make money if no one trusts you enough to borrow it?" She heard the pleading in her voice and despised herself for it. She sounded like her mother.

I need some cash, Allie girl. Just enough to break even. I know things are tight but all it takes is one big win. Please don't let me down.

"That old argument? Won't work this time. People need money. When you're desperate you don't care so much how you get it."

Her panic mounted. "I don't get paid for another week."

"Not my problem."

The squeal of brakes, the growl of an engine and a familiar blue pickup charged down the street. Allison gave an inward moan and aimed a glare at the house. All three women stood in the window. Two of them held plates of cake. The third held up her cell phone—no doubt in camera mode.

Mr. Muscle crossed the street and stood beside Sammy, arms flexed at his sides, jacket hanging open. Dear God, he didn't plan to pull a gun, did he?

Sammy straightened his tie. "This guy better not be trouble, blondie."

"Just give me a minute. I'll take care of this." Allison hurried over to the truck, but not in time to stop Joe from getting out. She pressed a hand to his chest. He didn't even look at her. He yanked off his shades and glared over her shoulder at Sammy and Mr. Muscle.

"What the hell is going on here?"

"I'm sorry Hazel called you. You need to leave. You're going to make things worse."

He looked down at her, the steel in his jaw and the frost in his eyes making him seem far less cuddly than Mr. Muscle. "Did they threaten you?"

"No." Not yet, anyway. "They're here for a, uh, business meeting. You can go, Joe. Please."

It would be a gross understatement to call his glance incredulous. "No way in hell I'm leaving you here." He squinted over her shoulder and raised his voice. "You two don't have anything better to do than play bully?"

Allison spoke through gritted teeth. "You. Are. Not. Helping."

He stepped around her. "What's the deal here?"

"The *deal* doesn't concern you." Sammy took off his shades, polished them on his tie and slid them back into place. "And this isn't helping her old lady any."

Joe stiffened, and Allison knew he'd noticed the same thing she had. He turned his back to Sammy and spoke in a low voice.

"What does he want?"

"An early payment."

"You don't have it." She shook her head and he exhaled. "Borrow from me. Against the signing bonus."

"What if that falls through?"

"It won't."

"But if it does I'll owe you instead of him."

"Wouldn't that be an improvement?"

"It wouldn't be anything more than a shift in power."

His head went back and his nostrils flared. "And you think I'd take advantage of that?" He cut off her reply with a string of swear words. "This control thing is getting out of hand. You need to let go."

"*You* need to let me handle this." She turned her back on his fury, faced a smirking Sammy and a somnolent Mr. Muscle. "You can threaten all you want, but I can't give what I don't have."

Sammy smiled, and jerked his chin at a spot up the

street, away from the others. "This is between you and me, blondie. Let's go work it out."

That's when she got it. He'd hoped to back her into a corner so she'd sleep with him. The bastard wouldn't take no for an answer.

Not only was she not following him anywhere, but if she didn't get rid of him soon, Joe would catch on and raise his hostile factor, and Mr. Muscle would pull his gun, and Hazel would call 9-1-1, and Allison really would get booted out of Castle Creek.

Though she shouldn't care. She was leaving in a week, anyway.

"That's not an option," she said coldly.

The loan shark popped a shoulder. "I'm not leaving empty-handed."

"You work with your uncle, right?" Joe's voice was deceptively smooth.

Sammy scowled. "It's a family business. So what?"

"Does he know you're on drugs?"

Silence. Sammy slitted his eyes and Allison tensed. No one moved. Sammy and Joe stared each other down. Then Sammy turned his head and spit, and glared at Allison.

"Better not be one minute late with that payment, bitch."

Joe surged forward. "*What* did you call her?"

Mr. Muscle finally made his move. But instead of reaching for his gun, he wheeled around and headed for the car. Sammy watched over his shoulder and when he turned back, a wariness had crept into his expression. With a less-than-subtle gesture he cracked a few knuckles, leered at Allison and strode after his driver. As the Mercedes disappeared down the street, Allison could hear Hazel and company cheering at the window.

But the trouble was far from over.

She grabbed Joe's arm and hauled him behind a spruce tree. "Thank you for coming to my defense," she said tightly. "But for the last time, I can't let you pay him off. Can't this be about honoring me instead of your stupid pride?"

"My *pride?*"

"All right, then, your need to make amends, or… You know what? It doesn't matter why you're so determined to have your own way because you're not going to get it. This is my problem. Not yours."

"Do you hear what you're saying? It's not your problem. It's your mother's problem. And I'm sorry, but I'm determined to have my own way so I can keep your ass out of danger."

"At my mother's expense."

He shook his head and turned away, slapped at the branches of the spruce. The smell of Christmas wafted past them. "The hell of it is, you're telling yourself it's all about doing the right thing. About paying your mother back for looking out for you. Which, by the way, is what parents are supposed to do. But the real reason isn't so admirable, is it?"

"What are you talking about?"

"You're not taking responsibility, you're hiding from it."

She folded her arms. This ought to be good.

"You have an instant out," he continued. "A built-in excuse for not making a decision about us."

She dropped her arms. "I have made a decision. *We* made a decision. We said we'd take advantage of the five weeks we have together. Afterward I'll be staying in D.C. and you'll be coming back here."

"*You* said that, not me. Think about it, Allison. Letting me pay off that loan means cutting the ties to not only your mother, but your job. Which would leave you with just one last reason for not giving us a second chance—the city you supposedly don't want to leave behind." He put his hands on his hips and dropped his chin to his chest. When he lifted his head again his face radiated a grave intensity. "Tell me you haven't fallen in love with Castle Creek."

It took Allison several seconds to realize she'd stopped breathing. For a second there she thought he'd figured her out. Yes, she'd fallen in love. And not only with the town. She'd known that even before she'd jumped Joe's bones.

But nothing had changed. Nothing except that in a month, when he left D.C., he'd be taking her heart with him this time.

She backed away, her heels catching in the thick grass. "You're making this all about you. Just like before."

"No, Al. I'm trying to make this about us."

"By conveniently forgetting the years I've dedicated to T&P?"

"And how much joy have they brought you? Judas Priest, you can't tell me you find it fulfilling, playing these asinine games with Tackett. I'm not asking you to give up your career. I'm asking you to give up T&P. Start your own firm. Offer your services online. I could help you."

"It's not that easy."

"It is if you want it badly enough."

She was shaking her head, her chin traveling from left to right. What was he trying to do to her? They'd *talked* about this. "You're not being fair."

"Fair? How can you expect me to be fair when I'm fighting for—" He broke off, and scrubbed a hand over his face. "You're not doing your mother any favors, Al. As long as *you* keep paying the consequences, she's going to keep racking them up."

"You're right. She's *my* mother. So back off."

"Are you trying to get her hurt? Or worse?"

A violent tremor of outrage jarred Allison's bones and she hugged herself to keep those bones from crumbling to the ground. "You are a son of a bitch. And I'm going back inside."

She swung around and plowed straight into the spruce tree. With Joe's help she untangled herself from the branches, then shook her elbow free of his grip and veered toward the front door. He didn't try to stop her. Hazel met her on the stoop, took one look at her face and tugged her inside for a group hug.

FOR THE LONGEST while Joe sat in his truck and stared at the door to #2. He had some heavy-duty groveling to do. He didn't begrudge Allison the groveling—she'd more than earned it. But he couldn't help wondering if they'd ever stop hurting each other long enough to enjoy more than a couple hours' togetherness at a time.

'Course he already knew the answer to that. She'd made it more than clear—their relationship was temporary. Until he accepted that, things would continue to be tense.

Little did she know he had no intention of accepting it.

He scooped up the bag he'd tossed in the passenger seat and got out of the truck. He'd left Marcus painting the bathroom in #4—might as well check on him before braving Allison's wrath.

Not that he was scared.

Much.

He moved toward the bathroom, stopped in the doorway just as Marcus was finishing up a patch on the wall.

"Hey, man. What's up?"

The way Marcus jumped, anyone would think he'd been caught stealing the tile off the wall. Poor guy would have backed into the corner if there weren't a shower in the way. "I leaned too hard on the roller," he said, his voice gruff, and though he met Joe's gaze squarely, Joe could tell he didn't want to.

Sadness, rage, helplessness. Joe wasn't sure how to handle the feelings that crowded in on him whenever he was with this kid. And if he couldn't handle his own feelings, how the hell was he supposed to handle Marcus's?

He leaned against the doorjamb, and chose his words carefully. "You figured I'd be mad because you made a mistake. Thought maybe I'd even want to hit you. Marcus, you know what I'd really like to do? I'd really like to beat the shit out of the person who made you think that way." First Allison's father, and now Marcus's…whatever. What the hell was wrong with people?

Marcus was staring at him. Joe recognized the emotions crossing his face like the stages of grief. An automatic need to deny, guilt at not being able to hide the truth, anger at Joe for figuring it out, hope… that Joe might be different.

It was the hope that put a chokehold on Joe. He swallowed against it.

"Anyway. It's all cool. Accidents happen." He made a point of checking out the paint job, ran his fingers over the patch Marcus had sanded. "This looks great. Nice job."

"Thanks," Marcus said, and cleared his throat. "I'll paint it later. After it's dry."

"I have some patching of my own to do." Joe grimaced. "Guess I'd better get to it."

"Thought I heard a door slam earlier…."

Joe watched Marcus struggle with forming a question and took pity on him. "I tried to tell Allison what to do because I'm worried about her. I could have been more diplomatic."

"So what're you going to do?"

"Apologize. Seventeen times, if I have to. Whatever it takes to convince us both I deserve her."

Marcus's head came up sharply. "You don't think you deserve her?"

"She's...special."

"Yeah."

"You see it, too?"

"What? Yeah. Her, too. I mean...yeah, I do. See it." He scrubbed his fingers through his spiky hair and very carefully did *not* look Joe in the eye.

Joe snatched up the shopping bag. "Well, I better get to it. Any ideas for dinner tonight?"

"Salmon okay?"

"Yeah, great. And, hey, I'm here if you want to talk about...anything."

Marcus gave a stiff nod. But Joe needed him to know he wasn't just feeding him a line.

"I'm serious. I'd show you how serious by giving you a hug but I don't want to end up with my balls in my throat. So how about we bump knuckles instead?"

"Why do you trust me?" Marcus asked suddenly.

Joe paused. "You haven't given me a reason not to. In fact, that caretaker job I mentioned? It's yours if you want it. Think about it. Let me know."

But the kid didn't look interested. He looked... pained.

All that talk of deserving. Did Marcus think he didn't deserve the job? Or kindness in general?

Joe hoped the kid would hang around. So Joe

would get the chance to convince him he deserved a hell of a lot more.

He was almost at the door when Marcus said his name. Had he decided about the job? Or maybe he just wanted to talk. Joe hid his impatience to get to Allison and turned around.

"What can I do for you, kid?"

Marcus drew himself up. "I'm not a kid."

No. Joe had a feeling he'd never had that luxury. "Point taken. So what's up?"

"Mind if I take the truck for a bit?"

So this was what it felt like to be a dad. Despite—or maybe because of—Marcus's insistence that he was a man, Joe was careful not to smile as he dug his keys out of his pocket and tossed them over.

"She's all yours."

Marcus nodded his thanks and turned away, muttering something that sounded a lot like, "I wish."

Seconds later, Joe hesitated in front of #2. He'd thought about what to say to Allison, had even rehearsed a decent mix of explanation and self-reproach. But he had a feeling that once she let him in—if she let him in—he'd end up on his knees, begging her forgiveness. Five weeks was short enough. She couldn't end things now.

Could she?

He licked his lips and tasted desperation. Glanced toward his office, and the emergency stash he hadn't been able to bring himself to dump. He hadn't thought about taking a drink since the day before. Not much, anyway.

One drink, for courage, and he'd get right back on the wagon. One drink, to give him the confidence to fix what he'd broken.

Hell, he'd sailed through the past twenty-four hours. What harm could one whiskey do?

MARCUS KNEW BETTER than to wear his hoodie into the diner. The old ladies would squeal and flap their hands and the old men would throw themselves into cardiac arrest trying to take him down. Someone would call the cops and the whole ugly truth would come out. He'd be screwed.

Maybe he was being paranoid. He hadn't shown his face around Castle Creek in a decade. But being paranoid had protected his ass in jail. In more ways than one.

Bottom line was, Cal could recognize him. Was it worth the risk?

He thought of what Joe had done for him. Allison, too. And remembered the hurt in Liz's big blue eyes when he'd made it clear he had no interest in being friends.

Yeah. It was worth it.

Walking into the diner was odd as hell. Everything looked the same, just...shinier. The floor was new. Same with some of the stuff on the counters. And the stools were red and yellow, now—when he was a kid they'd been covered in turquoise, and had a lot of rips. What hadn't changed was the noise—muddled conversations, silverware clacking and the squeak of the waitress's shoes as she hurried across the floor. And the smell. He'd always associated cinnamon with brightness and plenty.

And escape.

"Hey. You're not gonna be sick, are you?" A skinny chick with pale skin and pretty brown hair watched him from behind the counter, her eyes heavy with suspicion. She threw out her right arm, index finger pointed. "Men's room is that way, if you think you're gonna hurl. Olivia just finished mopping, so if you mess up the floor it'll be my turn to clean it up."

"I'm okay." Except he was standing there gawking like an asshole where anyone could see him. His body flushed hot and he moved up behind the register, snuck a glance at the pass-thru that opened into the kitchen. Someone was moving around back there, but it wasn't Cal.

Marcus exhaled, and a tingling of undeserved relief swept through his gut. He'd just told Joe he wasn't a kid, and here he was acting exactly like one.

He tugged his wallet free of his back pocket, and pulled out one of the twenties Joe had fronted him. Resisted the urge to look around and see if anyone was watching.

"Got any cinnamon rolls?"

The girl eyed him warily, as if expecting at any moment he'd spew all over the counter. "It's a little late in the day for those," she said, in a tone that hinted he should have known. "We usually sell out by lunch and it's almost time for the dinner crowd. But let me see if there are any in the back." She turned away, then spun back, her cheeks suddenly pink. "You that guy who's staying at Joe's?"

Shit. That was the thing about life in a small town—even if *you* didn't know what you were doing, someone else always did.

When he gave her a reluctant nod, she pushed her shoulders out of their slouch and straightened her black polo shirt. She glanced nervously at the diner door, as if talking about Joe might make him magically appear.

"You may not have a choice," she warned. "I mean, between regular and special. How many you want?"

He'd meant to buy three. One each for Allison and Joe, as a small token of thanks. And one for Liz Early, as a weak-ass apology. But why not get one for himself, too? He looked down at the bill in his hand, and thought about what he planned to do to the man who'd given it to him.

Had planned to do.

He set the bill on the counter and carefully smoothed it out. "I'll take three," he said softly. The girl turned toward the kitchen. "What's the difference, anyway?" he asked. "Between regular and special?"

She stopped herself mid eye-roll, the color in her cheeks going from pink to red. "Special means heart-shaped."

An image of Liz marched across his mind. He deserved that eye roll. "Just regular."

She shrugged. "I'll check."

Five minutes later, Marcus left the diner with a sweet-smelling box and strict instructions from the girl—Rachel, she said her name was—to make sure Joe knew she'd risked her entire hospitality career by raiding Cal's private cinnamon roll stash. Marcus shook his head. Joe certainly had a knack for inspiring devotion.

He set the box on the passenger seat of Joe's truck and was headed for the driver's side—thankful he'd made it in and out of the diner without being recognized, and disgusted with himself for taking the risk in the first place—when he heard a slapping sound, followed by a frustrated grunt. He looked around. A man knelt at the front bumper of a cherry-red compact, scooping up papers from the pavement. Marcus turned back to the truck. The dude seemed to have it under control.

Then a breeze kicked up and he heard the ominous rustle and flutter as papers scattered. The man swore. Marcus gritted his teeth and turned to help. What was one minute more? He joined the man in the chase for what looked like spreadsheets. Invoices. Tax documents.

Oh, shit.

He straightened his stack as best he could and thrust it at the gray-haired man, his body angled away.

"Here you go," he said gruffly, and as soon as the man accepted the papers he started for the truck.

"Wait, I want to thank you." Calvin Ames stepped in front of him, his expression harried but friendly. "It's not often—" He frowned, his gaze roving over Marcus's face, his eyes growing distant as he struggled to place him. Marcus sighed. Cal paled.

"Marcus? Marcus Watts? Is that you?"

Busted.

ALLISON HAD HER laptop open and her eyes closed when the knock came. She jolted upright and stared at the door, half expecting Joe to let himself in. Or try to, anyway. This time she'd thrown the bolt.

She stood, and wiped her sweaty palms on the seat of her jeans. Another knock. Should she let him in?

Grow up, Allie. She couldn't hide out in her room forever. He may be an arrogant so-and-so, but they did have a deal.

Besides, there was always the chance he'd come to apologize. And even if he hadn't, it was ridiculous to stay in here and sulk. She was hungry. She'd missed dinner.

Oh, who was she kidding, she'd missed *him*.

She ran her hands through her hair and opened the door. And blinked.

"Marcus."

He held a white bakery box, his shoulders hunched over it to protect it from the slow drizzle that had already created puddles in the parking lot. When had it started to rain? A gust of air pushed the cool mist against her and she stepped back.

"Come on in."

He set the box on the table and glanced around the room. "Joe around?"

"I thought he was with you." But apparently he was practicing his own avoidance techniques.

Marcus shook his head. "The office is dark. I didn't want to knock." Red streaked his cheeks. "Guess I shouldn't have come here, either, but—"

"It's okay. As you can see, you didn't interrupt anything." She closed her laptop and set it aside, perched on the edge of the bed and gestured for Marcus to take a chair. He sat, and fingered a corner of the bakery box.

"So your…talk didn't go well?" he ventured.

"What talk?"

"With Joe."

Her stomach reacted with a sour flip. She yanked a pillow free of the covers and curled it into her lap. "I haven't seen Joe since we got back from Hazel's and he said he had some errands to run. He told you he was coming to see me?"

"To apologize."

To apologize. She breathed a little easier. "I'm sorry he's not here, Marcus. He must have arranged a ride somewhere. Did you need him for something important?"

"I was hoping to talk to you."

"To both of us? Together?"

"Just you."

"Oh. Sure." She clasped her hands on top of the pillow and smiled. "What's up?" He didn't answer right away. He swallowed, then swallowed again, and when he looked over at her, his eyes were haunted.

"What's wrong?" she asked quietly.

He stood, shoved his hands in his pockets and wandered over to the door. "I used to live here," he finally said. "A long time ago."

Whatever she'd expected to hear, that wasn't it. "Do you still have family in Castle Creek?" Was that why he'd come? To reconcile with his family, maybe?

"You don't understand. I used to live *here*. My stepfather owned the motel. He—" Marcus looked down at the carpet and gripped at his hips.

Oh, God. Oh, no. "That little boy," she whispered. "That was *you?*" He nodded, and her heart squeezed as tight as the hands she'd fisted around the pillow. "Oh, Marcus. I'm so sorry."

"I survived," he said stiffly, and raised his head. "I'm not telling you so you'll feel sorry for me."

"I know. Of course not. Why are you telling me?"

He nodded at the box on the table. "Cal recognized me when I was at the diner, and I need to tell Joe before he does."

"Marcus, I…I can't imagine what you went through. But you were a child. What happened wasn't your fault. You don't have to be ashamed to tell Joe who you are."

Inwardly she cringed. Easy for her to say. But what else could she offer him?

"It's tough to talk about. And...there's more."

But he didn't say what "more" was, and there was no way she'd push him. "Do you want me to be there when you tell him?" she asked gently.

"I just wanted..." He jerked his shoulders up in a sad little shrug. "I don't know, the chance to practice saying it out loud."

"Did your stepfather go to jail?"

"Yeah. He died of liver cancer after he got out."

"Where did you go after they arrested him?"

"I left first, then they arrested him." Hands still in his pockets, he leaned back against the door. He held her gaze, an almost feral glint in his. "One of the motel regulars decided to 'rescue' me. He gave my stepfather five thousand dollars and took me home. Wasn't much of a rescue, but at least I wasn't passed around anymore."

Dear God in heaven.

A shocked, solemn silence gathered in the room, Marcus's revelations mocked by the homey scent of cinnamon wafting from the box on the table. Allison's muscles started to ache and she realized she was bent over the pillow, and it was damp with tears she hadn't even known she'd shed. Slowly she sat up, while Marcus paced in front of the dresser. Rehearsing the rest of it.

She wasn't sure she wanted to hear any more.

"When I was fourteen I ran away from the guy

who bought me," Marcus continued. "I lied about my age and got a job at a restaurant. I'm only telling you all this so you'll understand."

"Understand what?"

He stopped and faced her, that gleam in his eyes turning defiant. "Why I came back to burn down the motel."

She gaped. He nodded.

"Since I was eight years old I've dreamed of lighting that match. Of standing back and watching this place burn, room by room, the heat searing my face, the flames destroying what destroyed me. It's what kept me going. What I lived for. Imagine my surprise when I finally make my way back here and instead of an abandoned building, I find someone's pet project. I find Joe." He shot her a look that begged her understanding. "I checked. To see if he had insurance."

Slowly she pushed to her feet, crossed the room and pulled him into a hug. He resisted at first, then his body loosened and he wrapped his arms around her. They stood like that for a long while, until Marcus whispered, "He'll hate me."

Gently she freed herself. "You should know better than that."

His throat worked. "I'll tell him. I will. I'm just... not ready. You won't tell him, will you?"

"I promise."

"Thank you. For listening."

"Anytime." She bit at the inside of her cheek. That

wasn't true, was it? She wouldn't be in Castle Creek much longer. And she'd never expected that to make her heart ache.

MARCUS STEPPED OUT of Allison's room and into full-fledged rain. The gutters rattled and pinged under the onslaught and despite the overhang, the sidewalk kicked up the wet and his clothes were damp in no time. But he didn't mind. He felt lighter, freer, after talking to Allison. Meathead was one lucky guy.

If he ever got his head out of his ass.

Where was he, anyway? And why had he blown off that apology?

Marcus looked toward the office. It was hard to tell, what with the rain reflecting the beams from the security lights, but it looked like Joe still hadn't gotten back from wherever he'd disappeared to. But since he and Allison were both starving, he'd offered to try the lobby door, see if he could get in to cook up that salmon. Cinnamon rolls just wouldn't cut it for dinner.

He pulled at the handle and the door swung open. *Yes.* But before he could step inside, Tigerlily darted outside. She recoiled at the damp, then scampered up the sidewalk, toward the woods.

Shit. Shit, shit, shit. "Here, kitty." Where the hell had she gone? He squinted through the rain and caught a flash of orange at the tree line. The moment he stepped off the sidewalk, he was soaked through.

"That's it," he yelled. "No salmon for you."

He lost track of time as he slogged along the tree line, calling the cat's name. No sign of her. Screw it. He'd have to ask Allison for help. As he was turning back to the motel, someone behind him let loose a bellow and jumped him. Marcus landed face-first in the sodden grass and pain exploded in his jaw. His attacker straddled him and started punching, shouting like a crazy man.

"I know what you're up to, you son of a bitch. Either get your ass out of here right now or I'll *kill* you! Understand me?"

Marcus threw an elbow into the guy's gut and rolled out from under him. He followed, still shouting, still punching, then his hands went for Marcus's throat. Marcus shook his head, his vision blurred by the stinging rain and the blood seeping from a cut above his eye. He reared up with a head butt, going for the guy's nose—caught his cheekbone instead. As the guy recoiled, Marcus aimed a punch at his jaw and he slumped to the ground, groaning.

Marcus staggered to his feet, tasting blood and ready to kick more ass before calling the sheriff. What the hell? Where had this asshole *come* from? The guy on the ground mumbled something, and Marcus went still. Then he put a boot to his shoulder and pushed, rolled the guy onto his back.

Shit.

It was Joe.

CHAPTER FOURTEEN

JOE LAY IN BED, too afraid to move. The moment he opened his eyes, or raised his head or even swallowed, he'd start heaving and he'd never stop. His stomach hovered on the hairy edge of Armageddon, like when he was seven years old and ate four hot dogs and two ice cream cones before riding the Tilt-A-Whirl. The aftereffects hadn't been pretty.

Still, he had to move eventually. He had to take a piss. And there was a heavy, disturbing sensation pressing at him from all directions. Telling him he had something to take care of. Something that couldn't wait.

Something unpleasant.

Like the taste in his mouth.

Slowly, cautiously, he cracked open one eye. Found the room blessedly dim. Maybe he wouldn't have to clean puke up off the carpet after all. He blinked his eyes to chase away the haze and raised a palm to his throbbing head. What the hell had he been thinking, dipping back into the whiskey like that? Dipping? Hell, he'd dived in. And after he'd told her he was going to quit.

Allison.

He imagined the disappointment on her face and groaned. Then groaned again, when the noise ricocheted like a bullet inside his brain.

It took him a while, but he finally managed to push to his feet and stagger his way to the bathroom, where he dry-heaved for several minutes, then downed four ibuprofen and two glasses of water. He felt better when he stepped under the hot spray of the shower— until the water hit his hands. He held his knuckles up to his face, saw the shredded skin and fell back against the shower wall.

Ten minutes later he found Allison yanking paneling in #6. He stepped in between her and the wall and the misery in her expression nearly sent him to his knees.

"What did I do?"

She lowered her mask. "You attacked Marcus," she said quietly.

"I *what*?" Judas Priest. He looked down at his hands, then back up at Allison. *"Why?"*

With slow, deliberate motions, she set aside her tools and removed her goggles. "Our theory is that you mistook him for someone sent by Sammy." Her voice shook. His throat tightened.

"Is he all right?"

Her shrug was anything but casual. "I haven't seen him since last night. He helped me get you inside and into bed, then disappeared." She answered his unspoken question. "He was outside when you jumped him."

"Did I hurt him?"

"You hurt all of us," she whispered. "Yourself included."

He nodded, wanting to reach out but afraid she'd only flinch. "I—I don't know what to say." What *could* he say? He rolled the fingers of his right hand into a fist, watched the blood ooze and felt like his soul was bleeding.

"I have to find him." He looked up and into her eyes, hating what he'd done. What he'd become. "Allison. After I've talked to Marcus, will you…can I…"

"I'll be here," she said. He heard what she didn't say, too. *Because I wasn't before.* But damn it, he didn't want to be somebody's good deed.

He'd wanted so much for her to be a part of the reno. To see the before and after. Experience the difference for herself.

Right now, she was probably thinking the before and after looked pretty much the same.

IT TOOK JOE twenty minutes to find it. A cloudless blue sky mocked from high overhead and birds chided loudly as he tromped through the woods behind the motel. The smell of damp pine and his own whiskey-soaked sweat rose up around him. With each stick that snapped under his boots the pain in his head spiked, and every time he tipped his head back to scan the treetops, his neck muscles screamed.

But it was the dread that begged him to stop, that tempted him to sink to his knees and sob like no man had a right to.

It scared the hell out of him, what he might have done to Marcus.

When he spotted a weather-beaten wooden rung nailed to a tree trunk, he knew he'd found it. He craned his neck. The rungs led up to a small shelter he recognized as a deer stand. Looked to be in pretty good shape, too, considering it must have been there a decade or two. He inhaled and hoped he wasn't going to have to climb up to that thing. With the shape he was in—

"I'm here."

He swung around. Marcus watched him from just outside the woods. He stood with his shoulders in a slight hunch, his arms hanging stiffly at his sides. He had a bandage above his left eye and a nasty bruise on his jaw. Joe felt his hands start to shake. Marcus shook his head.

"It's humiliating," he said.

Joe swallowed thickly. "I know. I know, man, and I'm sorry. I can't even—"

"Not you. Me. The fact that you expected to find me here. Hiding in the woods, like a scared little kid. The worst of it is, you were right."

"You have every reason to keep your distance, Marcus. You okay?" He nodded and Joe rubbed a hand over his face, wincing as his fingers found the bruise on his cheekbone. Slowly he made his way back to the field, and looked Marcus in the eye when he reached him. "I won't make any excuses. I screwed up."

"So did I," Marcus said roughly. "I broke my promise."

"Promise?"

"I promised myself a long time ago I'd never hit anyone in anger again."

"Marcus, it was self-defense, man. What, you were supposed to just let me beat on you? And speaking of promises—" His breath snagged on an inhale, and he had to work to get the words past the hot ball of shame blocking his throat. "I promised you'd be safe from me. I broke that pledge all to hell."

Marcus squared his shoulders. "I know. And...I'm not sure I can hang around and wait for it to happen again."

Joe felt the cold, hard clutch of panic, deep in his gut. Why did he *do* this? Why did he ruin every good thing he had in his life?

"I understand," he managed. "However you need to handle this, man."

Marcus opened his mouth, closed it, looked away.

"Tell me," Joe said. "I need to hear it."

The kid hesitated then shook his head. "It's okay to ask for help," is what he finally came out with, then, "I need to find the cat."

Joe watched him walk away. All the spackle in the world wouldn't help him fix what he'd just broken.

HE NEVER DID get back to Allison. After Marcus walked away, Joe retrieved his keys, set a dish of cat food on the sidewalk and headed for the Pennsylvania Turnpike. Other than the two times he stopped for coffee and a restroom break, he spent the day in his truck. He drove for hours. The rumble of the pavement beneath his tires alternately soothed and scolded him. When it got dark and he got sleepy he rolled down his windows. The relentless rush of cool air stung his cheeks and burned his throat.

He ranted. Begged. Grieved. Prayed.

And realized.

He needed help. He didn't want to hurt himself or anyone else anymore. And he wanted Allison in his life more than he wanted to drink. He just didn't know how to make that happen.

When he remembered the brochure June had given him what seemed a lifetime ago, he turned the truck around and headed home.

ALLISON POURED HERSELF another cup of coffee and peered out the kitchen window. She had work to do—all that paneling wouldn't take itself down, and the electrician was supposed to come tomorrow to do the rewiring—but it was hard to feel motivated.

Joe's apartment was quiet. Too quiet. Marcus had headed out first thing, to pick up a special order of tile from some warehouse in Buffalo. At least he'd returned to his room in the motel. Meanwhile, poor

Tigerlily hadn't found her way home yet. Neither had Joe.

But he'd called the night before to let her know he was okay. Of course, she could tell from the unsteady timbre of his voice that he wasn't anywhere close to being okay. Neither was Marcus. Since Joe took off, Marcus had been moodier than usual, and Allison couldn't help wondering if he regretted confiding in her. If he was tempted to torch the place after all.

She knew *she* was.

Joe had her worried, but he also had her angry. After that scene at Hazel's he'd supposedly meant to apologize but went on a bender instead. And rather than talking with her about *that,* like he'd said he would, he'd decided to drive across the country.

Now she was feeling inspired to pick up a hammer.

Her stomach grumbled. Breakfast first, demolition second. When was the last time she'd eaten? She sipped at her coffee and opened the refrigerator door, stared with disinterest at the eggs and fruit inside. Then her glance slid sideways, to the box on the table. The bakery box Marcus had left behind in her room. The box that smelled like cinnamon.

She shut the refrigerator door and went on the hunt for a fork.

JOE INHALED, COUNTED to ten, exhaled and knocked on Allison's door. It took her a few minutes to answer. When she did, and he got a load of her red, swollen eyes and messy hair, his belly went sour.

"Shit."

"As in, I look like?"

"As in, I feel like."

"I'm glad. And by the way? Now's not a good time." She trudged to the bathroom. He heard her fill a glass with water, and the telltale *snick* of a cap being popped from a bottle of pain relievers. *Damn* it. He shut the door behind him.

"You okay?"

"No, I'm not okay," she snapped from inside the bathroom. "I'm worried and angry and sad and I just ate three of Cal's cinnamon rolls."

"In one sitting?"

She came out of the bathroom, glaring, and jabbed a finger at the door. He held up a hand.

"I'll leave you alone, but first I need to apologize."

"And I want to hang on to my mad awhile longer."

"Allison." He set aside the shopping bag he carried. "You said you'd hear me out."

She scowled, and opened her mouth—probably to tell him to go screw himself. And rightly so.

"Please," he said before Allison could get her words out. "I know I have a lot to apologize for. Just…give me a chance." He picked up the shopping bag and gave it a rattle. "I bought you a present. The least you can do is open it before you kick me out."

Her gaze traveled from him to the bag and back again, and some of the tension seeped from her shoulders. She sank down onto the bed and dipped her head, started running her fingers through her hair.

"Hey." He crouched in front of her. "You okay?"
She hesitated, then nodded. "Good. Marcus okay?"
Another nod. He had to ask, though he wasn't sure
he wanted to hear the answer. "Where is he, by the
way?"

"On his way to Buffalo."

The tile. Better and better. Joe would have another
chance to make things right there, too. "Okay. First
things first. Let's start with what happened at Hazel's."

She was shaking her head. "Joe—"

He pushed the bag into her hands. She accepted it
with a sigh, peered down at the contents and frowned.
"You bought me a pillow?"

"Thought maybe you could whack me with it while
I apologize."

"Is this some kind of kinky sex thing?" She said
it with what could barely pass as a smile.

"No. But I will keep that in mind." He plucked the
ridiculous square of fluff from the bag, needing her
to take a closer look. He set the pillow in her lap. It
was the same emerald hue her eyes reflected in the
sunlight, but that wasn't why he'd bought it. As soon
as her fingers encountered the tangled strips of fringe
that bordered the thing, he knew he had her.

"I outjerked myself again."

She gave him a "no kidding" look and bent over
the pillow, her fingers already busy combing out the
fringe.

"I never meant to imply that you'd intentionally

hurt your mother. I said a lot of things I didn't mean because I was scared as hell. The thought of Sammy or his goon putting their hands on you is enough to—" He rubbed a hand over his chin, then settled it on her knee. "Look, I get it. You were abused as a child. It makes sense, your having control issues."

Her fingers halted. She drew in a breath, smoothed a hand over the fringe she'd already straightened, rotated the pillow in her lap and started on the next row. She was making too much progress too quickly. He added his own fingers to the mix.

"But what gave you control issues also gave you a good heart. Which I've always admired. So I'll back off, and let you be who you are. But I need to know that you hear me—that you'll think about what I said, and that you'll...stay safe. After the five weeks are up, I mean." He held his breath, continued to fuss with the pillow.

She slapped at his hands. "You're making it worse."

"The fringe? Or this thing between us?"

She straightened her back and sighed. His knees had started to ache so he rose out of his crouch and settled beside her on the bed.

"I know what you're going to say, Al. That it's not worth the heartache. That we shouldn't see each other as anything more than coworkers from here on out. That being lovers will make it that much harder to say goodbye. Well, it's too late for that. But I don't want to waste any of the time we have left."

"And when the month is up and I tell you I'm staying in D.C? You'll hate me all over again."

"You know that's not true." He leaned in, scooped a tousled hank of hair out of the way and nuzzled her neck. "I'll be sad, bitter even, but I could never hate you." He closed his eyes. Sad? Bitter? He'll be damned lucky if he can manage to haul his ass out of bed every morning.

Allison jolted to her feet and swung to face him, the pillow clutched to her belly. "Sad enough to keep binge drinking?"

Direct hit. "Okay. Let's talk about that." He blew out a breath and stood. Faced her. Felt his knees go loose because nothing, *nothing* had ever meant more than this moment. Than convincing the woman he loved that he could change. That he *would* change.

Because if he couldn't convince her, how the hell could he convince himself?

"I have a drinking problem," he said, his tone steady. "I will always have a drinking problem. I can't cut back—I have to quit. And the thought of never having a drink again scares the shit out of me. But I'll take it one day at a time. Today, I won't drink. And I'll be that much closer to kicking this tomorrow."

He moved closer, staring into her cautious eyes. "While I was out driving yesterday, it struck me. This motel is all I have left of my brother and I don't want to lose him again." He reached down and took the pillow from her and placed it on the bed. Pulled her close. Inhaled her warm peach scent. "I know you're not mine to lose, but even though I can't have you, I would like to have your respect. I intend to win that back."

She put a hand to his face. He turned his head and kissed her palm and she shivered.

"Damn you, Joe Gallahan," she whispered, her voice thick with tears. "You made me care for you all over again and it's not going to end any better than it did the first time."

"We have five weeks," he said. "Something could change."

Her gaze roved his face, lingered on his bruises. "I think something already has. You seem to have a...a new sense of peace about you. That makes me happy."

"What would make me happy is if we could pretend all this never happened. Our argument about your mother, my drunken rampage. Can we pick up where we left off? You know, right before you left for Hazel's card party two days ago?"

"I believe where we left off was in the shower," she said primly. He wiggled his eyebrows and she huffed a sheepish laugh. "If you'd asked me that half an hour ago, I never would have—" She paused, glanced at the pillow on the bed and back at him. "You did that on purpose."

"Had to find some way to distract you."

"Oh, really?" She draped her arms over his shoulders. "That thing you were doing before? With my neck? That was working pretty well."

"Yeah?" He buried his face in her hair. "That was working for me, too."

"So you're saying we work well together?" She said it lightly, teasingly, but her words taunted a void he was damned weary of staring into.

His fingers flexed on her hips, and even he could feel the desperation in his grip. "Does this mean you accept my apology?"

"Actions speak louder than words, Gallahan."

Her hands dipped beneath his T-shirt and went exploring. He hissed in a breath, his skin burning where she touched him, gratitude and regret making it hard to find his voice.

"We don't have a lot of time," he said gruffly. "I promised Snoozy I'd help Noble build Mitzi's pen since we couldn't con anyone else into doing it."

"You wasted ten seconds right there," she breathed. "Ten seconds we could have used to—"

"Point taken," he muttered, and helped himself to her mouth.

AN HOUR LATER Allison lay panting in bed, her last few shreds of energy focused on admiring Joe's jean-clad ass as it headed out the door.

Best. Apology. Ever.

No way she'd ruin it by wondering whether Joe's newfound determination would last, or if Marcus would be able to forgive him, or how she would manage to say goodbye when Joe had put in his time at T&P.

She almost didn't answer her phone when it rang. For one thing, she'd have to stretch her arm all the way over to the bedside table to reach it. For another, she recognized the ringtone. But she might as well get the daily status check over with.

"Good morning, Mr. Tackett."

"Not for you, Kincaid. You're fired."

She gasped and shot upright. *"What?"*

"Mahoney called. Said he'd heard from Gallahan. Seems they worked out a deal where you and Gallahan would handle Mahoney's account together. That wasn't part of your assignment, Kincaid. You don't get to make those kinds of decisions. You're through."

"You can't—"

"I just did. You tell that boyfriend of yours that if he doesn't show up as agreed I'll sue his ass for breach of contract. I have an email trail and I'm not afraid to use it. Meanwhile, get your own ass back here and clear out your desk." He disconnected.

Allison stared down at her phone. Fired. She'd been *fired*.

No job. No paycheck. *Oh, God.* No way to pay Sammy—

Joe. He'd done this. On purpose? Allison ran shaking fingers through her hair as anger flared, like the match Marcus longed to strike. Joe *had* to have known Mahoney would tell Tackett. Had to have figured Tackett would blow a fuse. And from day one he'd made it clear he'd like nothing better than to get back at Tackett by convincing Allison to quit her job.

She jumped to her feet and paced, stopped long enough to kick at the emerald-green pillow that had fallen to the floor. No. She knew better. She was mad at herself, not Joe. He'd only been looking out for her. She should have guessed that Mahoney would mouth off to Tackett.

What a god-awful mess.

So much for having options.

She slumped down onto the bed and dropped her face into her hands. With no paycheck coming in, how was she supposed to make her next loan payment? And exactly what would Sammy do, when he didn't get his money?

HANDS ON HIPS, jaw set at an "I'm gonna kick somebody's ass" angle, Joe eyed his so-called helpers, who were lounging against the bar, cracking jokes and sipping brews. Meanwhile, the tub hadn't been installed in Mitzi's pen, the door hadn't been hung and the wood shavings and dust from their morning labors had been tracked all over the floor.

"Are you two kidding me? Looks like you didn't do squat while I was gone."

"Ate lunch." Noble toasted Joe with his beer before taking a swig, while Snoozy turned to face the bar and started stacking dishes.

"Noble had the chili." He gave Joe a look over his shoulder. "Two bowls."

"Judas Priest, just kill me now."

"Kiss my ass, Gallahan." Noble pushed a bottle in

his direction. "Have a beer. Then we'll finish up and you can get back to your pretty little guest. Have to say, you two make a good team."

A loud clatter as Snoozy fumbled a bowl. He snatched up a towel, scrubbed furiously at a water stain, then rounded the bar. "I'm going to check on Mitzi." He headed for the stairs.

Noble rubbed his chest. "Bring me some antacid, will you, Snooze?"

Joe winced as the door at the top of the stairs banged shut. "Snooze seems pissed. Regretting his decision to close the bar for the afternoon?"

"Nah. He's in love with your girlfriend."

"She's not my girlfriend."

"Well, she's a lot more to you than she'll ever be to Snoozy."

"'A lot more' still isn't enough."

"That have anything to do with your mysterious errand?" Noble sat up straight. "You didn't buy her a ring, did you?"

"No." Though he might have considered it, if he thought there was the slightest chance she'd accept it. But of course she wouldn't, and he couldn't blame her. He had some changes to make first.

Changes that would take time.

"What's it to you, anyway?" he asked Noble.

"The crankier Snoozy gets, the hotter he makes his chili. You and Allison get together and I'll have to swear off the stuff altogether."

"That's worth getting married right there."

"Watch it, tough guy."

A scrabbling sound overhead. They both frowned up at the ceiling as they heard Snoozy running across his apartment.

"Think she bit him?" Noble surged to his feet, losing control of his beer, which ended up all over the front of Joe's T-shirt. "Think she's after him?"

"Noble, man, what the hell?" Joe grabbed a handful of napkins and swabbed at his chest.

"Joe," Snoozy shouted from the top of the stairs, and practically fell down the rest of the way. "Joe!"

The alarm in the bartender's voice punched the air right out of Joe's lungs. He dropped the napkins and stumbled forward as Snoozy appeared at the foot of the stairs, thin chest heaving, face paper-white.

"Tell me," Joe demanded.

Snoozy wrenched his keys out of his pocket. "I just heard it on the scanner. We have to go. Your motel's on fire."

CHAPTER FIFTEEN

TWO MILES FROM the motel they spotted an ominous tube of smoke. Fat plumes of gray intertwined with black, connecting earth to sky like a sinister, ghostly version of Jack's beanstalk. One mile away they could smell it, the thick, stinging odor telling Joe what Snoozy had already guessed—the motel was suffering major damage.

· But that wasn't why Joe felt like he'd been body slammed by the entire volunteer fire department.

Please let her be okay. Please, God, please...

"She was pulling paneling," Joe said, his voice barely recognizable, even to himself. "The wiring... What if something shorted? What if the room went up before she could get out?" Noble put a hand on his shoulder. Joe shook him off and glowered over at Snoozy. "Can't you make this piece of shit go any faster?" He'd wanted to drive but they'd bullied him into the passenger seat. Poor Snoozy was so tense he was practically kissing the steering wheel. Joe gritted his teeth.

Damn it, he needed to be *there*. Now.

"She's okay, Joe." Snoozy risked a sideways glance. "The call over the scanner said nothing about injuries."

Injuries. Jesus, he'd never forgive himself if any-thing happened to her because of that lame-ass deal they'd made. He wanted to shout, wanted to put his fist through the dash, was climbing out of his skin with the need to *be there*.

And then they were. Snoozy turned the Jeep into the parking lot, and all three of them sucked air.

The last three rooms of the motel were engulfed in flames, and the fire was working its way to the woods. *Son of a bitch.* Two firefighters manned a hose hooked up to the tanker truck, blasting water at the burning building, while two others toted axes around the back of the motel and another two suited up. The fire chief stood in the middle of the sodden parking lot, talking to the sheriff beside him when he wasn't talking into his radio. Red and blue emergency lights flashed and flickered warnings that were no longer needed. An ambulance sat with its doors open and Joe went cold. He fumbled with the door handle, but his fingers had gone suddenly numb.

A deputy and several volunteers guarded a tem-porary perimeter that bisected the parking lot. The deputy waved Snoozy through when Noble stuck his head out of the window.

Joe stumbled out of the Jeep and a blast of hot air almost knocked him on his ass. And the noise—be-neath the roar of the water shooting out of the hose and the rumble of still-hungry flames, men were shouting, glass shattering and wood creaking and popping. Noble and Snoozy appeared on either side of him, eyes wide, mouths shut. What was there to say?

His dream…Braden's dream…was collapsing before his eyes. But at that moment all he gave a damn about was finding Allison. Thank God he didn't have to worry about Marcus, too—it was too soon for the kid to have gotten back from Buffalo.

Where the hell are you, slick?

"Help me find her," he begged, then took off toward the fire chief, all the while scanning the lot for Allison's Camry. Didn't see it. Had the fire department hauled it out of the way, or by some miraculous stroke of luck, had she been away from the motel when the fire started?

"Joe." Burke stepped into his path. "I'm sorry, man, I can't let you get any closer." He reached out but Joe dodged him. Rolled his fingers into fists and widened his stance, more than ready to flatten anyone who got in his way of finding some answers. Finding *the* answer.

"Where is she? Where's Allison?" His gut felt hollow and his throat burned, like he'd been breathing smoke for days.

"Not here." Burke took off his helmet and shifted again, into Joe's line of sight. "Joe. She's not here. We managed to check out all of the rooms before things got too bad, confirmed the motel was empty."

Joe sagged. "Thank God," he muttered, and scrubbed a hand over his face.

"You can say that again." The firefighter glanced

over his shoulder. "Looks like they're getting it under control. I'd better get back over there."

"Any idea how it started?"

"Once we've put the sucker down we can start checking for origin. We'll keep you posted. Meanwhile, you should give your insurance company a call."

"Thanks, man. For everything." They shook hands. Burke gave him a solemn clap on the back and jogged away, toward the fire chief.

"I don't know what to say, other than 'this sucks.'" Noble came up, shaking his white-blond head. "For damn sure the next round at Snoozy's is on me, on account of no one got hurt."

Not yet, anyway. Joe breathed a silent prayer for the firefighters. "I'm not drinking anymore, man." Noble gaped while Joe turned in a slow circle, scanning the parking lot, waved thanks in response to a parade of sympathetic looks. At least the curious were keeping their distance—he didn't think he could deal with all that goodwill right then. "I don't know where Allison went, but she's in for one hell of a shock when she gets back."

"I think she just did."

"Joe!" he heard. "Joe!"

He turned, saw her running at him and opened his arms. She threw herself into his embrace and held tight. The ache in his chest finally eased. "Thank God you're okay," he whispered.

"Me? What about you?" She pressed a kiss to his

neck, then slowly unwound her arms, and gazed at the sobering activity around them, the portion of the motel still in flames. Her chin trembled. "I—I can't believe this. I'm so sorry this happened."

"I'm thankful you weren't here when it did." He pulled her close again, dug his fingers into her shoulder blades, breathed in. But instead of her familiar scent he smelled smoke. "Where were you?"

"Ivy invited me to lunch." She leaned back and stared toward the motel. Her troubled gaze reflected the orange glow of stubborn flames. Joe angled her away.

"Thank God Marcus is in Buffalo," she said fervently. "He is still in Buffalo, isn't he?"

"Should be. I don't know. I haven't heard from him."

She scanned the parking lot, as he had earlier, her teeth digging into her lip.

"What is it?"

"Just…" She shook her head. "I hope Tigerlily's okay, wherever she is." He murmured in agreement. He missed that little so-and-so.

Allison swiped at her eyes. "So…what now?"

"Now we wait until the fire department says it's safe to go inside, and we see what we can salvage." He grimaced. "Your clothes and your computer… there's a good chance they suffered smoke or water damage. Or both."

"Considering that most of it was paid for by T&P, I guess I can't be too upset about it. Tackett might be, but since I don't work for him anymore I won't let that bother me."

He went still. "Want to run that by me again?"

She tried a smile that didn't quite come off. "I... don't work there anymore."

"You *quit?*" Despite the disaster playing out behind them, a hot, happy swell of hope damn near choked him. Had she decided to stay? Judas Priest, did she plan to give them one more shot? He wanted to haul her into his arms again, but something about that smile... Instead he reached out and cupped her elbows, gave her a little shake. "When did this happen?"

"I didn't quit, Joe. Tackett fired me. This morning, after you left. I was going to tell you tonight."

"What happened?"

"He found out we'd been talking to Mahoney. Which violates my confidentiality agreement."

"But I'm the one who talked to Mahoney."

"It doesn't matter."

"The hell it doesn't. I got you fired."

"I GOT YOU FIRED," Joe said again, slowly. He looked over at the smoldering remains of the motel, then looked back at Allison. Ran a shaking hand through his hair. "That job meant everything to you. Losing it, on top of everything else I've put you through... that must have really pissed you off."

Allison's tongue felt suddenly thick. The ugly suspicion in his navy eyes was zapping the strength right out of her muscles. "W-what are you saying?"

"You were here alone. You knew no one would get hurt."

"Oh, my God, *Joe*. You can't think that I... How could you even..." She lifted shaking fingers to her mouth. She couldn't believe what she was hearing. Couldn't imagine that he'd think her capable of something so monstrous. After all they'd been through... all they'd shared. Even after what Marcus had confided, she'd never accuse *him* of something like this. She *knew* him.

Apparently better than Joe knew her.

"You've been drinking," she choked. "You smell like beer. You don't know what you're saying."

"Tell me the truth," he demanded. "Do you know something about this?"

She couldn't keep the guilt out of her face. And the look he threw her was just this side of loathing.

She wished she could disappear, just tuck herself away, fold herself up like a wrinkled piece of paper and seal herself inside an envelope.

She had nothing to go back to, and she had nothing here.

She had nothing.

Someone, a man, came up and spoke to Joe, offered condolences, said something about Marcus. Allison managed to shake herself out of the heavy haze of hurt and disbelief, recognized Cal, saw the shocked expression on Joe's face and imagined she must be wearing its twin. She heard words, but they didn't register.

Her car. She had to get to her car. Then she could have her breakdown, in the quiet comfort of her secondhand Camry.

She passed the sheriff, Cal and Joe, heard the sheriff say something about vandals, heard Joe mention wiring. She stumbled, felt a hand under her elbow, squinted up into Joe's tortured gaze.

"Allison. Jesus." She jerked at her elbow, but he wouldn't let go. "Wait. Please forgive me. I was upset, I know you'd never—" His jaw pulsed. "Please. Listen to me. Let me apologize."

"It's too late for that." God, was that her voice? She swallowed, and tasted ash.

He swore under his breath, tugged her gently to a halt. "I was so damned scared. I heard about the fire and didn't know if you'd been hurt. Then you're here and telling me you don't work for T&P anymore and I thought…I thought you were going to tell me you quit. To stay here. With me."

She should feel something. She knew she should feel something. But she didn't, other than an icy deadness, creeping into her veins.

"Joe. Allison." Burke strode up, helmet gone, jacket hanging open. "Give us another hour and you'll be clear to enter the motel, check out the damage. It's not as bad as it could have been, in the part that's still standing, anyway. Hopefully you'll find something you can salvage." He hesitated, looked from one to the other, backed away. Allison was shaking her head.

"There's nothing worth saving." She pulled free.

"Al. Please. Tell me how to fix this."

"There is no fixing this. I said it from the beginning. We don't know each other."

"We do know each other. We love each other. I love you. I know you love me, too."

"No." She wagged a finger as she backed toward her car. "You don't get to do that. You don't get to use the L-word as a last-ditch effort. You never said it before and suddenly I'm supposed to trust that you mean it?" Everything inside her stung, every last piece of who she was scrubbed raw by his accusations.

It wasn't true. He couldn't love her. If he did he'd never believe she could so heartlessly torch his tribute to his brother.

"We need to talk about this. Let me take you to Ivy's. She'll let us clean up, give us a place to stay until we—"

"I have a place. In Alexandria." She swallowed a hot surge of grief and forced herself to move in close, brushed bits of cinder from his shoulders. "We both knew this was temporary. It just turned out to be a little more temporary than we expected." She lifted her chin, showed him the resolution in her eyes. "Good luck, Joe."

She managed to pivot without falling on her ass, despite the high heels she'd gotten out of the habit of wearing. She stuck her hand in her pocket, rediscovered the piece of tumbled green glass and walked away.

First stop: the lake. Where she'd finally see how many skips she could get out of this pathetic excuse for a good-luck charm.

ALLISON SMELLED LIKE smoke, which meant she had to breathe it all the way back to Alexandria. Really, it couldn't be more fitting, since more than Joe's motel had gone up in flames.

When she wasn't cussing and slapping at the steering wheel, she was rummaging for tissues.

How could he even *think* she'd do such a thing?

Truth was, she should have been angrier. She should have been mentally constructing a voodoo doll to skewer—complete with oversize head and minuscule penis. But her fury was tempered by a bizarre sense of relief. By acting like an ass, by accusing her of doing such a hideous thing, he'd saved her from having to say goodbye four weeks down the road. A goodbye she knew damned well would have been extraordinarily painful.

Because at the moment, on a scale of one to ten, her pain level was five hundred and forty-seven.

She scrubbed a tissue across her face. It was no more than she deserved. She had let loose and lost control. Allowed herself to fall in love with a man who had no follow-through. Claimed to believe, claimed to trust, claimed to have her best interests at heart—

Thing was, he did. She knew he did. But it wasn't enough. For either of them. She'd known this day would come. She just didn't expect it would come with a pink slip.

Speaking of which, she had to get to T&P before he did. Get her desk emptied and her accounts transferred before there was any danger of running into Tackett's prodigal son. Though Joe would have his hands full now, with cleanup and insurance matters. At least he had Marcus to help. Providing Marcus decided to stick around.

A rather upsetting peek at her reflection in the rearview mirror had her blinking madly and clearing her throat. She could do this. She could find another job. And to tide her over in the meantime she'd sell her condo. Pay Sammy off, and maybe even have enough left over to put her mother back in rehab. She didn't know why she hadn't sold the damned condo before.

Or maybe she did know.

It was all she had left. Except for one person. Whom Joe had begged her to shut out.

Control. She needed to get it back.

She pulled off the road, picked up her phone, selected a number and hit Send. Ran her fingers through her hair, over and over, while the phone rang.

"Mom? I'll be back in town tonight. How do you feel about lunch tomorrow?"

MARCUS HEARD THE key in the lock and got to his feet. Scowled down at his knees when he realized they were shaking. If he'd miscalculated, he was about to have a hysterical female on his hands. Not to mention the local sheriff.

But it was too late to back out now.

The door opened. He braced himself for a scream.

But when Liz hesitated in the doorway, she didn't look scared, or even mad. She looked relieved.

"Marcus. There you are." She shut the door, squinting as she dropped her purse on the floor.

"What are you doing here?" She blushed, and plucked a half-eaten bowl of cereal off the coffee table. "They're looking for you, you know."

"I didn't want to leave without saying I'm sorry. For being such an asshole."

Now she did look upset. She set the bowl back down and put her hands on her hips. "You can't run. You'll only make yourself look guilty."

"What do you mean, *look* guilty?"

"I know you didn't do it. Joe knows you didn't do it. It's that hardheaded sheriff you need to convince. She heard Cal tell Joe who you are and decided you had to be the person responsible for the fire."

"How do you know all that?"

"I was there. Half of Castle Creek was there, not that there was anything we could do to help. I looked for you. Do you have any idea what happened? Joe said it was probably faulty wiring."

"Was that before or after Cal and the sheriff told him about me?"

"It doesn't matter. Turn yourself in and let them figure it out. Besides, how far will you get without a car? And it'll be dark soon. You can't hitchhike in the dark."

He was shaking his head. "I'm not going back to jail."

"It won't come to that."

"You don't know that. And you don't know what it was like."

She walked up to him, put both hands on his chest and pushed. With a yelp, he fell back onto the couch. She settled beside him, and tipped her head.

"So tell me."

JOE SLOUCHED IN the straight-back chair, staring through the late evening gloom at the bottle of Glenlivet on the table in front of him. Every muscle strained toward temptation. Thirsted for the velvet bite of whiskey. Hungered for the slow, sweet slide into oblivion.

He'd worked hard for that oblivion. He'd let Allison down, not only by getting her fired, but by accusing her of arson. Not bad for a day's work.

He leaned closer to the table.

She'd agreed to trust him. And what had he done? Betrayed that trust.

Didn't matter that he'd been scared out of his mind, or angry that she kept insisting they had no future together. He'd done exactly what he'd vowed never again to do. Got close to someone. Put himself in the position of caring too much.

Proved himself a callous asshole.

She wanted him out of her life? Not a problem. He was done with letting her down.

He reached for the bottle. Wasn't done letting himself down, though.

What about Marcus?

He hesitated, then threw himself against the back of the chair. Damn it to hell. Wherever Marcus had disappeared to, he needed Joe. Because the rest of Castle Creek was pretty damned sure he'd tried to raze the tragedies of his childhood by razing the motel.

Maybe that had been his original plan. Who knew and who could blame him? Judas Priest, the kid had endured unimaginable brutalities. For years. But whatever he'd meant to do, he hadn't gone through with it. The Marcus that Joe knew, the Marcus he'd watched come out of his shell, the kid he'd seen behind those guarded eyes—he wasn't the destructive type.

He scrubbed his hands over his face. He'd lost a lot today. But as horrible as it had been to watch the motel burn, it had been a hundred times more painful to watch Allison walk away. Knowing they could have enjoyed at least another month together, if only he'd been willing to play by her rules.

"Feeling sorry for yourself?" Noble set down a

plate of sandwiches and took the chair beside Joe. The rickety thing creaked under his weight.

"Screw you," muttered Joe, but already he felt better. Less of a chance he'd drink himself blind with Noble there to watch over him. "Thanks for letting me crash here."

"Not a problem. Won't be long before they get your place in shape. Marcus is welcome, too, if he comes back."

"If Marcus comes back I'm afraid our fair sheriff will insist on hosting him."

"Kid didn't do it."

"Preaching to the choir."

Noble ate half a sandwich in one bite. Nodded at the bottle and swallowed. "Gonna drink that or stare at it, or what?"

"Or what. You can have it." He stood and stretched, fought the piercing regret that he wouldn't be falling asleep with Allison in his arms. "See you in the morning." He stumbled over to the couch.

Morning came a hell of a lot sooner than Joe expected. Not surprising, considering he'd fallen asleep just before dawn. He kicked off the blanket, sat up and reminded himself to tell Noble his couch sucked. He ran his hands through his hair and down his face, and grimaced. Two showers and he still smelled like smoke.

The loss hit him all over again. *Allison.* Her name crumpled his lungs, like a kick to the solar plexus. What the hell had he been thinking? No more saucy smile, no more counting or tapping or combing, no more prissy attitude—

The doorbell rang. Joe thought about ignoring it— hell, he hadn't even had his coffee yet. Plus it wasn't even his doorbell. Then he heard Marcus's voice on the other side, and staggered over to let him in.

"I didn't do it," Marcus said.

"Didn't think you did." Joe stepped back. "Want some coffee? I was just about to make some."

While they waited for the coffee to brew, Marcus told Joe he'd turned himself in early that morning, only to learn the true offender had already confessed. A teenager who regularly cut through Joe's field to get to the lake had tossed a cigarette. It hadn't taken long for the parched summer grass to ignite, and the resulting fire to spread.

"The sheriff said she'd give you a call."

"So you're in the clear." Joe grinned and offered his hand, thought better of it and pulled Marcus into a hug. A self-conscious embrace made even more awkward by Noble, who shuffled into the kitchen in a black bathrobe decorated with lime-green palm trees and wrapped both arms around his guests. And squeezed tight. And made mmm-mmm-good sounds.

Joe was having trouble breathing. "Get off me, man."

Once they'd disbanded and were able to look each other in the eye again, Joe nodded at Marcus. "I'm proud of you. Turning yourself in like that."

"Kid's got balls," Noble said.

Joe shook his head. "He's not a kid."

Marcus picked up a mug and smoothed a finger over the lettering on the side, which spelled out Where in the Hell Is Castle Creek, Pennsylvania? "I guess you know what happened when I was…" He looked up. "I was going to do it, you know. Burn it down."

"I probably would have felt the same." Joe kept his gaze on Marcus but thrust his chin at Noble. "We're sorry, man. All of us. For what you went through. You know if you ever need anything…" He let the sentence trail off. Had to. His throat had closed.

Marcus tightened his mouth in acknowledgment. Noble busied himself pouring the coffee.

"So what changed your mind?" Noble asked.

"Not 'what.' 'Who.'" Marcus dipped his head, seemingly mesmerized by the process of stirring milk into his coffee. "I…ran into Liz Early."

"Ah." Noble slurped his coffee. "True love."

"I dunno. Could be." He lifted his gaze to Joe. "I came back so I could maybe deserve her one day. Like what you said. About Allison. That you'd do whatever it takes to convince her you deserve her." He frowned. "Where is Allison, anyway?"

CHAPTER SIXTEEN

ALLISON HAD JUST kicked off her pumps and slumped down onto the sofa when her doorbell rang. Instantly nerves erupted in her stomach—sparkles of rocketing heat, like fireworks on the Fourth of July. She sat up straight and bit her lip, flinched when the bell rang again.

She seriously considered ignoring it. If it wasn't Sammy standing out in the hallway, it was likely Joe. She wasn't interested in seeing either of them. But if she ignored Sammy he'd get petulant and mean, and if she ignored Joe…well, he might not come back.

This could be the last time they saw each other.

You're a masochist, Allie.

Oh, yeah? Bite me.

A-a-and you just made my point.

Oh, for God's sake. She was out of her mind. Had to be, if she was considering letting Joe inside her apartment. He'd already abused her heart twice—was she really up for a third round?

Slowly she stood, and crept over to the door. A careful eye to the peephole confirmed what her belly already knew. *Joe.* Wearing a suit. Looking stern. Holding a box.

Probably the items he was able to salvage out of her motel room.

Emotion crowded her throat. She couldn't do this. Couldn't let him in. Seven long, lonely, wretched days had crawled by since she'd left Castle Creek, but it might as well have been an hour. If they talked they might manage to get some closure, but it wouldn't happen without casualties.

With the two of them, there would always be casualties.

She swallowed against the thickness in her throat and leaned her forehead against the cool, painted surface. And must have made just enough noise to signal she was there, because he didn't ring the bell again. Instead he spoke to her through the door.

"How about letting me in, Al?" *Way to go, Allie.* She dragged in a breath and peered through the peephole. He hefted the box. "I have chocolate." When she didn't say anything he faked a wince. "Don't make me tell Hazel I left her gift in the hallway. She'll never bake me another cake as long as I live."

Allison sighed, and opened the door.

He walked in, nodded once, glanced around and set the box on the coffee table, which gave her a few seconds to catch her breath. And to check him out. He looked devastating in a charcoal-gray suit and blue silk tie, his jaw free of stubble, his hair less rumpled than usual. She was glad he hadn't cut it.

He straightened, and shoved his hands into his pockets. She had hers linked at her belly, her fingers tangled into numbness. He cleared his throat and jabbed his chin at her lightweight suit, a favorite she'd worn to two interviews that morning.

"You look good," he said.

"So do you."

Several beats of silence. He cleared his throat again. "Here's the thing." He moved closer, yanking his hands out of his pockets and steepling his fingers. "I panicked. The motel was on fire, I couldn't find you and when I did you made me think, for just a moment, that you were staying. Then you set me straight, and I—" He exhaled. "What I said had nothing to do with the fire and everything to do with watching my world fall apart in front of me. I was so damned determined not to let you down again and I did it anyway. I'm sorry."

Her fingers were trembling. She put her hands behind her back, wishing she'd taken ten seconds to put her shoes on. She felt short, and powerless, and naked.

"You said what you did because I hurt you. And you wanted to hurt me back."

"Maybe. A little juvenile, but not impossible. I *am* sorry, Al."

"Apology accepted. I hope you'll accept mine, as well." She moved toward the door, suddenly glad she wasn't having to maneuver in high heels after all. "If there's nothing else you need…"

"I need you."

The words seemed to echo in her sparse apartment. Her heart shifted beneath a hot, aching slide of regret, and her eyes misted. "I need you, too. But more than that, I need this world I created for myself. And you need the one you created in Castle Creek."

"This world of yours is falling apart."

"You're rebuilding. I can, too."

He raised a hand to his forehead and squeezed. "Help me understand. That day at the diner, after we found Mitzi, you talked about penance. Said my move to Castle Creek was my atonement." He dropped his hand, used it to gesture at their surroundings. "Is this yours? Because you, living like this? Secondhand furniture—and very little of it—no knickknacks, or pictures of flowers on the walls? Driving a car too old to be reliable and worried every check you write might be the one that bounces? This is about more than being grateful to your mother. What is it you think you did to deserve this? To commit to paying this kind of price?"

Why had she let him in? "That's none of your business."

"The *hell* it isn't." He strode up to her, took her hands and pressed them between his. Bent his knees so they were eye to eye. "I love you. And I know you feel something for me. I'll never forget that look on your face when I accused you—" His jaw muscles knotted. "Is it the alcohol? Because I'm proud to say I haven't had a drink since that disaster with Marcus."

Dear God in heaven, if she didn't get him out of there soon she'd be nothing more than a hysterical mess. She tugged her hands free. "I've made it more than clear. I have responsibilities."

He straightened, and ran his fingers through his hair. So much for less rumpled. "I'm not asking you to choose between me and your mother. I'm asking you to let her live her own life, so you can live yours."

"I was trying. Then you showed up."

Joe took a jagged inhale. He followed it up with a bitter, dismal smile that freeze-dried her insides. She bit down on the inside of her cheek, battled to keep her chin from wobbling, the damp in her eyes from spilling.

"You don't love me, Joe. You can't love me and still believe I'd destroy your tribute to your brother. We don't... There's no trust between us."

"I get it," he said huskily. His hands went back into his pockets. "I guess you heard what really happened."

"A careless kid with a cigarette. Ivy emailed me. She told me about Marcus, too. She said he works at the diner now?" She couldn't imagine what he was dealing with, now that everyone in town knew about his wretched past.

"He's pissed at me because of what I said to you. He's not the only one. Then there's the whole drunken ambush thing." He grimaced, and leaned forward. "Just so you know, that day of the fire, I didn't have anything to drink. I smelled like beer because Noble spilled his on me when Snoozy came running to tell us about the fire."

"I knew you weren't drunk, Joe. I was just...hoping you were."

The room got quiet. He gave a sharp nod. "Listen, I talked to Tackett. Explained you weren't the one who approached Mahoney. He wants to offer you an apology, and the position of Account Executive." She started to protest and he shook his head. "You don't have to worry about me. I won't be at T&P while you're there. I made arrangements with Mahoney to do some freelance work from Castle Creek."

"But...what about Tackett's threat to sue?"

"We worked it out. Point is, you don't have to refuse the job to avoid running into me. You don't have to take it, either, but...you know what I mean."

"I...thank you. And thanks for delivering the cake from Hazel."

He waited, wanting more, but she didn't have more to offer. Finally he made his way to the door, where he pulled an oblong box from an inside pocket. "I realized in all the time I've known you, I never bought you anything other than food—well, besides that damned pillow. I got this for you before the fire. It's not an apology. It's...just a gift." He held out the box. "You can do what you like with it. Wear it, sell it, take a hammer to it..." He shrugged. "Your decision."

With unsteady fingers she lifted the lid. On a bed of deep purple silk lay a tennis bracelet, set with alternating diamonds and emeralds. The stones shimmered as tears threatened once again.

"Joe," she managed. "It's lovely." She replaced the

lid and pushed the box back into his hands. "But you have to know I can't accept this. It's too much. Even if we were together—" She pulled in her lips, fought to pull herself together. "Thank you for the thought, but it's far too much."

"I had you crawling around in filth, put you in close quarters with a killer snake, forced you to sleep in your car, practically called you a whore and got you fired. To top it all off, I accused you of arson. This is the least I can do. Please. Take it." He wrapped her hands around the box, leaned down and kissed her on the cheek. "Bye, my sweet." He gave her a lopsided smile. "Don't forget to bolt the door behind me."

Her entire body quaked with misery as she started to close the door. Then she wrenched it open again and leaned out into the hallway. "Joe!"

Slowly he turned, and she hated that glimmer of hope she'd put in his gaze. But she'd never forgive herself if she didn't tell him. "I'm proud of you," she choked, her fingers digging into the doorjamb. "For not drinking. I'm so proud."

After a long while he gave a vague nod, as if she'd answered a question he didn't remember asking. "That means a lot, slick," he said softly. He pivoted, and walked away.

Allison clapped a palm over her mouth, closed the door and fastened the deadbolt, her fingers clumsy because of the box she clutched in her hand.

Bye, Joe.

THE MORNING AFTER JOE'S unexpected visit, Beryl Kincaid called Allison and finally agreed to lunch. Her mother had been dodging her, which worried Allison—she'd never been one to pass up a free meal. Or an opportunity to finagle a little seed money out of her only child.

By the time she was due to meet her mother at the restaurant, the prospect of finding out what Beryl had been up to wasn't the only reason Allison had lost her appetite. An hour before her lunch date she'd stopped by the T&P offices to clear out her desk—and what a smirking Danielle Franks had told her made Allison realize what an unqualified idiot she'd been.

Tackett hadn't planned to offer her that Account Executive position—Joe had bartered for it. He'd signed a contract, committing himself to working at T&P a full week every month—which meant staying in D.C. Earning money for a company he loathed in a city he despised.

Because he wanted to make amends.

All the while Danielle had been talking, the woman had grinned like a Cheshire cat, as if she already knew Allison had turned down the job. It seemed Danielle was looking forward to having Joe to herself. She prattled on and on about what a good team she and Joe would make, but Allison didn't pay much attention. She was too busy kicking herself for doubting that Joe loved her. All she wanted to do was go home, crawl under an afghan and try to figure out how to set things right. She had a wretched feeling it was far too late for that.

When she finally made it to the restaurant, her mother had already ordered.

"There you are." Beryl Kincaid stood, setting aside the wrapper for the butterscotch candy she'd just popped into her mouth. Allison hugged her carefully—her mother was so thin that even as a little girl Allison had feared she'd break her. "I have somewhere else to be after lunch, so I went ahead and ordered for us. Potato soup and quiche. Doesn't that sound wonderful?"

Allison nodded absently. "Where's Carlotta?" She'd invited her mother's landlady, as well. The woman had opened her home to a flighty craftaholic with a gambling addiction—Allison figured it was the least she could do.

"She had other plans." Her mother avoided her gaze as she sat back down. Allison's heart dropped. Her butt followed. Thank God the chair held.

"What happened?"

"It's…possible I owe her some money."

"You haven't been paying your rent?"

"I have to buy supplies. You know, for my crafts. And everything's so expensive these days. Speaking of expensive…" Her gaze had snagged on Joe's bracelet. "Where did you get *that?*"

Allison put her hand in her lap. "It was a gift." She recognized the avid gleam in her mother's eyes and her throat started to burn. The fingers of her right hand started up a quiet drumming on the tabletop.

"How much do you think you could get for it?"

"Nothing, since I'm keeping it. Mom, have you been back at the tables?"

"Please stop that ridiculous tapping." Her mother waited for Allison to put her other hand in her lap, then shrugged. "Remember old lady Graham? She was our neighbor, when we lived in Falls Church. She died just after Christmas. I guess she remembered how well I looked after her because she left me a little cash."

"How much?"

"Now, Allie girl, I don't think that's any of your business."

"Not my business? Mom, Sammy came after me."

"Yes, but…nothing happened. And if you're suggesting I turn that money over to you, it's a little late for that. Anyway, she left it to *me*." She smiled to take the sting out of her words. "Care for a candy?"

Stiffly Allison pushed away from the table and stood, the disappointment—in both her mother and herself—ice-cold and rock-solid behind her breastbone. Why had it taken her so long to see it?

She'd stuck by her mother all these years, given her chance after chance after chance to change, to realize she needed to be accountable for her actions. During all that time, her mother had never shown even one-tenth of Joe's strength. Or any inclination to make things different. Joe had made his intentions to get his act together more than clear.

And yet it was Joe whom Allison had turned her back on.

She shook her head at her mother. "You don't get it. I gave up almost everything I had for you." Including Joe. God. *Joe.*

Her mother's pretty face hardened. "I gave up a husband for you."

And there it was. The reason Allison continued to punish herself. Her mother had loved her father deeply. But he'd abused his wife and child, and he'd gone to prison for it. They'd never seen him again. It wasn't Allison's fault he'd beat her. Nothing she sacrificed—not even Joe—would change the reality of her broken family.

From somewhere deep and dark within her came a bitter laugh. Joe's words rose to her lips. "Isn't that what parents are supposed to do? Protect their children?" She snatched up her purse. "Mom. I love you. But I can't do this anymore."

"Do what? What are you talking about?"

"You gamble and I lose. Why should you stop, when there aren't any consequences?"

Panic skittered across her mother's thin face. "Is this about the meetings? I'll go to the meetings, I promise."

"And rehab?"

Her mother pursed her lips, reached blindly for the piece of candy she'd shoved across the table. Allison shook her head. "I am grateful for what you did for me. How you protected me. But that was a long time ago. I've paid my debt. Now it's your turn."

"Uncle. Uncle. Kid, I give up." Joe bent at the waist and struggled to catch his breath, made a grab for Nat as she scampered by, giggling. He saw Parker come around from the front of the motel and raised a weary hand in greeting. He'd had to recreate Nat's hockey field to the left of the building, since the fire had razed the field around back. And it was just as well because, though this area was smaller, Parker's daughter was kicking his ass. Joe dropped his hockey stick and made a show of wiping the sweat from his forehead. "Good thing your mother's here to pick you up 'cause I was getting ready to kick your butt."

Nat rolled her eyes. "You mean you were getting ready to need a nap."

"That does it." Joe lunged at the nine-year-old. She screamed and took off across the grass but Joe caught up quickly, swung her into his arms and around in a circle, legs extended like spokes on a wheel.

Parker greeted them from a safe distance. "If she gets sick, it's on you. Literally."

Good point. Gently Joe set Nat down. She complained, until she tried to walk. He and Parker exchanged a grin over Nat's head as the girl stumbled over to her mother.

Parker smoothed a hand over Nat's hair. "Do you have something to say to Joe?"

She scooped up the hockey stick she'd let fall to the ground. "Thank you for teaching me hockey."

"I think at the end, there, you were teaching me."

After Parker and Nat left, Joe put the hockey sticks away, then stared across the blackened expanse of grass between the motel and the woods he'd always associate with Marcus. He lifted the hem of his T-shirt and swiped at his face, decided an iced tea and one of Parker's muffins would serve as the perfect excuse to get out of the late afternoon sun. And to sit his tired ass down. Maybe he did need a nap.

He was always tired these days. Not enough protein, Audrey would tell him. Too many regrets, more like.

Out of the corner of his eye he saw a figure approach. He smiled. The kid had come back for her stick. Probably wanted to sleep with it under her pillow.

"Couldn't stay away, could you?" He swung around, and froze. Not Nat.

Allison.

He felt a weightless, rising sensation, as if a giant had picked him up to get a closer look and let him dangle in midair. Joe wiped his palms on his jeans, made a vague gesture toward the parking lot.

"I thought you were Parker."

"I figured. I saw them leave." She tried on a smile. "I waved."

He closed the distance between them, taking in the neat sleeveless dress that hugged her curves, and the controlled smoothness of her hair, which she'd worked into some kind of twist at her nape. Even the leather case she carried boosted the impression of calm, cool and collected. But the slight tremble of her chin and the fingers tapping against her thigh betrayed her—she wasn't as self-possessed as she wanted him to think. A thrill of possibility flickered through him.

Don't assume anything.

He stopped a few feet away, and the words came out harsher than he'd intended. "Why are you here?"

A tiny wince. She gestured toward the far end of the motel. "That was quick work, getting the damaged part cleared away. When do you start rebuilding?"

"Crew's coming next week. I repeat. Why are you here?"

After a second's hesitation she patted the case, which he realized contained a laptop. "I have something to show you."

He scowled. "This have anything to do with Tackett?"

"Not directly. May I set this up inside?"

He hesitated, then tipped his head. For his own peace of mind he meant to keep his gaze above her waist, but his brain was already in chaos mode, so what the hell. He tormented himself by watching her gorgeous ass walk all the way to the lobby, where she pulled out the laptop and opened it, pressed a few buttons and stepped aside.

He'd left his reading glasses on the counter. He slid them on, and studied the screen.

She'd created a website for his motel. The photos on the main page weren't the best quality, but she'd have meant them only as placeholders, until the renovations were done. Everything else—the background, the fonts, the menu that offered reservation information, directions, sightseeing tips—all looked sleek and professional.

He scratched his jaw. Then peered closer. Son of a bitch. "Is that me?"

She smiled, albeit nervously. "Since Hazel provided the photos, I had to promise to use the topless one. If you decide to take this live, naturally I'll replace them all. Though Hazel will try to talk you out of it."

"This is great," he said sincerely, even as the muscles in his back pulled tighter and tighter as he fought the urge to reach for her. "When I'm ready to advertise, this will be a big help. But...why?"

She took her time shutting down the laptop. "I'm starting my own PR business specializing in online promotions. I was hoping you'd be my first client. Gratis, of course."

Hell. "You're not taking the job at T&P." She shook her head. He turned, and braced his palms on the counter. "Because of me?"

"You mean because I found out you signed a contract committing yourself for one week every month in exchange for my Account Executive position? Then yes, you're the reason I'm not taking the job."

"Because you can't handle working with me?"

"Because I can't let you make that kind of sacrifice. For God's sake, Joe, I know better than anyone how miserable you were there. Going back for a month is one thing, but that contract is for two *years*."

"I want you to be happy."

"I know you do." She crossed her arms, dropped them, wandered behind the counter, picked up a stack of business cards and started counting. "But I don't belong there. And neither do you. I hope that contract you signed—"

"Is contingent on your taking the job. If you're not working there, neither am I."

"Good. That's good." She looked up, then, her hazel gaze both sad and sincere. Something bad was coming. His fingers dug into the countertop. She licked her lips. "I did so many things, said so many things that were wrong. I swore you couldn't love me, but...I already knew that you did. How could I not? All you've done since I walked back into your life is try to protect me. Even this." She held up her arm, twisted her wrist so the bracelet sparkled in the light. "This is because you knew I'd be too embarrassed to accept a loan."

Slowly Joe pushed upright. She hadn't sold his gift. What did it mean? "Does that matter to you? Knowing I love you?" He held himself rigid as he waited for the answer.

"Of course it matters. You put yourself out there for me, time and time again. You accepted me, compulsions and all, and I...I'm such a coward. I never even—"

"Okay, stop. Just...stop." With every goddamned miserable jilted cell in his body, he wished she'd delivered her little "I'm grateful" speech over the phone. "You came to apologize. I get it. But just remember that everything I put you through, everything I tossed your way, you took it in stride. Coward? Screw that. You're one of the strongest women I know. And you did put yourself out there for me. I knew damned well you didn't want to get involved but still I *had* to push—"

"Thank God you did."

"What?"

Allison shook her head. She looked a little shell-shocked. Meanwhile, he wasn't sure what the hell to feel. "I didn't come just to apologize. I came to explain. You were right about my mother. I have been enabling her. The last time I saw her she made it clear she's not interested in rehab. She was, however, very interested in this bracelet. What it's worth, I mean."

"Sorry to hear that."

"I paid off her loan. I told her I would. I had to do that, for me."

"You don't have to explain."

"But I do. Because—" Her beautiful eyes went wide. "I just realized how this is going to sound." She bit her lip, then pushed out the words in a rush.

"Okay, here goes. I don't have a place to live. I rented out my condo, and the renters are planning to buy it. They put down a deposit. That's how I paid off Sammy."

Joe drew in a breath, held it, let it go in a long, gratified exhale. Things were looking up. Slowly he worked his way around to her side of the counter. "How do *you* think that sounds?"

"Suspicious. Convenient."

"I vote for intriguing."

She tapped the stack of cards on the countertop. The closer he got, the faster she tapped. "*And* you were right about something else. Castle Creek. I have fallen in love with it. The people, the pace, the view. Even the quiet." Tap, tap, tap.

He kept his smile inward and held out a hand. She flushed, and dropped the cards into his outstretched palm. He set the stack aside, then pulled off his glasses and rested them on the counter. Interesting, that little hitch in her breathing. He moved in, backing her up against the wall.

"If you tell me you're here to reserve a room, I might have to excuse myself and go hammer something."

"I don't belong in D.C." Her breathing had quickened. "I belong here."

Two inches closer and he'd be able to feel the rise and fall of her breasts. He closed the gap, felt the rhythmic puff of breath against his neck, her nipples poking into his chest. Every muscle went taut.

"Still not what I need to hear," he murmured. He groped for her hand, pressed his lips to her wrist. Beneath his mouth her pulse stumbled. "Where do you belong?"

"Here." She swallowed audibly. "With you."

With his free hand he coaxed her chin up. "And?"

She tangled her fingers in his T-shirt. "I love you, Joe. I love you so much."

An overwhelming surge of elation tempted him to snatch her up and swing her around in a circle, like he had Nat. But he needed to hear it again. "Want to run that by me again?"

"I love you." She pushed up onto her toes and kissed him sweetly. He slipped his arms around her and pulled her in tight.

"You couldn't have just said that, first thing?"

"I had a plan."

He let his chuckle graduate to a laugh and kissed her neck, her cheeks, her nose. "Why doesn't that surprise me?"

"I needed you to know everything, up front."

"Afraid I'd change my mind? Not gonna happen." He raised her hands over her head and pinned her to the wall with his hips. Kissed her mouth with a sudden frenzied need, his blood thundering in his ears. She responded like she always had, with passion and zeal, the rising pitch of her moans signaling they were quickly approaching the point of no return. They had a door to lock and condoms to locate.

But he had to know for sure.

He gritted his teeth and lifted away from her. She stared up at him, lips swollen, gaze unfocused as she remained plastered against the wall.

"You're staying." He didn't risk making it a question. When she hesitated he had to bite back a tortured grumble of protest.

Slowly she lowered her arms, and pressed her palms to his cheeks. "What you said, about punishing myself? I knew I wasn't helping my mother, but I didn't know what else to do. And you... I should have stuck by you, no matter what. I—I think I finally got tired of letting people down. Myself included."

"I know the feeling." He inhaled. "And my drinking problem?"

"I'm not crazy about it. But I am crazy about you. And you're determined to quit, which makes all the difference." A smile trembled across her lips. "Ivy tells me the Catlett sisters have been crashing poker night."

"The guys have been good sports about learning canasta. Probably because Hazel never comes without a cake. And June—" he swallowed. "I don't know what I'd have done without her. It's been tough, but she's helped me stay sober."

Her eyes glistened with sudden tears and her hands dropped away from his face. "I wish you could say that about me," she whispered. "I let you down again."

"No. No, my sweet. If not for you I'd still be wallowing in self-pity—and a whole hell of a lot of whiskey." He captured her hands, and snugged them against his heart. "You make me want to be a better man."

"I am proud of you, Joe."

He shuddered. "The last time you that said to me you nearly brought me to my knees. After all we'd been through I couldn't believe we were done."

"We weren't. We're not. I'm just sorry it took me so long to realize it. But from now on I'm here for you, no matter what." She tipped her head back. "I love you, Joe."

"I love you, too." He had to push the words past a rock-solid lump in his throat. *She was staying.* No more lonely bed. No more *lonely,* period. "How about we lock the front door and take this into the back? I'll show you my new tool belt."

"I think you can keep me entertained without it."

His wicked smile turned somber. "I just want to keep you."

"I'm not going anywhere, Joe." Her grip on his fingers tightened, even as she waggled her eyebrows. "Besides the bedroom, that is."

"And I'm right behind you."

"Because you want to stare at my ass?"

"Not like I haven't caught you checking out mine." He levered away from her. "Come on. We have a lot of lost time to make up for."

He pulled her down the hallway and into his bedroom, where she gave a squeal of delight and lunged at the bed. She turned back to face him, smile wide, eyes liquid and a drowsy Tigerlily cradled to her chest.

"She came back," she breathed.

"Yeah," he managed. "She did." His gaze never wavered from hers. "And I won't let a day go by without thanking her for it."

* * * * *

LARGER-PRINT BOOKS!
GET 2 FREE LARGER-PRINT NOVELS PLUS
2 FREE GIFTS!

HARLEQUIN®

super romance®

More Story...More Romance

YES! Please send me 2 FREE LARGER-PRINT Harlequin® Superromance® novels and my 2 FREE gifts (gifts are worth about $10). After receiving them, if I don't wish to receive any more books, I can return the shipping statement marked "cancel." If I don't cancel, I will receive 6 brand-new novels every month and be billed just $5.69 per book in the U.S. or $5.99 per book in Canada. That's a savings of at least 16% off the cover price! It's quite a bargain! Shipping and handling is just 50¢ per book in the U.S. or 75¢ per book in Canada.* I understand that accepting the 2 free books and gifts places me under no obligation to buy anything. I can always return a shipment and cancel at any time. Even if I never buy another book, the two free books and gifts are mine to keep forever.

139/339 HDN F46Y

Name	(PLEASE PRINT)

Address		Apt. #

City	State/Prov.	Zip/Postal Code

Signature (if under 18, a parent or guardian must sign)

Mail to the **Harlequin® Reader Service:**
IN U.S.A.: P.O. Box 1867, Buffalo, NY 14240-1867
IN CANADA: P.O. Box 609, Fort Erie, Ontario L2A 5X3

**Are you a current subscriber to Harlequin Superromance books
and want to receive the larger-print edition?
Call 1-800-873-8635 today or visit www.ReaderService.com.**

* Terms and prices subject to change without notice. Prices do not include applicable taxes. Sales tax applicable in N.Y. Canadian residents will be charged applicable taxes. Offer not valid in Quebec. This offer is limited to one order per household. Not valid for current subscribers to Harlequin Superromance Larger-Print books. All orders subject to credit approval. Credit or debit balances in a customer's account(s) may be offset by any other outstanding balance owed by or to the customer. Please allow 4 to 6 weeks for delivery. Offer available while quantities last.

Your Privacy—The Harlequin® Reader Service is committed to protecting your privacy. Our Privacy Policy is available online at www.ReaderService.com or upon request from the Harlequin Reader Service.

We make a portion of our mailing list available to reputable third parties that offer products we believe may interest you. If you prefer that we not exchange your name with third parties, or if you wish to clarify or modify your communication preferences, please visit us at www.ReaderService.com/consumerschoice or write to us at Harlequin Reader Service Preference Service, P.O. Box 9062, Buffalo, NY 14269. Include your complete name and address.

HSRLP13R